1st Ed.

6 .95
00
1
7B

D0426287

THE GREAT THIRST

THE
Great Thirst

WILLIAM DUGGAN

DELACORTE PRESS / NEW YORK

Published by
Delacorte Press
1 Dag Hammarskjold Plaza
New York, N.Y. 10017

Copyright © 1985 by William R. Duggan

All rights reserved. No part of this book may be reproduced or transmitted in any form
or by any means, electronic or mechanical, including photocopying, recording or by any
information storage and retrieval system, without the written permission of the
Publisher, except where permitted by law.

Manufactured in the United States of America

First printing

Library of Congress Cataloging in Publication Data
Duggan, William.
    The great thirst.
    I. Title.
PS3554.U396G7   1985   813'.54
ISBN 0-385-29387-9
Library of Congress Catalog Card Number: 84-26863

For Lynn Ellsworth

TLADI

Tladis

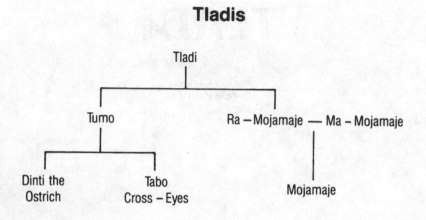

Tladi

Tumo — Ra – Mojamaje —— Ma – Mojamaje

Dinti the Ostrich — Tabo Cross – Eyes — Mojamaje

Potsos

Potso

Pule

1

The Battle of the Rocks

When the raiders emerged from the canyon, the boy could see that they had grown old and fat on their horses. He could hear them too, above the clatter of their horses' hooves, coughing and wheezing in the chill winter air. Even in the fading light of dusk he could see their pink necks and jowls flutter as they rode. They wore wide-brimmed hats, leather breeches, thick leather coats and shaggy beards. Each rider held in one hand the reins of his horse, and in the other he held a rifle.

The boy had never seen a Boer before. It had been nine years since they last descended on the BaNare to steal their cattle, a year before the boy was born. Since then the BaNare speculated that the Boers had grown too old and fat to raid. Standing with his goats at the mouth of the canyon, the herdboy was the first to see that the BaNare were wrong. The sentry posted at the entrance to the canyon should have seen the Boers first, but he had fallen asleep.

The herdboy froze, dropped his herding stick and ran in panic straight away from the Boers. Straight away from the Boers was straight toward the canyon wall, a sheer face of red rock rising up to the flat top of the ridge twenty yards above. The boy flew against the rock, too frightened to run any farther. He could only clutch the rock in fear. His arms spread wide to flatten him against the wall. Small for his age in height and girth, he wished right now he were even smaller.

The Boers rode slowly, cautiously, ready to fire their rifles. After a long, dusty ride with no water along the way, the sudden approach of night made them edgy. Never before had they raided so late in the day.

Their horses were edgy too, for never before had they ridden in such numbers, four hundred, pressed close in the narrow, darkening canyon. Some of the horses had also grown old, and faltered under the great weight of their riders.

The canyon was short as well as narrow, cut through a low ridge of scrub-covered hills. Behind the ridge lay the BaNare village of Naring. Though the BaNare numbered but a few thousand, their village spread out for miles. Their squat, round mud houses stood widely spaced, thatched loosely with brown grass. Surrounding each compound was an open courtyard of bare earth, fenced with thorn branches to prevent cobras, jackals and neighbors from approaching unnoticed. This one narrow canyon was the only entrance to Naring from the east, whence raiders always came, first the Zulu, then the Boers. The BaNare never worried about attack from the west because there, beginning just beyond the village, up a gentle slope of pale yellow sand, lay the endless Kalahari Desert.

The BaNare were able to send a thousand warriors to the field, but they counted only twelve guns to the Boers' four hundred. These twelve guns were old and rusty. The Boers should have come through the canyon full of confidence, then, but night hurried behind and they had not raided Naring for nearly a decade. They did not know what to expect. Perhaps the BaNare had accumulated more rifles. Maybe the BaNare had more soldiers now. Perhaps the BaNare had moved the village, or someone else had just raided the cattle and they had come all that way for nothing.

But the BaNare were there. The first thing the Boers saw as they emerged from the canyon was a sea of armed men standing atop the canyon wall, their spiked headdresses silhouetted against the last scarlet glow of daylight. Leaping from their horses in terror, the Boers jerked the beasts to the ground and collapsed in heaps behind them, wildly firing their rifles. Panting and swearing, they reloaded and aimed more carefully, squinting in the gloom.

"Black devils!" they shouted at the figures looming above.

"Savages!"

They raged and puffed and flushed deep and hot with fear. "I am too old for this," each one thought as he fired, tensed for the impact of a flying spear, imagining a long and horrible death.

They were lucky to have landed in the shallow bed of the stream that wound through the canyon, so they had some measure of cover. The summer rains had ended four months before, leaving pools of water in the stream bed. Some Boers landed in dry sand, some in mud, and a few in water. Expecting any moment for their ambushers to overrun them, the Boers did not take their eyes off the top of the canyon wall.

Although the Boers were good shots and some were only a few yards away, they fired at the top of the wall, not its shadowy face, so they did not hit the boy. His goats had rushed out of the canyon, bleating alarm, into his village, where the volley of shots drew the BaNare's attention. A thousand men grabbed their spears and a dozen grabbed their muskets. All raced to the mouth of the canyon. As they ran they cursed the sentry who had fallen asleep and let Boers pass.

The BaNare had no time to don their spiked headdresses. In fact, few owned them. They worked their way along the ridge to the canyon mouth, to take positions among the straight, single-trunked aloe trees, as tall as a man, whose silhouetted crowns of thorny, spiked leaves the Boers had mistaken for warrior headdresses. No one knows how many aloes the Boers shot before the BaNare soldiers arrived.

And so before the raiders realized their error, the sea of warriors began to return their fire. The gunshots woke the delinquent BaNare sentry, who made his way along the canyon wall to join the BaNare army. Passing above the Boers, he pushed down loose boulders, which fell far short but fed the Boers' panic. The sky darkened quickly and a cool breeze swept through the canyon. The Boers looked small, like children, from atop the canyon wall.

The BaNare commander raged and thundered and punched the sentry in the eye. He began to beat the man senseless, but then he thought of something else. "You will drive away the Boer horses," he ordered. "That will leave them no cover and no escape."

It was a good idea but a dangerous thing for the sentry, whose brother bravely stepped forward and insisted on going too.

The brothers crept down around the rocks, along the dry stream bed, as twilight turned to night. They could hear the Boers wheezing above the gunfire, the horses snorting and still catching their breath from the ride. The air smelled of gunpowder and dust. The Boers stopped firing as the night grew black, with only a dim glow of starlight in the cold, moonless sky. The two brothers crept without a sound along the stream bed and reached the first two horses. They listened to the Boers swearing behind the horses. Foul horse breath filled their nostrils, and blood: one of the nearby Boers was wounded. Separating, each to one horse, the brothers reached to their loincloths, drew their knives, and plunged them into the horses.

That very same moment a full moon rose up from behind the canyon walls, bathing the battlefield in gray light. Illuminated by the moon, the brothers' bodies snapped in the air and fell to the ground, pierced by a dozen Boer bullets.

The screams of the dying horses brought the other animals to their feet. The Boers jumped up to seize the reins and haul the horses back down, exposing themselves to fire from the canyon wall, with moonlight improving the BaNare's aim. By the time the Boers resettled their horses, a score were wounded.

Through the night the BaNare fired down on the Boers. Some crawled along the wall to push boulders down as the sentry had done. The Boers fired at every movement in the moonlight, and BaNare men fell from the wall to the canyon floor, wounded or dead, some close enough for the herdboy against the wall to turn around and touch. Until midnight the moon shone full onto his tiny, trembling figure. The rock cooled quickly, turning him cold as well. His spare loincloth offered no warmth. When he flinched at a rifle report, pressing his body into the rock, his tender private parts beneath the loincloth felt frozen, numbed with pain. The BaNare men above him also wore loincloths, but during the night young boys brought them fur blankets from the village.

The boy's mother had reported him missing. She told how she had sent him to the canyon to herd his goats just before the battle began, so when morning came the BaNare peered down to search the length of the battlefield for the boy.

"There he is!"

"He is dead!" they guessed.

"Poor luckless boy!"

There was no way to reach him, even to see whether he really was dead. He was so close to the Boers, in plain sight. Certainly, the BaNare surmised, the Boers had noticed him and dispatched a bullet to the back of his skull. The rocks held him up, spread against the wall.

When morning came, the boy's rock warmed slowly. By midday it glowed, hot to his mouth pressed tightly against it. The Boers' ammunition ran low, so they conserved their rounds, firing only when a shot was clear. For long periods they did not fire at all. During one of these lulls the boy opened his eyes. He studied the uneven grain of the red rock, the flies buzzing in the warm crevice between the wall and his body. He heard the Boers' every grunt, every word, every cry of pain when a spear found its mark. The BaNare aimed first at the horses, for their missiles flew in slow, lofty arcs and the crouching Boers could follow their flight and dodge them. Each time a horse screamed, the others panicked and the Boers made good targets when they stood to pull the horses back to the ground. The afternoon sky passed as cloudless as the previous night's, piercing blue, filling with dust and rising sweat.

As the day ended, as shadow crept up the canyon, the Boers decided to make their escape. Tying their wounded and dead to their surviving horses, they pushed the horses to their feet, swung on, some two or three Boers per horse, fired their last rounds, and disappeared down the darkened canyon. The BaNare hurled a final volley, and though many Boers were hit, they all stayed on their horses. The BaNare counted one hundred Boers wounded or killed—it was impossible to tell which. Seventy BaNare were dead, including the sentry and his valiant brother. More than one hundred others were wounded.

As soon as the Boers were gone, the men shouted and scrambled down. Women and children raced up from a safe distance to kneel by the BaNare casualties lying on the canyon floor. As they drew near the young herdboy against the rock wall, they saw that no blood stained his skin. They called out to him and gently tugged at his shoulders, but he continued to tremble with his eyes clamped tight, his hands and arms embracing the smooth rock face. "He is a shy boy," they remembered aloud. "We must wait for his mother."

By the time the boy's mother arrived, the entire village had crowded onto the battlefield. The BaNare stood watching as she rushed to the child who had miraculously endured a day and a night at the mercy of the deadly Boers. She whispered to him and gently pried his body from the rock, gathering him into her arms. Once free of the rock, his skinny, quivering arms flew to his mother's neck, and he buried his head in her bare breast. Tall and broad-backed, she blanketed the child almost completely. She turned to carry him to the village and the crowd parted to let her pass.

By this time the joy of driving away so many Boers had overshadowed the grief of so many casualties. And no cattle had been lost. As the BaNare followed the boy's mother, bathed in the same twilight that had met the Boers the previous day, the bearers of the dead disappeared into the surging crowd, which began to sing and dance in jubilation. By the time they reached Naring, they had composed a new song, praising the brave child who symbolized their victory, forgetting his original name and bestowing a new one: Mojamaje, "Eater of Rocks." The BaNare still sing today the chorus of this song:

All through the night
Through the terrible fight
Mojamaje kept watch by the door
First he ate a rock
Then he ate a bullet
Then Mojamaje ate a Boer

2

How the BaNare Saw the World

The BaNare like the story of the Battle of the Rocks because it features three of the most important characters in the story of the Great Thirst. These are Mojamaje himself, his mother, and his grandfather, Tladi, who commanded the BaNare troops that day. Mojamaje grew up to become the greatest hero in BaNare history, so that the story of his life and the story of the Great Thirst now are told as one. Although the story actually begins with Tladi, and some tellers go back even further, before the BaNare first came to Naring, the Battle of the Rocks marks the beginning of Mojamaje's career as a hero. The BaNare tell many stories and Mojamaje figures in most—slaying foes, making rain—but only the story of the Great Thirst sets the record straight. It gives a true picture of Mojamaje's heroism, a thing easily misunderstood but important to know, for he lived in a time when the world changed completely and the BaNare struggled to survive within it.

In Mojamaje's lifetime the Boers and then the English swept across South Africa. A century of chaos followed them, and the rolling grasslands reddened with blood. But the story of the Great Thirst is less about South Africa than about a people, the BaNare themselves, at their best and at their worst. It is a story they can never afford to let their children forget.

In ancient times, before coming to Naring, the BaNare lived in a part of South Africa known as Taung, one hundred miles to the east. There grass grew so green and luxuriant that corn poked like weeds through every inch of sweet red soil. Once a week the women cleared it away from the gates of their compounds, otherwise grain stalks sprouted under their fur-blanket beds on the mud floors of their houses, disturbing their sleep. Taung cattle stayed fat all year, even in the dry winter. Cows' udders burst with milk and children grew fat milking them, squirting once into the jug, once into their mouths, until they could drink no more. Women stored the rest in clay pots to thicken and sour and mix with porridge. There were so many cattle that Taung smelled of roast meat: each night somewhere in the village a family slaughtered an ox or old cow, dug a pit, filled it with dead wood and threw on chunks of beef. They lit the fire and their relatives and neighbors squatted around, each fixing one eye on a particular piece of meat, chatting, waiting until the morsel was done to perfection, snatching it out and stuffing it into a jabbering mouth. They laughed and sang and threw bones to their dogs. Red grease smeared their chins, reflecting the glow of the flames as the night fell dark around them.

The Taung people seldom ventured west, for even at such a great distance they feared the Kalahari Desert. No one knew where it started. West of Taung, red earth faded to sandy soil, then dark soil again, then broken rock, sandy soil, rock. Grass grew thinner and tougher. Trees grew farther apart, twisted, stunted, with tiny, leathery leaves. But these changes came slowly, so from mile to mile even careful explorers noticed little difference. Then suddenly, when they stopped to drink from a stream, the bed was dry as dust. They noticed now that the soil was not only sandy: it was pure sand, coarse and yellow, as deep as they could dig. They scratched away at the stream bed to find wet sand beneath, and they pressed their lips down, moistening them, but this did nothing for the thirst slowly choking their throats. The sun burned the backs of their necks as they knelt over the hole. The smell of water filled their parched nostrils, driving them wild with a great and terrible thirst.

Unable to find a trail with water along the way, the people of Taung abandoned their forays west, afraid to penetrate too far. But one summer a herdboy followed a stray cow's hoofprints across the empty plains west of Taung, toward the Kalahari. The cow's tracks wandered back and forth, north and then east, west again, always from water to water. The boy followed for days, munching berries, sleeping in trees, until he came to a ridge of hills with a narrow canyon cut through. Climbing to the top of the ridge, he gazed down the other side on a stream of water alongside a village of thirty round houses. This was Naring. The stream wound across a broad valley, a shallow bowl. The ridge walled its eastern rim. On the western side rose a gentle slope of pale yellow sand, covered with blue-green brush and stunted trees. It was a lovely spot, the last reliable water supply before entering the deep Kalahari on the opposite side of the village.

The herdboy made his way back to Taung and told his relatives. One night soon thereafter, while the rest of Taung chewed their beef, a dozen families packed their belongings into goatskin sacks and slipped away, unnoticed by the others. They paused at the enormous wooden pen where the whole village kept its cattle. Eyes shining with avarice, they selected the fattest half of the herd, some ten times their share, and drove the cattle slowly and quietly west toward Naring.

Near dawn, two of the greedy defectors returned to the pen, threw open its gate, set the posts on fire and ran back west to join the others. Crazed with fear, the remaining cattle charged against each other, froze where they stood, then escaped through the open gate, dashing in all directions, lowing in panic. The Taung people spent a week rounding them up. After counting them twice, then counting the number of families gone, they discovered the theft. This was how the BaNare first came to Naring, following the nimble herdboy back along the stray cow's route. The people of Taung never pursued their larcenous relatives, because approaching the Kalahari was treacherous business and a week of rain washed all trace of their trail.

The herdboy warned the BaNare that Naring was occupied, so they kept their spears and knives ready. When they reached the ridge, the men ran ahead through the canyon, thirty in number, cautiously, expecting ambush, crouched to strike back. They met no resistance. They marched into the village on the other side to claim Naring for their own.

"We are BaNare!" they shouted, thrusting their spears in the air.

"We come from Taung!"

"Get out before we eat you!"

This was an important moment in the story of the Great Thirst, for it marked the first meeting of the two sides of Mojamaje's family. His father's ancestors were among the BaNare who invaded Naring; his mother's ancestors were among the unfortunate villagers who suddenly found themselves invaded. In shock and disbelief they gathered around the BaNare warriors.

"How did they get here?" they asked one another.

"We thought we were safe," the women cried, clasping their daughters to their breasts.

The BaNare men continued to leap and shout, making menacing jabs with their spears toward the worried villagers assembling in a circle around them.

"What are they saying?" the villagers asked. They were BaKii, with a language like the BaNare's, but the invaders were yelling and this added to the difficulty of understanding them. Finally they calmed down, and an old BaKii man stepped forward.

"What do you say?" he asked slowly, to make sure the warriors understood him.

The invaders replied, also slowly and clearly, "Get out. The BaNare are here. Get out before we eat you."

The BaKii looked at each other with dread. They had no iron to tip their spears, and only twenty men of fighting age. It was futile to resist. They packed their belongings in goatskin sacks and departed. The BaKii had a name for the place but the BaNare never asked it. The conquerors named the valley Naring, meaning "Place of the BaNare."

The BaNare did not let the BaKii take their cattle, but only their goats. Some BaKii set out east, to South Africa, to throw themselves on the mercy of whoever would take them in. Others retreated west, into the deep Kalahari, Mojamaje's mother's ancestors among them. They wandered for months, living off roots and meat from the animals they trapped in tiny rope snares. They ate desert hares, bat-eared foxes, guinea fowl, duikers, ant-wolves, drinking their blood instead of water.

Their luck changed at a place they named Loang. This is an important place in the story of the Great Thirst, because Mojamaje's parents met there, and there Mojamaje was born.

The BaKii came upon Loang by chance, after many had died, first the oldest and then the youngest. There were other places that resembled it throughout the Kalahari. It was a broad, flat valley, very much like Naring, but without trees, grass, or a ridge of hills. The Kalahari had no hills, which were always made of rock. The Kalahari had only sand. It lay in waves like swells of a sea, an endless patchwork of wide, shallow basins. Loang was one of the widest.

One morning the BaKii came upon a herd of antelope on the glittering surface of the largest salt pan they had ever seen. Before the wind carried their scent to the animals, they were able to creep very close.

Then the first antelope snapped up its head, its pointed ears flapping to hear what its snout had just smelled. One by one the others did the same. A volley of spears flew through the air, and the herd galloped off, their hooves clicking loudly on the pan's surface. Two spears hit their marks. When the BaKii ran up to carve the antelopes into a meal, they noticed a flicker of light from the shallow holes the animals had scoured. Water.

Rain did fall over the Kalahari in summer, but not very much, and it quickly sank through the sand, out of reach. Sometimes it left pools on the surface, but these evaporated at once in the summer heat. The largest pools left a thick white crust of shimmering salt when they dried. The crust grew thicker every year. Huge brown antelope, their spiraled horns sweeping back from their high foreheads, came to the dry pools to lick the salt. They scraped their forehooves against the crust, digging down below to wet salt, the color of silver. Beneath the salt, centuries of rain lay trapped in mud, protected from the searing sun by the thick crust above.

Frenzied, wild, using only their hands, the BaKii dug three shallow wells in the Loang pan. The water was salty but drinkable, a parched oasis. Their journey had ended, in the deep Kalahari, perhaps fifty, perhaps a hundred waterless miles west of Naring. They had five goats left, only one female, but within a few years these multiplied to a sizable herd. The BaKii trapped game in the wilderness around them and gathered white roots and sour purple berries from the gnarled bushes and trees. They built a village by the wells, Loang, meaning "Place of Luck."

Years later the BaNare learned about the BaKii's luck at Loang. And so with Taung and South Africa to the east; Loang and the Kalahari to the west; Naring in the center—this was how the BaNare saw the world.

3

Lightning

Most tellers of the story of the Great Thirst do not go so far back in BaNare history: they begin with the Battle of the Rocks, and some begin with Mojamaje's grandfather, Tladi. Some tellers prefer to forget that the story of the BaKii is part of the story of Mojamaje's birth. Mojamaje was the first BaNare to have a BaKii parent. Some BaNare look down on the BaKii, whom they conquered without a fight. They like to forget how they stole the Taung cattle and drove the BaKii away, and also that almost all BaNare now have some BaKii blood. Tellers with the most BaKii blood leave Mojamaje's birth out of the story.

Every child has four grandparents: sometimes, though, one can be singled out as most responsible for the child's birth. This was the case with Mojamaje. Had it not been for Tladi, his father's father, the BaNare and BaKii would never have met again. Tladi brought them together, to produce Mojamaje, the BaNare's greatest hero. Unlike his famous grandson, Tladi received his name at birth. He was born at night during a violent thunderstorm, which the BaNare remember with this song:

> Lightning in the sky
> *Ah-eee-ah-yah!*
> Lightning beneath the clouds
> *Ooo-ta-ta!*
> Lightning in his heart
> *Paah-pah!*
> Lightning between his legs
> *Pooo!*

Tladi meant "lightning," and everyone agreed it was the perfect name for him. As soon as Tladi grew out of infancy, it was clear that he hated everyone. No one knew why. Some said it was the storm, a streak of lightning destroying his heart. It might have been his childhood, but no one remembers the details of his early life, perhaps because so many of his adult exploits ended up in the story of the Great Thirst. Both tellers and listeners could take only so much of Tladi.

He was born in Naring, a century or so after the BaNare arrived there. They had sprouted from a handful of families to nearly two hundred, grazing their cattle on the surrounding savanna, hoeing gardens in the valley. When summer rain fell, Naring reminded them of Taung, except that now the surrounding grass fed no herds but their own. Their cattle multiplied to a vast fortune. They scratched the earth and scattered seeds as they had always done and worried not at all that the rain fell more lightly, soaking the soil orange only a few inches down, so a kick with bare toes exposed dry sand beneath. Less corn, perhaps, but their cattle thrived.

Every winter, though, they fought off the suspicion that perhaps leaving Taung had been a mistake. As the summer rain faded, shallow pools in the pastures dried overnight, grass browned to straw and blew away, the cattle fell back on the only remaining source of water, the stream through the canyon. The Kalahari advanced from the west. A cold arid wind spread over the gentle slope of sand into the BaNare's midst, drying their skins and sweeping eddies of dust into the air. Women and girls wrapped themselves in hide blankets and hurried through the village carrying icy water, which sloshed out of the pots on their heads to sting their cheeks. Long months passed. The BaNare dug in the stream bed to expose muddy water, watched their cattle drink it, and waited anxiously for rain. The first summer storms revived their faith in Naring as the Kalahari retreated west, back over the sandy slope. Grass sprang back green and cattle returned to the pastures, shaken but reassured.

As years passed the BaNare learned tricks, some from the Bushmen, to lessen the impact of winter. They learned to appraise the roll of the savanna and find places to dig for water. They learned to keep goats away from the stream pools in winter, saving the precious water for their long-legged red cattle, whose teeth were too massive and smooth to pluck the tiny leaves from bushes and suck from them drops of moisture. During winter, goats lived on leaves, and the noise of their thirsty bleats forced the BaNare to wonder what fate would befall them if the summer rains ever failed. Even the lushest valleys of South Africa preserved the memory of ancient droughts, evil descending unannounced, undeserved, on its powerless victims. And all South Africa feared the Kalahari, source of the dry west wind, origin of drought. Drought brought thirst, but only a few great thirsts brought hunger and death.

Naring spread across the valley, the door of each new house facing east, to the rising sun, to South Africa. When women gave birth inside their houses, they pointed their legs east so their babies would emerge facing east as well. When a child began to come out backward, the mother spun quickly around so the child would still face east. Tladi was born backward, but he popped out too quickly for his mother to turn, so he faced west, to the Kalahari. Perhaps a bolt of lightning shocked her, forcing the infant out.

As soon as Tladi could walk, he probed the edge of the Kalahari, always facing west. He preyed on girls carrying water from the stream, clay pots balanced carefully on their heads. "Walk," he growled, a stick in one hand raised ready to strike. Older girls ignored him but the youngest were easy game when they came alone to the stream. Terrified, they obeyed. He dragged them over the sandy slope, out to the Kalahari, where they walked before him through the sand and coarse yellow grass. Tladi drank from their pots when he grew thirsty and turned back when the water was gone. The girls were left to carry their empty pots back home. Tladi never let them drink along the way.

As Tladi grew older he pounced on older girls, who carried larger pots, allowing him to penetrate deeper west. The girls told their brothers, who fell on Tladi in gangs of ten. Tladi won, fighting them off with the fury of an animal, gnashing his teeth, shrieking with glee.

He was short, very dark, with arms like knotted ironwood branches, lumps of muscle bursting through his skin. At the age of twelve he began as well to force himself on his water-bearers, until their brothers joined together in gangs of twenty that Tladi could not defeat. After four beatings he gave up his Kalahari walks. But he still faced west. Adults told the story of driving out the BaKii a century before, but still no BaNare had been to Loang. This was Tladi's goal, to discover the BaKii settlement and then use it as a base for exploring farther west.

The BaNare knew of Loang from the Bushmen, who came to Naring for water. Although today the Bushmen have nearly vanished, in Tladi's time, when the BaNare were few in number and never left Naring, the Bushmen kept them informed of the world around them. The Bushmen wandered everywhere, in bands of twenty or thirty, hunting wild animals, gathering wild roots, eating anything they could lay their hands on. They slept under mounds of grass and twigs and had no permanent home. Bushmen believed they owned the whole world: everyone else was a trespasser, squatting on Bushman land. They were frail and yellow-skinned, with cheekbones so high that they pulled their eyes tight into narrow slits. Bushmen were even shorter than Tladi, no taller than children, dirty, dusty, and wild.

The Bushmen hunted with tiny wooden arrows whose tips they smeared with poison made from a Kalahari caterpillar. Following antelope from pan to pan was a tough business, completely unpredictable, for the animals migrated in huge herds with no apparent aim. The Bushmen killed as many as they could, whenever they could, for they never knew when they might eat again. When they ate all they wanted, their bellies stuck out so far they could not see their toes. More often they went hungry.

When a Bushman band roamed close, the BaNare gave them water and occasionally a goat, not out of compassion but because the Bushmen had a reputation for eating anything. The BaNare did not want to end up on Bushman roasting spits. Eventually some BaNare learned to speak Bushman, a language composed of clicks and whistles instead of words. Tladi became fluent, so when Bushmen passed by Naring, he asked them about the Kalahari. The Bushmen explained that the BaKii thrived at Loang, with vast herds of goats. The Bushmen also begged water from the BaKii, who proved more generous than the BaNare. This was because the BaKii felt more exposed, surrounded as they were by the Kalahari. A few BaKii of every generation were even encouraged to marry Bushmen. The children of these marriages grew up and married in Loang, so eventually BaKii skin grew yellower, their cheekbones grew higher, their bodies grew smaller.

The BaNare laughed when the Bushmen told them this. "Bushmen!" they scoffed when the Bushmen were gone. "The BaKii are turning into Bushmen!"

Some say Tladi learned to speak Bushman because he was so short, like them, and felt more comfortable in their company. The real reason was the Kalahari: they were its masters, at home in its endless expanse. "Where does it end?" he asked them. "How far beyond Loang?"

The Bushmen laughed and jumped on one foot, thumping each other on the chest, whistling and snorting and singing this song:

> Where does the sun go?
> Into the sand
> Where does the sun go?
> Into the sand

Tladi understood this to mean that the Kalahari continued to the western horizon, as far as the setting sun, to the end of the world, where Tladi could see the sun vanish into the earth at the end of the day. Loang was the first step.

4
Lightning Strikes

Tladi grew into a brutal young man, the only BaNare to carry a knife in his loincloth. Girls covered their breasts when he passed, folding their arms across their chests to hide from his wicked leer. He married a cousin, who bore him two sons, and Tladi beat them all with a stick. The BaNare noticed the look in his eye, the dreamy ferocity, empty of vanity, reckless and sincere. Tladi never lied or played tricks. He was a violent man, secure in his strength and power. The BaNare remember no one else like him, but then he lived in an unusual age. Some say Tladi was a product of his times, while others insist that lightning produced him, in one terrible, deafening crack.

Before Tladi's first child grew to adulthood, a thousand refugees flooded into Naring from South Africa. A thousand more arrived the next year. They fled the Zulu, and the stories they told were horrible.

"The Zulu are tall and strong and do not hold life sacred."

"They are killers."

"They stop at nothing."

"They do not fight like human beings."

Instead of running and throwing their spears from a distance, as everyone else did, the Zulu held their spears under their arms and marched in step until they stuck the tips into whoever stood in their way. The refugees provided the BaNare with abundant details about which parts of human bodies the Zulu stabbed with their spears.

A throwing spear was a shaft of wood as tall as a man, with a flat iron tip as long as a man's hand. When a Zulu brute invented the stabbing spear, the days of the throwing spear were over. A stabbing spear had a short, thick handle, with a blade as long and broad as a man's forearm. Throwing spears stayed sharp forever, for they seldom hit their targets, but constant stabbing quickly dulled the tips of stabbing spears, which the Zulu thrust deep into men, deep into women and deep into children. As a result the Zulu were forever sharpening their spears.

Worse yet, they were multiplying. As soon as the Zulu ravaged a village, its surviving men organized themselves into the same formation as the Zulu, holding stabbing spears under their arms. They claimed that this was necessary to meet the next Zulu attack. It was kill or be killed. These imitators turned out as bad as the Zulu. In this way, wave after wave of Zulu and Imitation Zulu overran the South African grasslands. Their frightened victims called them all Zulu. The Zulu began at the coast a thousand miles from the Kalahari, and within a decade they approached Naring.

As they spread, the Zulu and Imitation Zulu met less and less resistance. They wore furs and feathers and stood on some prominent point, in plain sight of their prey, screaming Zulu war cries, thumping their Zulu spears against their Zulu oxhide shields, stamping the handles of their spears against the ground. It was an impressive display. The villagers below ran for their lives, shrieking, leaving their cattle for the Zulu to take. This reduced the blood they spilled, but not by much, for the Zulu liked to chase down the fleeing villagers and stab them with their spears.

The BaNare cringed at the news of the stabbing spear—all except Tladi, who wished he had thought of it first. He often remarked on the inefficiency of the throwing spear; how two bands of men ran into each other and hurled their spears across a distance small enough to be threatening but not small enough for accuracy. Most of these tosses missed their marks by yards, so after a man cast his own spear, he picked up one the enemy had thrown and threw it back. Whichever band had fewer men eventually scattered, leaving the disputed booty to the victors. Few men ever died in battle. As for the booty, this was cattle, women and children. The victors led away the cattle, took the children captive and burned the women on the spot. "Burn" meant forcing a woman at the point of a knife.

The only people to thwart the Zulu were the Wall-Makers, whom the BaNare remembered from Taung. They lived to the south, in the largest village in South Africa, a bustling metropolis with the finest singers and the fattest cattle history had ever produced. Their village crowned a massive flat-topped hill with ample water and grass. They built a rock wall around the rim of the hill and a smaller inner wall around the village itself. For countless generations they lived inside this fortress, their warriors trained to stab anyone who tried to climb over the wall. They beat back the Zulu time and again, to the envy and admiration of their less fortunate neighbors.

Tladi thrilled at the refugees' tales. His compound stood directly across from the BaNare chief's, and one morning Tladi woke Naring by strutting before the chief's home, shouting, "I demand, Chief Potso, to form a regiment! The men of Naring are not cowards. We are men, BaNare warriors, defenders of our people." The BaNare stumbled out of their blankets to rush outside. "Let them come," Tladi continued, his deep voice shaking the calm of dawn like the rumble of a rainstorm. "Let the Zulu come!"

A crowd quickly formed around Tladi, standing alone in only his loin-cloth, though it had rained all night and the morning air was cold. The young men whispered excitedly, discussing Tladi's proposal. Old men and women clucked their tongues and said to each other, "I knew he would turn out like this."

Chief Potso stepped out of his compound. The BaNare loved their chief and appreciated his many talents. Potso was descended from the clever herdboy who had led the BaNare from Taung to Naring, following the tracks of a stray. Potso's father died, passing the chiefship to his son, when Potso was a very young man. He accepted the role nobly, shouldering the burden of rule with natural grace and patience. "My soul is not my own," he often sighed. "It belongs to my people." Potso had a young son, whom he serenaded with songs and dressed in royal leopard skins. Potso himself dressed in a full-length leopard cape, clutching it closed with one hand. The other hand rubbed one temple or stroked his chin. The BaNare thought him chiefly and grand. He stayed trim, muscular, fit, a striking figure with cool brown eyes and a clear, penetrating voice.

He was no match for Tladi, though, and the BaNare knew it. The Zulu threat called for action. They could see that the refugees' tales gave Tladi ideas: he wanted to form a stabbing-spear regiment of Imitation Zulu. Was this not the only way to protect the BaNare from other Zulu? But the BaNare asked a second question: If Tladi formed a stabbing-spear regiment, who would protect the BaNare from Tladi?

Potso stepped out to face Tladi in the open lot between their two compounds. He looked magnificent. His leopard-skin cape was tied around his waist, its tails trailed behind in the dust, leaving his shoulders bare to the morning sun. His skin was smeared with goat fat, and also his hair, so his body gleamed as he walked, erect, head held high, to meet his challenger.

"BaNare," Potso called, raising his arms to the sky. "Why would the Zulu come here?" Tladi stood a few yards away, leaning back on a twisted log, on a woodpile that lay between the two compounds. He twitched with frustration, his eyes fixed on Potso, hatred boiling behind them.

"The Zulu will never come here," Potso continued. Now he strolled slowly along the edge of the crowd, peering one by one into each pair of eyes. "What do we possess? What do they want here? Nothing. We have the stream through the canyon, some grass in the pasture, some trees with sour fruits and berries. These trees are not very tall. They are few. It almost never rains. Our crops almost always fail. We live almost in the Kalahari, where the trees are shorter and fewer and there is even less rain. There is only grass here. Do the Zulu eat grass?"

When Potso spoke the word *Kalahari*, he pointed west, to the sand ridge, and the BaNare looked to Tladi. Then Potso swept his arm in a wide arc and pointed east. "Remember South Africa?" he continued. "The Zulu come from South Africa. Remember Taung? There are tall trees there. There is plenty of food. Why would the Zulu leave South Africa to come here? They will only grow weary with thirst and turn back. They are not stupid. The BaNare are safe because the BaNare have nothing the Zulu want."

"Except cattle," Tladi interrupted fiercely. "They will steal them all, burn our women, steal our children. And this idiot wants us to do nothing." The crowd had just fallen into Potso's rhythm, absorbed in the poetry of his soothing reassurance; now Tladi broke the spell with hard facts, the worst sort of medicine. The BaNare wavered, torn between their man of words and their man of action. Tladi stormed off, shouting curses into the morning, beating his chest with his fists.

Potso smiled serenely, pressing one hand to his temple. "They will not come," he said.

They came, of course, one morning a month later. The sentry on the ridge ran into Naring, crying "Zulu!" with the shriek of a dying bird. "Zulu! Zulu! Zulu! Zulu!"

He had spotted a column on the eastern plain, on the other side of the hills, marching straight for Naring. The refugees in the village screamed in reply and fled over the sand ridge into the Kalahari. The rest of the BaNare raced close behind. Naring was deserted when the Zulu arrived, except for about half their cattle, which no one had remembered to let out of the corral in the center of the village. The Zulu scoured the area around Naring, seeking someone to stab, but the BaNare had a good head start and were still running as fast as they could. The Zulu found no one to kill. They led the cattle away and set fire to Naring's thatched roofs. This took some time, for the village spread out for miles. Because the roofs were still damp from recent rain, only a few burned through.

Tladi spat in the dust. "Potso is a coward!" he shouted. "Kill or be killed!"

Potso grinned mysteriously, as if he knew a secret. "They will not come back," he said. "Now we are safe."

But the tide had turned in Tladi's favor. And his plan was surprisingly modest: instead of meeting the Zulu in force, he would lead a regiment west to Loang, to capture the wells from the miserable BaKii. The BaNare would send their remaining cattle there to graze and drink in safety from Zulu raiders. No Zulu would dare enter the Kalahari. But Tladi quickly found that the BaNare did not dare do so either. Only refugees answered Tladi's call to arms, eager to do unto others what the Zulu had done to them. As new arrivals to Naring, they feared the Kalahari less than the true BaNare did, except for Tladi, who had waited for this chance all his life.

Two hundred young refugee men put themselves under Tladi's command. They cut their throwing spears down to short stabbing spears and held them under their arms. The iron tips were far too small to be authentic, but the BaKii would never know the difference. The new regiment practiced stabbing the mud walls of the houses in Naring. "Eee-yah!" they shouted, thrusting their spears, terrifying the occupants of the houses on the other side of the walls.

Potso refused to endorse Tladi's plan. "He is a renegade," Potso calmly insisted. "He must be stopped." The refugees already outnumbered the original BaNare by a considerable margin: if they all flocked to Tladi, this would pose a grave threat to Potso's rule. But no one tried to stop Tladi. The BaNare admitted that the Kalahari was the only safe place for their cattle. And perhaps Tladi would remain in Loang once he conquered the place. The BaNare cattle would be safe from the Zulu and the BaNare would be safe from Tladi.

No one raised a hand against Tladi, but he hated Potso for opposing his scheme, for his weakness, his vapid poetry. But Tladi occupied himself with training his regiment, until one of his recruits showed him a pouchful of black powder, at night, in the secrecy of Tladi's house.

"What is it?" Tladi whispered.

"Fire," the eager young refugee replied.

"Where did you find it?"

"Boers."

Tladi whistled through his teeth, deeply impressed. This was many years before the Battle of the Rocks, long before Mojamaje's birth, so the BaNare had not yet seen a Boer. The refugees all talked about them, though only this one young man had ever seen one. There were thousands of Zulu, but only a few Boers, who kept to themselves, far to the south. Everyone talked about them with jangled trepidation, for they could do far more harm than Zulu. Boers rode horses and carried guns, while Zulu walked and carried spears. Boer skins were pale, like ghosts', and they wore clothes that clung to every part of their hairy, fleshy bodies, and wide-brimmed leather hats. Rumors flew the length of South Africa but the Boers remained far behind, far south. Everyone hoped they would stay there. None of the refugees had ever seen a horse or a gun, except for this one young man, who came from so far south that he did business with a Boer, trading four headloads of jackal pelts in return for a pouch of gunpowder. The Boer showed him how the powder went into his rifle, then filled a tobacco leaf with powder and tossed it on the fire. Even such a small amount of gunpowder made a tremendous noise. The sparks burned a hole in the Boer's shirt.

This young refugee gave Tladi his pouchful of gunpowder in return for appointment as the regiment's second-in-command. As he crossed the sand ridge with his two hundred Imitation Zulu, headed for Loang, Tladi sent a messenger to take the pouch to Potso.

"He cannot fool me," Potso announced to his advisors. He stood before the cookfire in his own compound. "Tladi sent me this powder in a pouch. Because it is in a pouch, it must be medicine. Because Tladi sent it, it can only be poisonous medicine." He took a grand step toward the fire. "He thinks I will bury it in a pit or throw it into the wilderness. But I know better. I know about these things. If I do that, the medicine will find its way back to its victim. Me." Potso hefted the pouch in his hand and smiled a knowing smile. "Only fire can destroy something like this." He tossed the pouch onto the fire. The explosion scattered the advisors and burned Potso's face to the bone, ending his life.

5

The Conquest of the Kalahari

After a century of separation, a BaNare set out again to meet the luckless BaKii. Tladi was the only true BaNare among the raiders, since the rest were refugees. He was the sole representative of the original BaNare who had driven the BaKii out of Naring. Among the innocent BaKii, ignorant of the regiment's advance, was Mojamaje's mother. Mojamaje would be the most valuable result of Tladi's conquest of the Kalahari.

It took the regiment a week to reach Loang, Place of Luck. Tladi drove them day and night, pausing only each dawn to eat. Each warrior carried his spear in one hand and a water gourd in the other. Tladi and his second-in-command drank whenever they wanted, but the soldiers themselves were instructed to drink only once a day. The Zulu threat had given Tladi the chance to organize a caravan of two hundred water carriers, whereas before, as a boy, he could coerce only one girl at a time.

The water ran out halfway to Loang but Tladi drove his men onward. They broke rank completely, to stagger forward in the deep sand. Twice a day Tladi let them sleep for a few hours and then prodded them awake with his stabbing spear. Without hills to mark the horizon, they were uncertain of which direction to march, especially after they fanned out and lost each other in the tall grass and brush. In some places scraggly trees grew close enough together to provide shade for a few extra moments rest out of Tladi's sight. They kept the rising sun to their backs all morning, to keep facing west. But at midday the sun moved high through the northern sky: dazed with thirst, some men lost their bearings. When night fell, they were still lost. They peered through the dark for their fellows, unable to call out for fear of attracting lions.

When they reached Loang, they did not bother to regroup. Stumbling down to the wells to drink, they pushed away the startled BaKii watering their stock.

"Not again!" the BaKii cried.

The BaKii moved off without resisting, sullen, disheartened, gathering their stock to retreat out of sight. "We thought we were safe," they mumbled aloud, wiping tears from their dusty faces.

Tladi's regiment stabbed no one. They drank and rolled in the water. Tladi sprang into the deepest well and lay facedown in the mud, motionless, clutching his spear above his head with both hands. The Kalahari was his.

6
A Wonderful Thing

And so, through the agency of Tladi's Imitation Zulu, the Zulu Wars reached the deep desert, the last ripple of a great wave that engulfed all South Africa. The day after they reached Loang, Tladi's men recovered enough to begin burning the BaKii women. The BaKii numbered a few hundred, so there were as many BaKii men as BaNare conquerors. But the unfortunate BaKii had no spears and only a few old knives. "We can do nothing," they sulked. The burning rapidly fell into a regular pattern, in which the BaNare men passed over any BaKii woman whom they knew another BaNare man claimed. Each BaKii woman thus had some choice of which BaNare invader would burn her, but refusing them all was out of the question. A BaKii woman who made no choice was fair game for Tladi's entire regiment. To protect herself from the others, a woman submitted to one. Some BaNare men began living in the same house as their conquests, almost like husbands, but most did not.

Tladi's men occupied the village the BaKii had built alongside the wells. The BaKii men and old women withdrew a mile away to build another. Tladi waited for the rains, then sent half his men back to Naring, following the trail of empty water gourds they had dropped along the way. It was summer and the men were able to follow a straight line back to Naring, without any meandering, drinking from rainpools before the summer sun dried them. Back in Naring, they gathered up the remaining BaNare herds, except for a few milk cows the BaNare needed in the village for the children. Tladi's men drove the cattle back to Loang, growing familiar with the route, watering the cattle at the rainpools. Tladi's men in Loang cheered when the cattle arrived.

"They are here to stay," the BaKii muttered, eyeing the cattle with despair.

But Tladi's men were too proud to herd these cattle. Conquerors gave orders. They did not work. So Tladi farmed the cattle out to BaKii men, who reported to the regiment. Each BaNare conqueror had a BaKii herder under him: the herder was allowed to drink the milk, but the meat and half the calves belonged to the BaNare soldier. The other half belonged to Tladi. In this way the BaKii men herded cattle while the BaNare forced themselves on the BaKii women. Everyone at Loang was fully occupied. This was another reason the BaKii men did not hatch insurrection: The more time Tladi's men spent burning, the less time they spent overseeing the cattle. Only the BaKii herders kept track of cattle births and deaths, and of course they lied when they reported these numbers to the BaNare. The BaKii men did what they liked with the herds. They ate meat every day, in secret, and traded cows to the Bushmen for warm skins and pelts.

Tladi's conquest of Loang thus proved successful for the BaNare at Naring, for his regiment at Loang, and for the BaKii men. The BaKii women groaned and tore their hair.

"This is no way to live," they cried to each other, fearing for their daughters, who faced the same fate in the future.

"What can we do?"

"When will it end?"

"How can we save our daughters?"

One of the little BaKii girls decided to save herself. This was Mojamaje's mother. "We have no future," she explained to her friends, carrying water from the wells, past the leering eyes of Tladi's men, who scouted the young girls to see which ones were old enough for burning. Mojamaje's mother was only eight years old, but she made this decision: "I will join them," she said to her companions. "I will marry a BaNare." The other girls laughed, in desperate, ringing tones, and turned her hope into a sarcastic song. But even as a little girl, Mojamaje's mother was calm, serious and ruthless.

When she looked among the thugs in Tladi's regiment, her chances seemed impossible. She had five years at most to find a real husband before she grew old enough for the regiment to assault her. Then Tladi sent for his two sons, alone, without their mother, to come to Loang. One was almost a man, the image of Tladi. The other was small and frail, about Mojamaje's mother's age, and this is the one she chose. She would marry Tladi's younger son, officially, and become a BaNare.

Tladi's elder son was named Tumo, meaning "Thunder." He imitated his father in every way, but the BaNare were not impressed. They said Tumo (Thunder) followed Tladi (Lightning), but the Lightning did all the damage. Tumo challenged all the boys in Naring, but this was no real test, for no one dared strike a child of Tladi.

Mojamaje's mother dismissed Tumo immediately. "Too old," she said to herself. "He cannot wait to start burning us." But the younger son was a perfect candidate. The BaNare forgot the boy's name, though he grew up to be Mojamaje's father. They also forgot Mojamaje's mother's name, but this was no surprise. All BaNare women lost their names when they bore their first child, taking the child's name instead. After Tladi was born, his mother became Ma-Tladi, that is, "mother of Tladi." This is why Mojamaje's mother is remembered only as Ma-Mojamaje. Fathers, on the other hand, kept their own names, but Mojamaje's was an exception. The BaNare remember him only as Ra-Mojamaje, that is, "father of Mojamaje." In this case, the son was far more important than the father, and the BaNare remembered each accordingly.

Ra-Mojamaje was Tladi's opposite. He recoiled from his father's ferocity, wilting like a flower in the sun. He barely spoke or raised his eyes. Tladi beat him continually, like a dog, outraged at the state of his issue. Time and again he caught the boy eating spiders. This made him fear the boy was mad, which only made Tladi more angry. "Idiot!" Tladi bellowed as he beat his son unconscious.

Tumo joined the men of the regiment, while Ra-Mojamaje slept in Tladi's house. Tladi was the worst burner in Loang, so that every night the house filled with grunts and moans and cries. Houses had only one small room then, so the boy could not help hearing across the empty blackness of the room. Tladi forced the boy to sleep there in the hope that he would learn about burning. Ra-Mojamaje buried his head in his fur blankets, struggling not to listen.

The boy grew more depressed and frightened each day he spent at Loang. This gave Ma-Mojamaje her chance. She befriended him and set out to win him with cleanliness and sexual trickery. She kept her yellow skin clean because she overheard the BaNare regiment speaking about BaKii women. They said they were dirty, like Bushmen, and in general this was true. It made little sense to stay shiny clean in the Kalahari, for the wind blew dust everywhere, so that moments after washing, women were gray again with dirt. And water was precious. Why waste it washing? Ma-Mojamaje began spending most of her time carrying water from the wells to the BaKii village to wash from head to toe. She was always immaculate, as she imagined BaNare women to be. The BaKii had once been darker than the BaNare, as dark as even the Zulu, but when they came to Loang the BaKii mixed with Bushmen. Their skins grew ever lighter, their cheekbones rose higher on their faces. Ma-Mojamaje feared that the yellow of her clean skin appeared to the BaNare to be a layer of Kalahari dust. She was too tall to be a Bushman, but her cheekbones were the highest in Loang.

She resorted to sexual trickery because Ra-Mojamaje was terrified of girls. He knew nothing of sex, except that his father used it to make women scream. He saw what cattle and goats did, but he did not connect this with human beings, or even with the birth of calves and kids. His ignorance was complete. Young boys learned these things by talking with older boys, but Ra-Mojamaje hardly ever spoke to anyone, and never about sex. He wandered Loang and its environs, chasing hornbill and hoopoe birds, swallowing spiders, a little boy alone.

Ma-Mojamaje befriended him immediately. She walked beside him through the grass, holding his hand, chatting away at fantastic speed. At first he was too shocked to speak, but then he grew used to her. Slowly he answered back. To Loang adults they were two little children, casual friends, but the BaKii girls knew Ma-Mojamaje's intentions. They watched her progress carefully, wishing her success.

After two years her breasts began to rise slightly off her chest. Like other girls, she wore nothing but a makgabe, a string around her waist with a short fringe of leather dangling to the tops of her thighs. Her budding breasts were a mixed blessing: on one hand, she could use them to entice Ra-Mojamaje; on the other, they would eventually announce to Tladi's men that she was ripe for burning. She pulled Ra-Mojamaje down onto the coarse grass, a mile from Loang, and lay her new breasts across his belly.

"When we grow up," she whispered, eyelids low, "I will show you the most wonderful thing in the world."

Her breasts were naked and smooth, completely clean, but Ra-Mojamaje never touched them. He was a tougher case than she had thought. He conversed easily now, but his loins failed to stir. After five years Ma-Mojamaje grew desperate. Tall and full, with breasts as round as a woman's, she feared her days were numbered. Tladi's men were about to pounce. If she failed to drive Ra-Mojamaje wild with desire, soon, she was finished.

She turned to Tladi for help. To this day, the BaNare shake their heads at this remarkable fact. "Imagine," the teller of the story of the Great Thirst explains, "nowhere to turn, so she turns to Tladi, the worst burner of all. Who but the mother of Mojamaje would think to do such a thing?"

One morning she carried water to Tladi's compound and started to wash. She knew only Tladi was home. He came out of the house. She was thirteen now, too old to wash in sight of men. She drew handfuls of water along her bare yellow skin, shining in the early sunlight. Tladi looked at her, cocked his head and sat down without a word.

"My son worries me," he began. Ma-Mojamaje pressed a handful of water slowly across her full, woman's breast. "He eats spiders," Tladi continued. "He will never be a man."

Ma-Mojamaje raised one leg, resting it on a block of wood, the remains of a tree stump. She continued to wash, drawing water along her bare legs, above Tladi's head. He looked up, a storm in his eyes.

Ma-Mojamaje grabbed one breast with each hand, crouched down to thrust them before Tladi's face, and hissed, "Keep your animals away from my body and I will make your son into a man."

And so she won a reprieve, but a shaky one, which Tladi could rescind on a moment's whim. Sometimes Tladi looked at her as if debating whether to burn her himself. While her friends all bore children, Ma-Mojamaje persevered. Finally, after five more years of painstaking work, she decided Ra-Mojamaje was ready.

"The time has come," she cooed, "to show you the most wonderful thing in the world."

He loved it. Once a day for four months she showed Ra-Mojamaje what he thought to be the most wonderful thing in the world. She drove him wild with desire. His heart opened like a ripe melon, a stream of words flowing out, a childhood of anxiety flooding away.

"This is better than spiders," he admitted, lying happily on the sand.

After four months she said to him, "I have a confession."

He sat upright in the dust, wiping the sweat from his eyes. "What do you mean?" he asked.

"I feel so evil," she cried slyly, throwing herself against the ground. "You are so good and I am so bad."

He lay down to embrace her. "Tell me," he whispered.

She rubbed her eyes, shook her head. "I lied. I have not shown you the most wonderful thing in the world."

He laughed with relief. "What have you shown me?"

"The second most wonderful thing. We have done only half of what there is to do. There is more, much more."

"Then show me!" he said. "Show me the most wonderful thing in the world!"

Calmly, passionately, simply, sweetly, after ten years of planning, ten years of waiting, she said at last, "Only if you marry me."

He agreed without hesitation. She had driven him wild with desire and he would do anything for more. But her real test would be Tladi, for Ra-Mojamaje would risk death when he told him, and perhaps the poor abused boy would back down. Tladi would be outraged: BaNare did not marry BaKii women. They burned them. But Ra-Mojamaje could not burn anyone. He was not exactly sure what burning entailed, except that it was noisy, disgusting, and his father did it every night.

Ra-Mojamaje asked Tladi's permission to marry Ma-Mojamaje. Tladi punched him in the eye and began to cut out his tongue with a knife. "You will marry a baboon first!" Tladi shouted, but then he stopped to think. Tladi's violence was always calculated. He never lost control. Pausing, he withdrew the knife from Ra-Mojamaje's mouth.

"How did she do it?" Tladi asked. "What did she do to you?"

Ra-Mojamaje was too embarrassed to answer. He was growing tall and healthy at last, filling in the outline of a man. Tladi looked at him carefully, almost, for the first time, feeling a twinge of pride.

"Speak, boy," Tladi boomed. "How did she do it?"

Ra-Mojamaje stood up straight and cleared his throat. "For four months now," he stammered, "she has shown me something wonderful. But she says there is more. She will show me the final thing only if I marry her."

Tladi howled, hurling his knife into the mud wall of the house. "Filthy cow!" he bellowed.

"She is very clean," Ra-Mojamaje protested.

"I should have known," Tladi scowled. "I should have burned her myself."

Narrowing his eyes, he searched his son's face for some reflection of himself. The boy was now a head taller than Tladi, with the same powerful lines to his face, the same snub nose, but a longer, drawn pitch to his skull and neck. Tladi seemed to lean forward, ready to lunge, even as he stood still, while Ra-Mojamaje leaned back, as if in recoil. But now the boy stood erect, as if in compromise, one-half Tladi and one-half himself. Tladi saw all this, and the boy's long arms and legs, thickening into a man's.

"Burn her!" Tladi exclaimed, slapping his son on the back. "I showed you but you never watched."

Ra-Mojamaje wilted now, overcome by the strain. He looked almost in tears, unable to sustain his brave composure. Tladi winced and turned angry again. "You do not know how," Tladi moaned. "My idiot son!" He called out the door for one of his BaKii women. "I will show you again. This time you watch."

"No!" Ra-Mojamaje declared. "Never. As long as I live, I will never touch anyone else."

The image of the boy as an old man, chomping spiders, cut Tladi to the core of his vicious heart. He hit his son again, on the other eye, pulled his knife from the wall and started again to cut out his tongue. And then again he paused to think. He could not fight facts. "He will never burn anyone else," he thought. "Perhaps she will give him a son. At least he will have a son."

And so Mojamaje's parents were married, the first official union of BaNare with BaKii. Tladi wanted Ra-Mojamaje to beget a child out of pride, not concern for inheritance, for Tumo, who had joined the rest of the regiment in burning BaKii women, had made sure to venture periodically back to Naring to marry and then burn a proper BaNare wife. She bore him two healthy sons. Tladi had asked himself again and again, "What does it say of a man whose son has no vital juices?" Not for inheritance, the illusion of immortality, but for his own self-confidence, Tladi agreed to Ra-Mojamaje's marriage.

Tladi presented five cattle to Ma-Mojamaje's father to make the marriage official. For the wedding feast, Tladi slaughtered an old cow, hastily distributed the meat, and within an hour the meal was over. Mojamaje's parents were officially husband and wife.

Ma-Mojamaje's friends whispered, "How did she do it?" It was a victory for them all. Now Tladi's men regarded their BaKii women with suspicious reserve bordering on respect. They feared trickery, marriage, the fate of Ra-Mojamaje. But still no one knew her secret. "How did she do it?" everyone asked. Word reached Naring, and here too the people shook their heads in disbelief, because tricking Ra-Mojamaje meant tricking Tladi, his overlord. "How did she do it?" the BaNare asked.

On their wedding night, Ra-Mojamaje said to Ma-Mojamaje, "Show me the most wonderful thing in the world."

"Not now," she replied. "Soon."

He flushed with embarrassment, retreating in silence. He asked her again the next night and again a week later. Every time she refused, for a month, until at last she showed him not another magical pleasure, but a belly swollen tight with his child. Four months before, when she had proposed marriage, she had indeed already shown the innocent lad all there was to see. Only now did he learn that she had lied by saying that there was more to show him after the wedding.

Tladi hit his son on both eyes and ripped off half his ear with his teeth. Luckily, he was not carrying his knife. "My idiot son!" Tladi cried. Had Ra-Mojamaje watched his father's demonstrations, he might have evaded Ma-Mojamaje's trap. But because he never talked to anyone but Ma-Mojamaje, he had fallen for her ploy. Tladi beat his son unconscious and cried to the sky, "Burning a woman for four months without even knowing it!" He gave a final kick to Ra-Mojamaje's motionless body, prostrate on the dust of his compound floor. "I should have burned her myself," Tladi growled.

Tladi could have annulled the marriage by taking back the cattle he had given to Ma-Mojamaje's father. But the damage was done. And there was a glint of relief in Tladi's cold eyes, for at least his son had made a child, even if Ma-Mojamaje had done all the work. "I should have burned her myself," he continued to mutter, but in the end he let the marriage stand.

Ra-Mojamaje recovered quickly from Tladi's beating, as he had done throughout his childhood. For him the tragedy was Ma-Mojamaje's deception. For ten years she had slowly won his confidence, becoming his only friend. Now he wandered for days in the wilderness, trying to regain his strength, his resolve, the feeling of purpose and hope that her friendship had once instilled in him. He despaired to think that after all those years she loved him not at all.

But also he remembered the touch of her skin, that first time she won his final surrender. The air had been cool from morning rain, as she washed herself and then washed him, and led him out beyond Loang to the spindly shade of a thorn tree. She cleared away the grass and cow dung, leaving only a soft bed of pale orange sand. She removed his loincloth and gently pushed him to the ground. Blue sky and a flash of sun rushed past his eyes before he closed them tight, then opened them again to see her standing above him. She untied her leather apron, which had replaced her fringed makgabe when her body turned into a woman's. Still gleaming wet, she lay down atop him, gently, smelling of flowers, her smooth, clean yellow skin cool to the touch, as she whispered to him, at the moment of Mojamaje's conception, "This is the most wonderful thing in the world."

7

Bushman Eyes

Though Mojamaje's fame came later in life, he faced exacting demands from his very first breath. Child of the first official marriage between the miserable BaKii and their conquerors, he bore on his shoulders the hopes of the BaKii. He was also Tladi's grandson, the proof of his hapless son's manhood. Would Mojamaje grow up to be like his father, or like Tladi? But most of all, he was his mother's son, her only escape, her investment in a respectable future. When he entered the world, at the end of winter, Ma-Mojamaje feared to look at him, afraid that he resembled her, the color of dust, with cheekbones as high as a Bushman's.

"What does he look like?" she asked the women attending her, as soon as she felt him escape her loins.

"See for yourself," they replied, wiping Mojamaje and bringing him forward.

"I cannot!" she cried, stunning her attendants with the first loss of composure they had ever seen her suffer. "Tell me, please, does he look like me?" She was crying now in deep, heaving sobs.

"He is very dark," the women reassured, pressing the child into her arms. Ma-Mojamaje's hysteria subsided. She wiped her eyes and regarded her son. His face was indeed dark, but his cheekbones were as high as her own, pulling tight his wrinkly infant's skin. He looked half BaNare but that was enough, more than she had hoped for. She laughed until she cried again, squeezing him so tightly the women pulled him away, fearing she would crush him.

As soon as the summer rains began to fall, Ma-Mojamaje took her son to Naring. After the discovery of her trick, Tladi had dragged Ra-Mojamaje back into his own house at night, watching him closely to keep him away from her. Ra-Mojamaje did not try to see her. She was sorry for the boy, but felt no remorse. She would leave him in Loang. Perhaps in time he might recover. Her sights were set on Naring, where her son would become a full BaNare. She had no time to waste salving Ra-Mojamaje's battered heart.

She bundled Mojamaje in black goatskins and lashed him to her back. Tladi's men had been back and forth to Naring often enough to leave a faint path worn in the sand along the entire distance. Once trampled underfoot, a tuft of grass took years to grow back. The faint straight-line path cut days from the journey.

Ma-Mojamaje walked slowly, so as not to exhaust herself and dry the milk in her breasts. The early rains were so heavy that rainpools dotted the path. She drank whenever she wanted and washed herself in the rain. The BaNare remember no wetter week than when Mojamaje's mother carried him to Naring. After five days, she paused on the crest of the sand ridge above the village, fearful but courageous. Resting on the coarse grass to nurse Mojamaje, she drank from a rainpool and washed herself from head to toe. The sun quickly dried her skin as she wound her way down to Naring.

Word of her trick had preceded her, so the BaNare expected her arrival. At the outskirts of the village she asked for directions to Tladi's family compound. Her accent, child, cheekbones, yellow skin, her destination—all gave her away. Everyone knew who she was.

"How clean she looks," the BaNare whispered, watching her walk past their compounds.

"That is dust—that is why her skin looks so light."

"She looks like a giant Bushman."

The news flashed through the village, so Tladi's wife knew she was coming before Ma-Mojamaje arrived at the gate. She ran out to Ma-Mojamaje as soon as she came into sight. "Poor child!" she cried. "Poor child!" Behind her ran a younger woman: the wife of Tumo, Tladi's elder son.

Ma-Mojamaje looked up to see them running toward her, holding their bare breasts, shouting into the air. A cold shiver ran down her spine. "They will kill me," she said to herself, thinking to turn and run. Suddenly they were upon her. Tladi's wife pulled Mojamaje from her back, Tumo's wife threw her arm around her as if she were crippled, helping her back to the compound.

They sat her down inside their house. "Did he beat you?" Tladi's wife asked. "Did he beat the child?" They pulled off the skins binding Mojamaje, examining him for bruises. Then they examined Ma-Mojamaje, tearing the leather apron from her waist. At last they were satisfied, relieved.

"A miracle!" they exclaimed.

Ma-Mojamaje retied her apron and took in her surroundings. The round mud house had rain-stained walls, thatched with grass rotting in places, letting through streaks of sunlight. Tladi's wife and Tumo's wife looked alike: hunched, frightened, with eyes of hunted animals. Tladi's wife rocked Mojamaje in her arms, her eyes closed, her cheek pressed against his soft skull, humming a sad song.

"You need food," Tumo's wife announced, jumping up to run outside. Two naked little boys skittered into the house, chasing a dog with bleeding sores across its back. When the boys noticed Ma-Mojamaje, they drew up suddenly, to stand and stare. These were Dinti and Tabo, Tumo's sons. Tumo's wife returned with a wooden bowl of corn porridge. "Your new home," she said, a tense smile on her lips, as she drew one arm over her head. Behind her frantic eyes she was a lovely woman, tall, sturdy and dark, as was Tladi's wife, who woke from her reverie to lean close to Ma-Mojamaje, her brow drawn low in painful distress, to ask, "Did he burn you?"

She meant Tladi, of course, and now Ma-Mojamaje understood why these women and their compound appeared in such shambles. They lived in dread that he might return. Ma-Mojamaje lifted a spoonful of porridge to her mouth. It was less than half cooked.

"Only my husband has ever burned me," Ma-Mojamaje replied.

Tladi's wife and Tumo's wife fell silent. They sat against the mud wall of the house, listless, exhausted. They fell asleep. Ma-Mojamaje took Mojamaje from Tladi's wife's arms, and stepped outside past the two little boys still staring at her. The sun shone high overhead, and tall white clouds raced across the eastern sky. It would rain again that evening. She looked past the compound's thorn fence: Naring seemed remote and foreign. She imagined it looked the same to the two unhappy women who lived here. No neighbors came around to greet her, not even the two women's friends. They probably had no friends. The BaNare never forgave Tladi for murdering Potso. They would never forget Potso's fine, expressive face, blown apart by Tladi's pouchful of gunpowder. He saved their cattle by conquering Loang but they would never forgive him his spiteful caprice. Potso raised no hand to stop him, but Tladi killed him all the same.

Ma-Mojamaje asked herself this question: "Do the BaNare punish these women for Tladi's sins?" Or perhaps the women felt guilty themselves, as Tladi's closest kin. Or fear of Tladi's return had left them unable to lead normal lives. Perhaps they ostracized themselves. Ma-Mojamaje had hoped that winning acceptance by Tladi's family would make her one of the BaNare, and also her son. But now she suspected that being a Tladi was worse than being a BaKii, or having Bushman eyes.

She strolled along inside the compound fence, tossing Mojamaje lightly in her arms, to make him laugh and gurgle. "My son," she whispered, brushing flies from his tiny face. "These people do not yet know that you will grow up to be a great man." A lizard skimmed across a thin branch in the fence. "They cannot help us, so we will help them." Mojamaje looked up at his mother, his Bushman eyes squinting in the bright sun, arms twitching, mouth puckering, his high cheekbones solid and prominent, giving mature slope to his infant face. "We will make you a beautiful home." The mangy dog with sores on its back crawled toward her, its dust-colored tail drawn up between its legs, its droopy eyes begging for food. She raised a foot and kicked it.

8
Stick by Stick

Make preparations
Brew beer, chase the girls from the forest
My son, my son,
Bring them to me one by one
My son needs blankets for his bed
Make preparations
Brew beer, chase the stars from the heavens
My son, my son,
Bring them to me one by one
To light my son's cookfire

Make preparations
Brew beer, chase the warriors from the field
My son, my son,
Bring them to me one by one
My son needs a footrest
Make preparations
Brew beer, chase these arrows from my heart
My son, my son,
Bring them to me one by one
No one suffers like a mother for her son

This was the song Mojamaje's mother sang as she rebuilt the Tladi family compound in Naring. Tladi's wife and Tumo's wife tried to help her at first, but they were still too distraught. They began one task, lost interest, wandered off. So Ma-Mojamaje limited them to sweeping, cooking and looking after Mojamaje. She became a familiar sight carrying headloads of cow dung in a huge clay pot from the cattle pen in the center of the village where the BaNare kept the few dozen cows for children's milk. She also carried water from the stream, to mix with dung and soil. She set the two boys, Dinti and Tabo, churning the mixture with their feet. She built three new mud houses, tearing down the old ones, and thatched them with new grass. These tasks took four months. Then she replaced the thorn-brush fence with a low mud wall as she saw some of the refugee BaNare begin to do. This was a new style, from somewhere in South Africa. But Ma-Mojamaje's wall was three times longer than the thorn fence she tore down, making the compound the largest in the village, thirty yards from end to end. Her neighbors were impressed. Her industry improved the whole neighborhood. A few women began to call greetings when they passed her carrying water or dung. Tladi's wife and Tumo's wife sang as they worked at their simple tasks. Sometimes children snickered as Ma-Mojamaje passed, calling her "Bushman," but she ignored them, holding her temper. Eventually they stopped.

The rains continued well into winter, a good sign. No hint of drought marred Mojamaje's first year in Naring. But acceptance eluded his mother. Her last hurdle was the highest, seemingly insurmountable. Chief Potso's widow refused to speak to her. Ma-Mojamaje greeted her again and again, but the woman continued walking as if she were deaf. How could she forgive Tladi for murdering her dear husband? Now

Tladi's three grandsons, his heirs, breathed the same air as she, drank from the same stream, woke to the same bark of dogs.

The Potso family compound stood directly across from the Tladis', with the remnants of a woodpile between. Long ago both families had used the woodpile in common. They had both collected dead wood from the surrounding countryside, twisted and dried in the sun, and piled it up on the patch of ground between the two compounds. Both families had used the wood freely, heedless of how much the other took. Relations could not have been friendlier. Then Potso died, in one terrible, blinding flash. The families became enemies, and the woodpile dwindled to nothing. Each compound collected its own firewood now and piled it within its compound fence. Outside, a few twigs remained scattered in a wide circle, showing how large the woodpile once had been.

Tladi's wife and Tumo's wife, and now Ma-Mojamaje, could hardly be blamed for Tladi's sins. Yet Dinti, Tabo and Mojamaje would grow to inherit Tladi's place. Potso's widow had her own sons to consider, especially the eldest, who stood to inherit the chiefship. The boy's name was Pule, so his mother, Potso's widow, was known as Ma-Pule. She played the part of a chief's wife, but she lacked Potso's charm. Imperious, austere, she refused to speak to refugees or children. She never lifted a finger to work, until Potso died and condemned her to an ordinary life. No longer the wife of a chief, she became instead the mother of a boy too young to be chief but in line for the job if no one usurped his place. Her servants deserted her. Her son disobeyed her. Ma-Pule became an ordinary BaNare woman, fetching her own firewood, sweeping her own compound.

But still she was Potso's widow. The BaNare knew it would be rude to accept Ma-Mojamaje, wife of the son of Potso's murderer, without Ma-Pule's approval. Ma-Mojamaje knew this too. After months of observation, months of rebuff, she decided her line of attack: the woodpile. Every day she carried wood from the countryside to the abandoned pile between the two compounds. First she covered the large circle that twigs still marked out, then she piled more wood on top. When the ground could no longer be seen underneath, she offered Ma-Pule some wood.

Everyone knew how much the woman hated working. She never carried more than a few slim sticks at a time, too few even to raise a sweat. Such dainty precaution kept her own woodpile puny. She was always running out. One day Ma-Mojamaje called out to her as she departed yet again to fetch wood, "Ma-Pule, a chief's mother need not carry wood. There is plenty here for us all."

Ma-Mojamaje stood before the massive woodpile, her hands on her hips, an inviting smile on her lips. Ma-Pule stopped short, blinking in dismay, considering Ma-Mojamaje's overture. Truly, she hated carrying wood. If only Ma-Mojamaje had not been a BaKii, with skin like dust, Bushman eyes, married to the son of her husband's slayer, living in the compound of that same vile criminal . . .

Ma-Pule flared her nostrils and replied, "No, there is not enough wood for us all."

The next day, Ma-Mojamaje collected more wood, and the next day more, and every day thereafter until the woodpile doubled in size. Every day she asked Ma-Pule, "Please, take this wood. There is plenty here for us all."

And every day Ma-Pule flared her nostrils and replied, "No, there is not enough wood for us all."

Who knows how long it would have gone on, the woodpile scraping the clouds, Ma-Pule's resolve growing with every inch the woodpile rose, if bogwera had not intervened. At first it seemed a coincidence. Nothing obvious connected the two things, the woodpile and bogwera. Years later, though, when the BaNare told the story to their children, they realized the two things were tied together and were actually part of a third thing, a larger problem that embraced them both.

This larger thing was the refugee problem. The woodpile stood as a battleground, the last redoubt for Ma-Mojamaje to capture in winning acceptance as one of the BaNare. She was the only BaKii in town, but clearly if she proved successful, others would come from Loang to try their luck. Even so, Loang was far away, and if Ma-Mojamaje had been the only newcomer in Naring, she might have melted into the BaNare more easily. But the village crawled with refugees, and more came every year. The BaNare had yet to decide what to do with them. Every time Ma-Pule said, "No, there is not enough wood for us all," she cast her vote, and that of dead Potso, against admitting the foreigners as BaNare. Their loyalty could not be taken for granted. Tladi had led the most troublesome out to Loang, and there their cattle were now safe from raids.

Bogwera was another part of the refugee problem: its cure. Bogwera was an initiation ceremony that turned each new generation of young men into full BaNare citizens. All the young men pledged their loyalty to

the BaNare and especially to the chief. If the chief was of their generation, initiated in the same ceremony, they were especially bound to him.
When Potso died, his heir, Pule, was still a small boy. Pule's senior uncle,
Roba the Restless, became the boy's head advisor until the day he would
be old enough to be initiated and become chief. Meanwhile, more refugees arrived every year from South Africa. But Roba and Pule's other
advisors put off bogwera until they could be sure that the village itself
was secure. This was because the ceremony took place out in the wilderness, thirty miles north of Naring. It lasted a month, during which the
village would stand defenseless. The threat within—disloyal refugees—
could not be settled until the BaNare were safe from the threat without
—raids from South Africa. Bogwera would turn refugees into honest
BaNare citizens, faithful to young Pule's rule. But until the raids abated,
it would not be safe to leave Naring.

Still more refugees came, confirming Roba's fears. But this new wave
did not flee the Zulu, who never raided Naring again. They explained to
the BaNare, their eyes bursting with terror, that the days of the Zulu
were over.

"They are smashed!" the refugees cried.

"The Zulu now wander the earth, homeless and hungry, begging for
water."

"Who did this?" the BaNare demanded, equally stricken, infected by
the refugees' panic.

"We cannot say," the refugees replied.

"The word hurts our lips to speak it!"

"Then show us," the BaNare insisted. The refugees slapped their
behinds, galloped in circles, pointing their fingers at the BaNare.

"Poowgh!" they cried, mouths exploding.

"Poowgh!"

"Poowgh!"

Consumed with dread, the BaNare whispered the awful truth:
"Boers."

Since stories of the Boers had first begun to circulate, all South Africa
knew it was only a matter of time. Everyone wondered when they would
make their move. But they stayed close to the coast, adjusting their
white skins, practicing with their guns, acquainting their horses with
patches of sand, coarse pastures, blazing summers. Then all at once,
without warning, soon after the Zulu spread like plague across the coun-

tryside, Boers leapt into the fray. Suddenly they were everywhere. Not even the Zulu could stop them.

Years after the Zulu raided Naring, refugees reported that Boers had conquered Taung. They had thousands of cattle in tow, accumulated from dozens of raids. They seized all the Taung cattle, set up camp alongside the Taung River and immediately began burning the young Taung women. Unable to resist, half the Taung people packed up their belongings in goatskin sacks and headed west for Naring. They took along half the Boer cattle, including those stolen in Taung.

Upon arrival in Naring, these Taung refugees said to the BaNare, "We forgive you, cousins, for stealing our cattle many generations ago."

The BaNare replied, "We forgive you, cousins, for leading the Boers to our village."

"They will not follow," the Taung refugees assured.

"You know these lazy Boers."

"The only cattle they own are cattle they steal."

"When they find these cattle gone they will only steal more."

"They will not follow."

For safety, though, they sent the cattle out to Loang. A week later, twenty Boers rode into Naring. The sentry on the ridge warned the BaNare, so the men stood ready with their spears. The twenty Boers rode slowly through the village, high on their horses, rifles cradled in their arms. Children ran screaming to their mothers. Dogs barked at the horses' hooves. They were fearsome beings, pale as ghosts, covered with cloth and leather, their wide-brimmed hats hiding their eyes. One of the young Boers, his chin still beardless, had learned the language of Taung, and he called out a greeting as the Boers drew near.

"We come in peace," he said. "Where is your chief?"

Young Pule's uncle, Roba the Restless, came out to speak for his people.

"We will give you a rifle," the young Boer said from his saddle, "if you give us the thieves who stole our cattle."

Old Roba shifted from foot to foot as he squinted up at the Boers. "I would like a gun," he replied. "Yes, I would like one. But we have no Boer cattle. Search the wilderness. You will see."

The Boers followed Roba's advice. Boer cattle were easy to recognize because only the Boers branded cattle with hot irons on the rump. Everyone else marked their cattle by carving symbols in their ears with a knife. The Boers searched for hours, but of course all their cattle were deep in the Kalahari at Loang. They found no cattle at all, except for the few dozen milk cows in the center of the village. Angry now, the Boers shot the herdboy tending these cows and drove the cattle out of the corral, east to Taung.

"We will be back!" they warned, firing their rifles in the air.

"We will bring all the Boers in South Africa!"

"We will burn this village to the ground!"

They rode quickly out of range before the BaNare men had time to hurl their spears.

The Boers returned once a year for the next eight years, hoping to catch the BaNare with their cattle. They never learned the secret of Loang, and even if they had done so, no horse could have survived the Kalahari. Once they came in a band of two hundred but usually they numbered only fifty. The BaNare met them with spears and arrows as the Boers rode in circles, shooting their rifles, until the BaNare turned and ran. But they never found more than a hundred milk cows in Naring.

A year before Ma-Mojamaje's arrival the Boers failed to appear. Another year passed and still the Boers did not come. Roba the Restless shifted from foot to foot, pondering this question: Had the Boers given up? If so, it was safe to hold bogwera. Young Pule was now old enough for initiation, which would allow him officially to become chief. Every year more refugees arrived; many had wandered for years before ending up in Naring, since their youth, and so some were thirty years old and still uninitiated. Bogwera would unite the backlog of young men and refugees safely under Pule's rule.

After two years without a Boer raid, Pule's advisors judged it was safe to hold the ceremony. "And Tladi?" Roba queried. During bogwera older men drilled the initiates as soldiers, teaching them tricks of sex and war: Tladi was certainly the best military instructor among the BaNare. And they did not want to anger him by holding the ceremony without him. They sent an invitation to Loang. Tladi accepted, agreeing to meet them at the bogwera site. But he would not enter Naring.

"Why is that?" the BaNare asked each other.

"Why will he not set foot in Naring?"

Meanwhile, Ma-Mojamaje's woodpile grew taller than any tree in the village. Every day she said to Potso's widow, "Please take this wood. There is plenty for us all."

And every day Ma-Pule flared her nostrils and replied, "No, there is not enough for us all."

The bogwera was a mixed blessing for Ma-Mojamaje. On one hand, it might soften Ma-Pule's heart by turning so many foreigners into loyal BaNare. On the other hand, bogwera was only for men, so Ma-Mojamaje would remain a foreigner. And the refugees were all from South Africa, whence the BaNare originally hailed, so their skin and eyes resembled those of everyone else in Naring—save Ma-Mojamaje. The refugees argued most forcefully that Ma-Mojamaje's tawny skin and Bushman eyes disqualified her from joining the BaNare. As yet the original BaNare were divided over accepting her. When the refugees became full citizens the balance would swing against her.

So Ma-Mojamaje kept herself clean and continued to build up her woodpile. The sentries on the ridge took a final look across the eastern horizon, then joined the other men, a thousand in all, for the march to the wilderness thirty miles north from Naring. The older men wore fur cloaks while the younger men wore only loincloths, which gave them no protection from the icy winter night. All carried their spears and their square oxhide shields. They left thirty older men behind to guard the village.

After a week a small band of refugees arrived in Naring. They were naked and hungry, trembling with fear. "Beware!" they exclaimed, clutching their empty bellies.

"Nothing can stop them!"

"The world is over!"

"Prepare to join your ancestors!"

They rolled in the dust, grinding their teeth and howling with pain.

"Tomorrow!" they cried.

"They will be here tomorrow!"

"Who?" the BaNare demanded, expecting the worst. "Boers?"

"No!" the refugees shouted in chorus.

"The Zulu?"

"No!" the refugees repeated.

"Then who? Tell us, who?" The BaNare held the refugees still on the ground, doused them with water, soothing them with quiet songs and bits of roast meat. "Who?" the BaNare asked again.

The refugees replied in one voice, "Wall-Makers."

Wall-Makers? Oh, what a time in South Africa, what desolation, the world thrown upside down—in all the generations, as far back as memory reached, no one ever imagined Wall-Makers acting like this. Everyone knew them as peaceful, stable, an inspiration to lesser peoples, guardians of order. Their flat-topped fortress, a hill with two solid walls, disciplined warriors stabbing anyone trying to climb over, kept them safe from even the Zulu. But the Boers were a different matter. Truly a new world had come, extinguishing the past. Across South Africa refugees fled to ancient strongholds famed for their might, new nations arose from the dispossessed, and one by one the Boers crushed them. The survivors escaped, regrouped, crowned a new warrior-king, then the Boers pierced his chest with a bullet.

When they came to the Wall-Makers' hill, the deadly Boer horsemen rode around it until the defenders grew dizzy watching them. Shooting at every crevice, forcing their way over the outer wall, the Boers pried out enough stones to make a gap large enough for their horses to ride through. The Wall-Makers retreated behind their inner wall, which stopped the Boers, who rode around the walled village for months, shooting. The Wall-Makers grew hungry and restless. One day they erupted over the wall, past the Boers, down the hill, to devastate everything in their path. They headed west, ten thousand disciplined Wall-Makers out of control.

The refugees grimaced as they reached the end of the story, spreading their terror to their hosts, so that soon the BaNare ran screaming along the paths, tearing their hair, casting themselves on the ground, rolling in the dust.

"They will burn us for sure!" the BaNare women shrieked. Only thirty men had stayed behind, too few to protect a village of women from a marauding horde.

"They will burn us!"

"Eat us!"

"Murder our children!"

One thousand BaNare women beat their breasts and pulled their children close for a final embrace.

Lona White Mouth fell on her knees to scrape at the ground behind her compound, digging a hole to hide her daughters.

Ipee Noo scratched bloody lines into her arms with her nails, the pride of her life, and climbed into her woven-grass bin alone. It had taken her years to grow her nails so long, the hardest thing was learning to hoe without breaking them, and now in dark privacy she bit them down to stubs.

Balada the Tart grabbed a knife in each hand and screeched like a cat, running in circles and stabbing the air.

It was dusk—a messenger would take all night to reach the men at bogwera, at the same time the Wall-Makers would arrive in Naring. The men would take all day to return, finding only the bones of their kin, Wall-Makers occupying their houses, ready to eat them too.

Suddenly the BaNare smelled smoke. Their wailing died to an eerie silence, as one by one they stuck their noses high in the air. Near the center of the village a tongue of flame leapt over the tops of the houses, flashing against the darkening sky. They ran to the spot, and there stood Ma-Mojamaje, a burning stick in her hand, setting afire her enormous woodpile.

"Eeee-laaanng!" the women cheered, tears of joy streaking their dusty cheeks. Their eyes danced in the fire's bright blaze, the largest woodpile in creation, now become the largest torch, the brightest beacon, to carry their message of distress to their distant warriors.

"Eee-laang!" they cried again, rushing to their own meager woodpiles, carrying more fuel to the towering fire. It climbed and climbed, until their skins grew hot and wet with sweat as they ran up to toss on their twigs.

"Burn!" they shrieked, their eyes wide with wonder.

"Wall-Makers! We will burn you!"

They composed songs as they worked, until the fire burned so full and hot they could no longer approach it to add more wood. So they formed a ring around it and danced in a circle, sweating with heat and joy, thankful for salvation, stamping their feet on the blistering sand. Their shadows skipped against the distant hills, on into the dark Kalahari. They sang again about burning, love, the white heat of passion, and now they threw off their leather aprons, the girls tossed away their fringed makgabe—a thousand naked women in one wide circle around the soaring beacon, tight against it, circling, singing, thrusting hips and breasts to the dark sky. Now they danced faster, light gleaming quickly against their shining skins, the dark, warm glow of their bodies bumping, nostrils filled with smoke and dusty sweat.

"Burn!" they sang, "Burn!"

"Burn us all away tonight!"

Now they sang forgotten songs, ancient refrains from a distant time, before villages, when everyone roamed like Bushmen, hunting like animals in the boundless wilderness, feasting on blood and raw meat, when cattle were nothing but fat, juicy prey, slow to escape the hunt, when no one wore clothes, when men spoke like lions and women hid from them in the tall summer grass. The circle closed and the women pressed together, one behind the other, their bodies meshed in one swirl of flesh.

"Kyakyo ea hle!" the oldest woman cried, and the others had no idea what these ancient words meant.

The thirty old men climbed the ridge to stand in a line on its crest, gazing down at the spectacle below. Then they peered north, straining their eyes, their ears bursting with the crackle of the blaze, the wail of the women, the blood pounding hard through their temples. One pointed out to the dark: there, a light, a flicker of fire far to the north, a small bonfire in the bogwera camp. The BaNare men had seen the blaze and answered. They were on their way.

The men on the ridge gave a hoot and threw their spears in the air. Now they started to dance, their loins remembering, responding to the women's lusty cries, faster and faster they pounded their feet on the rocks, the light from Ma-Mojamaje's woodpile bright on their faces, howling down at the women below.

9
Magical Child

Around the fire a woman screamed in alarm. *"Aayah! The child!"*

The singing stopped. The dancers froze and some reached abruptly for their aprons, suddenly shamed, hastily regaining their senses. The spell was broken. A woman dashed into the fire, dodging the shooting flames, to swoop up an infant and rush it to safety. This child was Mojamaje.

There are several fires in the story of the Great Thirst, but this first one is perhaps the most important. By the time the tellers reach this point in the story, the winter cold has swept through the night to envelop their listeners, who creep closer to the fire before them. Some tellers stoke the fire now, so that flaming shadows play across each face. In this first blaze, the burning of Ma-Mojamaje's woodpile, the infant Mojamaje first displayed his immunity to fire. His cousins Dinti and

Tabo were supposed to be tending him, but they ran to join the children holding hands to form a larger circle around the dancing women. The children knew none of the ancient songs, so they whistled and stamped their feet.

Then came the scream, the woman yanking Mojamaje from the fire. Everyone crowded round, expecting the worst, but miraculously the child was unharmed. Some BaNare say that Mojamaje had just begun to crawl toward the fire, past the ring of frenzied dancers, and was rescued just in time. Others insist he was found crawling away from the fire, having crawled straight through from the other side, first one tiny hand pushing forward in the dust, then one tiny knee, then the other hand, the other knee, the inferno's blaze sparkling in his wide Bushman eyes, his soft naked flesh glazed smooth and hot. . . . The BaNare debate this issue to this very day, but no one doubts that throughout his life Mojamaje proved unnaturally resistant to fire. This was a trait his grandson inherited, which proved very important later in the story of the Great Thirst.

10
The Battle of the Woodpile

The BaNare army marched all night to meet the Wall-Makers early the next morning on the plain east of Naring. They did not enter the village but swung east along the outer edge of the ridge of hills, certain that the attack the fire signaled could only come from South Africa. Tladi kept them in perfect formation, shoulder to shoulder, their long throwing spears tucked tight under their arms, chanting, bodies still chilled from the cold night's march, rising in temperature every moment the dusty speck on the horizon before them grew larger and larger. They kept their eyes fixed on that rising cloud of dust, chanting louder and louder, their feet rising higher from the ground until they were nearly running. Tladi chanted the loudest, racing up and down the columns, thrusting his spear in the air. One thousand voices cut the dawn, shouting for victory and blood.

The cloud of dust on the eastern horizon was the Wall-Makers. The sun rose behind the cloud, charging it with a bright yellow haze that drew the BaNare faster to it. The women of Naring climbed up the ridge to watch their regiment march into battle. The Wall-Makers outnumbered them ten to one, so when the BaNare drew closer they saw through the dust the Wall-Makers spread endlessly across the plain. They were not all men: the Wall-Makers as a whole had burst from their walled fortress past the Boers. Now the BaNare regiment saw children and women in the Wall-Maker ranks, then they saw that the Wall-Makers were not in ranks at all. They were not in formation. A hundred yards from the swarm of Wall-Makers, Tladi shouted for his regiment to halt.

The Wall-Makers had not come to fight. Tired, weak, hungry, they staggered forward like an army of the dead, aimlessly, without a sound. They were all very thin and naked. The BaNare warriors watched them shiver. They did not seem to fear Tladi's soldiers or even notice they stood on a battlefield.

Years later the BaNare pieced together the full story of the Wall-Makers, how they exploded from their fortress already starving from months of Boer siege, destroying three hamlets, but thereafter they were completely spent, marching to Naring not as raiders but as refugees, seeking safety on the edge of the Kalahari. There on the broad plain before the Naring hills, in the somber morning light, the BaNare turned them back. No blood flowed. Tladi simply refused to take them in. Naring was already too crowded. The Wall-Makers stumbled back over the eastern horizon, so slowly this time they raised no dust.

At first the BaNare felt shame for repelling the Wall-Makers. "What can we do?" they argued.

"We have too many refugees now."

"They cannot eat dirt."

"We cannot drink air."

"Naring is too crowded."

"Too many bellies go empty already."

No one mentioned the most important reason of all: The Wall-Makers brought no cattle.

Eventually the BaNare forgot what happened on the battlefield that morning, remembering only that Ma-Mojamaje's glorious woodpile saved the day. The only victor in the Battle of the Woodpile, Ma-Mojamaje found her apprenticeship ended. Despite her yellow skin and Bushman eyes, the BaNare accepted her as a full citizen. Her past was behind her.

11
Griqua Beads Lost

Or so Ma-Mojamaje thought. Everyone in Naring forgot her history, but Tladi did not. Out at Loang he stewed and fumed, his son's entrapment nagging away at the flesh beneath his skin. "What did she do to him?" Tladi asked aloud. "I should burn her myself."

He led his closest cohort on long hunting trips deep in the Kalahari. "Why did I let her win?" he grumbled, burying his spear in a buffalo's flank.

"What did she do to him?" he muttered, pulling a roasted fox thigh from the campfire.

"Why should I let her win?" he hissed, carving the liver from a gazelle's quivering belly.

"I will burn her myself," Tladi spat, flying through space to plunge a knife through a warthog's heart.

Back in Naring, the BaNare wondered, "Why will Tladi not enter the village?" He had met the bogwera not in Naring but out at the ceremony site, and after the Battle of the Woodpile he had marched his regiment straight back to Loang. Why did he avoid Naring? The Kalahari wind now carried Tladi's threats back to the BaNare's ears.

"Ma-Mojamaje is the cause," they concluded.

"He cannot face her."

"She has driven him wild with desire."

The BaNare waited, anxious, curious, for a final confrontation. "He will come here to burn her," half the village insisted, but the other half maintained, "He will never set foot in Naring again." Tladi would certainly not come for another initiation. After the Wall-Maker scare interrupted the ceremony, the BaNare feared risking another. They looked east, expecting more raiders, and also west, expecting Tladi to swoop like a vulture between Ma-Mojamaje's legs.

Pule was still not officially chief, though he was now more than twenty years old, with a child. Despite his uninitiated status, he began to assume the duties of chief. The BaNare accepted this. No one challenged his position. As long as Tladi ruled Loang, casting his menacing shadow over Naring, no one else wanted the job.

Pule resembled his father in looks, demeanor and aspect: the same trim, muscular frame, the same regal air, the same noble lilt to his voice. But Pule was stronger, more warrior than poet, though he wore copper wires in his ears and brushed back his hair with the same scarlet ocher women smeared on pots. He sprang as he walked, like an eager young leopard.

"A wonderful boy."

"Some day he will face Tladi."

"Remember his father's face when Tladi blew it apart?"

Pule proposed another bogwera. His advisors refused. "Too dangerous," they insisted. Pule itched for a challenge, a test of his authority, a problem worthy of a great chief, to allow him to win the respect that bogwera's postponement denied him. Hrikwa the Griqua answered his prayer. More diversion than crisis, Hrikwa's arrival boosted Pule's popularity nonetheless. Pule took credit for Hrikwa's boon.

Hrikwa was the only Griqua the BaNare ever saw. Mojamaje's generation was the last to have Griquas. After that they disappeared. They came from the south, where the Boers first settled generations before, when Bushmen still lived there, hunting in the hills. The Boers killed some Bushmen, some they drove away, and some they forced to herd their stolen cattle. A Bushman herding cattle was something the BaNare wanted to see—in a wink, they wagered, the cows would be on the roasting spit. But some Bushmen really did work for Boers, learning to speak the Boer language, wearing clothes that covered their yellow arms and legs. A few acquired horses and guns, and when they did, of course, they rode away from the Boers, never to return.

These Boer-like Bushmen who escaped to the wilderness called themselves Griquas. They were not completely Bushmen because the Boers fooled around with their servants, so most Griquas had some Boer blood. They looked and spoke just like Boers except for their dark skins and high cheekbones. When they settled elsewhere in South Africa, the Griquas tried to learn the local languages but spoke them with thick Boer accents. They lived hard lives, for no one would give them land to work, so they hunted and sometimes raided cattle, just like Boers.

Over the years, the Boers built a few towns along the coast where English ships brought items to exchange for ivory from the deep interior. Elephants once grew like fat weeds in the wetter forests, far from Naring, but they made such handy targets for rifles that they had quickly vanished, the last confused survivors retreating to the hidden swamps beyond the great northern rivers. After that the English ships took whatever came their way: buckskins, wolf fur, ostrich feathers, even corn. A few Griquas ventured back to the coast to buy wagons, loaded them with trade goods and set out to wander the plains to trade. It was not the safest of jobs, especially in Zululand, but it was better than working for Boers.

A few years after the Battle of the Woodpile, a Griqua trader rolled into Naring. He walked alongside his long wooden wagon, cracking his whip above the ears of a team of twelve oxen. The sentry on the ridge announced his entrance, and the BaNare ran from their houses to see. He wore leather trousers, a stiff leather jacket, a wide-brimmed leather hat, a scraggly black beard, and he carried a rifle in one scarred hand. Everyone thought he was a Boer. When he drew close, halting his wagon in the center of Naring, the BaNare crowded around him. He had the face of a frog, but with high Bushman cheekbones and skin the color of dust.

The Griqua whistled softly to himself, cradling his rifle in his arms. He had spent a few years near Taung, so he knew the BaNare language. Throwing his rifle to the ground, he proclaimed to the gathering in the voice of a frog, "I am not a Boer."

Pule bounded out, copper earrings dangling, red hair gleaming with fat, to jump in front of the Griqua, toss back his head and set his hands on his hips. "You look like a Boer," Pule snapped.

The trader assumed that Pule was chief, albeit a somewhat unusual one. "I am Griqua," he said. "We dress like Boers but we are black like you."

The BaNare repeated the word, struggling to pronounce it. "Hrikwa" was the closest they could come, so this was what they called him.

Hrikwa the Griqua reached up to his wagon to pull out a hat, identical to his own. "Here," he said, handing it to Pule. "You can dress like a Boer too. This is a Boer hat. A gift."

Pule hesitated, then swung his head around to the BaNare, making sure all eyes were upon him. He took the hat in his hands and pulled it onto his head. The crowd howled and shrieked, the women ululating, their tongues clicking furiously in their wailing mouths. Pule stood grinning, naked except for a loincloth, earrings, and an enormous Boer hat.

"What is this?" he asked Hrikwa, pointing to the wagon.

"This?" Hrikwa replied. "You never saw one before?"

"Never," Pule answered, shaking his head.

"We call it a wagon," said Hrikwa.

"Give me one of those too," Pule said.

Hrikwa the Criqua explained with great care that a wagon was far more expensive than a hat, so he could give Pule a hat and go buy another, but if he gave him a wagon he would not have enough money to buy another.

"What is money?" Pule asked.

So Hrikwa explained all about money, showing the BaNare some English coins from his pocket. They were fascinated. He went on to explain how he paid money for his goods, to trade them for skins and furs, which he sold back in South Africa for more money, then he bought more goods, and so on. In the end, everyone was satisfied with his explanation. Money sounded like a clever invention, but most of all the BaNare admired the Griqua's wagon, how each wooden yoke held the two oxen at once, how a wooden pole tied the yokes to the wagon, how the Griqua guided the oxen with cracks of his whip, how the wooden wheels rolled instead of dragging along the ground. These were the first wheels the BaNare ever saw.

They brought out their skins and furs to trade with Hrikwa, laying them on the dust before the wares that he pulled from his wagon. Pule oversaw the bargaining, calling over the bustle, "Here lies the bounty of Pule the Splendid! Come, my loving children, enrich your meaningless lives with precious things. Worry not that this stranger is ugly. Look to my face, the face of your father, your provider. No other chief ever brought you such wonders!"

Pule climbed atop the wagon to continue his boasting, but the noise of the trading drowned him out. The noise was mostly the moaning and sighing of the BaNare, swooning at the multitude of treasures Hrikwa offered. There were pots, shoes, knives, blankets, axes, tea, trousers, hoes, soap, sugar, hats, buckets, shirts, spades, flour, tobacco, dresses, beads, nails, pans, cups, hammers, spoons, matches, needles, thread, mirrors, yokes, chains and rope. The BaNare could not believe their eyes. They asked the Griqua about each item, its name, its use. A few of the refugees had seen some of these things before, and helped explain them to the BaNare.

"Who made these things?" they asked.

"Boers?"

Hrikwa laughed and clapped his hands. "Boers? They cannot even plant their own corn. No one is lazier than a Boer. No, the English made these things. The same ones who made the money."

The BaNare fell quiet. "Will they come here?" they asked.

"No," Hrikwa replied, "they stay in their ships."

"What is a ship?" the BaNare asked.

So Hrikwa described the ocean, how ships floated on it, carrying trade goods to the South African coast. No one believed him. But they believed in the English, remembering that once the Boers were only a rumor, far to the south, eventually spreading, wreaking havoc everywhere. Soon the sentry on the ridge would cry, "English!" and the BaNare again would run for their lives.

Hrikwa reassured them the English would not come, but his mind was elsewhere, on the fabulous bargains he found at his feet, magnificent furs and skins, dirt cheap. The BaNare did not know their value in South Africa, so he traded one for one no matter the item: one silver jackal fur for one pot, one bat-eared fox fur for one shoe, two furs for a pair, lion skins, red thware furs, panther pelts streaked with fine golden hairs.

"Where do these come from?" Hrikwa asked casually, tugging at his wispy beard.

"Loang," Pule replied, pointing west. "We catch them in the Kalahari. Sometimes Bushmen trade them for water."

"Can I go there?" Hrikwa asked.

"This is winter," Pule replied. "There is no water for your oxen to drink. This . . ."

"Wagon."

"This wagon," Pule continued, "will sink in the sand."

Hrikwa eyed Pule suspiciously, thinking to himself, "Why should this arrogant boy share his secret? He does not want me to find the source of his treasures." He said aloud to Pule, defiantly, "Will you stop me if I go?"

"I will not have to," Pule replied, pulling a red dress over his head.

"That is for women." Hrikwa said.

"I am chief," Pule snarled. "I wear what I wish."

So Hrikwa the Griqua stored half his trade goods and all his furs in an empty house in Pule's compound, the young chief promising to protect them. "Your oxen will die," Pule repeated. Hrikwa said nothing. He whipped his oxen westward over the sand slope, the half-empty wagon rumbling on into the Kalahari. He quickly found a faint path, the one Tladi's men carefully maintained on their journeys to Naring. He sang to himself in a thick, croaking voice, dreaming how he would spend his new wealth:

> Honey, a bath, a bottle of brandy
> Lick my bum like a stick of candy
> A pretty lass in a skirt of lace
> Kiss my cheeks then kiss my face

The BaNare elders descended on their chief, crying, "He will die!" "The Bushmen will eat him!"

"Why did you let him go?"

Pule raised a hand and smiled shrewdly. "Trust me," he said, "I know exactly how this will come out."

The trader's oxen moved slowly through the deep sand, but the wagon kept rolling. By the third day they grew weak with thirst but there was no place to water them. Hrikwa had never seen anything like it, three days of sand with no water. Yet an unmistakable path cut straight west through the tall yellow grass. Loang could not be far. All across South Africa he had followed dozens of paths just like this one. Paths led from village to village—it was as simple as that. And along each path water holes stood a day's trek apart. That was the point of the paths: sometimes they turned east, then north, then west, but always from water to water. A wagon set out at dawn from one stream bed and by nightfall it reached the next well. Wagon drivers called this distance a "day" regardless of how many miles. On drier plains water holes stood farther apart, and so there wagons traveled not by days but by what the drivers called "thirsts." A thirst was a journey of more than one day between water. To avoid the heat of the day, drivers set out from one water hole not at dawn but at dusk, and drove quickly through the cool of the night, halting the oxen at first light. Anxious for water, the animals slept fitfully all day in the shade of a tree. At sundown the driver yoked them up again and pressed on, reaching the next water by dawn.

On the evening of the fourth day, Hrikwa finally admitted to himself that the path to Loang was the longest thirst he had ever traveled. It now threatened to become his last. After resting all day, the oxen refused to stand up. They had chosen their spot to die. Hrikwa threw a dozen dresses and some beads in a sack, slung the sack on his back and began to walk. He was certainly more than halfway there, or so he hoped. He continued ahead, west. By sunup the sack grew heavy. His mouth grew thick and dry. He rummaged through the sack, pulled out a pouch of beads, and tossed the sack away. Beads were better than money in a pinch. In Loang he might need to buy water. He tied the pouch to his belt and walked on.

Two days later he arrived in Loang, crazed with exhaustion and thirst. Tladi's men picked him up and brought him to Tladi's compound.

"Boer!" Tladi growled. Hrikwa was too weak to explain. "In the well," Tladi ordered.

The splash of water revived the Griqua, and he struggled out of the mud. Tladi's men seized him and threw him back. He struggled out again, they threw him back, again and again. Each time he churned up more mud, until he sank completely, sucked into the slime. He started to drown. At the last moment Tladi's men pulled him out.

Hrikwa dozed by the side of the wells as the sun dried the mud that covered him. He awoke and crawled back to the well to drink. Struggling to his feet, he called out weakly to no one, "I am not a Boer." He wandered through Loang, searching for a place to sleep. Rolling onto his side, he felt at his belt. "My beads," he gasped. They were gone, absorbed into the mud of the well. He waded back into the well to look for them, but to no avail.

A few weeks later it rained heavily enough to leave rain pools in the sand. Hrikwa walked back to Naring, passing his wagon, the oxen gone, eaten by hyenas or Bushmen.

Pule welcomed the trader back and made this offer, "Take twelve of my oxen to fetch my wagon."

"Your wagon?" Hrikwa replied. "Not my wagon?"

But Pule's terms were generous. He would hire Hrikwa as official BaNare trader, to drive the wagon to and from South Africa, keeping as much money as he wished but serving no other master. He would work for the BaNare and no one else. Hrikwa accepted. To express his gratitude, he took eight leopard skins and hired a Boer seamstress in South Africa to sew a full-length suit for Pule, cut in English fashion, with tight trousers and a long, sweeping coat.

The BaNare sang praises to their chief's wisdom and wiles. Other traders began to reach Naring, including a few Boers, but Pule met them

in his leopard suit and tipped his leather hat. "We have a trader," he
said. "He gave me this hat, this suit and a wagon. So turn around and go
away."

12
Longing and Lust

Pule's deal with Hrikwa the Griqua won the BaNare's everlasting appreciation. Their compounds filled with English wares. The clothing took
longer to catch on. Wool blankets replaced fur in beds on skin mats on
the floors of houses, but Hrikwa's trousers and dresses and shirts lay
unsold on the ground before the wagon. The BaNare used the blankets
to cover their shoulders in winter, but clothes that clung close to the
body made them feel like Boers.

Pule's vaulting popularity settled the refugee problem. His rule stood
unquestioned. Tladi's brooding shadow no longer stretched from Loang
to stunt Pule's ambitions. His chiefship was secure. But still Pule had not
been to bogwera. Until he passed initiation, he was not officially a man,
and thus not officially chief. The Wall-Maker scare made his advisors
warier than ever of leaving Naring undefended for a month to hold the
ceremony.

For years after the Battle of the Woodpile, Tladi's ominous vow still
reached the BaNare's ears. "I will burn her," he muttered, his massive
brow knit in consternation. Every year the tension mounted. More irritable than ever, hunting more often, Tladi killed more meat than his men
could eat or carry back to Loang. They grew irritable too, resenting the
beatings he delivered them for no reason. "What did she do to him?" he
called out in the night as he burned yet another BaKii woman. The
BaNare in Naring received detailed reports of Tladi's ripening obsession,
expecting him any day to charge out of the Kalahari to force himself on
Ma-Mojamaje. Some placed wagers on when he would come.

At first, Ma-Mojamaje remained tranquil. Once the Battle of the
Woodpile confirmed her acceptance, she settled down to domestic
peace. Tladi's wife and Tumo's wife relaxed as well. Ma-Pule no longer
scoffed at Ma-Mojamaje's offer of wood, taking it gladly, extending her

friendship in return. The two compounds built up the woodpile again and used it freely, neither heeding how much the other took.

Mojamaje roved the village with other children, a normal BaNare boy except for his Bushman eyes. At first some boys mocked him, calling, "Bushman! Bushman!" but his cousin Tabo bloodied them with a tree branch. Several years older than Mojamaje, Tabo grew quickly to be the man of the compound, despite the seniority of his elder brother, Dinti. As Tumo's eldest son, Dinti was Tladi's direct heir, but he turned out nothing like his vicious grandfather, adopting indecision as a way of life. When asked his opinion, Dinti fluttered his arm and ran in circles, unable to make up his mind. The children called him Dinti the Ostrich. Tabo turned out a more complex child. He was first of all huge, a towering brute by the age of ten, with a deep voice, a massive chest, hair already receding from his forehead. His eyes were odder yet: one bad, with the evil leer of Tladi, displaying violent, grasping greed, contempt for all humanity; the other eye was good. Tabo could be mean, Tabo could be kind, almost two children in size and personality. The BaNare wondered which Tabo would win out when he grew to adulthood. His good eye watched over Dinti and Mojamaje, protecting them from injury and childhood enemies. The other eye waited, deep in its socket, for the moment to make its move. The children called him Tabo Cross-Eyes.

As for Mojamaje, the BaNare remember little about his early years. Only his Bushman cheekbones marked him out from the other children, scrambling through the village, fetching water for his mother, chasing dogs, slipping out at night to dance in a circle and sing to the moon. Some noticed that he was somewhat shy, and then it became known that he picked up a wide smattering of the various refugee languages spoken in Naring. This marked him as clever. Ma-Mojamaje rejoiced at the normality of her son; her quest ended, she and her son had become BaNare. The fate of the BaKii was no longer her own.

But five years after the Battle of the Woodpile, her neighbors began to hear her cry out in the night. At first she only moaned, faintly, but then they heard these words:

"Why does he not come? Why does he not come?"

They noticed too that she sometimes stopped to gaze, motionless, across the sand slope west, toward the Kalahari. She whispered again, "Why does he not come?" At night she lay on her blankets, heaving great sighs into the steamy summer air, sweat streaming from her yellow skin. She ran her hands up her thighs, to her smooth breasts, then up to her face, crying into her palms. "Why does he not come?" she called, waking the neighbors, who wondered whether Tladi's vow matched Ma-Mojamaje's desire. Perhaps they had heard the story wrong. Perhaps Tladi allowed her to marry his son and escape from Loang in return for a taste of her secret charms. Now she pined for more of the same, as Tladi did. He would come to Naring not to vanquish her, but as a lover seeking reunion.

These speculations were as far from the truth as the earth from the stars. Ma-Mojamaje longed for her husband, Ra-Mojamaje, Tladi's hopeless son. The BaNare had forgotten about the poor boy, but Ma-Mojamaje had not. Still a young woman, loins aching for a man, she lay in her bed, remembering his touch, the lonesome boy barely able to speak or look her in the eye. Ten years! She devoted her childhood to winning his heart, only to cast it away in the end. When at last she showed him the treasures of love, he learned quickly to caress her softly, gently, to follow her movements, though he did not know what he was doing until it was too late. She had no choice but to abandon him. Naring was her only hope. Once she arrived, she hoped that he would follow, to reclaim his willful bride.

"Why does he not come?" Ma-Mojamaje wailed, pounding her fists in her blankets. Gossip from Loang never mentioned Ra-Mojamaje, as if both she and the BaNare had discarded him at Mojamaje's birth.

"I killed his heart," she groaned in her sleep. "He will never recover. He never will come. Tladi himself never did such a thing. I am crueler than evil itself. But what could I do? How could I escape?"

She threw off her blankets and flew out the door, to stand naked in the half moonlight, her Bushman eyes and pale yellow skin glimmering with tears and sweat. "Why does he not come?" she cried to the moon, silent in a cloudless night.

Like the BaNare's, Ma-Mojamaje's speculations could not have been farther from the truth. He was coming. After her crushing blow, her grievous betrayal, her dirty trick, Ra-Mojamaje had wandered in the Kalahari until he was almost crazy. Blood and sand crusted his lips. But deep in his soul a flicker of life refused to die. He had returned to Loang with bitter resolve, a dim, painful hope that perhaps it was not too late. At last he woke up, seeing each thing in the world as if for the first time. Slowly he built up his strength, gathering his courage, observing how others lived life. He stole out at night from Tladi's village, where he finally built his own house. He walked across the flat pan floor to the BaKii settlement, where he asked to sit by their fire, listening. The old men told stories and the old women corrected their mistakes. He drank corn beer and tea from Hrikwa's wagon, asking his hosts what each story meant.

Back at Tladi's village, he walked more proudly, joining in hunts. Carrying only a knife, twice he chased down impala and slit their throats. He was not a great hunter, yet neither did the others laugh at him. Tladi paid him no mind. Ra-Mojamaje's confidence swelled in secret. His mind and eye grew quick and clear. The sour memory of Ma-Mojamaje's deception turned to passion, hope for a second chance. This time he was strong. He would not fail. Their intimate years would not fall to waste.

Finally his brother noticed the change. Tumo offered quiet encouragement, running beside him on the hunt, wordlessly accepting his comradeship. Though mimicking Tladi in every visible manner, Tumo had a heart more stupid than malicious. He tried to storm, thrash, take command, for truly he looked up to his father, failing to notice Tladi's cruelty. So Tumo's own venom never developed properly. Everyone dismissed him as Tladi's eldest son, born to follow his footsteps as thunder follows lightning, with no will or fate of his own. Tumo lived in Tladi's shadow, knowing no other life. His journeys to Naring were brief and cold: he burned his wife, beat his sons, drank beer with old friends. But somewhere in his soul lurked a lack of conviction, which he passed on to Tabo, the complicated boy with contradictory eyes.

As for Tladi himself, the details of his sons' lives interested him not at all. Never visiting Naring, he never saw Dinti or Tabo. He cared only that Tumo was rugged, tough, and held his head high. He demanded a minimum of manliness from Ra-Mojamaje, and that is exactly what Ma-Mojamaje delivered. Once Ra-Mojamaje had fathered a child, Tladi lost all concern for him. There was no ambivalence in Tladi's heart, icy and sour, whimless, as it had been since his earliest youth.

Seven peaceful years after the Battle of the Woodpile, Pule's advisors judged the scene quiet enough to hold another bogwera. They sent word to Tladi, who agreed to come, but this time to meet the initiation party in Naring, to march all together to the ceremony site. The news flashed like a crack of lightning through the village. Tladi was coming back.

13
Tladi's Return

Such was the state of the Tladi family compound when its founder returned to Naring after eighteen years' absence, from the Kalahari he called home. Up to this point, the tellers of the story of the Great Thirst allow all who remember parts of the tale to have their say. Now, with Tladi's return, they silence everyone but the oldest, most experienced teller. This event is too important to entrust to beginners. Every detail must be right.

Tladi's Loang regiment marched over the sand slope in perfect formation, their spears tucked tight under their arms, chanting. Tladi led them to the center of Naring, where they halted, sparkling with sweat. Tladi was magnificent: he wore a pointed jackal fur hat two feet high and a splendid fur cloak that reached to the ground, the long silver tails of the pelts still attached, dragging in the dust. He was as trim and muscular as ever, though his hair had receded and tufts of gray hugged his temples.

Studying the regiment, the BaNare identified each man. There was Tumo, his father's replica, and who was that beside him? Could it be Ra-Mojamaje, the frail boy who left Naring so long ago, whom Ma-Mojamaje promised to make a man but made a clown instead? He stood tall, erect, in line with the other soldiers, his shoulders as broad as his brother's. No shame or fear marred his face. His eyes peered ahead, narrow in the late afternoon sun, his jaw set firm on his neck, eyes shining with resolve.

A crowd quickly formed around the regiment and now it burst alive with talk of this new development. Had Ra-Mojamaje whipped himself into manhood, now come to claim his long-lost bride? The women swore she would be a fool to turn him down and if she did so they would gladly take him instead.

"What a lovely boy!"

"What about Tladi?"

The crowd stilled. Tladi had come for her too. Whom had she pined for, Tladi or Ra-Mojamaje?

Tladi barked a command to break rank. He sent Tumo off to guard duty in the hills, ever mindful to keep him safe from Naring's soft corruption. He called his lieutenants for final instructions on the next morning's departure for the bogwera. Meanwhile, Ra-Mojamaje raced to Ma-Mojamaje's house.

Mojamaje sat on the mud floor of his mother's house, watching her stand at the doorway, impatiently rubbing her hands. He knew all the rumors and regarded his mother with a new curiosity. For the first time she appeared a separate being, no longer just part of himself. What was she thinking? He no longer knew. Her bare breasts were suddenly those of a woman, not just his mother's, longing for the things older boys said men and women did. Mojamaje knew the story of her trick, his own birth, of Tladi's recent threats to repay her. He felt powerless, young, a child unable to reach beyond his years to assist her.

Ma-Mojamaje gasped and stepped back into the house. Her husband flew into the room. Warm tears rushed to her eyes. How wonderful he looked! Mojamaje guessed that this was not Tladi—too young, tall, pleasant. It must be his father.

"I knew you would come," Ma-Mojamaje sighed, but before she fell into his arms, Tladi burst through the door. He hurled his spear into the mud wall and his fur cloak onto the floor. His intentions were obvious: there was lust in his eye and his loincloth was no longer large enough to clothe his loins.

A moment of silence, the three adults stood their ground, their three faces jumbled in Mojamaje's eyes. A fury of helplessness assaulted the boy. He knew his father was good, Tladi was evil, his mother's desperate ache, and what would happen next. Ma-Mojamaje looked down at her son and softly said, "Go, take your goats to the canyon stream." Mojamaje dashed out, through Tladi's bodyguards lounging outside the house, away out of Naring. He ran to his goats and threw himself among them, chasing them down to the canyon, tears streaming over his high Bushman cheekbones.

Ra-Mojamaje moved between his father and his wife, but Tladi pulled him in one swift, powerful motion, tossing him out the door and barking to his bodyguards outside, "Keep this dog out." Ra-Mojamaje struggled but the thugs pinned him to the compound floor in front of the house, laughing and pouring sand into his nostrils and mouth.

Inside the house, Tladi turned on Ma-Mojamaje, who covered her breasts with her arms. Tladi reached for her leather apron, but she drew back, slapping away his hand.

"You owe me a favor," Tladi hissed, violence steaming from his eyes.

"I owe you nothing," Ma-Mojamaje replied, squinting hard in the dim light of the house, her mind racing to plan an escape. "They will rescue me," she said to herself. But the BaNare stood perplexed, gathering in small groups around the Tladi compound, discussing whether Ma-Mojamaje had yearned all those years for Tladi or for his son. They waited at a distance for signs of clear resolution.

"What did you do to him?" Tladi demanded, not wanting to force her as he did other women. The essence of her fascination, his nagging arousal, was the thought of some magical trick she had showed to his son. How else had she stirred the dolt to passion?

"Show me," Tladi grunted in a low, animal voice, almost purring, like the hum of a panther ready to pounce. "Show me!" he bellowed. "Filthy Bushman slut!" His eyes flashed white like sun burning through clouds, through Ma-Mojamaje's resistance.

"I am clean," she replied. "No one is cleaner. My skin is the color of dust." Fear gripped her throat as she realized grimly that the BaNare would not save her.

Outside, Ra-Mojamaje sputtered and writhed, finally clearing his mouth enough to cry out, "Save her, BaNare! He is burning my wife!" Tladi's men, thirty in number, all beefy, empty of sense or ambition, silenced Ra-Mojamaje with more sand, but now the BaNare around the compound picked up sticks from Ma-Mojamaje's famous woodpile. By now all Naring had heard the news, the crowd grew, Pule bounded into view, elegant in his full leopard suit, copper earrings dangling, his ochered hair glistening, head tossed high in imperial disdain.

"Stop!" Pule shouted. "Your chief commands you!" Tladi's bodyguards looked up at Pule, looked up at each other, then broke out in laughter. The BaNare moved closer, but still they feared these reckless toughs and their deadly captain inside the house. Then a figure leapt out from the crowd, the first to risk battle, and a scuffle broke out. The BaNare pressed even closer, but still they did not join in, peering first to determine who it was who had struck first and, more important, to see how he fared against Tladi's men.

It was young Tabo Cross-Eyes, still just a boy, who dove headfirst into the bodyguards' midst, a chaos of shouts. At first the thugs laughed but then Tabo held his own. The BaNare watching praised the good eye that pushed him to such valor, then they shuddered at the pleasure the boy took in the brawl, a product of the bad eye.

Tladi's men overwhelmed Tabo, but the boy's courage shamed and prodded the BaNare crowd to action. They shouted, rushed forward, waving their sticks in the air. The bodyguards stopped laughing and called out in fear, "Tladi!"

In a flash Tladi stepped from the house, spear in hand, his fur cloak thrown over his shoulders. He barked out an order and his men snapped into formation, their spears clamped under their arms, facing the crowd, which halted, silenced. But it did not retreat. A vicious leer covered Tladi's face, the taste of blood already in his mouth. It seemed as if every adult in Naring stood before the compound, stick in hand, signaling the end of Tladi's usefulness. After seven years of peace, there remained no reason to endure his separate empire, to live in fear of him turning on his own people. Potso's murderer at last faced his jury.

Tladi barked out another command: he ordered the column to attack. But they refused to move. Tladi had gone too far, sending his men against their own flesh and blood.

Voices called out from the crowd:

"Pheno, will you slay your own father?"

"Kemang, will you carve out your sister's liver?"

One by one, Tladi's men dropped their spears and melted into the crowd. Tladi watched the defection in silence, with satisfaction, even with glee. He faced the BaNare alone. Tossing off his cloak, revealing his massive, muscular chest, he held his spear in his left hand and drew a knife from his loincloth with his right. Meanwhile, Ra-Mojamaje recovered, struggled to his feet, took up a stick and stepped forward to face Tladi first.

Fearsome Tladi, Man of Lightning, rolled back his head and let loose a bloodcurdling laugh. He would kill thirty BaNare before they subdued him, and the first to perish would be his pathetic son. The BaNare shivered and caught their breaths as Tladi rocked back on his heels, narrowed his eyes and tensed for the kill.

Suddenly gunfire filled the air.

"Boers!" Tladi shouted.

The crowd turned toward the Naring hills. Tladi raced to the canyon as the BaNare men ran home for their spears, then followed behind him, to rush to take up positions among the valorous aloe trees on the ridge at the canyon mouth. The Battle of the Rocks had begun.

Tladi deployed BaNare warriors along the canyon walls and called together his lieutenants and the village elders for a quick briefing. As they stood in a circle atop the ridge, as the sky fell to deep violet and black, the BaNare women reached the top of the canyon wall and pushed Ma-Mojamaje toward Tladi's war council.

"My son!" Ma-Mojamaje cried. "I sent him to tend his goats in the canyon! No one has seen him, he must be down there. . . ."

Just then Tumo, Tladi's shadow in flesh, rushed into the clearing. He was the sentry who fell asleep at his post and let four hundred Boers thunder past. When the shots awakened him, he rolled boulders down on the Boers as he made his way back along the canyon wall, giving the battle its name. Now he reached the men and women huddled in two groups on the ridge, overlooking the battlefield. At first the twilight shadows hid his identity, then Tladi strode over and hit his son twice in the face, raised a rock to crush his skull, then paused to think. He gazed over the lip of the canyon, assessing the Boer positions.

"You will drive away the Boer horses," Tladi ordered. "That will leave them no cover and no escape."

A murmur ran through first the group of men and then the group of women. It was a good idea, though dangerous. Then Ra-Mojamaje stepped forward. "I must go too," he declared. "We will chase away the Boer horses and I will bring back my son." Tladi spat on the ground and turned away, back toward the battle.

The sky was now so dark that Ra-Mojamaje could not make out Ma-Mojamaje's face in the group of women across the clearing. There was no time to lose, he did not seek her out. He and Tumo crawled down, and as he smelled the first Boer horse he realized the night was too black to see at all. Perhaps when the dying horses screamed and chaos erupted on the battlefield, he could stand up and shout his son's name, calling him to him.

As he and Tumo plunged their knives into horseflesh, the full moon popped out, the Boers poured bullets through their bodies. As Ra-Mojamaje snapped in the air, his head turned to see his son in the moonlight, spread against the rocks, the last thing his eyes ever saw.

The BaNare on the canyon wall watched this moon-dance, and Ma-Mojamaje threw herself on the ground, beating her fists against the air, rolling in the dust that she spent her life washing from her tawny skin. The reunion she dreamed of for so many years had lasted only a moment, a blink, a breath, without even a final embrace. She cried bitter tears, the hopes of her happiness vanishing in the night. Then abruptly she sat up on her knees.

"My son!" she screamed, and the other women held her back as she made to dash away. They knew, had expected, that now she would try to reach the boy herself, wherever he was. She collapsed in their arms, delirious with fear for her only son, the product of all her desires. They carried her back to her compound.

When the Boers made their escape in the pale light of dusk, the BaNare warriors sent word to Naring that the battle was over. The women roused Ma-Mojamaje, telling her that her son lived. She flew to the battlefield and there, as she pried the boy gently from the rock, she whispered in his ear, "I am safe, he did not touch me. Come, my Eater of Rocks, we can go home."

His arms flew tight around her neck, he clung to her as to the rock, buried in her bosom, his legs wrapped around her waist. She turned from the canyon wall and declared to the BaNare assembled around her, "I knew they could not harm him. I knew he would be a great man."

As she carried the boy back to Naring, the crowd pressed behind, the sorrowful deaths slipping from their memories, especially Ra-Mojamaje's, the end of an unhappy life. Then the BaNare began to dance and sing in celebration of their victory. By the time they reached the village, they had composed the song still sung today:

> All through the night
> Through the terrible fight
> Mojamaje kept watch by the door
> First he ate a rock
> Then he ate a bullet
> Then Mojamaje ate a Boer

14
Mojamaje's Refrain

The dancing and singing continued through the night. When the icy winter wind whipped across the sand ridge, from the empty Kalahari, the BaNare fell back to Ma-Mojamaje's woodpile, which the Tladi and Potso families now kept fully stocked. They set it afire, and the flames leapt high to warm their skins. The blaze was smaller this time, nothing like the towering beacon that saved the BaNare in the Battle of the Woodpile. Men and women danced together, in one circle close around the fire, while their children formed a larger ring around them. Sweat bathed every dancer, every singer's voice grew thick and hoarse. As the night wore on, feverish steps faded to slow, languorous whirls, dragging feet, memories of the dead. Then someone remembered how they found the infant Mojamaje crawling out of the fire on the eve of the Battle of the Woodpile.

"The very same child!" the BaNare cried, their exhausted bodies picking up the tempo again.

"Eater of Rocks!"

"Eater of Fire!"

"Magical Child!"

The fire burned to red embers, but still the BaNare danced, their shimmering skins barely visible in the gloom. Morning came and they dispersed, to sleep away the sorrows still grasping at their hearts.

Mojamaje lay in the house of his mother, listening to the wails of her fitful sleep, across the floor on her cold blankets. Some BaNare claim this was the moment he decided to become a great man. He could not know what adventures lay ahead, there on the floor of his mother's house, the brief, radiant image of his father still fresh before him, cries of despondency filling his ears, gunshots, fire, the terrible spectre of Tladi. Mojamaje closed his Bushman eyes, rubbed salty tears from his Bushman cheeks, to stare out at the world with new knowledge, a new passion for the future and for the chance to win for himself, for his mother, for the

BaNare too, a peace of mind, a measure of contentment, a world stripped of false hopes and bitter endings.

Other BaNare argue that little boys never think such things. They say instead that Mojamaje buried his head in his blankets and cried himself to sleep, his head filled with nothing but sadness and fear.

15
A Knife Between the Legs

Tladi returned to Loang with his men. The Tladi family compound in Naring mourned its losses with bewildered restraint, for Tumo and Ra-Mojamaje had not lived there since childhood. Suddenly their mother was sonless, their wives widows, their sons fatherless. The compound lost what it had never really possessed. Their deaths made no daily difference. The greatest loss was a nightly one, in Ma-Mojamaje's dreams. After ten years spent capturing Ra-Mojamaje's heart, after eight years of waiting for him to come claim her, she realized how much she loved him. Now he was dead.

The summer rains commenced, filling the air with the musty smell of dust turned to mud. Out in their fields, bent at the waist, their hoes falling rhythmically against the damp earth, the three women of the Tladi compound buried themselves in work. The sun rose straight over their backs. Tladi's wife, now a childless mother, lost the glow of life that Ma-Mojamaje had instilled in her while reviving the Tladi compound. Now her hoe rose slowly in the air, to fall with only the pull of the earth. Tumo's widow raised her hoe higher and brought it down harder, now and then stopping to stare across the empty field, wondering how life might have looked with a real husband by her side. Ma-Mojamaje's hoe began the season as feebly as her dead husband's mother's, but by the end of planting she had picked up the pace to a fury, the dark iron hoe blade worn shiny and smooth, glinting in the sun each time it rose above her sweating yellow back. She hummed, then quietly, so no one else could hear, she sang to herself these words:

At least I am BaNare
At least I have my son

Out at Loang, Tladi fell sullen and silent. Weeks, months passed, and still he remained subdued. No one had ever seen him like this. He never shouted and barely spoke. The BaNare searched for an explanation, debating long into the night what could be the cause of Tladi's quiescence. Some blamed the loss of Tumo, Tladi's only pride and only joy. Others doubted that Tladi was capable of feeling such emotions. There was the question of immortality, still others suggested, and now Tladi's sons were both dead. But Dinti the Ostrich, Tabo Cross-Eyes and Mojamaje were still Tladi's grandsons. Tladi's blood flowed in their veins. Someone argued that Ra-Mojamaje's final heroism made Tladi feel ashamed. Still others said it was Ma-Mojamaje's refusal, lust undone.

There was yet another view of Tladi's melancholy and this one finally won out. Tladi failed to draw blood in the Battle of the Rocks. The BaNare troops were so disorganized that Tladi spent the entire battle positioning them, bellowing orders, leaping from cover to cover, seizing the twelve ancient rifles from the men pointing them at the Boers. Hrikwa the Griqua had been able to smuggle only these few rusty muskets to Naring, two of which exploded when the BaNare tried to fire them before Tladi was able to locate the guns and pull them from the reckless hands of his soldiers. He was forced to rely on the lowly throwing spear against the Boers. The greatest battle the BaNare would ever fight, his greatest chance at war, had flown by without Tladi partaking of the slaughter.

Weeding followed planting, harvest followed weeding, winter followed harvest, another year passed with reports from Loang describing Tladi as quiet, moody and sober. This was good news for Ma-Mojamaje, for as her son grew up she faced a painful dilemma. When a BaNare boy grew old enough to herd cattle, he moved out to join the older boys and men in the pastures. It was still not safe to bring the cattle back to Naring, only two years after the Battle of the Rocks, so BaNare boys went out to Loang to herd. Dinti the Ostrich and Tabo Cross-Eyes were old enough to start work, and older boys took along any younger boys they had watched over as they grew up. Mojamaje should go with his cousins, but was Loang safe? Would Tladi take revenge on Mojamaje? Tladi's silent brooding was good news, so Ma-Mojamaje sent her son to Loang. Certainly she would miss him, certainly it would tear her heart, certainly the compound would ring hollow without his small voice. But BaNare boys herded cattle, girls stayed with their mothers. Mojamaje would be a normal BaNare boy, to grow up to be a great BaNare man.

And so at the age of ten, Mojamaje returned to his birthplace. Loang quickly added weight to his bones, and he grew taller, for herdboys ate meat every week and drank all the milk they wanted. His black skin glowed, his Bushman eyes sparkled, but his brow knit deep lines across his forehead. Far too serious for a child so young, only Mojamaje listened at the lecture given to novices before their first herding assignments. They were told to remember three things: First, always keep all the cattle in sight; second, keep the calves close by their mothers; third, wave a stick in the air to show lions that a human being was present, otherwise they would help themselves to the herd. The sight of a human kept lions away only if they knew in advance. If they came upon a herdboy suddenly, they attacked.

Only Mojamaje followed these instructions. He ran through his herd, waving his stick, cracking it down on the cattle's rumps, keeping them in sight, keeping calves beside their mothers, alerting lions. Every other herdboy dozed under a thorn tree, a dry reed between his teeth, while his herd wandered off to graze where they pleased, to be rounded up at the end of the day. Mojamaje was the first herder in history to follow instructions, running in circles from dawn to dusk, wagging his stick furiously, dust flying from his little heels.

Years later the BaNare looked back to realize that Mojamaje had worked hard as a herdboy to sharpen his skills for the greater challenges ahead. He learned to speak BaKii as well as Bushman from the bands that frequented Loang to trade skins for water, and he learned to sew furs into blankets and capes. One cape he fashioned from thirty silverbacked jackals earned awe from the older men, especially because Mojamaje trapped each jackal himself over several winters with an eye-loop snare and stake pit. He caught each animal in the dead of winter, when their coats grew thick and luxuriant, smelling sweet, warm, so that each man who tried on Mojamaje's cloak, admiring its beauty, swore he heard the quiet beating of thirty jackal hearts inside it. Mojamaje left on the heads and tails, which flapped as if the cape were alive.

And so beyond reach of his mother's eyes, Mojamaje grew to the shape he would be as a man. Long-limbed, thin but strong, he waited out the rest of his childhood, impatient for it to end. He watched the other boys and learned to act and talk like them, but in secret he remained unconvinced that he wanted to be like them. He needed a better reason. Although his adolescence, his inexperience, loosened his grasp on the full chain of reason, he understood that emulating his elders would seal his fate as an accomplice of the past. Something was wrong in the world, whatever it was, and Mojamaje wanted to find it and make it right. He hunted, sewed skins, and wandered for hours in the wake of his red cattle, lost in thought and speculation of what adulthood would be like. Sometimes the solitude formed like a drop of honey on his tongue, so sweet under the endless blue sky. There was only the rustle of grass, yellow straw dried in the winter air, to muffle the echo of cowbells across the Kalahari plain. Then he would run, waving his stick and slashing the brush, bursts of sun and twisted trees flying as he raced away his loneliness, savoring the pleasure and pain of lungs heaving and feet slapping the warm sand, a limitless world embracing him, empty, until distance silenced the cowbells and Mojamaje stopped to listen.

Catching his breath, he whispered, "I am alone." A knowing smile formed on his lips, a suggestion of selfishness. For all his sympathy he knew above all to avoid his mother's fate. And to the still air he added, "I will not live my life alone."

The most remarkable thing about Mojamaje's early years at Loang was that Tladi ignored him completely. Though his quiet mood slowly faded, Tladi remained aloof from Loang affairs. He hunted all the time now, even in early summer, when the great herds of blue-maned antelope broke into smaller bands to drink from the myriad rainpools across the Kalahari. A large herd was easier to find and follow, whereas bands of ten and twenty appeared and vanished without a trace. Still, once a month at the waning half-moon, Tladi hunted.

Back at Naring, the BaNare guessed that Tladi's venom had finally run dry. Then Pule revived the idea of bogwera. At first no one paid attention to Pule's suggestion, for every time the BaNare men left for the ceremony, some pack of marauders made a beeline for Naring. Despite Pule's fear that an uninitiated chief was not a real chief, no one disputed his rule. The refugees had settled down as loyal citizens, marrying BaNare and each other. Pule persisted, nagging his advisors, until finally they gave in. They sent word to Tladi, who agreed to meet them at the bogwera site. Women sighed in disappointment: he would not come to Naring. There would not take place another drama between Tladi and Ma-Mojamaje.

This bogwera came about just as Mojamaje grew old enough to participate. Four times a year he had visited Naring, spending the entire time in his mother's compound while the other boys waited in ambush, bleary with stolen beer, to pounce on the girls least resistant to seduction, who walked with their new breasts thrown far ahead before them.

Mojamaje was one of the youngest initiates; Pule was one of the oldest. Copper earrings still dangled from the avid chief's ears. Oil and red ocher still stained his hair and also his Boer hat. Still strutting, he spoke like a king, and the BaNare applauded his every flourish. They feared for him at initiation, though, for there he would be not chief but a mere novice. Every night the initiates would lie naked by the fire while the older men beat them with clubs and sticks. Bogwera always took place in midwinter, when the night would be painfully cold to the naked novices. Old men would drill them in military tactics, rousing songs, tricks of seduction and hunting. At night they would beat them agair., until the end of a month, when the initiates would lie naked in a row. One by one they would be circumcised. This would turn them into men. In Pule's case it would turn him into a chief. But throughout the bogwera ceremony, he would suffer the same humiliations as the other novices. Young men whispered that one initiate always died and the others were forced to eat him. What if this dead one were Pule?

BaNare circumcision was a delicate operation. A man's foreskin is tougher than an infant's and sometimes required some sawing with the knife. One slip meant disaster. Fortunately, the older men always entrusted the knife to the most experienced cutter. Unfortunately, it had been more than twenty-five years since the BaNare circumcised anyone. The backlog of uninitiated men meant that some novices were more than forty years old.

Fortunately, they had Tsulu. Tsulu was a Zulu, a real one, not an imitation. Tall and dark, he carried a stabbing spear under his arm. Tsulu was a refugee who had arrived in Naring soon after the Battle of the Rocks. Such hard times in South Africa, that even Zulu ranged the plains as refugees! Tsulu was the only genuine Zulu to reach Naring. The BaNare called him Tsulu because they could not pronounce the word *Zulu*. When they tried to say "Zulu," it came out "Tsulu." So that was his name.

No one circumcised like a Zulu. The Zulu turned initiation into an art, circumcising thousands of new recruits in one ceremony. This was how they made conquered peoples into Zulu, by capturing and initiating young men. During their initiation all new Zulu warriors received instruction in the art of circumcision, so they could make more Zulu wherever they raided. Zulu bands swept across South Africa, rounding up uncircumcised men to initiate into Zulu regiments. As for circumcised men, the Zulu slaughtered them on the spot. The naked recruits lay on their backs in the dust, the Zulu taught them war songs, beat them with sticks and circumcised them with knives. This made them Zulu.

Though Tsulu was still a young man, the BaNare appointed him circumciser. They piled high Ma-Mojamaje's famous woodpile in case Naring had to signal again, and departed for the wilderness with Tsulu in the lead, still clutching his stabbing spear under one arm. He wore a spotted wildcat coat that Pule loaned him for the occasion. The initiates and teachers left Naring at a half run, shouting wildly, taking two quick steps to match one of the Zulu's long strides.

Night after night the BaNare initiates lay naked by their campfires, shivering with cold until their skins numbed and they fell asleep to fitful dreams of freezing to death, imagining their fellows chewing their bones the next morning. Only Mojamaje stayed warm, because of his immunity to fire, first demonstrated at the Battle of the Woodpile, when a dancing woman found him crawling through flames. The other initiates tried to creep close within the circle of warm air around each campfire, but the heat drove them back. They lay on the edge of the fire's heat: one side of their bodies faced the blaze, warming; the side turned away grew frigid and numb. They rotated often, switching sides, but never beat back the frightening chill that threatened to snuff out their breaths. Only Mojamaje was able to bear the heat near the campfire's center, lying close to its flame, his flesh glazed smooth like the inside of a fresh goatskin, his whole body bathed in deep heat.

After three weeks of chants, beatings, drills, and cold nights, the time for circumcision arrived. A thousand initiates lay naked in a clearing between two low hills. By midday the sun had still not appeared, hidden behind a gray ceiling of clouds that stretched from horizon to horizon. The novices shivered. Tsulu stepped forward, tossed off his wildcat cape and strode briskly to the first figure. Clad in only a loincloth, Tsulu's magnificent Zulu body, his long Zulu neck, the knife in his hand, made an impressive sight. The older men nodded to each other, congratulating themselves on their choice of circumciser.

Several of the initiates at this bogwera were important characters in the story of the Great Thirst, especially Mojamaje himself, his cousins

Dinti and Tabo, and Chief Pule. So it is odd that a Bushman turned up first in line for Tsulu's knife. The BaNare debate who arranged this order, for what happened next could only have occurred with a Bushman first in line. Some argue that one of the instructors, most likely Tladi, maneuvered him into this position, while others claim that he pushed his own way to the front. In the end, the BaNare abandoned both theories. It was chance, pure and simple.

This Bushman's name was Xo. He was the first Bushman to settle in Naring, or half settle, for now and then he vanished into the Kalahari to rejoin his band for a hunt. "Once a Bushman, always a Bushman," the BaNare said. The bogwera was open to all now, so BaKii from Loang and all the Naring refugees joined in, but no one expected the Bushman to come. When Xo showed up, no one thought he would stay for the whole ceremony. At any moment, they expected him to jump up and disappear into the wilderness again. Strict obedience and iron discipline were essential during bogwera: no initiate spoke unless spoken to or moved a muscle without permission. During circumcision the initiates lay perfectly still, eyes closed, no matter how much it hurt. Bushmen, of course, did not have an obedient bone in their bodies. Because Xo had the yellowest skin, the shortest legs and the highest cheekbones, everyone expected him to act like a Bushman. When Tsulu approached with the knife, Xo did something no other initiate would ever do. The other initiates were glad he did.

As Tsulu bent down, the Bushman opened his eyes, raised his head, and looked up. This was completely against the rules. With a wild Bushman yelp, clicking his teeth and smacking his lips, he grabbed Tsulu's loincloth and vanished into the wilderness. The other initiates opened their eyes and looked over at an astonished Tsulu. With one voice they gasped in horror. Tsulu was uncircumcised. Xo had looked under Tsulu's loincloth to see his ragged Zulu foreskin still firmly attached to his sleek Zulu body. Tsulu was a fake. He was Zulu all right, but he had become a refugee before being initiated. He was no Zulu warrior. He was just a Zulu, an uncircumcised Zulu. He knew nothing about circumcision. The Bushman had exposed him.

The naked initiates trembled to think how close they had come to disaster. Tsulu would have made a terrible mess. They flushed with fear, from their loins through their bowels.

Tladi walked up to Tsulu, who backed away stammering, "I can explain. . . ." Tladi grabbed the knife from Tsulu's hand and smacked him square on his broad, flat Zulu nose. The other men led him away.

The ceremony proceeded without further incident. Tladi performed the circumcisions. A bit rough, never having done it before, Tladi was fed up with repeatedly postponing bogwera. He would finish it this time, one way or another. No one protested, least of all the initiates, who did not think Tladi qualified for the job, but once he bent over them with the knife, they decided that this was not the best time to say so. There was some blood, but not much, and no one died from his wounds.

Except perhaps for Tsulu. No one ever saw him again. When the initiates sat at their fires for the next meal, they were too frightened to ask whether the meat was Tsulu. They stared at it roasting on the fire, and none dared touch it.

Of all the initiates, Mojamaje was most terrified by the knife in Tladi's hand. He was the only one who would have preferred Tsulu, or even the Bushman. Anyone but Tladi. As his grandfather moved down the line, Mojamaje broke into a feverish sweat, cursing his high Bushman cheekbones, identical to his mother's, which would only inflame Tladi's frustrated lust, remind him of Ma-Mojamaje's trick, the disappointment of his sons, the slow-burning bitterness that ruled Tladi's soul.

"He will punish me," Mojamaje thought. "He will kill me, cut me apart, rub my flesh in my face." Mojamaje quivered in the dust, helpless, his back to the earth, his belly exposed to the sky, as vulnerable as when he clung to the rocks with the Boer shells bursting in his ears. Eyes shut tight in perfect discipline, he heard his neighbor cry out in pain, then felt the warmth of Tladi's sweat, heard his hard breathing, smelled his breath, the breath of an angry man, searing like fire against Mojamaje's taut eyelids.

Tladi spent an hour on Mojamaje's foreskin. He spilled not a single drop of blood. Perspiration streamed from Tladi's brow and bare back as he sawed away at his grandson's foreskin. After finishing Mojamaje, Tladi grew tired, and farther along the line he left a few boys bathed in blood.

16
One Heart Too Many

By this time the tellers of the story of the Great Thirst judge that their listeners have heard enough to begin answering questions about some finer points of the tale. So they ask:

Why did Tladi circumcise Mojamaje so carefully?

The BaNare tellers ask this because it gives them the chance to discuss relations between Mojamaje and his grandfather. Some listeners suggest that Tladi loved Mojamaje's mother, that Mojamaje's Bushman eyes looked the same as hers, that he reminded Tladi of his mother, while others contend that Tladi hated Ma-Mojamaje and Mojamaje too. Still others argue that Tladi first hated her because she outwitted him, then he loved her, thinking of the magical tricks she used to woo Ra-Mojamaje, begging for her love before the Battle of the Rocks, and so at bogwera Mojamaje reminded Tladi of Ma-Mojamaje and at that moment Tladi loved her again.

The tellers, of course, know the truth. They explain that Tladi charged into Ma-Mojamaje's house that day of the Battle of the Rocks bursting with lust, not love. These two things are not the same. He hated Ma-Mojamaje, always, and only kept his men from burning her to serve himself, to spare himself the shame of a sexless son. He did not circumcise Mojamaje carefully out of love for his mother. Tladi loved no one. He prolonged Mojamaje's circumcision to show his contempt for the boy and his mother. The teller directs the listeners to think how it feels when a tooth rots and must be pulled out. The same with circumcision, a practice long forgotten now. Every scrape of the knife against Mojamaje's tender flesh—tensed tight, like a goat with its hind legs tied, expecting the butcher knife and the roasting spit. The cold tip pressed against the skin, twitching, struggling to escape. Tladi drew no blood, but the hour he spent cutting the boy was torture, vicious torture, a grievous insult to Mojamaje.

The tellers of the story of the Great Thirst delve in such detail into Mojamaje's circumcision not out of prurience, but because his relation-

ship with his grandfather is so important to the story. The BaNare did
not accept the tale of Tladi's contempt for Mojamaje until well after the
initiation. Because Tladi paid Mojamaje no attention at Loang, and
singled the boy out for such precise circumcision, at first the BaNare
failed to appreciate the consistency of Tladi's hatred, how he hated
everyone equally. At the time, the BaNare suspected some reserve of
affection for the boy, however stifled and twisted. This judgment led to
widespread confusion in the final confrontation between Tladi and Mojamaje, soon after Hrikwa the Griqua brought unusual news from South
Africa.

The trader rolled into Naring, spread his wares on the ground before
the wagon, and announced to Pule, "The English have come."

BaNare assembling to bargain cried, "English!" and turned to flee into
the Kalahari.

"Not here," Hrikwa said. "In South Africa. They will not come here."

The BaNare returned to crowd around the wagon as Pule asked suspiciously, "How do you know?"

The trader pulled down a stack of dresses and replied, "They have
built a town south of Taung and chased the Boers away from it."

"How did they do it?" Pule asked.

"Cannons," Hrikwa replied. He went on to explain how a cannon
worked, as the BaNare listened in silence. First came the Zulu stabbing
spear, then the Boer rifle, now the English cannon. For years the English
had been only a rumor, now everyone expected them to sweep across the
countryside like the Zulu and Boers before them. The BaNare shuddered.

Hrikwa insisted they wanted only one town.

"Why only one town?" the BaNare asked.

"Diamonds," the trader replied. "White stones like water. They are
digging the biggest hole in the world. They find diamonds there."
Hrikwa did not know why they wanted the diamonds, but he had seen
the hole. "They pay men money to dig," he concluded.

The BaNare listened carefully. "How much do they pay?" they asked.

Hrikwa whistled through his lips. He told them of men leaving the
dozens of shops in the town with armloads of blankets, clothes and tools.
A thousand men worked for the English, he said, and every one lived like
a king.

The BaNare whistled through their teeth.

"I am going," each young man said to himself.

"Do not take my word," Hrikwa warned. "You cannot know for sure until you work in the hole yourself. Maybe the pay is good but the English beat you night and day. I do not know. How many men fall down the hole? I do not know. Maybe Zulu work there, and at night they stab you with spears. I do not know."

"I will wait," each young man said to himself. It was one hundred miles to Taung, another fifty miles to the diamond town, too far to go only to turn back.

"Who will go first?" the BaNare wondered. This was the question village after village asked, throughout South Africa and across the Zambezi far beyond, everywhere word of the diamond hole spread. "Who will go first to bring back the news?"

For the BaNare, as in the past, Tladi provided the answer.

Rain had been so sparse the previous three summers that soon after Hrikwa brought his news the Loang wells ran dry. Mojamaje supervised one of the three wells, having moved up from herdboy after initiation. Mojamaje's well was the first to run dry, followed swiftly by the others.

This was a brief drought, nothing compared to things to come, but serious nonetheless. Tladi considered sending the cattle back to Naring: it had been more than fifteen years since the last raid, the Battle of the Rocks, so the cattle would be safe there. But first he tried to deepen the wells, to reach water beneath the mud. He ordered the herdboys to round up the cattle while the men built a gigantic stockade of thorn brush and tree branches. The younger boys guarded the periphery of the new corral to keep cattle from breaking through its weaker spots. Men and boys took the fences away from the wells and began to scoop out mud. They used slabs of wood, held in two hands, bending over at the waist to scrape up soil and throw it out behind, between their legs. They dug until they were waist-deep in sludge, then chest-deep. There was water below, but they churned up so much mud that they began to sink beneath the surface. Stepping up to stand at the edges of the wells, covered in muck, they debated how much deeper they had dug. It was impossible to tell before the silt had a chance to settle. The mud dried on their skins and there was no clean water for washing. They had nothing to drink but the thick muddy sludge in the wells.

They looked up from the mud to see a dark line descend to the other end of the pan, across the flat floor. The line wiggled toward them. They shaded their eyes from the sun.

"Xo," one of the mud-covered men announced.

The Bushman band moved in single file toward the Loang wells. Each squinting man remembered the Bushman's performance at the initiation and reached down a hand to confirm that his private parts were still in place. The Bushmen drew near, their narrow eyes flashing with hunger at the stockade of cattle. Tladi greeted Xo and the two men stood face to face, both the same height. The Bushman explained that the drought had driven away all their game to the deepest Kalahari where no one could follow. The Loang men slipped away to reinforce the boys around the perimeter of the stockade.

Tladi fed the hungry Bushmen corn porridge. They sat down by the wells to eat. The Bushmen wore swatches of hides on their shoulders and waists. Their yellow skin hung in long creases from their tiny frames. The men carried bark quivers filled with delicate reed arrows tipped with iron heads, tiny bows of gut strung on short branches, and skin bags filled with equipment for making smelly poisons. The women carried sticks worn at one end and pointed at the other. The worn end was for holding, the pointed end was for digging in the sand for food. The younger children clung to the backs of the older, their skin as old and wrinkled as their elders'. Every Bushman eye sparkled with greed as they gazed at the cattle, eating their porridge.

When night fell, Xo sang to the Loang men the story of exposing Tsulu's foreskin and the Bushmen danced around the fire, clapping, spinning, smacking their lips, howling, whistling, until they fell into a trance, humming, their tiny feet kicking sand into the fire. Toward midnight they fell asleep. Toward dawn, one Bushman crept up to another and ripped open his chest with a knife. Although the victim died without a sound, the assassin's screams woke the camp. The murderer screamed because he had wanted the victim's heart for some foul medicine, but when he opened the man's chest, the heart was gone. He shrieked in terror and ran away.

The Bushmen searched Loang for the missing heart, as dawn filled the air with quiet light. The victim's sons set off to hunt down the murderer. The search yielded nothing. Xo thanked Tladi for his hospitality, apologized for the commotion, his tongue clacking and clicking, and led the band back into the Kalahari.

At midday the men of Loang took down the stockade and began watering their thirsty cattle in the newly deepened wells. After Mojamaje watered fifty cattle, he spied something floating in the sludge of his well. The herders around paused to watch as Mojamaje waded out to investigate. Chest-deep in the muck, he reached over, picked up the muddy object from the well's surface, and held it in his hand for a moment before realizing what it was. He dropped the thing and tried to run back to solid ground but his legs stuck in the muck. He stumbled twice, submerging himself in the same foul slime where the horrible thing had hidden all day.

Loang was aghast. They closed down the well. What next? At first no one accused Mojamaje of stealing the heart. Everyone agreed that it reached the well under its own power, escaping from its owner's assassin in the early morning dark. But why Mojamaje's well, and how did the heart end up in his hand? No one wanted to think about this, but the heart haunted them now. It was still out there, in Mojamaje's well.

Then one by one, over the next two days, fifty of Tladi's cattle disappeared without a trace. Mojamaje had watered exactly that number before discovering the heart. Were they the same fifty cattle? The coincidence was too perfect for doubt. And Mojamaje certainly had a motive for bewitching his grandfather's cattle. Tladi had killed his father and uncle and almost burned his mother. However innocent Mojamaje's face, no one denied that he stood in the well with one heart too many, one in his chest and one in his hand. Who would blame Mojamaje for seeking revenge? But holding a human heart in his hand was going too far.

Some BaNare disagreed. They pointed out that Xo's hungry Bushmen were still in the neighborhood. Perhaps they circled back to pick off the cattle, roasting them on the spot, burying the bones. Only Tladi's opinion counted, though, and he blamed Mojamaje. A week after the incident, the silt finally settled in the wells to reveal only four inches of murky water, enough for only a few weeks more. This too was blamed on Mojamaje. Tladi gave the word to abandon Loang and drive the cattle back into Naring. Twitching with bitterness, his BaNare followers rounded up their herds, cursing Mojamaje for spoiling the wells with his extra heart.

Tladi sent for Mojamaje. Still covered in dried mud, Mojamaje quaked with fear, unable to forget the feeling of the heart in his hand.

"You!" Tladi spat, wrapped in his long fur cape, his hair now gray like a thundercloud above his brow. "Just like your mother. Nothing but tricks. You ruin my wells, send me back to that stinking pit, that nest of worms, cowards. Naring!" Tladi spat again.

Mojamaje said nothing. He stood trembling before Tladi, thinking of the heart.

"You will pay," Tladi continued. "You will go to South Africa, dig for the English, bring back money to pay for the cattle you killed. If because of you I must live in Naring for the rest of my days. . . ." Here Tladi paused, turning to the west. "I will kill you."

Mojamaje joined in driving the BaNare cattle back to Naring, still covered with mud. The herders washed the mud from their bodies in the stream that ran through the canyon, telling Naring the story of the heart and Mojamaje's sentence.

In his mother's house, wrapped in the beautiful jackal-fur cape he had sewn as a young boy, Mojamaje related his version of the story.

"I am not sorry," he said to his mother. "I am finished at Loang. There is nothing more for me there. It is time I go to South Africa."

Ma-Mojamaje sat on her blankets, wrapped in confusion and sadness. The day was cold, with a thick ceiling of gray clouds hiding all trace of sun. She sat with her back against the round mud wall, her legs stretched out straight before her, feet bare, their soles worn hard and smooth, gray with years of work. It was true, she thought. Soon the BaNare would go there to work. Mojamaje had proved himself a normal BaNare boy. It was time for him to become a great man. The young men his age had begun to marry: if Mojamaje did the same, he would turn out a normal BaNare man. Perhaps that was all she wanted after all, all she should want. The aches of her youth dulled to distant remorse, her burning desire to prove herself, for her son to prove more, receded to memory. She felt different now. The compound echoed, empty. Tabo Cross-Eyes had just married and soon his children would enliven it. Did Ma-Mojamaje hope for the same for her son? For the first time in her life, she did not know what she wanted.

Yet, gazing across the house to her son seated against the opposite wall, Ma-Mojamaje could see that it was too late. Her son was already the man he would be. South Africa was his frontier. He would be the first to go there. She sighed at the sight of his Bushman eyes, the gentle dark skin. Despite the loss of Ra-Mojamaje, she was still alive, full of life, her heart strong and ready for more, beating for her son.

"I will miss you," she said at last.

"I will not stay long," Mojamaje replied.

Though her hopes matched his words, she knew that this would not be so. He would indeed become a great man, but not in Naring. The world stood beyond, away in South Africa, ready for her son's arrival. In dim light he looked like his father, her only love, the sweet young man she had left behind. Now Mojamaje did the same to her.

17
Griqua Beads Found

Hrikwa the Griqua rolled into Naring and agreed to take Mojamaje along to the diamond town. He loaded the wagon with pelts, cracked his whip over the oxen's ears, and set off again east, through the canyon, to South Africa. Mojamaje walked alongside the Griqua, his fur cape draped over his shoulders.

"Nice cape," Hrikwa commented. "You catch them?"

"Every one," Mojamaje replied.

"Sew them?"

"Every stitch."

"Ten shillings," Hrikwa offered.

"I will have all the money I want at the English hole."

"What a hole!" Hrikwa exclaimed. "The biggest hole in the world. All the white men in the world, looking for diamonds. All the black men in the world, digging. All the money in the world, waiting." He cracked his whip and spat a stream of tobacco juice. "Watch out," he continued. "White men are trouble. I am too old to fight them. See this rifle?" He pointed up to the wagon, where an old musket stuck out from a slot in the wooden side rail. "I carry a gun but if I shoot one they will hang me for sure. Only a matter of time. They rob and kill. Nothing to do. They do not want Griqua trading. They think I smuggle guns to black hands."

Mojamaje walked alongside the wagon, lost in thought.

"Why so quiet?" Hrikwa asked.

Mojamaje turned to the trader. "The heart," he replied, speaking loudly above the rumble of the wagon.

"Oo hoo!" Hrikwa howled. "Interesting case."

Mojamaje continued, "It did not feel like a heart."

Hrikwa whistled, touching one hand to the brim of his hat. "How do you know? How many human hearts have you held in your hand? Please, boy, leave mine alone. Old and cranky. Wait for the diamond town, plenty there. Big hearts, little hearts, English hearts, Boer hearts, black hearts, Griqua hearts—"

Mojamaje interrupted. "It should not be much different from a cow heart."

"True," Hrikwa admitted.

"This one was soft," Mojamaje continued. "Big enough, but too soft, covered in mud, I did not see it. More like a goat liver, or a hare's stomach. A heart should be harder."

"Which well was yours?" the Griqua asked, a smile spreading slowly across his stubbled face, ending in a wide crooked grin.

"East," Mojamaje replied, "where the path to Naring meets the pan."

Hrikwa could hardly contain his laughter, dancing a high-step Bushman step, long forgotten by the Griqua, giggling to himself.

"What is funny?" Mojamaje asked, but Hrikwa did not answer.

Here the tellers of the story of the Great Thirst pause to ask their listeners the same question: Why did Hrikwa laugh?

The answer follows Hrikwa's history, his first long thirst to Loang, how he took a pouch of beads from his wagon, to buy water there. He tied it to his belt. When he thrashed in the well, the pouch came loose and stuck in the mud. When the men of Loang deepened the wells, they churned up the mud, freeing the pouch to float to the surface. When Mojamaje picked it up . . .

He thought it was the heart.

18
The Edge of the World

A month after Mojamaje's departure the summer rains arrived in a powerful storm. Lightning exploded in the BaNare's ears, setting fire to a dozen thatched roofs, which the wind tore away and sent swirling through the village. The stream flooded its banks, lapping against the canyon wall where Mojamaje had stood through the Battle of the Rocks.

"To Loang," Tladi ordered when the storm abated. Most cattle remained at Naring this time, for the danger of raids was past. The Tladi family herds alone were immense, including Tladi's younger brothers' and cousins' and their children's. These cattle returned to Loang. He led his men back, to find the three wells overflowing with rain.

Tladi spent his time hunting again, setting out at each waning half-moon with his cohort of bodyguards. Every time he pushed farther west, deeper into the Kalahari, searching for game trails that might lead to water. He encountered Bushman bands that drank only the blood of their prey and sometimes the juice of sour melons growing wild in the sand. He asked them about water holes, but they insisted Loang was the last one. Tladi tried ranging farther west, drinking blood and melon juice like the Bushmen, but thirst drove him back each time. His bodyguards grew weary of following, and often he left them behind, pushing on alone, singing to himself the Bushman song he learned as a child:

> Where does the sun go?
> Into the sand
> Where does the sun go?
> Into the sand

Four months after returning to Loang, Tladi set out on another hunting trip. Heavy rain had left small pools everywhere in the sand, so his party penetrated quickly west, farther than Tladi had ever gone before. Then the rainpools dried up and their progress slowed. The hunting was fair, with a large antelope speared every other day. Finally they halted, unable to find another pool ahead.

On the night they planned to turn back, Tladi woke suddenly, his bladder lately losing some of its strength. He struggled to his feet, rubbing sleep from his eyes, as the campfire glowed bright, tended by the youngest member of the party, who woke periodically to stoke it. Tladi stumbled away from the circle of firelight into the dark wilderness beyond. An upside-down half-moon hung in the western sky, ready to sink below the distant horizon, drawing Tladi toward it, the Bushman song ringing in his head. He remembered back to his childhood, forcing young girls to carry water west, into the Kalahari. He had conquered Loang for this purpose, for a base to take him farther. The other parts of his life—grooming Tumo, hounding Ra-Mojamaje, lusting after Ma-Mojamaje, the first BaKii BaNare, woman of the west, Loang, fighting the Battle of the Woodpile and the Battle of the Rocks, punishing Mojamaje —these had all been distractions, interruptions, bees buzzing before his eyes. He waved them away, to concentrate on his true goal, to discover

the end of the Kalahari, to see the sun set below the horizon, at the edge
of the world. He knew now he would never succeed. His short, muscular
body was still fit and strong, though deep lines marked his face and
hands and eight teeth had recently fallen out. His hair was almost gone.
He was calm, sad, as he faced the moonlit horizon, realizing he would
never conquer it.

A cool breeze swept through the underbrush, rustling the coarse grass
at Tladi's feet. His eyes adjusted to the darkness, the campfire's glow
mixing with the hollow moonlight. The air smelled of wet sand still fresh
with rain.

Tladi's bladder pulled him back from his reverie. Sighing deeply, he
lifted his loincloth, began to urinate, then gasped silently, drawing his
breath through his teeth. A pale shape crouched in the brush a yard
before him. Tladi heard a second stream of urine crackling onto the
grass.

"A peeing lion," Tladi explained afterward as he related the story back
at Loang when his party returned home. His men understood the significance of this fact, for Tladi had never killed a lion. Several lions were
slain each year but never by Tladi. His luck had simply been bad.

"There I was," Tladi continued, "the first lion of my life, and my
knife was back at the campfire."

Tladi prided himself a careful hunter, never taking unnecessary
chances, never risking his companions' lives. He appreciated fully the
danger of wildcats, especially lions and leopards.

"The only thing to grab," Tladi joked, "was between my own legs.
And that was no help at all." Tladi tried to make light of the incident,
but his men all perceived his embarrassment at the lion catching him so
completely off guard.

The lion was off guard too, but still armed with terrible claws. For one
fleeting instant the pissing lion and the pissing man peered across the
gloom to where they assumed each other's eyes set in the dark shadows
of a face. Then, like a bolt of lightning, the lion flashed through the air
to sink its claws into Tladi's eyes, neck and belly, in one forward lunge
with paws outstretched. Then it loped off into the night.

Tladi's men carried him back in an antelope-hide sling. He bled for a
day and a half, soaking the sleeping mats in his house in Loang. Then
the bleeding stopped. He sat up to recount the tale of his mauling. A
week later several of his internal organs burst, bleeding Tladi dry.

MAKA

Tladis

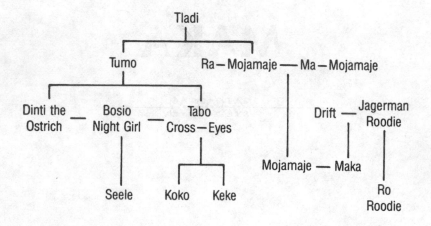

Tladi

Tumo — Ra – Mojamaje — Ma – Mojamaje

Dinti the Ostrich — Bosio Night Girl — Tabo Cross – Eyes

Drift — Jagerman Roodie

Seele

Koko   Keke

Mojamaje — Maka

Ro Roodie

Potsos

Potso
|
Pule
|
Pia the Scornful

De Swarts

Old Man Piet
|
Paulus the Lover

1

What Was on Mojamaje's Mind

Some BaNare imagine their hero, Mojamaje, venturing forth with the intention of ridding South Africa of English and Boers. Where others took two steps Mojamaje needed only one, rain clouds followed him and soaked the earth. As he strode past, cows bore twins, corn ripened, Boers and English trembled and turned to stone. Then Mojamaje pushed the invaders to the edge of the sea, then onto ships, and with one breath he blew them away forever.

Other BaNare, when they sit down on winter nights to tell the story of the Great Thirst from beginning to end, dispute this view. They suggest instead that Mojamaje struck out from Naring not to save South Africa but to forestall its terrible fate from descending also on the BaNare. Certainly this goal stood closer to the truth. Still others argue that he was still but a young man, almost naked, ignorant of what lay ahead. Visions of heroism struggled against common sense. Ambition wrestled with fear. Mojamaje knew only vaguely that both danger and opportunity lurked in South Africa. As he rode atop Hrikwa's wagon, his mind raced with questions, but each time the same infuriating answer arose— wait and see. Things will happen.

Already Mojamaje looked ahead to wonder how his life might come out. His escape from Loang remained incomplete, for he feared that his mother's unhappiness condemned him to the same fate, that something would always be wrong, that however hard he fought, his triumph would vanish like the image of his father. The seed that carried his fate grew from years spent at his mother's side. As he looked up from childhood,

piecing together her story, the loneliness of her nights, Mojamaje understood the circumstances of his own birth, the dilemmas of his parents'
lives, and he understood Tladi. The world made sense and Mojamaje felt
small within it. He leapt out into South Africa so that actions might
force themselves upon him, pointing him in one, many, any direction.

Such were some of Mojamaje's thoughts as he headed for South Africa. Of course, there were other, less weighty things on his mind as well.
He jumped down from the wagon again and asked the Griqua, "Do you
have a woman?"

The trader's frog face sparkled and his mouth croaked a laugh as he
looked into Mojamaje's eyes. "Hold on, boy. Diamond town has plenty
of that too."

2
The Truth About the Hole

South Africa! South Africa!
The white man in South Africa
Wants everyone to come to dig a big hole in the ground
South Africa! South Africa!
I am going to South Africa
To go and dig the hole and be the richest man around

This is the song the young BaNare men sang on their way to Kimberley, the diamond town. They did not wait to hear from Mojamaje, for as
soon as he left they began to think: If he does become rich, why would
he come back to tell us? If he came back to say that the work was
dangerous and the pay was low, why should we believe him? If Mojamaje
never came back, we would have to go anyway to find out for ourselves.
As it turned out, each young man would go see for himself.

A week after Mojamaje's departure, eight BaNare slipped out of Naring at night, without informing their relatives. The first to come back
told the BaNare that the work was hard and dangerous, the pay was
terrible, and the sleeping quarters were more treacherous than the hole

itself, with knife and spear fights every night. No one believed them.
The young men continued to go.

Each man who went found out for himself that the worst of the tales
was true. They signed a six-month contract upon arrival at the hole. A
wire fence ringed the mine compound, patrolled by armed guards and
savage dogs, so no one could smuggle out diamonds or leave before the
six months ended.

This is the song the BaNare men sang at work in the English mine:

> South Africa! South Africa!
> Why did I come to South Africa?
> Digging in this hole is just as good as being dead
> South Africa! South Africa!
> Take me from South Africa
> I took too long to realize the hole was in my head

3
Drift

"Down," the white man ordered, pointing a pistol at Mojamaje, who
stood atop the furs on Hrikwa's wagon. He spoke in English, which
Mojamaje had never heard before. Because Mojamaje did not obey his
command, the white man pulled the trigger and Mojamaje tumbled
down, striking the earth with a thud.

A second Englishman stood pointing another pistol at Hrikwa. When
the shot rang out, Hrikwa threw down his whip and ran away. The first
Englishman tied his horse's reins to the back of the wagon, picked up
the whip, and lashed it over the oxen's ears. The wagon resumed its
lurch and rumble south to Kimberley. The second Englishman remounted his horse and rode alongside.

When the wagon had disappeared from sight, Hrikwa ran back to
Mojamaje, who lay motionless, facedown, his beautiful fur cloak still
draping his shoulders, blood staining the dust around him. Hrikwa
turned him over. Mojamaje moaned. A quick inspection revealed that
the bullet had passed clear through Mojamaje's left hand.

"English?" Mojamaje inquired weakly, pain dulling his speech. Hrikwa nodded. "Pistol?" Mojamaje asked, and again Hrikwa nodded. That morning on the road to Kimberley, Mojamaje became the first of the BaNare to hear English, see a pistol, and meet an Englishman. These two English looked like Boers, except that their cheeks and jaws were shaved clean, leaving only long black moustaches above their lips. In the brief moment he saw them, Mojamaje noticed their marvelous boots, shiny dark leather reaching to their knees. The Boers who raided Naring wore floppy, coarse hide boots reaching barely above their ankles.

"It hurts," Mojamaje said now, sitting upright, holding his bloody hand before his eyes.

Hrikwa knew the story of the Battle of the Rocks. He replied to Mojamaje, "Lucky once, dead twice. The head is the worst. Chest bad too. The neck is worse than the gut. Legs are terrible because you cannot run away."

Mojamaje asked, "Did they shoot you in all those places?"

"Most," Hrikwa replied.

Mojamaje determined not to complain again about his scratch. He turned his head to take in the countryside. A green, nearly treeless plain, flatter than the Kalahari, extended to every horizon, except to the east, where a few isolated hills stood in the distance.

"Where are we?" Mojamaje asked, feeling weaker, his head beginning to spin.

"Taung," Hrikwa replied. He swung his arm in a wide arc. "All this is Taung. The diamond town's fifty miles south." Then he looked to the sky, where tall white clouds gathered in darkening clusters. He sniffed the air. "Rain," he judged.

Mojamaje brought his good hand to his forehead, leaned back down to the ground, and passed out.

He awoke in a light shower, propped against a low thorn tree, whose tiny pointed leaves offered little cover from the rain. Hrikwa had torn away his own shirt to make a bandage for Mojamaje's hand. He crouched against the opposite side of the tree, smoking, speckles of rain wetting his leather coat.

"Let's go," the Griqua said, noticing Mojamaje's open eyes, and he trotted off. Mojamaje pulled his fur cloak tighter around his shoulders, struggled to his feet, and shuffled after Hrikwa, holding his throbbing hand steady in the air.

"Worse than Boers," Hrikwa mused when Mojamaje caught up. "English run the diamond town. Police, judge, all English. If even a Boer looks cross-eyed, they throw him in jail. I'll never get the wagon back. They would laugh me out of town if I tried. Maybe hang me."

Mojamaje stumbled along beside the trader. "So this is South Africa," he said to himself. Despite his bloody hand and the lost wagon, perhaps because of them, he felt exhilarated, wary, inspecting the horizon for the next adventure.

"Where are we going?" he asked, straining to contain his eagerness.

"Drift's," Hrikwa replied. "My nephew works there."

Mojamaje noticed the grass, green and soft on his bare feet, not brown and coarse like Naring's or Loang's. And it grew dense, one continuous mat, not scattered tufts with sand in between, as in the Kalahari. The earth smelled sweet from rain, thick red mud that clung to his toes as he trotted along.

They came to a field with turned soil distinct from the unbroken ground around it, as large as a village, the largest field Mojamaje had ever seen. Three workers moved in its center. Beyond them, off in the distance, similar teams worked in other fields. The Griqua halted at the edge to stand silently watching the work. Mojamaje drew up beside him. The team of three was a large woman, a thinner, very young woman, and a little boy. At the time, Mojamaje had no way of knowing how important all three would be in the story of the Great Thirst.

The large woman was dark, with heavy breasts and hips clearly outlined under her long yellow dress. A red scarf hid her hair, tied behind in a knot. She held the handles of an enormous blade of metal that cut through the soil, turning it over as a team of twelve oxen pulled the thing on a long metal chain. The woman danced behind, guiding the blade. The younger woman was almost as tall as the older one, but her skin was paler and her frame was slim. When the team swung close, Mojamaje saw small black freckles dotting this younger one's face and arms. She also wore a yellow dress, but her breasts and hips were invisible beneath it. As with the older woman, a red scarf hid her hair. She walked beside the oxen, cracking a cowhide whip over their ears, guiding them across the field. The boy was very young and looked like a Boer, with bright white skin and huge red freckles covering bare arms, chest, legs and face. He wore a pair of worn trousers, cut off at the knee, and around his waist hung a small bag. He walked ahead of the oxen, rhythmically reaching into the bag to scatter handfuls of seed on the bare soil ahead.

Thus did Mojamaje become the first of the BaNare to see a plow. The

Griqua explained how it worked, ripping up the soil much faster than the hoes that BaNare women used to plant their corn.

After a few moments, Hrikwa called out, "Drift, this boy's been shot!" But none of the three workers looked up. "Damn," Hrikwa muttered. Then, turning to Mojamaje, he said, "We wait. She will stop when she finishes the field. Not before." He crouched on his haunches and pulled a pouch of tobacco from his jacket. Mojamaje sat on the ground beside him. The sun broke through the clouds, warming Mojamaje's wet fur cloak, filling his nostrils with the wild smell of the animals that once wore the pelts.

"Who are they?" Mojamaje asked.

Hrikwa sat down, leaned his elbows back on the ground and told Mojamaje the story of Drift.

She was a member of Taung's oldest family, one of those who remained behind when the original BaNare stole half the Taung cattle and marched them to Naring. When the Boers arrived in Taung, they shot Drift's grandfather. Half the remaining Taung people stole half the Boer cattle and marched them to Naring. Again Drift's family stayed behind. The Boers realized that their cattle would continue to disappear unless they negotiated with the remaining people. The bargain ended up that the Boers would keep the cattle and land they had already claimed but would seize no more of either. And they would leave the Taung girls alone. In return the people of Taung would leave the Boer cattle alone.

Some wept bitterly at this accommodation, but there was no other choice in range of the Boers' deadly rifles. Then Drift scandalized her family by marrying a Boer. This was bad enough, but she chose Jagerman Roodie, the meanest, ugliest, laziest, poorest, stupidest Boer in Taung. Why? Drift was a beautiful woman, voluptuous and fierce, desired by every man who saw her. Then someone pointed out that Roodie was the only Boer who had brought a plow to Taung. Drift set immediately to plowing, using twelve of her father's oxen because Roodie owned no cattle at all. The Boer yoked the team to the plow and walked alongside with the whip while Drift held the handles, guiding the plow through the furrows. Even when other Boers began buying plows, none plowed as skillfully as Drift, in perfect lines at a fast, even pace, working fields larger than anyone had seen before.

Roodie could not keep up. His white skin flushed deep pink and his huge red freckles glowed purple as he lumbered along with the whip, stumbling and puffing and cursing the oxen. Their first child, Maka, was the pale, slim young woman whom Mojamaje saw driving the oxen in the field that day. Her skin was lighter than her mother's but darker than her father's, with freckles much smaller and darker than Roodie's. The Boer was tall and fat, Drift's breasts and hips were full and round, but Maka was as slender as Kalahari grass, stiff, strong, turning the narrowest of faces to the sun and wind. When Maka grew old enough to handle a whip, she replaced her father in the work team, guiding the oxen in perfect step. Roodie retreated to his chair, drinking brandy and sleeping until noon in the sturdy square mud house Drift had built.

The people of Taung worried for Drift, questioning her choice of Roodie, plow or no plow. Then someone suggested that she wanted a lazy Boer who would not interfere in her business. But why a Boer at all? There were other ways to acquire a plow, such as ordering one from a wagon peddler. But when Drift began to sell her corn, they understood her strategy. The English had just discovered diamonds and began building Kimberley fifty miles south of Taung. Drift needed a white face to sell her corn in town. She bought cattle with her first harvests, then sent Roodie to Kimberley to buy a wagon with thirty of the cattle. After that, Roodie drove the wagon to town to sell Drift's corn.

But Roodie was smarter than Taung suspected. The English judge in Kimberley gave Boers in the area six months to register claim to their land, so that English speculators could begin to buy it from them. Roodie drove a wagonful of corn into town and while the shopkeeper counted the sacks, he walked to the courthouse to register the fields that Drift plowed plus a thousand acres around them. In the English records, Roodie became the farm's sole owner. Then he walked to the outskirts of town to the shanty village where his Griqua mistress lived. He visited her each time he drove Drift's corn to town. Now she packed her belongings into a blanket and walked with Roodie back to the empty wagon. She rode on top, back to Taung.

Roodie announced that the Griqua woman was his new wife. He passed around a marriage certificate from the English courthouse that called his wife a Boer. Though no one knew how to read, Drift had no marriage certificate, so she was not his wife.

To Taung's surprise, Drift welcomed Roodie's deceits. She gave up the house she had built and withdrew to a corner of Roodie's farm. Here she built a small round house, more magnificent than the first, with beautiful thatch. Roodie was out of her bed and she was able to run her business without his interference. Roodie now followed the lead of neighboring Boers who invited tenants onto their land to farm it. Roodie's new tenants built houses near Drift's, forming a small village. Roodie allowed these tenants to plow as much land as they wished, charging them rent, which they paid in cash or by working in Roodie's own cornfield. All the tenants chose to work off their rent except for Drift, who paid cash. She hired some of the other tenants to work on her own fields as well.

Roodie's Griqua wife quickly bore a son as pale as any Boer. His skin was pure white with enormous red freckles like his father's. Roodie named him Roman, but everyone called him Ro. When the boy grew old enough to walk and talk, Drift befriended him, feeding him milk and meat and wild honey from towering trees that grew along the Taung River. Roodie confiscated Drift's wagon, so she saved up for another and enlisted young Ro to ride along to Kimberley when she sold her corn. A white face on a wagon protected it from attack. In town Ro bargained with the shopkeepers who bought the corn. Ro claimed that the corn was his father's, but everyone knew it was Drift's. A white face was still a white face, so Ro won a higher price.

Ro also helped Drift plow. He was the little white boy whom Mojamaje saw sowing in the field that day. Ro spent all his time with Drift because his father had collapsed into drunken sloth. Roodie was now a solid Boer citizen with a pale wife, a farm, a pale son, tenants, and a soft armchair bought in Kimberley. But more and more he sat in the chair, swigging brandy, imagining himself back in Drift's bed, rolling over on top of her, feeling below for her . . .

"Drift!" he bellowed in a drunken slur, rousing from his carnal drowse. Pulling himself to his feet, he aimed his enormous bulk out the door and across the darkened fields. "Drift!" he cried again, falling into the tenant village to pound against her door, dreaming again of her womanly charms, her lovely breasts, the round of her . . .

"Drift!" he called, throwing his shoulder against the door. Drift's house was the largest in the tiny village, with thick mud walls and a heavy door she had bought in town. It was the only door in Taung with a key, in a solid wood frame that shook not at all when Roodie hurled himself against it. He stumbled back home, blubbering into the dark.

Night after night the Boer made a fool of himself, beating in vain against Drift's door. He embarrassed his son, who preferred the company of Drift and Maka. Like everyone else in Taung, Ro waited for the day when Drift would take her revenge. His Griqua mother moved silently through the house, seeming to wait too. Drift ruled the fields, the Griqua woman ruled the house, and Roodie ruled nothing, not even his own soggy urges.

The expectation of Drift's retaliation doubled with the arrival of Vlei. He was a Griqua, a nephew of Hrikwa the BaNare trader. Roodie hired Vlei as foreman to oversee the tenants who paid their rent by working Roodie's fields. No one knew whether Vlei was completely human. He walked like a hyena, hunched, snarling and snapping his jaws. There were scars all over his body, his chest was one enormous muscle, his forehead sloped forward, his teeth and ears were long and pointed, his hands were as large as his face.

The worst part of Vlei was his knife. He had killed a Zulu warrior with his own Zulu stabbing spear, then cut off the shaft, and now carried the blade in his belt like a knife. As long as a man's forearm, as wide as a man's palm—it was a terrifying weapon, in terrible hands. Vlei's knife was famous far beyond Taung, so when he arrived on Roodie's farm everyone wondered who would be first to feel it cut.

Vlei and Drift immediately joined forces, or so everyone guessed. He ran Roodie's fields so efficiently that Roodie was even more unnecessary than before: surely Vlei and Drift would kill the Boer and take over the farm. They spoke together often, in private, hushed voices, and some said that Vlei visited her at night. But Vlei burned other women in the tenant village and no one ever saw him enter or leave Drift's house. Still the rumors persisted, because they made so much sense.

Drift's harvests grew larger every year. She hired more helpers. As more people bought plows, young men came to work first for Drift to learn how to use them. She paid very low wages and worked everyone to death, but every worker left her fields an excellent plowman, ready to go into business for himself.

Watching Drift made it worthwhile, too. She worked herself into a heavy sweat every day until her yellow dress clung close to her skin, showing every curve of her body. She gleamed in the sunlight, filling her apprentices with lustful fantasy. Every young man who came to learn plowing hoped to learn a few other tricks from Drift as well. None succeeded. When she caught one staring at her, desire glazing his eyes, she tossed back her head and laughed him to shame.

Hrikwa concluded the story with a spray of tobacco juice against his boot. He rubbed the juice into the leather with the palm of his hand.

As Hrikwa spoke, Mojamaje watched Drift work, moving along the furrow, heaving her weight against the handles to keep the plow moving at a smooth, constant pace. Then the oxen stopped. The field was finished. Drift turned the plow on its side, wiped one hand across her brow, and walked toward Hrikwa and Mojamaje. Moisture glistened dark on her long, full arms, her breasts heaved as she caught her breath, her hips swayed, her eyes danced with the sensual thrill of exhaustion, the pleasure of work. Hrikwa stood up to meet her and Mojamaje did the same. Before she reached the edge of the field, Mojamaje decided not to dig in the English hole. He would work for Drift.

4
Dagger and Cloak

Drift stood before Hrikwa and Mojamaje, catching her breath, hands on her hips, one foot impatiently tapping the ground.

Hrikwa said something in Boer, so did Drift in reply, then Hrikwa switched from Boer to say to Mojamaje, "Show Drift your hand." Mojamaje held up his bandaged hand.

"Looks all right to me," Drift said, also switching from Boer. "He can walk."

"The hole will not hire him with a hole in his hand," Hrikwa argued. "Take him until his hand heals."

"Then he disappears to work in the hole," Drift replied, "and never pays me back."

At this point Mojamaje blurted out, "But I want to stay!"

Drift regarded him for the first time full in the face, an eager young man in a loincloth, bare feet, a fur cloak, staring at her like all the young men who came her way. Drift rolled back her head and laughed Mojamaje to shame. She walked off, chuckling to herself, across the field.

Hrikwa laughed too and clapped Mojamaje on the back. "Good luck, boy," he said, turning back toward the road.

Mojamaje stood confused, watching Drift disappear in one direction and Hrikwa disappear in the other. Almost out of sight, Drift turned around and whistled. "Bushman!" she called, waving one hand in the air.

He ran after her, the throbbing in his hand submerged in the pounding of his heart.

That was how Mojamaje came to work on Roodie's farm. The BaNare did not know much about his life there: most of their reports came from young men on their way to and from the Kimberley hole. They would stop at the farm's tenant village to greet Mojamaje and tell the tenants stories of Mojamaje's exploits.

"As an infant, Mojamaje walked through fire."

"At the age of two, he slew a thousand Boers at the bottom of a canyon by rolling rocks down on top of them."

"His grandfather burned his Bushman mother, then Mojamaje killed a thousand of his grandfather's cattle."

"Once he tore out a Bushman's heart."

"See his beautiful cloak? He caught the jackals with his bare hands, skinned them with his teeth, sewed them together with spider webs, a delicate job, one slip and the whole thing falls apart."

Perhaps these stories convinced Drift that Mojamaje was no ordinary young fellow, for she rapidly awarded him a privileged position. He slept in a grain storehouse behind her own house and shared the meals that her daughter Maka cooked. Drift gave him an old pair of trousers, a frayed shirt of gray cotton, but no shoes and no money. Even before his hand healed, she sent him out to herd the cattle that she bought with the money she earned from selling her corn. Drift was very careful with her cattle and out on the range they were easily stolen, so she trusted very few of her workers to herd them. The other tenants noted well how quickly she promoted Mojamaje to this honor. As at Loang, he proved himself an excellent herder. He soon learned how to yoke and unyoke oxen and thus became the first BaNare to learn to plow. Everyone spoke Boer on the farm, so Mojamaje also became the first BaNare to learn to speak Boer.

Mojamaje worked hard, learning quickly, and had trouble keeping his eyes off Drift. Citing his present privileges, the other tenants encouraged him to press for still more favors.

"She wants you," they insisted.

"She wants you to come at night."

"By moonlight."

Mojamaje nursed his doubts, enough to prevent him from taking chances, especially with Vlei. The fearsome Griqua sometimes also shared the meals that Maka cooked. He squatted by the fire, shoving pawful after pawful of dry porridge through his cavernous jaws, tearing apart chunks of meat, growling like a dog, saliva frothing over his stubbly chin. His terrible Zulu knife hung on his belt like a warning. Vlei's intimacy with Drift was still confirmed only in rumor, but his knife kept all other suitors at bay.

After crop weeding, Drift bought two black horses. Vlei taught Maka to ride, then he taught Mojamaje, who became the first BaNare to ride a horse. Drift sent Maka and Mojamaje riding the pastures together to herd her cattle. The people of Taung decided that Drift had finally gone too far. She had raised Maka to be like herself, almost a man, and now she had put her on a horse. Soon she would buy Maka a rifle and send her out raiding villages. No, they concurred, Drift was ruining her, turning her into an oddity that no man would think to marry.

Maka raced through the meadows, learning to run circles around stray cattle, confounding them, easing them back toward the herd. Mojamaje rode as close to her as he could, studying her face while she looked out over the rippling fields of golden grass. Her face was lovely, smooth, pale, and long, with a maze of tiny black freckles, thick eyelashes, and a wide mouth. She braided the kinks of her black hair into intricate crosses and swirls, tight against her head, covered with a red scarf that the wind sometimes blew off. Sometimes Mojamaje pulled his horse to a halt and watched, transfixed, this young woman on a horse on the rolling South African plain. Sometimes in silence he stared at her face, silhouetted against an endless expanse of blue. His eye moved from her nose, small and flat, to her ears, swept back like a fox's, then from tiny freckle to tiny freckle on her cheek. Her frame was slender, true, but sinuous, firm, her muscles taut from work. When the wind blew her dress against her breasts, showing their smooth outline, Mojamaje's eye lingered there too. Once Maka turned suddenly and caught Mojamaje staring, his mouth hanging open. She rolled back her head and laughed.

Mojamaje was of two minds, and the other parts of his body responded accordingly. Drift's magnificent womanly figure still dominated his dreams, as nightly he lay separated from her by only the mud wall of his storehouse, then the wall of her own house, nothing more, so close. And the tenants chuckled and goaded him on. But Drift was the stuff of fantasy: Maka was sixteen, old enough to marry and bear children, and in Naring she would have married someone Mojamaje's age, nearly ten years her senior. Some young men herding at Loang had trouble finding a Naring wife until they were nearly thirty. Mojamaje was ready. At night he now imagined Maka's naked body lying a few yards away, but as he drifted off to sleep the image grew in the hips and chest to take her mother's shape.

The rains ended but the wind stayed warm, drying the corn quickly but threatening to bring more rain. A cool wind was better. Sure enough, a night shower fell, then two more in the space of a month. The corn-stalks turned brown and ants began to climb them. When Drift judged the corn finally dry, she hired extra hands and ordered work night and day, to bring in the crop before the ants ate it all. Women cooked meals right alongside the fields, and everyone returned to the tenant village only to sleep.

Roodie's nearby fields, of course, suffered the same threat from ants. But Drift had hired all the casual labor in the neighborhood, moving the Boer to make a rare appearance at the fields to beg her to release some help.

"Drift!" he bellowed across the plain. The first sound in response was Drift and Maka's laughter from somewhere in the tall corn, ridicule mixed with honest joy, and then a wind rustled the dry stalks and drowned out the Boer's shouts. Roodie's drunken assaults on Drift's door had trailed off so much during that season that Mojamaje had heard only four. As he paused from his work to watch the Boer now, Mojamaje almost felt sympathy, for he knew well the laughter of Maka and Drift. Sometimes he looked up to see mother and daughter conspiring in low voices, laughing and gesturing toward him, throwing their heads back together and showing their teeth. Alone against the world, they needed no one but themselves, and Mojamaje wanted them both, or wanted to be one of them, or wanted something from them that they offered only each other.

Roodie wandered away, night fell, the work went on. From somewhere in the field, Mojamaje heard a cry of pain, Maka's voice. As he rushed through the stalks he heard other voices, then female hands pushed him away. The women formed a circle around Maka. Mojamaje could not see her for this barrier and the dim moonlight. Someone took his arm, a man's hand. A man's voice told him that Maka was bleeding in her monthly way, as all women do, because of the moon. Mojamaje went back to work and later saw Maka's form moving slowly through the night shadows, back to the village. Drift would not spare another woman to go with Maka, so she made her way home to rest alone. It was all harmless enough, yet Mojamaje wanted to go with her. But a man was not allowed near a woman during her monthly bleeding.

Mojamaje worked until dawn, then Drift went home to check on Maka. She returned soon thereafter to shout that work was over for the day. She was in a foul mood, her eyes bleary with overwork and some other, new anger, or perhaps she only feared that the ants would win. As Mojamaje had worked, breaking off ear after ear of corn, the ants had crawled up his legs and leapt from the stalks onto his shoulders, biting him everywhere. The harvesters were all exhausted. Mojamaje collapsed on his blankets and slept until dusk.

Maka stayed in Drift's house a full week. She emerged as furious as Drift, who continued to snarl at her workers and even smacked one on the jaw for sleeping on the job. But when Maka came back to work, Drift slowly regained her humor and then Maka did too. A week later the harvest was done. Drift now awarded Mojamaje another privilege: he would take her place on the trip to Kimberley to sell the corn. The other tenants advised him as he left, "Drift wants you, boy."

Mojamaje shrugged off these blandishments and shook his head. But a grain of hope lingered. A look in his eye confirmed it.

Out on the road to Kimberley, Mojamaje walked beside Drift's wagon, loaded with sewn goatskins stuffed stiff with grain, even into the arms and legs, headless goatfuls of corn. Maka walked alongside Mojamaje or sometimes climbed up to sit on the mountain of skin sacks. It was too dangerous for her to ride her horse to town—an Englishman would certainly steal it. Ro Roodie skipped along behind the wagon, then far ahead, hunting crows and lizards with a slingshot, in ragged shorts, torn shirt, and bare feet. His curly red hair tossed as he ran. The boy was devoted to Drift. When he sold her corn in Kimberley, he spoke to the shopkeeper as if to a servant, haughty, defiant, while Drift stood in silence at the door. Ro bargained hard for a good price: the merchant mocked him but eventually gave in, partly out of amusement at the little boy's vehemence, partly because Drift was his largest supplier of good-quality corn. And a white face was a white face, regardless of what lay behind it.

Ro was also devoted to Maka, his half sister, daughter of his father. Their freckles marked them as kin. When Mojamaje sat in Drift's compound, watching Maka bend to spoon porridge into his bowl, he moved his eye from mark to mark, her freckles like dust sprinkled with fine rain, each one hiding a secret. Curious, Mojamaje tried to read Maka's face like the night sky, each dark mark challenging him to discover her secrets. Time and again she turned her head to catch him staring, and each time she smiled, winked in mock seduction, and laughed at him.

"Bushman!" Maka called from atop the wagon, her slender legs rigid against its roll and pitch, standing tall above the sacks of grain. She pointed one arm toward the track far ahead, where Ro disappeared over a rise in pursuit of a hare. "See that rise?" she continued. "See how the earth right here is red and the grasses that grow here are yellow, and the sun is behind us so the sky ahead is darker than behind? It is a beautiful place, and watch when we reach the rise. Everything will change. The sun will be lower, the sky will be darker, it all changes over the rise."

Mojamaje whistled and twirled the whip, cracking it a hairsbreadth above the oxen's ears, as Maka had taught him to do. "I see," he replied, pleased at her attention. The afternoon was cool, the first breeze of winter crouched in the shallow valleys that the wagon crossed, jerking over one stream bank, across the dry sandy bed, struggling up the opposite bank, the wagon's wooden joints moaning with work. A few scattered trees stood off to the east. Flat-topped hills rose in the distant west, the cloudless blue of the sky ending where the yellow grass met the horizon. White-necked crows and black sparrows dipped and spun close to the ground.

They reached the rise and Maka called out, "Stop here!" Mojamaje snapped the whip, the oxen fell motionless. "Climb up," she commanded. He did. She looked out ahead, and Mojamaje followed her gaze with his own. He stared at the plain below.

It was more than a rise on this side, a cliff, and the line of the track wound back and forth to descend gradually to the treeless plain below, endlessly flat, fading to the distant horizon. "See," Maka explained, "the grass here is white in winter." Mojamaje looked down at the ground ahead. The grass was topped with strands of white floss, knee-high and feathery, letting the earth show beneath. "See how the soil is black and dark blue, how dust from the plain makes the late sky look red." Mojamaje watched the plain of grass tossing in the wind, the low sun caught first at one angle then another. Mojamaje and Maka stood silently on the wagon and the sun fell lower, finally turning the world below into a shimmering blanket of silver, rippling like the fur of an animal.

"It looks like my cape," Mojamaje said. "Silver-backed jackals."

Suddenly one of the oxen tugged at its yoke and the wagon jerked forward, sending Mojamaje and Maka tumbling down onto the sacks of grain. He fell forward but pulled his hands away, trying not to touch her as he fell, but this effort only left his body free to land against her, his hands held away and unoffending, his chest, thighs and face pressed close to hers. He began to laugh at his herdboy shyness. But then eye to her eye, he saw in it anger and fear. Mojamaje moved away and jumped down onto the ground. He grabbed the whip and lashed the oxen forward without looking up at Maka. Their descent to the plain passed in silence. Ro waited at the base of the escarpment with a campsite picked out, a cookfire blazing, and two fat rock hares sizzling on spits.

A shallow stream flowed under the cliff, and Maka collected water to cook porridge and tea. Mojamaje guided the wagon under a copse of willows along the stream bank, the last trees until Kimberley. He unyoked the oxen and they drank from the stream and then sat down under the trees to sleep. Maka and Mojamaje ate in silence, staring into the fire, as night descended and the air grew cold. Ro whistled, then sang a song about brandy, candy, lasses and lace. He fell asleep, exhausted from chasing animals all day. Mojamaje carried him to his blanket under the wagon. Maka lay down too, beside the boy. Mojamaje returned to the fire to drink tea. He sat with his hands wrapped around his warm cup, watching the firelight play across Maka's face, her closed eyes. Brightly lit, her skin appeared dark; in shadow, light. He remembered the warm glow of her skin as he fell against her, the closest he had ever come, a ripe essence of earth and sweat. But why the fear in her eye? She had been so fearless, so luminous until the end of harvest, the night he heard her cry out in the field. Since then she had not been the same.

"Something happened," Mojamaje whispered aloud, tossing more wood on the fire. "That night Roodie came to the fields. The night Maka bled. Something no one else knows."

On the afternoon of the following day, the wagon rolled into Kimberley. A dozen wide, treeless streets lay at perfect right angles to another dozen, lined with one-story square buildings, plastered white. Ruts dug in the summer mud had dried in the autumn air, pitching the wagon from side to side as it crept slowly through the town. Men and women, Boers, English, Griqua and everyone else, even some Zulu, hurried along the edge of the street, almost all dressed in clothes, a few men clad only in loincloths mixing in the crowds. Wagons and horses crossed at every corner, Mojamaje felt joyfully inconspicuous: he fit right in with his trousers, shirt and wide-brimmed hat. His feet were still bare, but he noticed happily that half of Kimberley was shoeless as well.

They drove to the shop, where Ro launched into negotiations and Maka stood at the door as Drift always did. Mojamaje wandered off through the town, into the shops where bolts of cloth and all the goods that Hrikwa brought to Naring lay stacked on tables and shelves in fantastic abundance. Away from the center of town, the shops merged with houses, all painted white, yellow or gray, with glass in all their windows. At the edge of town, the straight streets ended in a maze of paths and twisting roads. This was the township. English and Boers lived in the substantial houses on the wide, straight streets, while everyone else lived in the township. Mojamaje walked on. The odor of fried meat, smoke, beer, the sound of wagons creaking, sheep bleating, children shouting, pots clanking, a harmony of loud chatter, drew snug around him like a blanket, warming, inviting, looking like home. The houses pressed together: some were identical to those in downtown Kimberley, some were mud rectangles with thatched roofs, like Boer houses, some were mud circles, some were only straw and sticks. Women in long dresses and head scarves of every color called out to him in a dozen languages, offering food and drink and perhaps their charms for sale. It seemed as if all South Africa had come to Kimberley.

Mojamaje walked on and the township dwindled to bare ground. Across an open field stood a wire fence. Mojamaje drew his breath. Beyond the fence lay the hole, a mile across, like enormous jaws. An endless web of ropes hung across it, men clambering like ants across the lips, down the throat. Mojamaje ran to the fence. A cloud of black dust floated above the hole like breath on a winter morning. The noise was terrible from a thousand picks, axes, pulleys and ore crushers, the beginning of a cough that would end in the miners blown high in the air. Or perhaps the hole was clearing its throat, preparing to swallow them.

The heavy wire-net fence encircled the hole completely. To one side of the opening stood long rows of miners' barracks. Mojamaje peered carefully at the workings: tiny boxes on rails pulled blue earth to the surface, men also carried sacks on their backs. Others attacked the sides of the hole with picks. Mojamaje took one last look and turned back to town, satisfied that he had made the right choice. On the farm he had learned to ride, plow, yoke and drive oxen, speak Boer. In the hole he would have learned how to carry blue dirt and swing a pick.

Mojamaje returned to the shop as the storehands removed the last of the sacks from the wagon. Ro stepped out of the shop with a handful of bills, which Maka seized, counted, and rolled up in a handkerchief. She reached one hand down the collar of her dress and passed the cloth through the sleeve to tie it onto her back.

Four more times Mojamaje drove Maka and Ro to Kimberley before all Drift's grain was sold. The trip each way took two days, so a total of three weeks of walking made Mojamaje's legs taut and the heavy whip left his arms tense. Exhilarated, exhausted, the onset of winter tingling his lungs with cool air, the cloudless sky burning his face with sun, Mojamaje hummed with energy, even passion, as the wagon rolled back toward Drift's compound after the last trip.

As he unyoked the oxen, as he rushed to his bed, throwing off his clothes to lie naked and warm beneath his magnificent cloak as he closed his eyes, Mojamaje knew he was ready. He had waited too long already. The tenant village swarmed with romance, dance and songs, drunken brawls in defense of honor and love, more than one girl had caught Mojamaje's arm as the workday ended and pressed his hand against her breast, purring, "Take me, Bushman." But Mojamaje waited for Drift, or maybe for Maka. No, Drift was only fantasy. Then why not Maka? On each trip to and from Kimberley they stopped at the same spot on the rise to look over the silver plain, alone on top of the wagon, and each time the moment was right for an embrace, then her eyes warned him away, her body tensed, and he jumped down to lash the oxen on.

"But why not tonight?" Mojamaje asked himself, stroking the soft fur of his cloak as the air chilled, forcing him to bury his head deeper in its dark folds. But by now his body had sunk to inertia, his sore muscles melting, his eyes rolling back in their lids.

"Mojamaje, get up."

A hand moved along the cloak, found the edge and pulled it back to expose Mojamaje's sleepy body. It was too dark to see, but the voice he knew as Maka's. He sat up. "Have you come to me at last?" he said.

"My mother wants you," Maka replied, feeling for his hand along his bare skin. She found it, grabbed it, yanked him to his feet and headed for the door. Mojamaje reached his free hand back to clutch his cloak and draw it around his shoulders.

"So it will be Drift," he said to himself. Outside, a bright full moon gave shape to Maka draped in a gray blanket. Wordless, she led Mojamaje into her mother's house, bolting the door behind. The house was completely dark. Maka dropped his hand and Mojamaje waited, naked but for his fur cloak. Something was wrong. Why was Maka present? Was Drift even there? So maybe it really was Maka who wanted him. He listened for Drift's breathing, but he heard instead the barking of dogs in the village outside.

Suddenly the door shook in its frame. "Drift," boomed a deep voice, which Mojamaje recognized as Vlei's. "Locked?" the voice roared and Vlei growled like a lion, pounding the door with his fists.

"My new man is here," Drift's voice called from the darkness beside Mojamaje. "Go away, pig."

Vlei roared again. The door moaned on its hinges. Then it cracked.

"My door!" Drift cried. She grabbed Mojamaje's arm in the dark and said to him, "I paid five pounds for that door. Make him stop." Then she called out to Vlei, "Stop, animal, he will come out." She pushed Mojamaje toward the door. Maka's invisible hand released the bolt and opened the door. Mojamaje stepped out into the moonlight, face-to-face with the murderous Vlei. Then he remembered the knife.

When the BaNare tell the story of Vlei's knife, they recount in great detail how Vlei killed the knife's original Zulu owner, how both Vlei's hands bled from deep wounds in the fight, leaving only Vlei's mouth to drive the knife through the Zulu's heart. Vlei bit off the shaft as he did this, leaving only a short stub below the blade, which he carried thereafter as a knife. This monster now stood before Mojamaje, itching to carve him to pieces.

"Vlei!" Mojamaje called out. "I want your knife. I will give you my cape for it."

Vlei's hideous grunting fell back to hard breathing, which Mojamaje took as a sign of hope. He smelled beer on Vlei's breath. Then a slim shadow darted toward him. The knife! But it stopped short of his ribs and Mojamaje reached out to grab it. With his other hand he swept off his cloak and held it out to Vlei, who seized it from Mojamaje's hand and tossed it across his own massive shoulders.

Mojamaje stepped back inside Drift's house. He was completely naked now, with Vlei's huge dagger clutched firmly in his trembling hand. He took a deep breath, proud of his quick thinking, and then suddenly the knife disappeared from his grip. Maka's hand took its place. She pulled him back outside, back to the storehouse, and left him there. She returned to her mother's house and bolted the door behind.

Mojamaje threw on his trousers and shirt, wrapped himself in a thin wool blanket and lay down to think. He huddled for hours in the cold night air, listening to Vlei and his friends drinking and singing in a nearby compound. Vlei told the story again and again, and each time his

companions laughed harder when he described Mojamaje standing naked in the moonlight. Mojamaje could not help laughing too. Toward
dawn the revel died, as Mojamaje struggled to piece together the puzzle
of why Drift had called Vlei and himself to her house at the same time,
and why she took the knife.

Just before dawn a single gunshot tore through the silent dark, rousing
the tenants from sleep.

"They killed the Boer!"

The tenant village came alive as everyone ran outside to cry out the
news. Some ran to Jagerman Roodie's house to investigate, while others
packed their belongings onto carts or wrapped them in blankets and tied
them to their backs.

"The Boers will kill us all!"

"Run for your lives!"

Mojamaje stood before Drift's compound, the thin blanket around his
shoulders. He looked to the east, where the first blue glimmer of morning light spread across the horizon. The crowded village swirled with
commotion and from its midst Maka rode toward him on one of Drift's
black horses. Without a word she reached down her arm, onto which
Mojamaje clamped his own to swing up behind her onto the horse's
back. She dug her heels into the horse's flank, turning east toward the
dawn.

5

What Mojamaje Felt Along Maka's Spine

They rode until the sun climbed high before them, then looked for a
place to hide. Clusters of hills appeared in a line stretching the length of
the horizon. Maka headed for the tallest clump, a mound of huge gray
boulders strewn at odd angles with caves and passes between them. They
dismounted and climbed, pulling the horse behind, to discover a deep
cleft in the hill's center, reaching down almost to the level of the surrounding plain. They descended. A shallow pool of water lay in the
bottom of the cleft. The horse drank noisily and Mojamaje and Maka

pressed their faces down beside it. Maka tied the horse's reins to a thorn bush poking through the rocks. It began immediately to doze on its feet.

The sun's rays bounced off the cleft's slanted walls and warmed the air to summer heat. Thick brown flies buzzed lazily around Mojamaje's eyes as he watched Maka climb back up to the lip of the cleft to peer out over the plain they had just traversed. Motionless, silent, she fixed her eyes on the western horizon, but no one rode after them. Mojamaje waved away the flies and sat down to think. The still air smelled fragrant and he looked up to see a jwana bush hidden in a crevice. Its fragile violet flowers dangled like cowbells above his head.

They had spoken not a word on the ride from the farm. With his arms locked around Maka's slim waist, his chest pressed against her spine, which felt like cold steel in the early morning chill, Mojamaje ran over the details of the puzzle in his mind, satisfied that he knew the important parts if not every twist. The gunshot, for instance, surprised him. He would have expected a clean cut with Vlei's knife.

Mojamaje rose and climbed slowly to Maka, to sit beside her astride the rock lip. Her eyes remained set on the empty steppe.

"She killed him," Mojamaje asserted.

"Yes," Maka replied.

"Why the gun?"

Maka turned to face him, eyes violent.

"I followed her," Maka began. "She thought I slept. She slipped out the door. I ran behind, keeping to the shadows, until reaching the fields. The moon was bright. I saw the knife in her hand. Every few steps she stopped to look behind, like a wildcat prowling, so I circled around the field through the brush alongside, where she could not see me. She disappeared inside the house. I ran to follow. Before I reached it I heard the shot. That Griqua bitch came out with a pistol in her hand. I ran past her on the step. She looked at my face, clear in the moon, laughing like a devil. I ran inside, but the house was dark. Some moonlight came through a window. My eyes waited to get used to the dark. My father lay with Vlei's knife in his heart. My mother lay with a bullet in her head. I ran after the Griqua bitch to slice her to bits but she was gone."

Maka brushed a fly from her ear. Mojamaje watched her closely, observing how her ears swept to points, the tiny black freckles scattered back from her cheeks, veiling her face in black mist, behind which her eyes rose to his directly for the first time.

"Your cloak was lovely," Maka said, facing out to the plain again.

"They say you caught the jackals with your bare hands. You skinned them with your teeth. You sewed them with spider webs."

"They are misguided," Mojamaje replied. "See these eyes?" And he pointed to his face with one finger. "They are Bushman eyes. We Bushmen speak to animals. I asked the jackals to catch themselves. I asked a crane to skin them with its sharp beak. I asked the spiders to sew the skins."

A grim smile formed on Maka's lips, then she turned to face Mojamaje again. "Take the horse," she insisted. "I am sorry my mother did this to you."

Mojamaje reached out one arm, but she brushed it away.

"Did he burn you?" Mojamaje asked.

Maka placed her lips against the rock again, shutting her eyes. "Yes," she replied.

"I remember the night," Mojamaje said.

Maka sighed and shrugged her shoulders. After a long pause she said, "The village was empty. I did not think to lock the door." She commanded again, "Go, take the horse."

They sat all day on the top of the boulders, dozing and waking, lost in silence. When the sun finally set, Mojamaje stood up. "It is safe to ride," he said. He climbed down to the horse, drank again from the pool, and worked his way up and over the boulders, down to the plain. Maka followed in silence. They remounted, Maka again in front, and rode away.

When the BaNare tell the story of the Great Thirst, they debate at length the importance of Mojamaje and Maka's conversation on the rocks. Some say they fell in love there, entrusting their hearts, their fates, to each other. Others point to Maka's rigid limbs, her resistance, her command that Mojamaje ride away alone to gainsay this early assertion of love.

When women tell the story, they argue not only that love bloomed on the bare, lonely crag, but also that the story of the Great Thirst gained its second hero there. From this point on, they say, Mojamaje and Maka are equals. Their souls forge to one. They live one life, together. Other characters continue to be crucial, such as Ma-Mojamaje, but Maka and Mojamaje march in such close step thereafter that it becomes senseless to speak of one without mentioning the other. What Mojamaje touched, Maka felt; what Maka's eyes discovered, Mojamaje saw.

Women tellers also take special care to explain Drift's motives. After

Jagerman Roodie begged in vain for Drift to free some hands to work his fields during the ant invasion, he went home to drink himself numb. Deep in the night he awoke and stumbled down to the tenant village to throw himself against Drift's door again. He lurched against it, and it swung open, for Maka had neglected to turn the bolt. She lay on her blankets, asleep. "Drift!" Roodie cried in drunken joy, stumbling, thrashing in the shadows, falling to his knees. He found her just as she came to her senses, too late. Even in his stupor he must have known she was not Drift. Maka's slim body was nothing like the mounds of soft flesh that Roodie remembered from the nights when Drift was his wife. Maka cried out once and he clapped a hand on her mouth, almost suffocating her, his weight crushing her lungs. Crippled with pain, Maka stared with numb eyes into the dark above, smelling the stink of brandy, foul breath, listening to his deep grunts, the sound of her own flesh ripped apart by her father.

He staggered out and Maka lay bleeding. Toward dawn Drift came to look in on her and found the door open.

From that moment on, Jagerman Roodie was a dead man. It was only a matter of when and how. Since he had abandoned Drift years before, everyone expected she would kill him: if Roodie were murdered, Drift would be the first and last suspect. Neighboring Boers would hunt her down. She feared not for herself but for Maka's life afterward. For the first time, Drift wondered whether she had made a mistake in the way she had brought the girl up. She raised her to be another Drift when across South Africa the era of Drifts rushed to a close. Eventually the Boers and English would drive her out, to take her precious fields for themselves. Drift might last another ten years, but Maka had no future at all.

So what would become of Maka? Mojamaje's appearance answered this question to Drift's satisfaction. For all Maka's independence of spirit, Drift knew she would be better off other than alone. Maka imputed heroism to her mother's manlessness, while her mother would have loved to live life with a man by her side, before her fire, between her legs. A good one just never came along. Drift's plans for Mojamaje at first assumed no definite form. She merely took every opportunity to throw him and Maka together. She would never have hired a man unable to hold a plow, but she snapped Mojamaje up in spite of his wound, taking a chance on this earnest young man.

Then Roodie's heinous crime changed everything. Drift sent Mojam-

aje and Maka off to Kimberley and planned her revenge. She stared at
Vlei's fearsome knife dangling from his belt and decided that it belonged
in Roodie's heart. She would give Mojamaje his chance to prove himself
worthy of Maka, first by taking the knife from Vlei, and then by plung-
ing it into Roodie's chest. That night she waited until Vlei was drunk,
and thus less dangerous, and called him and Mojamaje to her door.
Mojamaje passed the first test: he came back with the knife in his hand.
But Drift then suffered a panic of second thoughts. She suddenly sensed,
like a cold wind down her neck, some unknown peril lurking in the
Roodie house. Whatever it was she could not send Mojamaje to face it.
She would go herself.

The nameless danger was Roodie's new Griqua wife. From her first
day in Taung, she had known that someday Drift would take her vengeance. She knew nothing of Maka's defilement: Drift had reason
enough to strike without it. Her pale Griqua face, her squinty eyes,
retreated to quiet vigilance. She kept a loaded pistol under her mattress,
waiting for Drift to make her move. The moment Drift drove the knife
through Roodie's foul heart, the Griqua wife shot Drift through the
head. Thus the only two rival claimants to the farm died within moments of each other. Jagerman Roodie was worthless. The Griqua
woman wanted the place to herself.

One question remained: Why did Maka ride up to Mojamaje with
only one horse? When they stopped to hide in the clump of rocks and
she urged him to ride away without her, was she already sure that he
would not? Drift's two horses were always corralled together, so she
could just as easily have taken them both.

As they rode away from the rocks Maka said to herself again and
again, aloud, "Drift needed no one," the words lost in the wind. Then
louder she said, "I need no one," and this Mojamaje heard. He felt again
the coldness of her spine, the stiffness of her body as he held his arms
around her.

6
The Potato Test

There was only one place to ride: east to the Taung mission. This was the home of the first Englishman to settle in Taung. His name was Bogg, and he had arrived on a horse more than thirty years before, even before diamonds, a skinny young man with curly black whiskers and a watch in his waistcoat.

"I will protect you," he announced in Boer. "Fear Boers no more."

Everyone laughed. They called him "Namane Setlhobolo," meaning "That Skinny Boy with No Gun."

"I need no gun," Bogg insisted. "I bear something more powerful."

"Cannon?" the people of Taung asked.

"The love of Christ," Bogg replied.

"Who is that?" they asked.

The missionary explained, but no one believed him. After hours of his lecturing, they decided he was a lunatic. They stopped laughing, fearful that whatever wild spirit infected his brain might burst out to enter them if they treated him roughly. Bogg begged for land, but Drift's grandfather refused, offering instead indefinite hospitality in his family compound, hoping the Englishman would tire of waiting and go away.

Then a dozen Boers rode up and shot Drift's grandfather. Bogg rushed out to confront the raiders, who turned and rode off as soon as they saw him.

"How did you do that?" the people of Taung asked.

"The love of Christ," Bogg replied.

The Taung people discussed the matter, concluding that fear of the English army, not the love of Christ, had driven the Boers away. So the people of Taung decided to give Bogg his land. They chose an enormous tract by the Taung River surrounded on four sides by Boer farms.

Bogg built a square brick house and a square brick church and offered garden plots to anyone who joined his mission. He dug a slim canal from the river to irrigate the gardens. But no one wanted to hoe vegetables in a garden, a useless skill, backbreaking work for a handful of cabbages.

A few old Griqua, too old to marry Boers or anyone else, accepted Bogg's offer. He insisted on Christian marriage for every mission member, accepting converts only in pairs, performing the wedding the moment they arrived, uniting bald, toothless Griqua men with stooped, sagging, spent Griqua women. But even some Griqua he turned away. "Only the oppressed," he declared.

Each time new candidates arrived, he held a potato against their skins. Anyone lighter than the potato, Bogg judged able to pass for Boer. He accepted the darker ones into the mission.

Each old Griqua couple received a garden plot, goats, and space to build a house. Bogg had firm rules about construction. "A brick's not a brick without straw," he chanted. "Without corners a house is a hut." The Griqua left out the straw whenever he was not looking, because the mission goats ate all the nearby grass and the only decent straw was miles away. And round walls made more sense than straight ones: corners wasted bricks and space. When Bogg came to check, he knocked down the walls, crying, "This is a mud hut! Christians live in brick houses!"

Neither did the Griqua learn the prayers or hymns. Bogg translated them into Boer but the Griqua barely mumbled. "Lord, send me black ones," the missionary prayed, speaking in English, eyes lifted to the thatch roof of his church, his Griqua converts listless and quiet on wooden benches, dozing in the summer heat.

Years passed, Bogg grew fat, and the people of Taung forgot about the mission. Then Drift made a gaping hole in Roodie's chest that only could have been made with the famous dagger last reported in Mojamaje's hand; then Drift's daughter and Mojamaje rode away on a horse. Everyone knew they would head for the mission. By the end of the day, word reached Bogg, who waited, fidgeting, for their arrival. "Thank you, Lord," he prayed aloud, raising his hands to the sky. He knew that Drift was a member of one of Taung's leading families, the granddaughter of the old man the Boers shot before Bogg's own eyes. Perhaps she had been one of the children scampering through the compound under his feet. Bogg was overjoyed at the prospect of her daughter becoming his first authentic Taung convert. True, Maka's father was a Boer, so her skin was somewhat light, but he had no doubts she would pass the potato test. As for Mojamaje, he was not a Taung citizen but his skin was completely black.

The moon rose above the horizon just as Mojamaje and Maka rode through the mission gates. Two rows of brick houses, four houses to a row, stood back a hundred yards from the river. They rode to the largest house and dismounted. Bogg rushed out to greet them, a Bible in one hand, a potato in the other.

Mojamaje had never seen a potato before, but he knew all about the mission and Bogg's rules. The Englishman would force him to marry Maka, here and now, that very night.

"Welcome, my children," Bogg called. "Enter my humble house." Slipping behind them, he pushed each with one hand, gently, toward his open door. The horse wandered off toward the river to drink.

"This is delightful," Bogg cooed, seating them in straight-backed chairs. The house was two rooms, separated by a heavy door, closed now, with two small glass windows curtained with blue lace. The walls were plastered white. A bookshelf climbed one wall, the other walls were bare, and a long oak desk stretched half across the room. Bogg sat behind the desk, facing Mojamaje and Maka on the other side. A single oil lamp, a stout metal base and a tall, dense glass, stood amid papers and books on the desk. Its yellow light fell short of the ceiling and corners while the desk cast a vast shadow on the floor. Bogg's face looked old and worn, his eyes deep in dark sockets.

"Shall we begin?" Bogg said cheerily. He held up the potato, expecting the dim light to make Maka appear darker than normal. But the mysterious shimmer of her powdery freckles made her skin look light in the dark, almost yellow like a Bushman's, as yellow as her faded dress. Perplexed, Bogg walked cautiously around the desk to bring the potato up against Maka's cheek. "Remarkable," he murmured. Close up she looked darker. The skin itself was paler than the potato, the mask of freckles was much darker, almost black. Bogg moved the potato to Mojamaje's face. Then he walked back around the desk and sat down.

His brow unfurled and he smiled again. "Splendid," he declared. "Now for the wedding. We shall use the chapel if you like." Bogg chatted on about the sanctity of marriage, the love of Christ, as Mojamaje and Maka sat in depressed silence. Hungry and thirsty, covered with dust, exhausted from the ride, cold in the chill evening air, barefoot, Maka clad only in her thin yellow dress, Mojamaje in torn trousers and shirt, hatless, Maka's tight braids covered with the red scarf—all along as they rode, each envisioned their arrival at the mission, their impending union. Neither spoke and their silence bespoke acceptance. There was nowhere else to go. Tonight they would be husband and wife. Now in their chairs, facing the energetic missionary, they sank into lethargy.

They were in Bogg's hands. Their eyes strained in the gloom, in the shadows of the room. The Englishman's voice droned as the cold of the night slowly conquered them. Their lids fell over their eyes.

Bogg finished reading a passage from his Bible, looked up, noticed his guests slumping in their chairs. "Just like the bloody Griqua," he muttered, slamming the book shut.

Mojamaje and Maka snapped open their eyes, struggling to remember where they were. Bogg married them where they sat. He entered their names on the certificate as Jeremiah Tladi and Ruth Drift.

"You are in luck," Bogg said, closing his book one last time. "We have had a death—two. Six months ago and then last week. Odd how one follows the other. Anyway, there is an empty house. Mind you, only temporary. You must build your own. Industry, my children, industry. Christians are industrious. We have an example to set, a world to conquer. In our hands rest the fate of . . ."

Mojamaje and Maka tumbled from their chairs, asleep.

7

Perfect Christians

Taung learned immediately of the mission's new converts. Days passed, but no Boer commando appeared at the mission gates. Jagerman Roodie's Griqua widow buried him hastily and within a week his younger brother Brakman was sharing her bed. Neighboring Boers were glad to be rid of the older Roodie, whom they never forgave for marrying Drift. A few Boers suggested hunting down Mojamaje and Maka, but Drift was dead and that was retribution enough. Besides, Brakman and his new wife wanted everyone to forget that Jagerman Roodie and Drift had ever existed. They merged their adjacent farms and never mentioned the incident again.

Months passed, and Taung concluded that Mojamaje and Maka were safe to leave the mission. Maka had nowhere else to go, but Mojamaje was a good worker and could find a job on another farm, or work in the diamond hole, or return to Naring. But still he remained at the mission. Then someone reported seeing Mojamaje and Maka in Kimberley driving the mission wagon, dressed in shiny shoes, hats and new starched clothes. Maka carried a parasol.

"No!" the people of Taung exclaimed.

"Yes," the witness insisted.

The news reached Naring, carried by BaNare men back from the Kimberley hole.

"Mojamaje is an Englishman now," they reported.

"With an English wife."

"He killed a dozen Boers with a Zulu stabbing spear."

"The English rewarded him with a new set of clothes."

"And a woman."

"They gave him an Englishwoman."

The BaNare whistled in amazement. Ma-Mojamaje gulped back a sigh at the mention of her son. Already his exploits in South Africa were famous. She would never have him back now. When someone mentioned Mojamaje to her directly, she replied, "Yes, I raised him well."

Bogg was delighted. He marveled at his good fortune. Perfect Christians at last—well, almost perfect. Mojamaje and Maka showed little interest in prayer, but their industry was truly wondrous. Their house went up in no time, with perfect corners and sturdy, straw bricks. Their garden bloomed with lush vegetables and Mojamaje asked Bogg to teach him to read the Bible in English and Boer. Mojamaje repaired the mission fence, replacing rotten posts and restringing wire, redigging the irrigation channels. Maka swept into Bogg's own house, chased away his ancient Griqua maid and imposed on the place a firm Christian order. She asked Bogg to show her the chores of a Christian lady, and he did. She washed Bogg's clothes, starched his shorts, cooked his meals of fried spiced meat and stiff corn porridge, kept a pot of tea always steaming, made his bed, swept the floors twice a day, arranged the books on his desk, darned his socks. She woke him in the morning, set out his ink for the day's correspondence, placed his nightshirt on his bed at night.

After four months of this regimen, Maka set Bogg's teacup before him and said brightly, "Brother Bogg, I must ask you two favors . . ." She hesitated and then added, "In the name of Christ."

The missionary looked up to see Maka standing close by his chair, a sparkle of earnest charity on her face, one smooth shoulder bared completely by a rip in her yellow dress, at exactly the level of Bogg's eyes. She had carefully torn the dress just for this occasion. Bogg cleared his throat and looked quickly down at his cup. He had been unable to find a suitable Englishwoman willing to accompany him to this remote mission station: now Maka was more like an English wife than most English wives.

"Brother Bogg?" Maka repeated as the missionary, struggling against impure thoughts, sweated over the table before him.

Finally he regained his composure enough to reply, "Yes, my child?"

Maka began, "My two requests are Christian requests, you can be sure of that, sir. First, the church needs a new roof. The rains were heavy last summer. The roof will not last another season. A master thatcher in Kimberley owes my family a favor. I can ask him to pay back the debt by thatching the church roof." She paused. He did not look up. She waited for some sign of attention.

Finally Bogg sighed and said, "I hear you, my dear. Go on."

Maka continued. "Second, my husband and I are good Christians now, but we still dress like savages. Look at these clothes." Bogg tried not to, but he did, and broke out again in a sweat. "When we go to Kimberley," Maka said, "we can see the thatcher and then my husband and I can buy Christian clothes. For these things we need the mission wagon, for I am a lady now and I will never shame myself again and ride a horse. And we need money for the clothes, so may we take some mission vegetables and sell them in town for the money?"

Maka leaned over Bogg to pour tea into his cup, her bare shoulder flooding his vision. His nostrils filled with the scent of her skin as he weakly replied, "As you wish."

The next day, Mojamaje drove the wagon to Kimberley, loaded with carrots and cabbages. Maka rode on top. The mission wagon protected them from Boers, or so they hoped. They discussed their plans out loud, above the creak of the wagon, as Maka idly sorted through the vegetables, tossing infested carrots and cabbages one by one over the wagon rail and onto the road behind. "I hate carrots," she interjected once, and Mojamaje launched into a description of the gnarled roots the Bushmen taught him to locate in the Kalahari sand, brown and tough as bone. His teachers ate them without cooking and so Mojamaje did too. Then he resumed the argument that they had had since Maka first concocted her plan. "It is too dangerous," he repeated. "And if the Boers are defeated, the English army will only march right in to take their place. And you cannot defeat the English. You hate Boers, I understand that, but this cannot work."

Maka said nothing. She continued tossing vegetables. Despite his protests, even if it was against his better judgment, he had come along. She had already won the argument.

They slept under the wagon halfway to Kimberley and drove into town the next day, heading straight for the township, where they inquired about for a master thatcher to mend the church roof.

"Papa Zulu is best," they were told. "But slow and expensive. Ferera is fast and cheap but very bad. My-Baboon is worst of all—expensive, slow, and useless."

They drove to Papa Zulu's house, small and round with immaculate thatch, shaped to a perfect point, trimmed in a straight line around the bottom edge. The thatcher came out to greet them, a frail, dark old man in blue shirt and trousers, a wide-brimmed hat in his hand. Tufts of gray hair dotted his head.

"You are looking for me," he asserted in a high, squeaky voice.

"Yes, Papa Zulu," Maka replied, jumping down from the wagon. "We are from—"

"I know who you are," the thatcher interrupted. "The roof you want will take one month. Go to Ferera if you want it faster. The cost will be fifty shillings. Go to Ferera if you want it cheaper."

"Papa Zulu," Maka replied, "we think the roof will take six months. That makes three hundred shillings. If this is too fast, you can take more time. If you need more money, we will get it for you."

Papa Zulu stroked his chin. This strange offer fueled his suspicions: he knew the church roof was not very old and probably needed a few new lashes, a dozen patches, the kind of job even My-Baboon finished in a day. But these Christians wanted the whole roof replaced, which Ferera could do in a week.

"Why do you suppose it will take six months?" Papa Zulu asked.

"The English missionary wants you to use the motsiki style. This requires the use of the motsiki grass that only grows in the hills behind the great hole. Once a month we will drive this wagon from the mission to fetch the grass."

Mojamaje and Maka stood close to the old thatcher, speaking almost in whispers as onlookers gathered around their wagon on the township path.

A smile spread slowly across Papa Zulu's craggy face. There was no such thing as a motsiki style. It was true that this grass grew only in the Kimberley hills, near the hole, but ordinary grass that grew everywhere else was tougher and longer, much better for thatching.

"Motsiki grass?" Papa Zulu asked, returning Maka's whisper, joining the conspiracy.

"The Englishman insists," Mojamaje replied with a wink.

Papa Zulu clapped his hat on his head, rubbed his hands together, laughed and whispered, "I am very impressed. You do know your grasses. Motsiki is a very good grass for smuggling." Then he turned to the crowd to announce, "The Englishman wants the motsiki style. Does Ferera know it? No. Only I, Papa Zulu, Master of Grass, sewing his first roof before Ferera tasted mother's milk—only I know the secret of motsiki, the most difficult style in the world. English appreciate quality. Motsiki it will be."

Mojamaje and Maka slept the night in Papa Zulu's compound, then drove the next morning into Kimberley proper, up to the shop where Drift had sold her grain. They dusted off their clothes and entered the shop.

"Dear Lord, 'tis true!" the shopkeeper hooted. "Christians!"

"We want guns," Maka replied.

The shopkeeper fell back against his counter, narrowing his eyes, searching Mojamaje's face, then Maka's, deciphering whether they were serious. Then he motioned them into the back room.

"Sixty," Maka said. "Six pounds each. We will take ten now. We will pay you the money in one month. We will take ten more and pay in a month again. We will do this for six months."

The shopkeeper wiped his hands on his apron, adding up the dangers, the costs, the profits of the scheme. Everyone knew the traders of Kimberley bought rifles for one English pound at the coast and sold them to Boers and Englishmen for three pounds. The English forbade the sale of guns to anyone else. This merchant would hang if they caught him, but who could resist a profit of five hundred percent?

The shopkeeper agreed and arranged for the first shipment. They walked out to the front room. "Anything else?" he asked.

"Christian clothes," Mojamaje replied.

"And one of those," Maka said, pointing to a parasol.

The shopkeeper brought out a black suit, a long white dress, a black bowler, a straw hat, and a bright pink parasol with an ivory handle.

Once a month Mojamaje drove the mission wagon to the Kimberley hills. Maka rode on top, her white collar circling her long neck, parasol high in the air. They filled the wagon with motsiki grass, then drove at night past the back of the English store, pushing a case of rifles under the grass without stopping the wagon. Driving north to Taung, they paused along the way at the cluster of hills where they had rested the day they escaped Roodie's farm. They found the deep cleft in the rocks with the pool of water at its bottom. Concealing the rifles there, they returned to the mission.

Then Mojamaje rode at night to the Roodie farm, to creep through the tenant village to the compound of Rejiletlhapi, meaning "We-Have-Eaten-A-Fish." He was kind and honest, with two young sons. His wife had died of fever a week after Mojamaje first arrived in Taung and he stumbled thereafter in a purposeless daze. Mojamaje now appeared in his suit and bowler with something for We-Have-Eaten-A-Fish to do.

"Of course," the man whispered, crouched in the dark of his house. "Thank you for thinking of me."

We-Have-Eaten-A-Fish and his sons drove five cows to the cleft in the hills. The boys scooped water from the bottom of the cleft with metal buckets, carried it down to the plain, and sloshed it into a drinking trough made from a hollowed-out log. Their father watched the cows graze. Toward midday he led them to drink from the trough.

Then Mojamaje rode to Kimberley to search the township for a BaNare. He found Ologo, son of the sister of Tladi's brother's wife's sister's daughter's husband's sister's husband's brother.

"Cousin!" Mojamaje said, then he pushed the boy behind a thorn fence to whisper, "Are you going to work in the mines?"

"No," Ologo whispered in reply, "I just came from there."

"Can you go back?"

"If I choose," the boy replied.

"Do it," Mojamaje said. "Look through the diggers for men you can trust. Tell them this: They can buy guns in Taung from a man called We-Have-Eaten-A-Fish, off the road from Kimberley, in the hills that look like the teats of a goat. He herds cattle there. Choose wisely. This is a dangerous thing." The boy's eyes widened. "Do you understand?" The boy nodded his head. Mojamaje pushed a shilling into his palm. "This coin has a hole. Give it to the first digger you tell. The first man must come with this coin. We will not start to sell unless this coin with a hole comes back."

A week later, We-Have-Eaten-A-Fish came at night to the mission to give Mojamaje the coin.

This was how Mojamaje and Maka used the Taung mission to smuggle guns. Word spread slowly among the miners. When they finished their contracts, they passed by the cleft in the hill, at night, to buy rifles. The price was high, seven pounds each, so men from the same village pooled their wages. Mojamaje and Maka made a profit of one pound, which they used to pay Papa Zulu and his helpers and to feed We-Have-Eaten-A-Fish and his sons. There were a few pounds left over each month, which Mojamaje used to buy cattle, which We-Have-Eaten-A-Fish herded for him. At the end of six months all the rifles had been sold, every cow had borne a female calf, and Papa Zulu had rethatched every roof in the mission. More miners came, eager for guns. So Mojamaje and Maka renewed their contract with the shopkeeper and hired bricklayers to build more buildings for Papa Zulu to thatch. The mission grew, the herd grew, miners carried rifles home to every village in South Africa.

8

A Touch

"So leave," Maka snapped, then shrugged, dismissing the issue.

Mojamaje sat on the floor of their square mission house, a blanket around his shoulders. An oil lamp glowed from one corner, its light reflected by Maka's white dress. She stood above him, at once sympathetic and angry. Still she had not let him touch her. The crime of her father still bound her limbs. By day Maka and Mojamaje ruled the mission as full partners, overwhelming Bogg with their bustle and quick answers for the changes around him. By night they slept apart, in their mission house, when they camped on the road to Kimberley, in Papa Zulu's compound, her blankets in one corner, his in another.

"I do not want to leave you," Mojamaje replied.

"You always argue," Maka replied. "You think me a fool. So go. Find someone else."

"I can read the Kimberley newspapers now," Mojamaje continued. "Not just the Boer ones. The English too. They talk of other gun smugglers in South Africa. I think the English ignore it, to weaken the Boers. I know you want to kill all the Boers. You blame them for . . . everything. I understand that. But you are playing into English hands."

Maka shrugged again. "They can use the guns against the English too. I do not care. They can use them against each other." She folded her arms over her chest. "At first, yes, this thing was to punish Boers. But now—now I like it here. I can live like my mother here. Because of the guns this place is ours." And now her voice softened as she repeated, "Go."

Mojamaje struggled to remain calm in the face of her obstinacy. He watched the flickering flame from the lamp darken then lighten the freckles of her cheek. He cleared his throat and resumed his entreaty. "Ologo, the boy from Naring who took the coin—he tells me that Tladi is dead. My grandfather, who sent me away. I can go back to Naring. Come with me. South Africa is doomed. Some day the Boers will seize the wagon and shoot us."

"So go," Maka said a third time.

"No!" Mojamaje declared, rising to his feet, naked from the waist, wearing only his black flannel trousers. He stayed at the mission to be with Maka. He loved watching her, moving beside her, with her. She ignited him from thought to action, filling his life. She even taught him to laugh at himself. He was not laughing now. "I have waited long enough," he said. "If I stay, if I risk my life with you, at least you will be my wife. Do you see these eyes? These are Bushman eyes. We see into souls. You want to love me. The time is now."

He reached out to embrace her, his hands pressing against the cold iron of her spine. She sprang back, pushing him away, then turned to face him. "You will never touch me!"

"I will touch you now," he said calmly, stepping forward again. She pulled back, against the corner of the house, standing on her blankets. He grabbed her arms and pulled her down, firmly, as she struggled to kick at his groin. He reached for the buttons at the back of her dress. She fell limp, turning her face to his.

"Let me go," she said. "I will do it."

Mojamaje lay back, stretched out on her bed, watching her reach both hands behind to unfasten the buttons. The dress fell over one shoulder as she pulled from its sheath, strapped tight against her spine, a long, flat blade of dark metal.

It was Vlei's knife. She sprang onto Mojamaje's belly, to kneel atop him, holding the knife against his throat, remembering the grunts of her father, the stink of his breath, her mother's face with a hole in her forehead, the blood on her hand as she drew Vlei's knife from her father's chest, her father's blood. She had concealed the weapon under her dress, tying it around her back. Every night Mojamaje lay beside her, underneath the wagon, in Papa Zulu's compound, in their separate beds in the mission house, she had been prepared to defend herself, vigilant, ready to pounce at his slightest advance.

Now Mojamaje lay still, Vlei's enormous knife poised against his throat. The sinews of Maka's hands pulsed taut in the gleam of the oil lamp. Her eyes were closed, lips quivering, bloated, her hands ready to strike at his slightest movement. He struggled to slow his lungs, to calm his heart. Slowly he relaxed, swallowing hard, the skin of his throat rising to graze the tip of the knife. The heave of their lungs fell into harmony, rising and falling in the same rhythm. Maka sighed, stood up, her eyes still closed, and threw the knife against the door, which rattled with the impact.

The white dress slid from her shoulders to her feet. Maka lay back down beside Mojamaje, her face calm now, her skin yellow behind its dark mask. Mojamaje ran his callused fingers along her cheek, down her chin, over her eyes, tracing the lines of her worry, smoothing them back to a trusting calm. The oil burned low in the lamp, smoking the glass, returning the room to darkness.

9

The Ugliest Herder

When word of the Taung gun trade reached Naring, the BaNare smirked with pride. Ologo told them the whole story, how it was really Mojamaje who sold the guns. BaNare diggers bought rifles and on the way home they stopped at the mission to thank Mojamaje, who warned them not to come there ever again. "The Boers will become suspicious," he explained.

And so the BaNare turned their attention to matters closer at home, such as Chief Pule's popularity, which had plummeted disastrously since Hrikwa the Griqua lost the wagon on the road to Kimberley and disappeared without a trace. Mojamaje was the last BaNare to see him. Chief Pule instructed young men on their way to Kimberley to look for another trader. None turned up. Just as Pule commenced to despair, tearing the ochered hair on his balding head, tugging on his copper earrings, swearing at his children—just then De Swart appeared.

Piet De Swart was a Boer. He came from Taung, near the road to Kimberley. His father had died, leaving nine sons who carved up his land among themselves. The father left many debts as well, so the English bank in Kimberley seized two thirds of each brother's plot. Then Piet himself fell into debt and the bank took another two thirds of what remained. Piet's worst curse came from another source, though, in the person of his only employee, Jeedo Parido. Because Piet was so poor, with so little land, no tenants came to work for him except Jeedo. As they worked together in the fields, Jeedo sang this song:

> Take me back to the empty veld
> Where bashee-birds fill the air
> Dear Plakenburg, those golden hills
> A beauty sweet and rare
> Take me back to the empty veld
> Where the grass runs green through the glade
> Dear Plakenburg, those golden hills
> The finest place God ever made

Jeedo sang this hideous song every waking hour until De Swart quivered with rage and disgust.

"Shut up!" he bellowed as Jeedo sang on, holding the plow or steadying a fence post for De Swart to drive into the ground, or tying the yoke as De Swart held the oxen's horns. Once Piet asked Jeedo whether the song had more verses, but the answer was no. He asked whether Jeedo knew any other songs but the answer was no. He asked whether Jeedo had ever been to Plakenburg but the answer was no.

De Swart could not fire Jeedo Parido because no one else would work for him. And only poor De Swart would hire the unbearable Jeedo. He was a Wall-Maker, a refugee from the long Boer siege that had sent the Wall-Makers staggering toward Naring, only to be turned away at the Battle of the Woodpile. They had wandered for years until finally settling in a new village halfway between Naring and Taung, in close range of Boer marauders. Between two attacks the Wall-Makers drove Jeedo Parido out of their territory, his awful song ringing in their ears.

"Where is Plakenburg?" De Swart asked one morning.

"Beats me," Jeedo replied.

"Where did you learn the song?"

"I made it up," Jeedo answered.

Then one night Jeedo Parido vanished with De Swart's cattle. In the old days De Swart would have rounded up his neighbors and set off after the thief. De Swart himself had ridden in countless raids to reclaim cattle, including the Battle of the Rocks at Naring. He was the youngest horseman in the Boer ranks that day, desperate to recover his father's herd, stolen by the Taung people enjoying refuge among their BaNare cousins. After the Battle of the Rocks, from which the raiders escaped in furious humiliation with nothing to show for their heavy casualties, the De Swarts were a destitute lot.

Straining to banish Jeedo's song from his head, Piet De Swart mounted his horse, a tired brown mare, and rode off after his cattle. His neighbors never answered calls to arms these days, content to sell meat and corn in Kimberley. None would bother to help recover De Swart's miserable herd of fifty cattle. He rode alone to the Wall-Maker village, calling out his peaceful intentions long before reaching the first compound. He asked whether Jeedo Parido was there.

"He will never come here," the Wall-Makers replied. "He knows we would cut out his tongue."

De Swart rode on to Naring. He called out his greetings again and Pule bounded out to meet him, his leopard suit torn and too small for his swelling rotundity, his ochered hair receding from his crown, copper earrings dangling. De Swart explained his plight and begged Pule's assistance.

Pule eyed the Boer carefully—old horse with graying fetlocks, clothes of home-tanned leather, not cotton cloth from the English, old musket, inferior to the modern rifles that BaNare miners bought from We-Have-Eaten-A-Fish, fat crimson face, gray hairs mixed with yellow in his beard. "My trader," Pule thought, a white face safe from wagon robbers. But he needed more time to assess the Boer's character. Was he foolish to consider trusting a Boer?

Pule also thought hard about De Swart's request for the return of his cattle. Since the end of the raids, refugees like Jeedo Parido came all the time, driving Boer cattle into BaNare territory without notifying the chief. Pule had no idea how many cattle and refugees inhabited his pastures. They no longer needed the safety in numbers afforded by Naring itself. Such insolence posed a grave challenge to Pule's authority.

Pule said to De Swart, "We will find your cattle."

De Swart tied up his horse and walked with Pule out of Naring into the countryside, from herder to herder, demanding information about a recent Wall-Maker immigrant named Jeedo Parido in possession of fifty . Boer cattle. Everyone directed them to a place called Stinkface. Jeedo saw them coming, but too late to run. Then the name of the place gave him an idea: he screwed up his face to make it as ugly as possible, sucking in his lips, crossing his eyes, jutting his jaw to one side.

Pule lined up the twenty herders. He recognized not a single one. He had taken action none too soon. His country crawled with strangers. Then De Swart walked beside Pule down the line once, twice, but none looked like Jeedo. He thrust his face before each man's nose, staring into his eyes, except for one herder who was so ugly that De Swart could hardly look at him. Pule grew impatient, tugging on one earring.

Then De Swart remembered Jeedo's song. He cleared his throat, hummed a note and sang out loud:

> Take me back to the empty veld
> Where bashee-birds fill the air . . .

At the end of the line, the ugly herder's face relaxed as he sang in response:

> Dear Plakenburg, those golden hills . . .

Before Jeedo could sing the next line, De Swart was on top of him, clutching his throat. The other herders pulled the Boer away. Jeedo ran off, never to be seen again, warbling with glee the rest of his song.

Pule ordered the herders to search the surrounding pasture for De Swart's cattle. The Boer drew his brand in the dirt, a *D* and an *S* hooked together. They rounded up forty, which Pule ordered them to drive to Naring.

Walking back with Pule, De Swart said, "Chief, I give you five cattle as thanks."

Pule declined, saying, "Keep them all. But do not take them out of my country. They have eaten BaNare grass, so they are BaNare cattle."

De Swart grimaced. "Chief Pule," he replied, "I am a Boer. How can I live here?"

"You can be my trader," Pule said. "Build a shop like the English in Kimberley. Keep your cattle. My people will love you." Pule opened his arms to the sky.

De Swart had no choice. He gazed at the Naring hills ahead. "I have a wife," he said. "And children. Little Boers."

"Fetch them," Pule replied.

They approached Naring through the canyon where De Swart had ridden twenty-five years before to the Battle of the Rocks. "Times have changed," he mused aloud.

"Yes," Pule agreed. He looked down at his elbows poking through his leopard coat, resolving to order another suit as soon as the Boer set up shop.

10
The Pig Feast

That was how a Boer from the Battle of the Rocks came to settle in Naring. No one recognized him, for a Boer was a Boer, and at first the BaNare questioned the prudence of inviting one into their midst. Pule reassured them.

"Think of him as a refugee," he said.

De Swart arrived with a wagon full of his wife and ten children. Four of these children were married and they brought their own spouses and children along. In all, twenty Boers arrived in Naring, forming their own small village on the outskirts of town, against the ridge of hills.

The De Swarts called Piet "Old Man," so the BaNare did the same. He became fast friends with Pule. The BaNare decided that the two men looked alike: about the same age, growing fat and gray, boisterous and cheerful. Old Man De Swart brought chickens, ducks and pigs on his wagon, explaining each one to the BaNare. They liked the ducks best of all, but they all died within a month. The chickens thrived and Old Man De Swart passed out eggs. Soon Naring swarmed with chicks scratching the dust for seeds.

The pigs were another matter. There were six and they never stopped eating. The younger De Swart children spent long hours carrying water for the animals to drink and slop. The pigs sweated and groaned in the summer heat, finally flopping onto their sides. The De Swart children secretly cut back the pigs' water, hoping to hasten their inevitable demise.

Old Man De Swart was despondent. "How low can I fall?" he asked his stout wife, who stood in the squat cookhut, a mud cubicle that he had built behind their rectangular mud house. Inside it, a three-legged black pot stood over a crisscross of smoldering logs. An enormous blue dress with faded white flowers covered his wife's body and a green scarf covered her hair. Her red face sweated as she stirred corn porridge with a long wooden spoon, dreaming of sausages.

Old Man sat on a stump in front of the cookhut. "We are Boers," he continued. "Boers ride horses. Boers carry rifles. Boers keep pigs. My horse is old, my rifle is rusty, my pigs are dying."

His wife stirred in silence, imagining the pigs held up by their forelegs, sliced down the chest and stomach, skinned and quartered, their intestines cleaned and stuffed stiff with bits of spiced pork.

"Kill them," she said, without turning from her pot.

Old Man jumped to his feet. "Are you mad?" he cried. "Boers keep pigs!"

He stormed off into the village. Winding his way along the paths, he lamented that although the BaNare called out greetings to passersby from their compounds, no one greeted him. "Boer-haters," he mumbled. Old Man De Swart was a gregarious fellow, dejected that no one but Pule wanted to make his acquaintance. How could he blame them? Though no BaNare knew, he himself had attacked this very village more than twenty years before.

"She is right," he concluded. "I must slaughter the pigs. I will give the BaNare a feast. After that they will love me."

He announced the event and sent his children to collect wood. A week later he dug a shallow trench in front of his compound and made a fire, spreading long branches over the pit as a platform for the meat. The BaNare came to watch the preparations, crowding around the trench. The pigpen stood a dozen yards away. The BaNare all agreed that pigs were the ugliest animals in the world. There were wild pigs out in the Kalahari, but these had tough gray hides like elephants. De Swart's pigs were pink, like Boers, sickly and pale, lying grunting and sweating— certainly they were diseased, and that was why their skin was so light.

Then two De Swart boys opened the pen and pulled out the first pig. They placed a bucket of corn on the ground and the pig snorted and thrust its snout down to eat, unmindful of Old Man swinging one leg over to straddle the animal like a horse. He held in his hands a long broomstick with a massive hand-hewn wooden mallet head on one end. As the pig gulped down the corn, one of the boys gently placed a plank of wood over its head. On the top side of the plank, a long thick nail stuck up into the air, its pointed tip barely gripping the wood. Old Man grinned with glee, exposing short, tobacco-stained teeth, grasped the mallet with two hands over his head, and swung the thing down on the unsuspecting pig's head, driving the nail through the plank and deep into the pig's brain.

A cow groans when slaughtered, a sheep bleats, a goat dies in silence. But the Boer pig squealed like the spirits of the dead, a horrible squeaky roar that sent the BaNare audience howling and scrambling for cover as the pig bucked once and hurled De Swart into the air, to land crumpled on the lip of his freshly dug pit. Then the pig collapsed, dead.

Each pig perished in the same manner, with the same hideous squeal. The pigs were ugly on the inside too. There were rolls of translucent fat and the meat was surely diseased, pink and pale like the skin. It did not look like meat at all. The BaNare whispered, their stomachs churning with revulsion. Old Man Piet fluttered around the pit, singing to himself, poking the chunks of roasting pork with a long stick. There was a tremendous amount of meat, covering the pit completely. The BaNare felt sorry for the Boer, who had worked so hard butchering his pigs he loved. But no one dared even taste the ghastly stuff. As the meat blackened with smoke, they dreaded the moment when De Swart would finally realize the truth.

Then a cry came up from the back of the crowd.

"Bushmen!"

The BaNare parted to let the Bushmen band past, laughing, "They never miss a meal." Xo led the band, and a few BaNare stopped laughing, for they blamed him for stealing Tladi's cattle, causing Mojamaje's banishment. But most BaNare blamed the extra heart, so they continued to laugh as the Bushmen sat down close around the fire and began to pull the pig meat from the racks. Hooting with amusement, the BaNare watched the thirty Bushmen, half of them wrinkled children, stuff the greasy meat into their greedy mouths. By the time they had consumed all six pigs, they were completely covered in grease and the BaNare rolled in the dust, their sides splitting with laughter. The Bushmen rose to go, their stomachs sticking out so far that they could not see their toes, then waddled away, back to the Kalahari, burping and smacking their lips.

Henceforth, whenever Old Man walked through Naring, adults and children alike ran up to shake his hand and thank him for throwing the best feast in BaNare history.

11
More Than a Touch

At the time, the BaNare had no way of knowing the importance of De Swart's arrival in their midst. For this they would have to wait until his youngest child grew up. In the meantime, the Boers slowly faded from daily conversation to occasional mention in idle gossip. As with all the refugees who came to Naring, the novelty soon wore off.

The only BaNare who from the very first paid no attention to the Boers was Ma-Mojamaje. Her thoughts were already fully occupied. She sat in her compound, her legs stretched before her, sipping tea from a tin cup. With one hand she smoothed her dress against her thighs—a bright green dress, bought from Old Man De Swart's shop. The young men had returned from Kimberley wearing trousers and now encouraged other BaNare to buy them from De Swart's wagon. They bought dresses for their sisters, mothers and wives, who would not wear them at first, only gradually falling in step. Ma-Mojamaje still wore her leather apron beneath her dress and remembered back to the first days she noticed her girl's breasts rise off her chest, bare for all Tladi's men to see, how Ra-Mojamaje stared at them, afraid to reach out his hand to touch them. She had rubbed them instead against his chest, lying in the grass, whispering, her careful plot dissolving to love as she removed her apron, then his loincloth, and lay down atop him, to show him the most wonderful thing in the world.

"My son!" she cried, but Mojamaje was far away. She tossed her cold tea into the fire. The embers hissed and the low flames turned to smoke.

On their way to Kimberley some BaNare young men visited Mojamaje at the mission. They told him news of Naring, and that his mother asked about him the moment they returned to the village. Mojamaje warned them again never to come to the mission, for fear of attracting Boer suspicions. They wanted to know when he was coming home, but he sent them away without an answer. Once the gun trade fell into routine, once the fear of discovery faded to a dim uneasiness, life was good where he was. Bogg spent more and more time praying, while Maka and Mojamaje ran the mission.

They admitted more converts to fill the houses that Papa Zulu built and thatched, and now not only Griqua came to fill them. A new kind of refugee had appeared. Zulu and Boer raids had disturbed everyone in South Africa, shifting them in every direction. As things settled down, some places were overcrowded, while in others land went begging, so refugees left overcrowded places and searched South Africa for space. They did not run in terror like refugees of the past, but wandered slowly, sometimes driving a cow with a stick, children in tow, following rumors of empty fields and free pastures. When they turned up at the mission gates, Maka and Mojamaje offered refuge to all who vowed to follow their two cardinal rules. The first rule was attendance every morning at Bogg's prayer hour, which kept the missionary convinced of the piety of his flock. The second rule barred cattle from the mission grounds, for the area was too small to accommodate the growing body of faithful as well as their grazing herds.

As the mission thrived Mojamaje read the Kimberley English papers to keep track of the skirmishes and risings across the country. The Boers and English police began sweeps to disarm villages. Zululand on the coast and Kgama country in the northeast Transvaal proved the most resilient. Then an army of ten thousand Kgama, led by a Wall-Maker refugee, a charismatic vagabond with ochered hair and hawk-feather earrings, defeated a force of five thousand Boers. The Kgama had thousands of guns. The English finally decided that there were too many guns in too many hands. An English army marched through Kimberley, then northeast to the Kgama hills, to defeat the Kgama army. They caught the Wall-Maker refugee who had organized the Kgama troops, tore off his feather earrings and marched him back to Kimberley for trial. In the English jail, the refugee tormented his guards by singing over and over:

> Take me back to the empty veld
> Where bashee-birds fill the air
> Dear Plakenburg, those golden hills
> A beauty sweet and rare . . .

The guards shouted for him to stop, he refused and they beat him to death in the cell. Word spread through the countryside:

"The English cannot be trusted."

"Worse than Boers."

The English defeat of the Kgama army was one thing—a fair fight on an open battlefield—but murdering a prisoner was something else. A week after the murder, a mixed rabble of Boer and Zulu riflemen, all on horseback, attacked an English army post, sacking and burning the English shop alongside it.

The Taung mission gun trade fell victim to the surrounding unrest. It was no longer safe to smuggle guns in the wagon, for the Boers no longer feared English missionaries or the English army. Not even a white face insured safe passage anymore. Desperate, the Boers had nothing to lose. For months at a time, the mission wagon lay idle and We-Have-Eaten-A-Fish sold no rifles. The cattle he herded, though, continued to multiply. Half belonged to Mojamaje and Maka. Then the English shopkeeper in Kimberley refused to renew the rifle contract.

"Too dangerous," he insisted. "Crazy Boers everywhere."

Kimberley itself grew perilous, crawling with angry Boers who sometimes raided the fanciest houses in the township. They hated anyone darker than a potato who gave any appearance of wealth. Mojamaje and Maka received threats on the Kimberley streets because they dressed like Christians, in good, clean clothes. They discussed moving to another town, perhaps to set up a shop, but reports in the papers made them all seem the same.

Then Mojamaje read that suddenly, in the middle of a Boer farm two hundred miles east of Taung, an English prospector had found gold. He scratched a rock and there it was. Then another prospector scratched a rock a mile away and then another, until English and Boers and everyone else fell on the place like buzzards on a dead elephant. Within a month gold claims stretched for fifty miles. In the center the English built a new town, Joburg. To secure their bonanza, determined to prevent more trouble, the English declared all South Africa the property of their Queen.

"That does it," Mojamaje concluded. The English would soon be everywhere, as the BaNare had feared from the very first time Hrikwa the Griqua mentioned them. The mission gun trade would never revive. Englishwomen were no longer rare. Worse yet, Bogg's superiors, recognizing the new strategic importance of Taung, smack along the road from Kimberley to Joburg, sent a more worldly missionary to take Bogg's place. The new man's name was Dale. He arrived with a proper English wife, who banished Maka from their house. Papa Zulu and his thatchers returned to Kimberley. The time approached for Mojamaje to move on.

The final prod came from the English army, which marched into Taung to camp on the mission grounds. A stately gray-haired officer with a long gray moustache and eyes of blue marble, in an immaculate white uniform, rode ahead of the column and up to the main mission house. Dale came out to meet him. Mrs. Dale stood in the doorway. From years and years of Papa Zulu's rebuilding, the house was magnificent, with twenty rooms, arching thatched roofs set at varied angles, verandas and porches in every direction. Dale's straight brown hair was closely cropped, combed and lacquered in place, and he stood as erect and soldierly as the officer now approaching him.

"Reverend Dale?" the white-haired soldier called, swinging down from his horse. "Colonel Sweete, Her Majesty's Commissioner of Rhodesia, Southern Tanga and Kalahariland Territory. We march to inform the native tribes of this fact. You will accompany us as interpreter. Departure Sunday." Sweete spoke in staccato bursts, clipping each word with the shears of his moustache.

"Sorry, Colonel," Dale replied sharply. "I take my orders from a higher authority. My wife and I arrived only last month. I know not a word of a single native language."

Sweete opened his jaws to reply, but Dale continued. "I do have an excellent man for you. A native. Superb English. I believe he comes from Kalahariland."

"Very good," Sweete snapped. "Send him to me."

Dale knew what he wanted. He was well aware of Sweete's mission to bring Kalahariland, Rhodesia and Southern Tanga under English rule. These were territories bordering South Africa proper, worthless in themselves but potentially troublesome if left undefended. England's borders were now South Africa's and Sweete's job was to secure them. Dale had no intention of setting foot outside South Africa. And this was the perfect chance to rid himself of Mojamaje.

Sweete complimented Mojamaje on his command of English and added, "The English language is England's greatest gift to the world." He gave Mojamaje a comradely wink and ordered him to report for duty on Sunday.

"Do I walk or ride a horse?" Mojamaje asked.

"You walk."

"Do you have a guide?"

"Of course," Sweete replied.

"A Boer?"

"Of course."

"That is dangerous," Mojamaje warned. "No one will talk. They will attack. They hate Boers. I will be your guide instead."

Sweete sneered. "Is this true?" he demanded. "Or do you just want a horse to ride?"

"It is true," Mojamaje replied. "Also I want a horse."

And so the English army hired Mojamaje as guide and interpreter for their march. Sweete's force comprised one hundred cavalry and two hundred foot soldiers, all in bright red uniforms that attracted flies in the summer heat. They were covered with dust from the march from Kimberley and Sweete insisted on cleanliness, so they washed their uniforms in the Taung River and hung them to dry on the mission fence. The summer was drier than usual, so the wind whipped dust into the folds of the wet cloth. The soldiers washed the uniforms again, hung them to dry, and again the wind filled them with dust.

Now came Mojamaje's most difficult question—would Maka come with him? Despite their conquest of her deepest fears, Mojamaje and Maka had failed to conquer them all. Their embrace on that night he first touched her, after she nearly slashed him with Vlei's enormous Zulu dagger, had ended only in sleepy caresses. Night after night they tried to consummate their love, but each time Maka's memory flared to violent wrath. She hurled herself against Mojamaje, flailing against his arms, still dreading the final submission, cursing her father, mourning her mother, lapsing into despair, into hatred, vicious remorse. Sometimes as they tossed, locked in futile embrace, she erupted to beat on his chest with her fists, tear at his eyes with her nails, kick at his groin with her knee. Eventually she stopped trying. She separated their blankets again to opposite corners of their square mission house. Mojamaje yielded, exhausted, despondent, unable to try again.

"I will wait," he said.

"You will wait forever," Maka replied calmly. But then she added more softly, "Remember, it is hard for me too."

Mojamaje spoke with Sweete at dusk, and he returned to the house to find it completely dark. In the corner he heard a faint rustling of Maka in her blankets. Without lighting the lamp, he crawled into his own.

"I am leaving," he said. "The missionary will throw you out. Where will you go?" He reached out to touch her across the empty space between their beds, his hand brushing against her blankets. He lay down, tense with anticipation, exhausted by the thought of renewed battle. Certainly she mirrored him, thirsty for respite, cringing at the creak of the door, at the fall of his body across from hers.

But Mojamaje was wrong. Maka stood up, and he saw the faint outline of her long white Christian dress fall to the floor. She lay back down, her bare skin exposed to the night air, her small breasts heaving with silent sighs. She whispered softly, "Will you leave me, Eater of Rocks? Will you leave me to my failure? Will you sleep well at last?"

Maka's anxious voice, redolent with memory, made Mojamaje fear Vlei's knife. Was it there in her hand, ready to end his sorrows?

Maka continued in a stronger whisper. "Do not leave me, Mojamaje. Sleep in my arms, lie with your head on my breast, love me. As I love you."

The fear of his leaving softened her limbs, melting them over his body, raising his back to the surface of hope. She floated across him, fluid at last. He kissed her breasts, they rose to meet him, then her thighs, his lips brushed along her mist of fine freckles, finding them everywhere. Years of relief flowed through his veins and out, release, entwined, release. And some BaNare insist, although others vehemently deny it, that at the moment of final victory, joined in love at last, Maka whispered in Mojamaje's ear, "This is the most wonderful thing in the world."

12

Why Tall Trees Shade the Road to Naring

A night of ecstasy, the shackles of memory broken, he loved her warm breath on his face, sometimes their noses touched, she blinked and her lashes grazed his cheek. Toward dawn he fell asleep, at first light he woke up alone.

"Maka?" he called out, sitting up abruptly. The room was empty. "She has left me," he muttered.

There was nothing for Mojamaje to do but leave with the English army. Sweete gave him a gray horse to ride, a bit old but healthy.

Mojamaje rode at the head of the column with Sweete, whose white uniform still shone with immaculate fury. Behind rode the hundred cavalry and behind them walked two hundred infantry in two rows, their red uniforms wringing wet. Behind the infantry rolled ox wagons of supplies and behind them walked the army's servants and cooks, recruited from Kimberley township.

Mojamaje was on his way home. To this day, the BaNare do not understand completely why the discovery of Joburg's gold moved the English to conquer their country. But the English army did not bring cannons and they denied any interest in stealing cattle or land. When the BaNare tell the story of the Great Thirst, they do not argue about the English army, because it arrived as a fact, unstoppable, backed by thousands more soldiers in Kimberley, Joburg, on the coast, in England itself. The English were able to do what they wished. No, the BaNare do not discuss the English. Their concern is Mojamaje. After so many years in pursuit of Maka's heart, after finally placing his skin against hers, he rode out the mission gates without her. Surely this was as sad a day as Mojamaje had ever lived.

When the column was two days out of Taung, a cloud of yellow dust appeared ahead on the horizon. As the soldiers approached it the cloud seemed to recede in the same direction, west to Naring. Next morning they reached its fringe, the hum of lowing and the tinkling of cowbells wafting behind. Manure lay everywhere, the smell of cattle hung in the dust as the column caught up with the gigantic herd that was raising the cloud. Herdboys waved to the soldiers. By the end of the day the head of the column reached the head of the herd. Dust filled the soldiers' nostrils and hair and stained their uniforms orange.

There at the front of the herd rode Maka on her black horse, barefoot, her old yellow dress hugging her thighs, her old red scarf tied over her braided hair. The cattle were those herded by We-Have-Eaten-A-Fish, bought from smuggling profits, multiplied over the years. Mojamaje rode ahead, searching for her in the haze, the noise of the cattle drowning his shouts. Finally he found her, the pale yellow of her skin darkening as he approached, until her black freckles stood out from her face. The herdboys pressed close to overhear their words, but cattle bells drowned them out. Mojamaje jumped from his horse and pulled her to stand on the ground, where they looked into each other's eyes, laughed in joy and relief and embraced like the lovers they were.

Never before had so many cattle moved so far at one time. Never before had so many cattle dumped so much dung. Along the path from Taung to Naring, when rain fell that summer and summers thereafter, the wagons traveling the road churned the dung into the mud. The stink remained overpowering until the rains stopped. After five years of good rains, small trees sprouted from the fertile manure, and ten years later they had grown tall enough to shade the road along its entire length.

13
What Ma-Mojamaje Knew

The army column pushed ahead and reached the Naring hills in advance of Maka's herd. The English red coats sparkled in the sun and alerted the BaNare sentry on the ridge. He called others to look. The most recently arrived refugees cried "English!" and turned to run for their lives.

But two thousand BaNare men had rifles. "We will shoot them as they come through the canyon," they said.

"Like the Boers at the Battle of the Rocks."

"Now we are ready."

Then someone exclaimed, "Mojamaje!"

The crowd looked carefully down onto the plain, and there at the head of the column, before the red coats, rode a black man in a black English suit and bowler hat. Fearing exactly the ambush that the BaNare planned, Mojamaje had told Sweete to camp on the plain while he rode ahead to arrange a meeting with Chief Pule, and he spurred his horse forward. For one brief moment it looked as if Mojamaje was leading the entire column, followed by the white uniform and then the red ones.

This is the moment the BaNare remember from Mojamaje's return to Naring. He rode from South Africa commanding an army of English soldiers—one of their own, a BaNare, the infant who crawled through fire, the boy who won single-handedly the Battle of the Rocks, the young man who slew a hundred Boers with a Zulu knife, had become an En-

glishman, married an English wife, smuggled rifles that gave all South
Africa defense against the Boers. The English had recognized his powers
and given him an army to lead.

Mojamaje's presence softened the BaNare's belligerence to suspicion.
They watched as the English army stopped, the cavalry dismounted, the
foot soldiers sat down, the supply wagons formed a circle, on the broad
plain where the Battle of the Woodpile had taken place. Then the
BaNare rushed down to meet Mojamaje at the canyon mouth. "Mojamaje! Mojamaje!" the crowd shouted, surrounding his horse, men thrusting their new rifles in the air.

Mojamaje shouted back, "I must see Chief Pule!" But the tumult
drowned him out. He caught the eye of Ologo in the crowd, the distant
cousin whom he had recruited to begin the gun trade, and motioned him
forward. Mojamaje shouted to him, "Tell Pule to meet me here. To talk
to the English. I will come back with their chief. Tell him not to shoot.
The English do not want to fight."

Sweete selected fifty cavalrymen with the cleanest uniforms to ride
with him and Mojamaje to meet the chief. Sweete's clean white tunic
gleamed brightly in the sun, as did his teeth as he grinned broadly,
proudly, a soldier serving his Queen. They met Pule at the canyon
mouth, against the rock face where Mojamaje had spent the Battle of
the Rocks. Pule sat on a wooden sling chair, slats of wood held together
by leather straps. He wore a new leopard suit, the old hat that Hrikwa
had given him, copper earrings, and no shoes. At his shoulder stood his
eldest son, Pia ya Pipa, known as Pia the Scornful. Pia wore a black
English suit, a bowler, shiny black shoes, and held a straight black cane
in one hand. The cold avarice in Pia's vain eyes brought shudders to
every BaNare who looked in them, so no one did. The crowd of BaNare
stretched into the canyon behind. The English soldiers stood at attention, facing out to the BaNare, their rifles resting on their shoulders.
Mojamaje and Sweete approached Pule and Pia.

"Tell your chief," Sweete said at once to Mojamaje in English, "his
country belongs to the Queen."

Mojamaje folded his hands, turned to Pule, greeted him formally,
then greeted Pia, who responded with a contemptuous harrumph. Pule
said, "Why do these English face my people with rifles?"

"What did he say?" Sweete asked.

Mojamaje turned back to Sweete and replied, "Chief Pule greets your
Queen. He welcomes you to his country."

"Does he accept English rule?" Sweete demanded.

Mojamaje turned back to Pule. "My Chief, this man has serious business. The English chief sent him to thank you for fighting Boers. The English chief wants to help us fight them."

Pule leaned forward on his chair, wagging a forefinger at Mojamaje. "The Boers do not bother us now. This is not South Africa. We drove them away, right here. You remember, Mojamaje. You stayed on this rock behind me. Tladi killed your father and uncle."

Mojamaje remembered. He raised his eyes to the red rock wall behind Pule's head. Then he looked into Pia's face. "Ha!" Pia scoffed.

One by one, BaNare men fetched their rifles and stood face-to-face with the English soldiers, holding their own rifles on their shoulders, standing at attention, mimicking the soldiers' military stance, protecting their people. Sweete noticed this new development and asked Mojamaje, "Why do these men face my soldiers with rifles?"

"A salute," Mojamaje replied. "A military salute." He turned back to Pule. "Chief," he hurried on, "I have very bad news. The English hate the Boers so much they want to put soldiers along the South African border. They claim this land for their chief. They say they will not take land or cattle. They will protect us."

Pule exploded in rage. "What!" he bellowed. "Never! I will feed this insect to the Bushmen."

Mojamaje crouched before Pule, negotiating terms. He spoke quickly, urgently, struggling to convince Pule not to fire on the English, to control his men, that the redcoats were trained troops, that thousands more English soldiers waited in South Africa.

At last Mojamaje turned, took a deep breath and declared to Sweete, "Chief Pule is honored. He welcomes the rule of your Queen. From the Chafwa River to the Xan-Xan pan, the BaNare bow to the English."

"Chafwa?" Sweete queried. "To where?"

"I will draw a map," Mojamaje replied, and the map he drew gave the BaNare far more territory than they had ever occupied, including the new Wall-Maker village along the South African border and the farthest landmark the Bushmen reported in the deep Kalahari, the bleak Xan-Xan pan. This was the trick that Mojamaje proposed to Pule, cooling the chief's ire, BaNare recognition of English rule in exchange for English recognition of a vast BaNare realm.

And then Mojamaje made his gamble. He had waited for this moment of conciliation to risk it. He said to Sweete, "Pule is so glad to have

English rule that he deserves a reward. Let the BaNare keep their guns. They will be loyal defenders of England."

Sweete wiped his handkerchief across his dimpled chin and paused to think. His orders strictly instructed him to disarm all chiefdoms. But Mojamaje's logic impressed him, to count armed chiefdoms as English allies. "Done," the colonel said at last, and Mojamaje inwardly exploded with relief. If Sweete had tried to take away the BaNare's rifles, they would have resisted. The result would have been senseless tragedy. Sweete thanked Pule and ordered his men to remount. They rode back to join the main force, leaving Mojamaje behind.

The BaNare had watched with admiration as Mojamaje spoke English to the white officer, but the moment they most eagerly awaited was a very different one. As Mojamaje had squatted before Pule, his mother moved quietly to the edge of the crowd, between two redcoats. As Mojamaje glanced up now and then while negotiating, his eyes finally met his mother's. The crowd sighed. Still straight but growing stouter, with deep lines drawn back from her narrow Bushman eyes, Ma-Mojamaje stood with her arms folded across her chest, her eyes locked on her child. Mojamaje glanced up again and again, meeting his mother's gaze. Then Sweete led his soldiers away.

Mojamaje stepped forward. As on that day nearly thirty years before, on the same spot before the red canyon wall, Ma-Mojamaje reached out to bring her son's head down into the crook of her shoulder. He threw his arms around her neck as the BaNare circled completely around them. She whispered in his ear, "Mojamaje, my son, I knew you would be a great man."

Whereupon the BaNare began to sing the song they had composed that day, in the aftermath of the Battle of the Rocks:

> All through the night
> Through the terrible fight
> Mojamaje kept watch by the door
> First he ate a rock
> Then he ate a bullet
> Then Mojamaje ate a Boer

14
English

Sweete's soldiers camped on the site of the Battle of the Woodpile. The next morning, the cloud of dust that Maka's herd stirred appeared on the eastern horizon.

"Wall-Makers!" some of the oldest BaNare cried, remembering the swirling yellow haze that announced the Wall-Maker horde at the Battle of the Woodpile. Then the first cattle became visible through the dust, red and black with magnificent horns, then brown and white, then herdboys, and the BaNare's mouths fell open as they crowded onto the ridge to gaze upon the spectacular herd filling the plain below.

"Whose cattle?" they asked excitedly.

"Who owns so many cattle?"

"It must be the English chief."

"Mojamaje, who owns them?"

And Mojamaje replied, "My wife."

All heads snapped back to the plain, all eyes searched for a woman. The sound of tramping hooves now reached the spectators, then cowbells, as the herd entered the canyon to fill it from wall to wall, the dust rising above the ridge to darken the sky. Children ran through the canyon mouth to mix with the herd, jumping atop the largest cattle, shouting, giving them names, inventing songs about Mojamaje's wife, and then suddenly the BaNare saw her. She emerged from the canyon mouth, high on a horse. As the herd spread to Naring's outskirts and slowly enveloped the village, the BaNare strained to see her clearly, to mark her features, but all they made out was a dress and a figure erect, a scarf, then the swirl of dust hid her again. Now the cattle occupied every path in Naring, as the BaNare laughed and beat them away from their compounds with sticks, rejoicing in the good fortune Mojamaje brought back from South Africa.

Mojamaje found Maka in the commotion. She swung down from her horse and he led her to the Tladi compound, into his mother's house.

The BaNare tell a story of a lion meeting a leopard on a dark winter night. Each ferocious cat trembled with cold, eyeing the other for its warm fur coat. But the lion winced at the thought of covering a beautiful lion fur with a shabby leopard skin, and the leopard thought the same about the lion. So they each skinned themselves, planning to put the other's skin on first, and their own magnificent fur on top. They exchanged furs and then crouched ready to tear apart the other, to steal its warm coat. But now the lion wore the leopard skin and the leopard wore the lion skin. The lion-turned-leopard now thought the fur of the leopard-turned-lion too ugly to wear on top of its own beautiful coat. The leopard-turned-lion thought the same about the other. So they skinned themselves again and exchanged coats. Again and again they repeated this, until they both fell panting on the cold sand, exhausted and confused. They slinked away in opposite directions, neither sure whether it was a leopard or a lion underneath its fur, hoping never to run into the other again. This is why lions and leopards inhabit different places. Leopards keep to tall trees and hills, while lions roam flat, open spaces.

Ma-Mojamaje had kept to the village she conquered so long ago. Maka had kept to the Boer farm and English mission she mastered. Now they were to meet. What would Mojamaje's mother think of Maka's yellow skin, her mask of freckles, her ignorance of village life, the stilted Boer accent she had acquired on the Roodie farm, tightly braided hair, her childlessness. . . .

A small cookfire glowed in the center of Ma-Mojamaje's round mud house. The smell of smoke and roasted meat filled the close, warm air. Ma-Mojamaje sat against the wall, her legs stretched before her, her bright green dress tight against her thighs. Her scarf hung low on her forehead, just above her eyes. She held a tin cup of tea in her hands. Maka knelt before Ma-Mojamaje, the fire to her back, so shadows shrouded her face. Its yellow hue stood out from behind the black freckles, tinging her face as yellow as her faded dress. Her red scarf was pushed back high on her head, revealing the maze of dense braids in her hair. She spoke formal greetings, the heavy roll of her Boer accent clanking against Mojamaje's ears.

Now Ma-Mojamaje opened her mouth to speak.

"They said you were English," Ma-Mojamaje said. "The BaNare from the hole said you were an English lady." Maka smiled. "They said my son was an Englishman, with an English wife. I see this is untrue. He is the same boy I held to my breast. His wife looks like me, a plain . . . BaNare."

The BaNare claim that all Naring heard Mojamaje's sigh of relief, like a gust of turbulent wind heralding a storm, rattling the roof poles of every house in the village.

Ma-Mojamaje continued. "We BaNare are simple people. I came here like you, a girl with nothing but yellow skin and Mojamaje. The BaNare mixed me up. But I washed myself three times a day and watched my manners. I knew I had what no other BaNare had—this boy, Mojamaje. When the BaNare confuse you, children stare and giggle, remember this boy, Mojamaje, your husband. They are jealous, you see. Yellow skin is not the reason. They can never forgive you for having him as your own."

Mojamaje slipped out, leaving his mother and wife to converse. He thrust his hands in his trouser pockets, whistled a tune, then added the words a Wall-Maker refugee at the Taung Mission had sung as he worked on his vegetable garden:

> Take me back to the empty veld
> Where bashee-birds fill the air . . .

At this moment Old Man De Swart drove a wagonful of firewood past the Tladi family compound on his way back to his house along the hills. When Jeedo Parido's song floated to his ears, the old Boer cursed the sky and did not even bother to look around for the singer, convinced that the song had come back on its own power to haunt him, to hover at his ear, driving him to madness and an early grave.

Mojamaje and Maka slept the night in one of the Tladi compound's storehouses. Mojamaje left the next morning with Sweete's army, leading them along the edge of the Kalahari, north toward Rhodesia. The BaNare know nothing of his adventures on this journey, for no one from Naring ever visited these places. They know only that he returned a month later with his horse's tail cut off and a festering sore on the animal's flank. Mojamaje's fine English clothes were in tatters.

"What happened?" the BaNare asked in dismay.

Mojamaje dismounted, tore off his black coat and threw it on the ground in disgust.

"English!" he spat.

Ologo ran up, took the reins from Mojamaje's hand, and led the horse down to the stream to drink. Mojamaje spoke not another word about the expedition. But Ologo found out the truth, or so he claimed, by drawing out details from Mojamaje over a span of several weeks. Ologo reported that the Kgama army had regrouped beyond the South African border after their initial defeat by the English army that preceded Sweete's column. When Mojamaje led Sweete into Rhodesia to meet them, the Kgama promised to keep out of South Africa. Sweete demanded they turn in their rifles as well. They refused. Sweete attacked. "English!" Ologo spat, his eyes wide with excitement. "They butchered the Kgama like cattle."

The BaNare never asked Mojamaje again about his travels with Sweete. They appreciated now how well he had handled the English when Sweete's column stopped in Naring. They pitied the brave Kgama, about whom they knew nothing, for no Kgama refugee ever settled in Naring. And so they tried to forget Ologo's horrible story.

But the English did not forget. Searching the Kgama battlefield, they failed to find Mojamaje among the dead. Back in Kimberley, Sweete reported him a deserter. It was not worth another trip to track him down in Naring, so instead the English filed the report away. They established in Taung, near the mission grounds, a headquarters for administering the distant Kalahariland Territory, and moved the report of Mojamaje's desertion to a file in the new office.

15
Dinti the Ostrich

Mojamaje distributed the great herd among the BaNare, entrusting a dozen animals to each herder. The first female calf born became the property of the herder, and all its offspring thereafter. The others belonged to Mojamaje and Maka. Then Mojamaje and Maka taught the BaNare to plow. The BaNare had taught themselves to yoke their oxen to wagons and drive them with whips, but never in a straight row, and no one knew how to handle a plow.

On the day he and Maka revealed the secret of the plow, Mojamaje borrowed the wagon of his cousin Tabo Cross-Eyes and drove it past the BaNare hoe fields clustered around the village. He whipped the oxen over the Stinkface plain to the Moseke pastures, renowned for their red-black soil. A caravan of BaNare wagons followed. The Tladi family unloaded the wagon and Ma-Mojamaje and Leana, Tabo's wife, began to build a home. Mojamaje and Maka set out to plow. They unhitched the oxen from the wagon, yoked them to the plow, and took turns guiding the team with the whip and holding the plow. The BaNare sat down to watch. In a week the Tladi family had a rough compound built and forty acres plowed and planted. In that same time a hand-held hoe could plant one acre. Camped by the side of the growing field, taking turns holding the plow as Mojamaje and Maka shouted instructions, tripping and stumbling over the furrows until finally catching the rhythm, the BaNare saw endless possibilities in the new device, a sprawling countryside to turn up and plant.

The women watched the plow blade, which they blessed for the work it would save them. Men, who never hoed anyway, watched Maka. Truly the daughter of Drift, her dress wet with sweat against her slim breasts, eyes shining with the pleasure of work, Maka skipped along the furrow or snapped the whip in perfect precision, swinging her hips like her magnificent mother. When she showed the young men how to guide the plow, they watched her instead of the blade. She rolled her head back and laughed the breathless, enrapt boys to shame.

When the BaNare returned to Naring, they rushed to De Swart's shop to trade their cattle for plows. They fanned out everywhere and plowed. Soon Naring was awash with corn. And then at night, first out in the plow fields but then back in the Tladi compound, Mojamaje began to tell stories. At first he waited for the old men to finish, until a long silence begged for a new voice. Then he introduced a plowing tale, illustrating some fine point of turning the soil, then expanding the story to describe the plowman, then the plowman's people, then all South Africa. One by one he explained the fates of villages, whole peoples no longer at large, names vanished forever, and slowly the BaNare understood. These were things he learned in Taung and he wanted the BaNare to know them.

An old man pointed a wrinkled, crusty finger to his eyebrow and said, "Does Mojamaje mention the BaNare? No. His tales of destruction say nothing of us. The boys back from the diamond hole say that other miners laugh at us because the Kalahari is our home. But they are only jealous." The old man kept his finger against his eyebrow. "We BaNare survived the Boers. We are still in one piece."

Mojamaje slipped away as others disputed the old man's conclusion. Debate ensued, then someone said, "But what about the English?"

They called Mojamaje back and he explained, "I do not know about the English. We will see. I think they will leave us alone."

Maka told stories too, of love on the Roodie farm and the mission. BaNare men had ventured to Kimberley but the stories they brought back to Naring lacked female appeal. Women did not thrill to hear about knife fights in the mine compound, wild carousal in the township, stupid Boer foremen and the price of beer. BaNare women inquired about more intimate matters. Maka showed the whites of her huge eyes as she told of the tenant village on the farm, of Bintu and Zhefa men from distant places with ideas about love play very different from those of the Taung girls they pursued, how they tried to stick themselves into all the wrong places, how the girls' brothers defended their honor and sent the miscreants running for their lives.

Ma-Mojamaje told stories too, but to Maka alone, instructing her in BaNare ways. In this she was truly the leading expert, for no one else had struggled so hard to become a true BaNare. She was now more BaNare than the original BaNare. Now that young men came and went from South Africa, bringing back all sorts of bad manners, as refugee slang corrupted daily speech, no one watched over the pure BaNare life as did Ma-Mojamaje, BaKii child of an earlier age. She shepherded Maka through her rounds, down to the stream for water, to the cow pen for building dung, to Old Man De Swart's shop for tea and salt, standing beside her at weddings and funerals. And when women came to press Maka openly about her childlessness, Ma-Mojamaje rushed to her defense.

Harvest, another winter, a new Englishman arrived in Naring. He drove a wagon into the center of the village and began to build a shop. He wore a long moustache like Colonel Sweete's, above a cleanly shaved jaw, and his brown cowhide boots were beautiful, reaching to his knees. The BaNare took one look and named him Dithakotseditona, meaning "Big Boots." He bore a shop license from the English office in Taung. Pule summoned Mojamaje to read the license and he did so, confirming the Englishman's claim to trade in Naring. Pule cursed the English.

"I am chief of Naring," Pule cried, thumping his chest with one hand, waving the license in the other. Mojamaje suggested that Pule issue his own license and wrote one out for Pule to sign with an x. Pule did so and waved it in Big Boots's face.

"How much?" the Englishman asked.

"Five pounds," Mojamaje replied.

Big Boots extracted a roll of bills from his pocket and handed a five-pound note to Mojamaje, who handed the money to Pule. "I am chief of Naring," Pule repeated, stuffing the note into his leopard coat.

The BaNare marveled at Big Boots's new shop, twice the size of Old Man De Swart's, fully stocked with everything shops in Kimberley sold. The BaNare traded cattle and skins, which Big Boots sent on to Joburg. No one but De Swart objected to his presence until Pule's son, Pia the Scornful, wandered by, up the steps, into Big Boots's back room. Once a week Pia sneered his way through the village to the English shop, swinging his cane, brushing dust from the sleeves of his suit. What did he do in Big Boots's back room?

The BaNare debated this question long into the night.

"English," someone suggested. "Big Boots teaches him English."

The other BaNare agreed immediately. Sure enough, Pia's "Ha!" took on an odd accent, and then he began insulting passersby in a foreign language. One day he did so near Mojamaje and the BaNare rushed to ask what Pia had said.

"You do not want to know," Mojamaje replied. "I do not wish to repeat it. Yes, it was an insult. Yes, an English insult."

Big Boots was teaching Pia English: what could Pia offer in return? The BaNare shuddered. Pia would someday be chief and who knows what tricks he and the trader might concoct?

The BaNare's apprehension turned to raw fear when a third conspirator appeared in Pia's company. This was Tabo Cross-Eyes, Mojamaje's cousin. Tabo had fulfilled the promise of his childhood, growing into a man of enormous size, ambition and contradiction. He sometimes seemed a friendly giant, his good eye beaming to all around him. Other times he glowered and fumed, his bad eye bubbling with violence and greed. He married a distant cousin, Leana Nna, who was the only BaNare who believed that both Tabo's eyes were good. Her friends had begged her not to marry him, warning that Tabo Cross-Eyes was destined to follow in Tladi's footsteps, regardless of how kind he sometimes appeared. Leana stared into Tabo's face, at one eye and then the other, straining to detect the evil leer that everyone else insisted was there. Try as she might, she never could see it.

Tabo Cross-Eyes crossed Ma-Mojamaje's famous woodpile, entered the Potso family compound, and spoke in low whispers with Pia the Scornful. The BaNare wondered what they were up to. Then someone pointed out that Pia had two healthy sons, while Leana had borne Tabo

Cross-Eyes five sickly boys who each died before his first birthday. Clearly, Tabo's bad eye had killed the infants. He was waiting for daughters, to marry Pia's sons. He and Pia were discussing the deal. Sure enough, soon after Tabo became a regular visitor at Pia's house, Leana bore a daughter. A year later she bore another. Leana held her breath and prayed for their health, unable to bear the anguish of burying another child. As the BaNare expected, the infants enjoyed perfect health. Before either girl grew teeth, Tabo announced their betrothal to Pia the Scornful's two sons.

The seeds of conspiracy sprouted beneath the BaNare's feet: Pia's sons and Tabo's daughters would marry to merge the two largest herds in Naring. Pia's was the chiefly herd, passed down from Potso to Pule and someday to him. Tabo Cross-Eyes' daughters stood to inherit the Tladi family herd. As the son of Tladi's eldest son, Tabo was senior to Mojamaje, who was the son of Tladi's younger son. Tabo did have an older brother, Dinti the Ostrich, but everyone knew Dinti would never find a wife. Dinti had only made it through childhood because Tabo, guided by his good eye and brandishing a tree branch, protected him from the teasing and torments of other boys. Without a wife, Dinti the Ostrich would not leave an heir. The daughters of his younger brother, Tabo, would inherit the Tladi family herd.

And so the BaNare cringed as Pia the Scornful, Big Boots and Tabo Cross-Eyes joined forces. Pia's sons and Tabo's daughters would marry and inherit a fabulous fortune in cattle. Big Boots, Pia's crony, was the BaNare's only outlet for cattle sales to Joburg. And Pia and Big Boots spoke a language no one but Mojamaje could understand. Bit by bit the BaNare pieced together a frightful future.

Then suddenly, miraculously, the BaNare discovered a way out. It was really so simple. After one of the many debates on the subject, as the dejected participants wandered away, someone muttered, "If only Dinti the Ostrich would find a wife."

The others turned, and the idea came to them all at once. "We will find him one," they said in chorus.

If Dinti produced an heir, Tabo's daughters would not inherit the Tladi family wealth. And so the BaNare's last hopes fell on the blubbery shoulders of Dinti the Ostrich. Such a serious situation demanded drastic action. He would never find a wife on his own. No one disliked Dinti, but young women testified that they would not marry him if all the other men in the world turned to scorpions and vanished into cracks in dead trees. Just hearing tales of Dinti's wavering, how he thrust his head into the sand when the smallest decision came his way, drove women mad with frustration.

The BaNare thus faced two problems: forcing Dinti the Ostrich to decide to marry, and finding a woman who would take him. They began with the first question.

"Who can we offer him?"

"Who would he ever propose to?"

A few names were mentioned, but then the choice became obvious: Bosio Night Girl, the beautiful face.

At the time, the BaNare had no way of knowing the importance of this choice for the story of the Great Thirst. There should have at least been a few suspicions, though, because soon after Bosio's birth everyone admitted that her face was the loveliest in the world. Her parents were refugees, and the BaNare are not certain that they had even given her the name Bosio, meaning "Night." But everyone called her Bosio, for obvious reasons. Her skin was so dark that it shimmered with hues of black, violet and blue, giving her face an unearthly glow. Her eyes were enormous, wide, white circles against the black of her face, with pupils as deep black as her skin. Her nose was flat and narrow, above full, dark lips that parted to reveal perfect long teeth. Her face held the calm mystery of shadows on a moonlit night. Other BaNare children were shy around her, conscious of her beauty.

Long before the Dinti crisis, though, the BaNare had decided Bosio's future. She would grow up to marry Paulus the Lover, youngest child of Old Man De Swart, whom the BaNare all agreed was the handsomest boy in the world. This was quite a compliment, for white skins reminded them of ghosts and pigs. They called him Paulus the Lover in anticipation of his destiny, eager to exchange rumors about his romances. Mothers feared for their daughters, expecting Paulus the Lover to break hearts. Even by the age of five he looked like a strong, handsome man, with clear blue eyes, a square jaw, skin burned tawny and rough by the dry winter wind, thick yellow hair that glowed like the sun. Paulus inspired in other children the same distant awe that Bosio Night Girl did. Were they not ordained to meet, to fall in love?

So it seemed at the time, but their childhoods passed without the two gorgeous youths meeting. Both retained their bashful ignorance of their beauty. Playmates recoiled at their magnificence, and Bosio and Paulus took this to mean no one liked them. Quiet, withdrawn, they became brooding adults, but this only added to their mysterious appeal. When the Dinti crisis arose, some BaNare protested the choice of Bosio to solve it. She deserved to marry Paulus the Lover. But most BaNare were more worried about the sheer enormity of the task, of how to push Dinti and Bosio together. Surely he would find a thousand excuses for procrastination. Saying a single word to the girl would take him a year of preparation. The BaNare cringed at the prospect of convincing Dinti the Ostrich to act.

In the end, they asked Mojamaje to do it.

"Why Bosio?" Mojamaje asked.

"Her beautiful face."

"Does she have other suitors?" Mojamaje inquired.

"Not one."

Mojamaje said, "Why not?"

"The boys are afraid to pursue her."

"She will reject them."

"In favor of the handsome boy of her dreams."

"And who is that?" Mojamaje asked.

"Paulus De Swart, the Lover."

"So she will marry Paulus the Lover," Mojamaje concluded.

"No!" the BaNare cried.

"Dinti needs a wife!"

Reluctantly, Mojamaje agreed to speak with Dinti. He found him in Tabo Cross-Eyes' compound, adjacent to the large compound that Ma-Mojamaje had built for the Tladi family her first year in Naring. Dinti was already bald and fat, with enormous black trousers hanging to his ankles, an old gray shirt buttoned to the neck, and bare feet. He sat on the mud floor of the compound, holding on his knees the daughters of his younger brother, Tabo, bouncing them gently, stirring a pot of porridge on the nearby cookfire. Mojamaje greeted Dinti and Leana, sat down beside Dinti, and took one of the children in his lap. The girls were named Koko and Keke and the BaNare already referred to them as the wives of Pia's eldest sons, Pono and Peke, foreseeing the day when Koko, Keke, Pono and Peke would rule all Naring.

As Mojamaje and Dinti chatted, the girls continued to sing, Leana continued to hum, happy and proud finally to present Tabo with healthy children. She had heard the rumors of conspiracy between Tabo and Pia the Scornful, but she still insisted that both Tabo's eyes were good. There was still no evidence to the contrary, only idle speculation and that terrible name, Cross-Eyes, which Tabo had borne since childhood. She was pleased now, and wished only that the BaNare would trust Tabo as she did. He was her gentle giant, matching her loyalty with gentle affection.

"Dinti," Mojamaje said at last, "I must tell you the truth. Tladi's eldest son was Tumo, who was my father's elder brother, the sentry at the Battle of the Rocks. Tumo's eldest son is you. The BaNare think that the senior heir of an important family like ours should marry and leave an heir. I told them to mind their own business. They asked me to talk to you. I tell you this now to let you know what the people say. I do not urge you to marry." Koko and Keke cut short their song to eye each other with concern. "But Dinti," Mojamaje continued, "I want you to be happy. Do you want a wife?"

Dinti's plump smile faded to consternation as Mojamaje spoke. Now he grimaced as if struck a deadly blow. He sighed, shrugged his shoulders and replied, "Who?"

"Any wife," Mojamaje said. "Just a wife. Do you want one?"

"I would not want just any wife," Dinti replied.

"The wife of your choice. Do you want a wife?"

"It depends," Dinti said.

"On what?"

"Who she is," Dinti asserted.

"If you had the choice of all the unmarried women in Naring," Mojamaje said slowly, searching for words that might overcome timorous Dinti's evasive logic, "would you choose one or remain unmarried?"

"I do not know all the unmarried women in Naring. Not every one would have me. I do not have this choice."

Mojamaje changed his approach. "Dinti, if a girl asked you to marry her, would you agree?"

"It depends on which one."

"If you liked her," Mojamaje added.

"How could I know?"

"If you saw her every day," Mojamaje pressed.

"Leana is the only woman I see every day. She is married to my brother."

Mojamaje began to see that the BaNare were right: if they did not force a woman on Dinti, he would never marry.

"How about Bosio?" Mojamaje asked.

Dinti cowered. "She is beautiful," he stammered.

"Would you marry her if she wanted you?"

Dinti recovered to reply, "She does not know I exist."

Judging his duty done, Mojamaje left Dinti to think, Leana to stir, and Koko and Keke to worry. He reported the conversation to the BaNare, concluding, "It is hopeless."

The BaNare thanked him, rushed to Tabo's compound, pulled Koko and Keke off Dinti's knees, picked Dinti up and carried him across the village to the compound of Bosio Night Girl. They chanted and danced, tied Dinti in blankets, burst into Bosio's house, tied her in blankets too, carried them both to the top of the ridge and along its crest to an empty cave. They pushed the two bundles into the cavern and ran away. By the time Dinti and Bosio had unwrapped themselves and struggled to their feet, they were completely alone and the sun had set.

16
Girl of the Night

The marriage of Dinti the Ostrich and Bosio Night Girl was marked by one of the largest feasts the BaNare had ever thrown. Almost every family in Naring contributed a goat, adding their blessing to the miraculous union. At the feast, they watched carefully for Tabo Cross-Eyes, Pia ya Pipa, or Paulus the Lover to show some sign of disappointment. But Tabo seemed as genial, Pia seemed as scornful, and Paulus seemed as bashful and handsome as ever, unaffected by Dinti's sudden change of fortune.

To the BaNare's surprise and delight, Dinti and Bosio had spent the night in the cave and announced their betrothal the very next day. Perhaps, the BaNare thought, they had underestimated Dinti the Ostrich. Or perhaps they had misjudged Bosio. She had been available for marriage for years but her life had been lonely. In truth, she thought the cause to be her own ugliness. Who might have set the poor girl straight? When Dinti the Ostrich appeared in a blanket, she concluded that this was as close to a proposal as she would ever receive. She suggested marriage and lay beside Dinti in the darkened cave arguing him to acquiescence.

After the wedding the BaNare waited for Bosio's first child. A year passed but her belly stayed flat. One night, two years after the wedding, the house of Bosio erupted in flames. Of the several fires in the story of the Great Thirst, this one remains the most mysterious. No year passed without at least one grass roof catching fire from lightning or cookfire sparks, but the fire that burned Bosio Night Girl's house occurred on a still summer night with no clouds in the sky and Bosio kept her cookfire outside the house, even on cold winter nights. With no good reason for her roof to catch fire, the BaNare looked for bad reasons. They did not look far. Tabo Cross-Eyes wanted his daughters to be principal Tladi family heirs. He set fire to the house to kill Dinti and Bosio before they produced a child.

But Tabo was the hero of the fire. He rushed to tear the door away and dashed inside as the roof collapsed. Sheets of fire flared in the dark. Tabo dragged Dinti and Bosio to safety, but not before burning thatch fell across Bosio's face. Why would Tabo set fire to the house, only to risk his life in the rescue of his victims? This question troubled the BaNare until they reached this conclusion: Tabo's bad eye led him to murder his rival brother, then his good eye moved Tabo to rescue him.

Dinti the Ostrich was dazed but unscarred. He lay with his eyes closed outside the burning house, unable to decide whether he was alive or dead. He remembered the flames, the strong arm beneath him, did it carry him to safety or to another world? He listened carefully to the commotion around him. Recognizing familiar voices, he opened his eyes. He was alive.

"Bosio!" he cried in a frenzy of worry.

Leana rushed to throw her arms around Dinti, saying, "Bosio is well. She is in my compound. There is a small burn on her face. It makes her shy. We must wait, dear Dinti."

"What shall I do?" he asked, distress choking his throat.

"Wait," Leana replied.

So Dinti waited for Bosio to recover from the shock of her wound. She allowed no one into the storehouse in Tabo's compound, except for his daughters, Koko and Keke, skinny, bashful girls, unable to raise their eyes to meet an adult's, their hands always covering their mouths. Although they were a year apart in age, no one could tell Koko and Keke apart, thin-faced, wide-eyed, with the hushed voices of bandits in conspiracy. At such a tender age, their waists where their knees would eventually grow, the girls inspired no suspicion of what in fact they discussed so furtively under their breaths.

Koko and Keke devoted themselves to Bosio's care, reporting her progress to the concerned people of Naring. Koko and Keke described the scar as light lavender, covering one cheek and running down her neck to end in a point between her breasts. They swore that the scar made Bosio more lovely than before. Bosio herself thought the opposite. Her lonely childhood, the aloof awe of her peers, had convinced her that she was a hideous hag. Now this horrible scar marked her as such for life. Even Dinti the Ostrich would disdain her now, averting his eyes from her disgraceful wound. She resolved never again to allow the light of day to strike her face. Koko and Keke relayed this verdict to the BaNare, who recoiled in astonishment and pity.

Dinti collapsed in despair. The BaNare urged him to force his way into the house.

"I cannot," Dinti replied. "She hides her head. I have turned her into an ostrich. It is all my fault. Look what I have done."

The BaNare paused to digest this declaration—strong stuff, coming from Dinti. He followed these words with another revelation: "I have decided to become a man. I will deserve Bosio Night Girl. Then she will pull her head from the sand."

"Shades of Ra-Mojamaje," the BaNare lamented—yet another unfortunate boy realizing too late the rigors of love.

Dinti disappeared. Months passed, then a young man back from the Joburg gold mines reported seeing Dinti at work there. He was no longer fat, he worked hard but the other miners gave him a hard time, teasing and tormenting him about his vexing indecision. They stole his clothes, tools and food, locked him underground at the end of shifts, leaving him alone for hours in the dark, steamy tunnels. Months later another man back from the mines reported that Dinti was injured in a knife fight. A year later another miner reported that Dinti was dead, crushed by an explosion in a supposedly abandoned, empty tunnel where the men in Dinti's barrack had locked him inside.

The news struck Naring to silence. Koko and Keke told Bosio, whose cries filled the night for weeks thereafter.

"I killed him," she moaned. "My ugly face drove him to death!"

No amount of protest by Koko and Keke could alter her judgment. Leana, Ma-Dinti, Ma-Mojamaje and Maka stood at her door, shouting the truth to the forlorn woman. But Bosio refused to believe them. They would say anything to cheer her.

When Bosio's crying stopped, Koko and Keke reported that she began walking at night. They woke from their tiny beds alongside hers, watching with curious eyes as she stole out the door, into the dark. The BaNare recognized walking at night as the first sign of lunacy. Afraid to face human beings, Bosio roamed like an animal, conversing with bats and spirits of the dead.

17

Seantlo

A year after Dinti's death, while Mojamaje wandered deep in the Kalahari to trade with the Bushmen, fox and jackal skins for plugs of tobacco, Tabo Cross-Eyes made an announcement. "The Law of Seantlo commands me to act," he said.

This was all the BaNare needed to end once and for all the debate on Tabo's character. "At last," they concluded, nodding their heads in grim confirmation, "the bad eye opens to reveal its intent."

Leana threw herself against Tabo's massive bulk, beating her forehead against his chest. "No!" she cried. "They cannot be right. This cannot be true. Show me your good eye, Tabo my dear!"

But Tabo's eye gleamed with a new oily luster that not even Leana could ignore. The BaNare tried continually to forget the ancient Law of Seantlo. When a man died without an heir, the law entitled his brother to claim Seantlo, by which he entered the house of the dead man's widow to raise an heir in his stead. This Seantlo child belonged to the dead man, not to the living brother who fathered the child.

Tabo's announcement surprised only Leana. Every man in the village longed to stroke Bosio's exquisite face, to rescue her from her lonely madness.

The evening after his announcement, Tabo threw open the door to the storehouse in his compound, now Bosio's house, and ordered Koko and Keke to leave. Tabo slammed the door behind.

When the BaNare interrogated Koko and Keke the next morning, the two girls spoke with one tiny voice, in soft whispers behind their hands. "She hit him," they said. "We heard a sound, like the iron cooking pot hitting our father's head. Then we heard another sound, like our father hitting the ground. The door opened just before dawn. He crawled out, rubbing his head."

The BaNare considered the possibility that the girls had invented the story to spare their father the ignominy of his deed. Lately the girls' perfect synchrony, their conspiratorial glances, had aroused the first glimmers of BaNare suspicions. But Tabo wore a hat for a month after the incident: no one remembered him ever wearing a hat before. The true test was Bosio's belly, and sure enough a few months later Koko and Keke reported it swelling.

Leana fell ill, swooning with anguish. Maka and Ma-Mojamaje attended her, mopping her fevered brow, dripping water onto her thirsty lips, holding her down when she erupted in fits. Tabo roamed the village in silence, a wounded buffalo reeling from beer pot to beer pot, retching into his hands, rubbing his hands on his face. Leana's fever and Tabo's dissipation lasted through Bosio's pregnancy. Finally Koko and Keke rushed out to announce that the Seantlo child was coming. The women burst in to assist the birth.

It was a girl. In acknowledgment of their loyal service, Koko and Keke were given the privilege of carrying her out to the crowd assembling before Ma-Mojamaje's famous woodpile. The girls faced each other, their skinny arms laced beneath the swaddled infant. Inching their way forward out of the compound, they stood before the BaNare. Ma-Mojamaje pulled aside the blanket to show the infant's face.

It was white. The crowd gasped. Or almost white, but certainly not black like Bosio or black like Tabo. The father of this child could only be white. The BaNare pondered this puzzle, calling out to each other for clues. In no time they solved the riddle: first one neighbor, then another, twelve altogether, reported a shock of yellow hair on top of a figure walking at night out toward the Kalahari, in the direction Koko and Keke reported Bosio walking, at about the same time that Tabo attempted Seantlo. Two of the witnesses insisted they recognized the hair as belonging to Paulus the Lover.

The BaNare reached rapid consensus that Paulus was the father of Bosio's infant, although legally, by the Law of Seantlo, the child was Dinti's. The BaNare looked again at the child in Koko and Keke's arms, pushing back the blankets to reveal its full form. The tiny face was beautiful, the same graceful shape as Bosio's, with the same mysterious glow to its skin. The BaNare looked closer, closer, and gasped again: along one cheek, down its delicate neck, a faint pink mark stood out against the ivory of the Seantlo child's skin. It was the brand of beauty, identical to Bosio's scar. The BaNare immediately named the infant Seele, meaning "mark," and composed this song to remember her:

> Face of beauty, child of woe
> Dinti the Ostrich dead below
> Face of nighttime, empty dreams
> Tabo Cross-Eyes what he seems
> Face of lonely, blind allure
> Paulus, bashful Lover, Boer
> Face of blackness, jealous sun
> Bosio Night Girl trusts no one
> Face of beauty, marked for life
> Seele child of Seantlo wife

Thereafter the BaNare watched carefully for Paulus the Lover to acknowledge his deed, but he never did. Nor did he ever deny the truth of the tale. The child's beauty proved once and for all that Paulus was Bosio Night Girl's perfect match.

Bosio Night Girl remained in her house. Koko and Keke reported that she no longer walked at night. She loved the infant but ran her fingers again and again along Seele's pink mark. The BaNare feared the child would grow up as odd as her mother, convinced of her ugliness, recoiling from all human contact save the most furtive kind. They vowed to ease the girl's passage to adulthood, to shepherd her to a normal life. But they lost their opportunity a year after the child's birth. Koko and Keke reported one morning that Bosio took Seele away in the night. She tied the infant to her back and slipped out the door, then away, out of Naring, at home only in the same enchanted darkness that imprisoned her face.

18
Maka's Hope

These tragedies worried Mojamaje and Maka by day, but by night they lay immune, untouchable, lost in each other's arms and legs and delighting in the fruits of their love that Maka's memory once had denied them. Still no child, and they wondered why. Ma-Mojamaje mixed potions from ancient BaKii recipes she had learned in her youth, adding pinches of Bushman secrets, a dab of BaNare spice. Maka drank them, spread them between her legs, sprinkled them over her blankets, rubbed them into her hair. Nothing worked. Her belly stayed flat. If nothing else, she envied Bosio Night Girl her child.

Each year, after plowing, while the corn sprouted and took care of itself, Mojamaje took long journeys deep into the Kalahari to trade with the Bushmen for skins and pelts. The quiet of the desert soothed him, as in his youth, alone with his cattle, the tiny desert birds, the wind. He left the Tladi compound early in the morning, to reach the crest of the sand slope just as the sun appeared over the hills on the opposite side of the village. He waited until the rock wall at the canyon mouth, where he spent the Battle of the Rocks, broke from shadow to explode in a flash of orange, the low sun reflecting its smooth face to Mojamaje. Then he disappeared into the desert.

Once while Mojamaje was gone, Chief Pule fell sick, his face ashen, suddenly developing a crop of hairy moles, blood spurting like rain from his nose. Pule refused to die, so week after week the sorcerers burned potions in goat horns, danced the sholasha, cut scars in his cheeks, and vomited lizard bones. Nothing worked. Yet he grew no worse.

Pia ya Pipa declared himself Acting Chief. His first official act was to announce that only Big Boots had official authority to sell cattle outside the district, and that anyone selling cattle to Big Boots had to buy a license from the Acting Chief for half the price of the cattle. The BaNare howled. They refused to sell a single beast. Then Tabo Cross-Eyes delivered thirty fat oxen to Big Boots's store, waving a license from Pia. The BaNare were outraged. Their fears of conspiracy had been well founded. And news from South Africa made the whole thing seem even worse. Prospectors had found some gold in Rhodesia and the English quickly convinced themselves that another Joburg lay waiting beneath the ground. Hundreds of wagons drove from Kimberley through Taung to Rhodesia. A railway had just reached Kimberley from the coast, and now the English began extending it to Joburg and Rhodesia. Thousands of wagon travelers and thousands of railway workers needed meat to eat, and Pia, Big Boots, and Tabo planned to sell it to them, excluding everyone else in Naring from the trade.

BaNare met in small groups, some armed with rifles, plotting to foil the treacherous scheme. Naring exploded with rumors. Someone fired a shot through Tabo Cross-Eyes' roof. Big Boots slept in his shop with his rifle across his chest, and awoke one morning to find eight of the cattle Tabo had delivered thrashing on the ground, their shin tendons sliced through with a knife.

Then suddenly a hush fell over Naring. The BaNare stopped to notice, falling quiet. Not a leaf stirred. All stood still and listened as the silence turned deadly and in one fell gust a wind rushed down from the north. Too warm for a winter wind, too dry for a summer wind, this gust blew down the great forest rivers and swamps far beyond South Africa, to lick lightly every blade of grass, every grain of soil, every tree and rock on the face of the land, sweeping up the nostrils of horses and cattle, graying their hides, peeling the hide away, leaving the beasts skinless, glistening like maggots in the sun.

This was the rinderpest, plague of destruction. It blew to Naring, out to Loang, to Taung, Joburg, Kimberley, Rhodesia, across South Africa to the coast. Everywhere wagons lay still, everywhere cattle lay dead.

The BaNare blamed the English. They blamed Pia. They beat their fists in the lethal breeze and blamed themselves. They struggled to think of an explanation, some reason for this ghastly visitation, a scourge that defied all memory. The BaNare had no word for it. No one knew what it was. One by one, BaNare men departed for the Joburg mines. Their wealth vanished, they cursed every step that took them farther from home, they cursed the mines where they signed on to dig. They cursed the Boer foremen, brawled with fellow miners, and saved every shilling they earned. When their rage subsided to grief, they asked whether others had seen the same thing.

"Yes," other miners replied. "We are paupers too."

A drought came slowly but the rinderpest plague came in a flash. A drought lasted years but the rinderpest lasted only a month. It swept past and the odd cow that survived struggled to its feet and chewed grass as if nothing had happened. Which was worse, drought or this plague?

The rinderpest ended Pia's plot. There were no cattle left to sell. Mojamaje found out about the rinderpest while walking home from a Kalahari trading trip, encountering carcasses of antelope every mile, some heaped in herds of thousands. The other desert animals escaped completely. Vultures feasted until they could no longer fly, hyenas until they could no longer walk. Then, approaching Naring, Mojamaje came across dead cattle, and he learned the full measure of the disaster.

Dozens of fires glowed through Naring, the cookfires of somber feasts, songless, danceless. The BaNare gorged themselves on roast meat, carving up other cattle into long strips to dry on hooks. But animals died so quickly that most rotted where they fell.

At night, in their house in the Tladi compound, Maka reached for Mojamaje's hand and drew it to her face, pressing his fingers against the lines behind her eyes. "Yes," she said softly, "you should go. You are educated. You can earn much more than the other men." Mojamaje lay down beside her. The room was completely dark. He said nothing. "And you are curious," Maka continued. "The way you ask about South Africa. You want to see it again. You wander the desert, you are so restless."

Still Mojamaje said nothing, and his silence bespoke assent. "I will miss you," Maka said at last.

"I will not be gone long," Mojamaje replied.

He gently ran his fingers over her face, up the points of her ears, her breasts, fixing every detail to memory. Neither spoke a word about their greatest concern—they took action instead, another hopeful attempt, and on this night, the eve of Mojamaje's return to South Africa, they conceived their first child.

NALEDI

Tladis

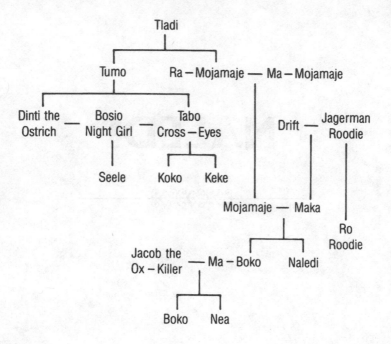

Tladi
├─ Tumo
│   ├─ Dinti the Ostrich — Bosio Night Girl — Tabo Cross-Eyes
│   │   │   ├─ Koko
│   │   Seele   └─ Keke
│   └─
Ra–Mojamaje — Ma–Mojamaje
Drift — Jagerman Roodie
Mojamaje — Maka
├─ Ma–Boko
└─ Naledi
Ro Roodie
Jacob the Ox–Killer — Ma–Boko
├─ Boko
└─ Nea

Potsos

De Swarts

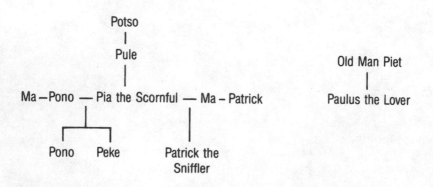

Potso
│
Pule
│
Ma–Pono — Pia the Scornful — Ma–Patrick
├─ Pono
├─ Peke
Patrick the Sniffler

Old Man Piet
│
Paulus the Lover

And so once more Mojamaje set out for South Africa. Months passed, and Maka's belly swelled to a staggering girth. The BaNare women feared that her narrow hips might burst when the child finally forced its way through. Maka's spirits soared with pride and relief, bathing her in a glorious glow that reddened her skin and darkened her freckles. She hummed, sang, rubbed her stomach with mud and ashes, danced in the rain, brewed wild herbs into broth and smeared it on her face.

Maka was attended by Ma-Mojamaje, Ma-Dinti, Leana, and Koko and Keke. Except for Ma-Mojamaje, she was in the hands of Tabo's family, his daughters, wife and mother. Tladi's wife had died soon after Maka arrived in Naring, while Ma-Dinti, Tumo's wife, remained like a sister to Ma-Mojamaje. She was nothing like the frightened rabbit that Ma-Mojamaje had found when she first entered the compound with Mojamaje on her back. The two women grew old together, looking more and more alike. Their breasts sagged low beneath their faded dresses, their head scarves hung low over their foreheads, almost covering their eyes, they walked with their hands clasped behind their backs, bent forward at the waist. They attended Maka with merry delirium, eager to cuddle the coming infant, for the Tladi family compound had less than its share of children. Koko and Keke were the only ones since Mojamaje, Dinti and Tabo grew up, except for the brief appearance of Seele, Seantlo child.

On a rainy summer night, Maka awoke with piercing pains in her belly. Her screams drew women from all over the neighborhood. They mixed up a salve and an elixir, administered both, then Maka began to bleed. Frightened now, Ma-Mojamaje tried the most powerful remedy the BaNare knew, the product of centuries of sorcerers' wisdom. Maka drank it. The bleeding doubled in force. The women decided Maka was dying. They had seen this happen so many times before.

Ma-Mojamaje cried, "The English doctor!"

The women gasped in dismay. Two months before, the Taung station had sent a missionary to Naring. He claimed to be a doctor, but the BaNare had not yet let him touch them. And men were forbidden even to set eyes on a woman in childbirth.

"Though he is a man," Ma-Dinti declared, "Maka is dying. There is nothing to lose."

The rain poured down in torrents outside, turning the earth to mud. Thunder and lightning assaulted the sky. Every wagon in the village sank to its axles in mud. The vicious rain deafened and blinded all the oxen that might have pulled the wagons out. Without a wagon, how could they take Maka to the Englishman? His tiny brick church stood on the far end of Naring, three miles away, too far to send a messenger. By the time the missionary arrived at the Tladi compound, Maka would be dead.

Leana called, "Tabo!" and dashed out into the rain. She yanked her husband from their house and ducked back in to push him toward Maka. Tabo Cross-Eyes filled the room with his enormous bulk. A candle lit by Maka's bedside revealed her freckled face contorted with agony. Bending down, dripping with rain, his huge bald head reflecting the candle-light, Tabo picked Maka up, blankets and all. The women threw more blankets on top, covering them both completely save for a narrow space for Tabo to peer out.

Tabo stepped out into the night with Maka in his arms, taking long sure strides through the mud. Again and again lightning sparked the sky as BaNare looked out from under their grass eaves to see his massive shape, doubled by the bundle in his arms, marching across the village. Again and again he sank to his knees, steadied himself, pushed on. Men and women ran out to help, supporting him until they themselves fell one by one. Others took their places, the driving icy rain cutting their eyes, they fell, others took their places. Tabo moved quickly through Naring, almost at a run, leaving behind a trail of BaNare helpers sprawled in the mud.

The missionary was sitting at his lamplit desk when the door burst open and a mass of dark crimson mud, six feet tall and six feet wide, charged at him with the speed of a horse. The missionary recoiled in terror. In one swift motion Tabo swung Maka down onto the desk and disappeared again into the rain. Women who lived near the mission rushed inside and closed the door.

The missionary, Dr. Stimp, cleared his desk and set water boiling on the stove. "It is true," he said as he worked. "She was dying. You were right to bring her. Only I can save her."

The English doctor had learned the language during five years in Taung, a fact that impressed the women beside him. But they did not know whether to believe his verdict on Maka: perhaps he said this only to encourage other patients to come. His treatment looked suspicious, too, pouring liquid down Maka's throat and over her skin, remedies they had already tried.

Maka lay unconscious, soggy and cold, as Stimp pulled out a tiny infant girl, whom he slapped, shook, and swung in the air until she sputtered and coughed. The women grabbed the tiny thing from his hands. Her skin was dark, like Mojamaje's. She was fat and healthy, bursting with life, her tiny hands groping, feet kicking, her mouth puckering as if to speak. She opened her eyes and peered around the room.

At this moment the Tladi women came sloshing in: Ma-Mojamaje, Ma-Dinti, Leana, with Koko and Keke skittering behind. Maka groaned, the women gasped: another child lay ready to leave her womb. Stimp quickly plucked it out. Another girl, but pale and thin, not like the first one at all.

The women nervously eyed Maka's second twin, they eyed each other, for in past times the BaNare killed second twins or gave them away to neighboring villages. The first twin belonged in the womb, while the second twin was an intruder, a demon, worming its way in to steal what the legitimate child deserved. The women now feared to let the child live lest it grow up and someday turn and damn them. Their hands itched to strangle the thing, but it looked too much like a child, a helpless infant.

Who knows how different the story of the Great Thirst would have turned out if the Tladi family contingent had arrived any later. Ma-Mojamaje pushed the women aside and reached out to grab the infant from Stimp's hand. She cradled the second twin gently on her breast, thus announcing that this child would stay in the Tladi compound, that she would watch over it and see that no evil developed within it. The other women sighed in relief that someone else made the decision.

They laid both newborn twins against Maka's breasts, slowly rising and falling in sleep. The first, dark twin crawled and grabbed at her mother's skin, as active as her first moment out of the womb. The second, pale twin lay motionless, unconcerned with life on this earth. The women named the first one Ma-Boko, meaning "Mother of Brains," for she seemed the most intelligent child ever born. The second one, perhaps an intruder in the womb, seemed lost in another world, a child of the heavens, so they called her Naledi, meaning "Star."

When Maka awoke the next morning, she accepted the women's choices for names in gratitude for their aid on the previous night. After a week, when the ground had dried and Maka had regained strength, Tabo Cross-Eyes brought his wagon to take her home. He lifted Maka onto the wagon, handed up each infant, cracked his whip, and walked along beside the rumbling wagon. A gray blanket over her shoulders, a red scarf covering her braided hair, Maka sat upright atop the wagon, cradling her twins in her arms, as the BaNare came out of their compounds along the path to call out greetings:

"Dumela, Mother of Twins!"

"Show us those babies, dear wide-legged wonder!"

"Dumela, BaNare woman!"

"Maka, they are beautiful!"

"Dumelang BaNare," Maka called back weakly, holding the infants up for them to see, grateful to have two. Tabo kept his eyes on the oxen. His heroic feat on the night of the twins' birth both impressed and confused the BaNare. As the only other Tladi children, Maka's twins would certainly grow up rivals of Tabo's daughters, Koko and Keke.

At the Tladi family compound, Maka, Ma-Mojamaje, Leana and Ma-Dinti all showered the twins with attention. But Koko and Keke did most of the work, milking goats for them, cooking their porridge, bathing them, washing their blankets. Tabo's daughters looked more like twins than Ma-Boko and Naledi did, scampering elbow to elbow, hands covering their mouths, their skinny legs moving in perfect unison, sounding like chirping birds when they spoke, their eyes cast down at the ground. Adults thought them cute, but children were short enough to look Koko and Keke in the eye, and there they saw the glint of smug evil that BaNare adults claim they perceived in the girls' father's bad eye. The children counted four bad eyes in Koko and Keke. Adults counted none, because Koko and Keke never looked up.

It was difficult for adults to see the cast of Ma-Mojamaje's eyes as she looked at Naledi, for she bent lower and lower at the waist as she walked and her head scarf fell lower and lower over her eyes. Yet no one doubted the results of the night of the twins' birth, that Naledi immediately became Ma-Mojamaje's child. Ma-Boko demanded so much attention that Maka, Leana, Ma-Dinti, and Koko and Keke ended up concentrating their care on the first twin while Ma-Mojamaje tended to Naledi. The BaNare noticed that Ma-Mojamaje never stopped whispering to the pale infant, the color of herself, of Maka, of Kalahari dust.

"What does she say?" the BaNare queried.

Koko and Keke offered an answer: "Ma-Mojamaje teaches Naledi how to be a witch."

Adults laughed at the girls' imagination. Children cursed Koko and Keke for slander. No one guessed how close the brats came to the truth.

None of these intrigues reached Maka, lost in bliss, a mother at last, grateful to survive such a perilous childbirth, happy to deliver children of Mojamaje.

"Mojamaje?" the BaNare suddenly remembered.

"Where is Mojamaje?"

They worried now for Maka, who begged each returning miner for tidings of her husband.

"No word," the miners reported.

"We have no news of Mojamaje."

2

The Eyes of Death

Where was Mojamaje?

On his way to South Africa, approaching the border, he had come upon the railway to Rhodesia passing alongside the Wall-Maker village. Despite his curiosity about how South Africa had changed, he stopped to poke around instead of hurrying on.

"They pay us double now," a Wall-Maker worker offered, smiling and wiping the sweat from his brow. He was busy nailing to a post a sign that proclaimed LOROLE STATION. The Wall-Makers called their village

Loroleladinaledi, meaning "Dust of the Stars," but the English short-
ened it to Lorole.

"Why do they pay you so much?" Mojamaje asked.

"Because the Kgama are at it again," the Wall-Maker replied. "They
are killing all the English in Rhodesia. The Shona are joining them.
Rinderpest killed all the oxen. No wagons to haul cannons, so the English want to finish this railroad fast. To reach the Kgama and take care
of them once and for all."

Mojamaje strolled around the new train station, mud-brick buildings
with white plaster still wet, tracks disappearing east but no train. Suddenly four English redcoats rode up on horses weakened by the rinderpest plague but tough enough to survive. Mojamaje stood in awe of the
resilient beasts as one rider called out, "Here's one!" The redcoats dismounted, grabbed Mojamaje by the collar, and demanded his papers.

"This is new," Mojamaje thought, for as far as he knew only miners
needed papers. Something was wrong. Mojamaje shrugged his shoulders,
mutely pretending not to understand English. The redcoats gave him a
few shoves and took him across the border to a police post, where Mojamaje stood listening to their discussion of his fate.

"Fourth company," one soldier insisted. "Trenches and sandbags."

"Addington's Raiders," another replied. "Pots and pans."

Mojamaje sickened to realize that he was being drafted into the English army.

"See here," he piped up in English, "I can read and write English and
Boer."

The soldiers fell silent, to regard each other with shocked faces. One
redcoat approached Mojamaje and wagged a dirty finger in his face.
"You sneaky bugger," he said. "You sneaky little bugger." He stood
shaking his finger at Mojamaje, repeating his admonishment. Mojamaje
shrugged his shoulders again, tugged at the broad brim of his hat and
hoped that the soldiers would not thrash him with their rifle butts.

They sent him to Kimberley headquarters, where the English army
signed him on for one year as a guide and interpreter. His new commander sent to Taung for the Kalahariland Territory files, among which
he found the yellowed report of Mojamaje's desertion from Sweete's
column. Instead of sending Mojamaje to jail, the English commander
extended his tour of duty to three years. The pay was excellent, but the
commander explained that Mojamaje would receive it in a lump sum at
the end of three years. They would shoot him if he tried to desert.

The English army issued Mojamaje a gray horse, a long gray coat of coarse wool, a broad-brimmed gray hat, gray trousers, a gray shirt, gray socks, gray boots, a gray metal bowl and a gray blanket. He sat in Kimberley headquarters for three months, eating gray soup and gray bread, already planning an escape. South Africa crawled with English soldiers and soon he discovered why. Boers around the Joburg gold mines had banded together to form a council that called itself a government, demanding that English mine owners pay taxes. The council used its first revenue to buy uniforms and rifles. From all over South Africa, destitute Boers who had lost their land to English banks flocked to join the new Boer army. The Boer government raised the gold taxes, bought rifles, enlisted more Boer soldiers, and on and on. The English mine owners complained to the English government, the English government sent company after company of English soldiers. Six months after signing up Mojamaje, the English army occupied Joburg.

The Boer army melted into the countryside. They burned their uniforms, slept in caves and dry riverbeds, rode in circles at night, shooting down redcoats one by one. All over South Africa, Boers jumped on their horses and rode off to kill English. Without fighting a single major battle, English soldiers died like flies. The English responded by sweeping the countryside. Boer women, old men and children remaining on the farms smuggled food to the Boer commandos, so the English decided to move them all to fenced camps, burning the farms behind. Farm by farm, district by district, they would drive the Boer raiders into the open.

Mojamaje was assigned to a Scorch Squad operating out of Kimberley headquarters. There were four English redcoats, ten unarmed black troopers and Mojamaje himself. The English soldiers and Mojamaje rode horses while one trooper drove a wagon and the others walked behind it. After the English army swept through a district, Mojamaje's squad moved from farm to farm, collecting Boer prisoners on the wagon, burning houses, food, and crops in the field, driving cattle back to Kimberley. The cattle were the trickiest problem: as soon as the English army appeared, all the tenants on all the farms led the Boers' cattle into their own corrals. When Mojamaje's Scorch Squad arrived, the Boer pens were empty. If the English seized the cattle in the tenant corrals, the tenants might join with the Boers. The last thing the English wanted to do was to draw all of South Africa into the war on the side of the Boers.

None of the English soldiers spoke anything but English, so Mojamaje ordered the Boer prisoners onto the wagon and negotiated with the tenants for a division of the cattle. The usual bargain was half for the English and half for the tenants. The English commander of the squad then issued the tenants a writ of safe passage out of the district, with the number of cattle faithfully recorded.

When the English army occupied a district, Mojamaje's squad first scorched the farms closest to headquarters, then moved farther out, spending more and more days in transit between farms. The squad carried no food of its own, depending instead on the cattle they rounded up. They were authorized to kill as many as they required. The Boer prisoners on the wagons were to be fed at the fenced camp at headquarters, so the squad was prohibited from sharing their meat. When the squad scorched the most distant farms, the prisoners spent five days on the road with nothing to eat. Most were starving already when they climbed on the wagon because they had given all their food to Boer commandos. By the time they reached the fenced camp, the youngest, oldest and weakest prisoners were limp and listless. They never died on the wagon but lay in the dust behind the wire fence, their tongues too thick for them even to swallow their own spit, dying within a week.

Had the squad moved faster, more prisoners would have survived. But the English soldiers tried to spend as many days as possible on the road. Back at headquarters they received standard rations of bread, brandy, and a morsel of meat every other day. The more time they spent on the road, the better they ate, roasting chunk after chunk of lean, juicy beef.

By the time the squad finished scorching a district, a vast herd of cattle had accumulated at Kimberley headquarters. Once a month a convoy of cavalry drove the herd toward Joburg, for distribution to other English army units. Each time, Boer commandos attacked the convoy and led off the herd. They split the cattle among Boer farms that lay beyond English lines. Then the English army swept in and scorchers confiscated the cattle again. Round and round went the cattle, to end in the stomachs of Mojamaje's and other Scorch Squads.

Mojamaje carefully planned an escape. He noted especially the positions of police posts and army camps, knowing that even if he managed to slip away from his squad without being shot, reaching the border was another question.

There was nothing for him in this war, no side to choose. Whoever won, South Africa lost. Everyone hated Boers, but why help the English steal from the Boers what the Boers stole from everyone else? Yet the slow march of destruction moved Mojamaje to contemplate action, one act of humanity. His position in the war placed him squarely in the eyes of death. As the Boer prisoners gazed out the back of the wagon at the cattle trailing behind, Mojamaje rode at the head of the cattle, and sometimes the prisoners' dying eyes strayed to his. He might have missed moments to make an escape, perhaps he stayed on to look for his chance for compassion. Or maybe he could try both.

Mojamaje's squad began in the Hurunang Hills west of Kimberley, then south through the Yellow Tsa Valley, east to where the Little Tsa headlands meet the Foelberg Plateau, then north to the Taung Plain. He had waited for this, too, to reach the scene of his first love, to see once again the land of Drift. Devastation reigned. The Taung Mission lay in ruins. Papa Zulu's roofs were burned away. Curls of black smoke smoldered from the blackened shells of the mission houses. The fence had been pulled up, and piles of bones marked the spots where hungry refugees had roasted the mission goats. Day after day, Mojamaje's squad burned farms farther and farther from the mission, past the cluster of hills where he and Maka had hidden, where We-Have-Eaten-A-Fish sold rifles. And at last, one day, they reached the Roodie farm. The squad pulled up to the house Drift built, where she killed Roodie, where Roodie's Griqua wife killed her.

The Boer occupants had already set the house afire, a gesture of defiance the squad had not encountered before. The Boers stood in front of the burning building, their bones sticking through their rags. Mojamaje recognized none of them: two very old men, four women, three young girls and two young boys. The troopers marched to the tenant village where Mojamaje once slept, in a storehouse in Drift's compound, and counted out the cattle there. Mojamaje wrote out a writ of safe passage. The English soldiers leaned against the wagon, smoking.

Mojamaje ordered the Boers into the wagon. As the redcoats mounted their horses, one of them snapped his fingers and said, "Wait, I know this trick. They try it in Transvaal." He ran back to the house, now a smoldering mud shell. Rummaging through the rubble, he found a wet blanket on the floor and yanked it back to reveal a Boer soldier lying in a hole. The redcoat dragged him outside, onto the wagon.

The Boer was covered in bloody bandages, long hair and a beard hid his face, but the huge red freckles against the pale white skin alerted Mojamaje that this was Ro Roodie, Maka's half brother, the precocious scamp who had sold Drift's grain in Kimberley. He had grown into a large man, with thick bones and a wide face, but now his ribs showed deep corrugations behind his tight bandages. His feet were bare and his eyes barely opened as the English soldier pushed him onto the wagon.

Back on the road, two English soldiers rode in front of the wagon, one rode on each side, one black trooper lashed the oxen, Mojamaje rode directly behind the wagon, and behind him walked the cattle, driven by the other black troopers. Mojamaje stared at Ro Roodie's eyes until they rolled open to stare into his own. Neither spoke a word. Mojamaje rode as close to the wagon as his horse would allow, close to the English soldiers who rode alongside. One by one, Ro caught the eyes of his fellow prisoners, even the children's, directing them to Mojamaje's face. One by one, they nodded their heads in comprehension.

That night the English soldiers roasted a calf. They always kept the prisoners on the wagon while they ate, guarded by the black troopers, who built their own cookfire at the back of the wagon. The redcoats had grown confident that the black troopers would not risk summary execution to assist the hated Boers. The black troopers only nibbled at their meat, conscious of the starving eyes upon them. But this night the Boers slipped down off the back of the wagon, in full view of the black troopers, who looked in panic to Mojamaje. Ro could not walk, but the four women and two old men crept along the wagon's shadow toward the English soldiers. Mojamaje looked up, tossed a sliver of meat into his mouth, and began to sing a song. He waved for his black troopers to join in and they did so, tense with anxiety, poised to run for their lives. The women threw themselves on the English soldiers as the old men grabbed their rifles. The black troopers jumped up and ran off into the night.

Mojamaje helped the Boers tie the red-coated soldiers to a tree. Ro struggled onto one of the English horses, the two old men mounted two others, and the oldest boy mounted the fourth. The women tossed roasted beef onto the wagon as another boy grabbed the lash, whipped the oxen, and the wagon jerked away, leaving the cattle grazing and the English cursing in the dark.

"This is Mojamaje," Ro announced to the other Boers.

"Mojamaje!" one of the boys exclaimed. "Show me your knife."

"I left it home," Mojamaje called back. "If the English stole it from me they would win the war." The Boers laughed and Ro resumed the song Mojamaje had started as they pounced on the English.

Mojamaje drove north, then west across a rocky wasteland, to enter the Kalahari at a place called Mmi. The rains were about to begin and if enough rainpools formed in the sand, they might wind their way along the edge of the Kalahari and approach Naring from the empty northwest. An ancient, dry valley ran from Mmi to BaNare territory, and summer rain often collected in its sandy bed.

Their difficulty was an English police post at the entrance to the valley. When they approached Mmi, Mojamaje and the Boers jumped off their horses and tied the reins to the back of the wagon. Mojamaje had taken the English commander's pencil and paper and now he wrote out a writ of safe passage for the Boers, explaining that Ro was a spy whose valuable services to the English had turned the tide in a number of skirmishes; now Mojamaje had orders to drive him and his family to safety in the Kalahari, for the Boers had discovered his activities and vowed to assassinate him. Ro was wounded from a nearly successful attempt. Mojamaje signed the writ with the name of the commander of his Scorch Squad. Then the Boers all climbed into the wagon, Mojamaje walked alongside, lashing the oxen forward, a rifle slung over one shoulder. The other three English rifles lay in the wagon, under the women's tattered skirts.

Mojamaje stopped the wagon in front of the low brick building that comprised both barracks and office of the police post. A redcoat emerged. Mojamaje saluted, explained his mission and handed the soldier the writ. Mojamaje's script was crisp and clear, with tall, elegant letters. Five more redcoats came out to investigate. Each read the writ. "Most unusual," one of them said at last. "We shall send to headquarters for confirmation."

Mojamaje looked over at a wire corral beside the office: it held only one horse.

"Good," Mojamaje replied, smoothing the front of his uniform shirt. "These horses will die in the Kalahari. If headquarters does not fetch them, I must leave them here with you."

Eager to accept Mojamaje's bribe of five horses, five of the redcoats advised to let the wagon pass immediately. But this left one soldier who already had a horse and he of course was the senior officer. He read the writ of safe passage again, speaking aloud the signature. "Lieutenant Bryce," he said. "We have had things from him before." He disappeared into the office and emerged with another piece of paper. He held the two writs side by side. The handwriting and signatures were identical. Mojamaje's Scorch Squad had grown so dependent on him that he not only wrote all the writs but also signed his commander's name.

The English soldiers took the horses and let the wagon pass. By the time the Scorch Squad redcoats had freed themselves from the trees and walked to the nearest police post, the wagon was deep in the Kalahari, where the English would never follow.

3
Long Arms

As BaNare men returned from the Joburg mines with terrible tales of the South African war, they still had no news of Mojamaje.

"Only Joburg is safe," they reported.

"The countryside is still in flames."

"No one has seen him."

Maka and Ma-Mojamaje occupied themselves with the twins, but worry invaded their every thought. Soon they lost track of what they were doing, placing empty pots on the cookfire, forgetting their neighbors' names.

Mojamaje was worried too. After passing the Mmi border station, he drove quickly through the dry river valley toward Naring. Rainpools dotted the terrain, but the heavy wheels sank deep in the sand so the oxen tired quickly. Mojamaje rested them whenever he found a pool of water. They finished off the English soldiers' roast meat, then shot guinea fowl, antelope and sand hare with the English rifles. After a week the game disappeared, so they slaughtered an ox from the wagon team. The meat revived the Boers, who drank deeply from the pools along the way. Ro pulled off his bandages to reveal festering scabs on his chest and back scattered among the huge red freckles of his skin. They slaughtered another ox and then two more, so the eight remaining grew weaker and weaker from pulling more weight. At last the valley intersected the path from Naring to Loang. Mojamaje turned the wagon east.

"You sure?" Ro asked.

"I am sure," Mojamaje replied. "I know this trail."

Ro asked, "Will Maka remember me?"

Mojamaje assured him she would.

"I saw her," Ro added, stomping through the tall brown grass alongside Mojamaje, who cracked the whip above the oxen's ears. "That night. She ran out after my mother. She saw them both dead."

Mojamaje kept his eyes on the oxteam. "Do not mention it to her," he said. "Please."

"Maka wanted to kill her."

"I know."

Ro insisted, "I knew it would happen," remembering back now, drifting from the present, back to his youth.

"We all did," Mojamaje replied calmly. "Only not like that."

Ro shoved his hands deep in his pockets and skipped a step. Suddenly he was back along the road to Kimberley, a boy playing beside the wagon that Mojamaje drove, loaded with Drift's grain. "Any children?" Ro asked.

Mojamaje smiled slightly and then laughed. "Not when I left. Maybe when we reach Naring I will find one."

Ro slapped Mojamaje on the back in consolation. "Sorry, old man. But take my advice: Love it just like it was your own."

They rolled over the sand slope into Naring, nearly two years after Mojamaje's departure. Ro and the old men walked behind the wagon while the women and children huddled on top, all fearful of the reception they would receive. The BaNare noticed the wagon as soon as it reached the crest of the sand slope. Children ran out to meet it as it thumped down into Naring. Recognizing Mojamaje, they shouted his name, running and skipping alongside the wagon. It was early afternoon. BaNare adults came out of their compounds, wrapped in blankets, to wave and call out as the wagon rolled past:

"Dumelang, Mojamaje and everyone with him!"

"Mojamaje, where did you find these Boers?"

"In the Kalahari?"

"With the Bushmen?"

"Eating snakes?"

"Mojamaje!" the children cried. "Mojamaje brought us some Boers!"

The Boers were all ragged and dirty, covered with Kalahari dust, with burned red faces and thick, curly hair. Mojamaje looked tired and old, in a frayed gray uniform, his heavy gray coat pressing down on his shoulders, his gray hat pulled low over his eyes. Deep lines cut through his face, pushing higher his Bushman cheekbones.

By the time the wagon reached the Tladi compound, a crowd of BaNare had gathered there, curious about who the Boers were. Pia the

Scornful appeared in his elegant black suit, swinging his cane, and cried, "Ha!" when the wagon appeared. Chief Pule was still sick in bed, surrounded by sorcerers rubbing sheep dung in their ears and spitting up stones.

"Boers," Pia muttered when the wagon halted in front of Ma-Mojamaje's famous woodpile. "More Boers," he called out loudly, turning to the crowd. "I will send them back. We have too many Boers already."

The BaNare knew this to be false. The Naring Boers had barely multiplied at all. Old Man De Swart's children, and now even the children of his married children, refused to marry BaNare. This was fair enough, for BaNare parents would never allow their children to marry Boers. Hospitality was one thing, marriage another. The BaNare cheered at the prospect of Mojamaje's wagonful of Boers settling in Naring to provide suitable partners for the De Swarts. Pia's remarks were especially insulting because Old Man De Swart and Chief Pule remained the best of friends. The old Boer visited the dying chief every day.

Mojamaje turned his tired eyes to Pia, said nothing, then turned his attention to helping the Boers down from the wagon. Some BaNare men stepped forward to join in. Then Maka and Ma-Mojamaje appeared at the Tladi compound wall, each with a twin in her arms.

Until this moment, the BaNare had never noticed the great length of Mojamaje's arms. Certainly he was tall, but no one would have guessed that they would have reached as far as they did, as he stepped over to his wife, his mother, and his daughters he had never before seen, and leaned over the compound wall to embrace them all. One arm surrounded Maka's shoulder, the other curled around his mother's, as he pulled them and the infants they held against his chest. Their faces all beamed. Some BaNare began to cry, some to cheer, and then some BaNare still dispute what happened next. Some decry the story as impossible, others insist with vehement certainty that Ma-Boko, the lively dark child in Maka's arms, the most intelligent ever born, turned her tiny face up to greet her father, her tiny voice piping, "Mojamaje," and then in clear English, "Eater of Rocks."

4

Secrets

The wagonful of Boers quickly settled alongside the De Swarts' sprawling compounds. Ro Roodie set himself up as a blacksmith, to fix wagons and plows, and immediately married the youngest daughter of Old Man De Swart. Paulus, the taciturn Lover, married one of the Boer women from the wagon. Old Man De Swart threw a feast for both weddings, using beef this time instead of pork. Since the rinderpest had now passed, and some BaNare miners had returned from South Africa with surviving cows to rebuild their herds, they too contributed their first surplus oxen to the Boer marriage feast.

As song followed song at the event, the women fixed their dreamy eyes on the marvelous figure of Paulus the Lover, stiff in a starched white shirt, on a straight-backed chair beside his plump, fair wife. They mourned the end of his romantic youth and began humming to themselves, then aloud, then adding the words of the song composed to remember Seele, the product of his ill-fated love:

> Face of beauty, child of woe
> Dinti the Ostrich dead below
> Face of nighttime, empty dreams
> Tabo Cross-Eyes what he seems
> Face of lonely, blind allure
> Paulus, bashful lover, Boer
> Face of blackness, jealous sun
> Bosio Night Girl trusts no one
> Face of beauty, marked for life
> Seele child of Seantlo wife

As the feast wore on into the night, it also celebrated Mojamaje's return, the arrival of his wife's half brother, the birth of his twins, recovery from rinderpest. Attention shifted from Paulus the Married to Mojamaje and Maka as the BaNare sang at last the celebration of their marriage, laying the wedding feast at their feet. Seated on straight-backed chairs far from the roasting fires, they sat with their hands folded across their laps, Mojamaje in his gray English uniform, washed and mended, Maka in her old yellow dress and red scarf. They spoke softly to each other through the feast, greeting BaNare who danced or reeled drunkenly by, their eyes filled with calm, their serenity drawing the light of the fire.

For days after the ceremony, BaNare strolling past the Tladi compound noticed that Mojamaje and Maka paid attention only to each other, speaking in low voices close to the cookfire. Chickens scratched at the compound floor by their feet, children chased dogs through the gate, wagons rumbled past, neighbors called out greetings, night fell, and still they sat. When they finally retired, falling into their blankets, Mojamaje and Maka clung to each other as to life itself, grateful to conquer the past. "It is about time," Mojamaje whispered in the dark.

Ma-Boko grew quickly, then stood up and walked, chattering endlessly. A broad chestful of lungs powered her voice. She spoke to other children with her hands on her hips, like a wife berating her husband, ordering them around, assigning them nicknames, organizing them to carry water, collect firewood and sweep the Tladi compound in return for the porridge that Ma-Mojamaje fed to all the children. Her dark skin was smooth and clear, her cheeks were round and healthy, her lips full, her nose wide, her arms and legs were already muscular and thick.

Naledi, Ma-Boko's opposite, neither spoke nor walked. Her yellow skin slowly developed a random scattering of large black freckles. Her hair grew out in wispy brown strands curling weakly at their tips. Her limbs and fingers moved stiffly. Her eyelids remained half closed, like a sleeping lizard's. Her eyes peeked out dully from their deep, dark sockets. As her arms and legs grew larger, as her twin sister ran and danced like a full-grown girl, Naledi sat propped up against the compound wall, uninterested even in crawling.

But once a day Ma-Mojamaje sat down before the child and spoke. Every day she seemed older, bending lower and lower at the waist as her scarf fell lower and lower on her eyes. Sometimes she wandered out of the compound and out through the village, lost in memories and daydreams. At first everyone else ignored what Ma-Mojamaje said to Naledi, since it was mostly mumbles anyway. But Naledi looked up at her grandmother, her ears perked, and appeared to listen to every word. The first outsider to sit beside Naledi and listen was Ma-Boko, curious and eager to learn. It was she who reported the content of Ma-Mojama-je's lectures.

"Secrets," Ma-Boko explained.

One by one other children sat down to listen, but they grew bored and restless, stood up and ran off, replaced by others, so only Naledi heard every word.

At first Ma-Mojamaje's lectures seemed only a series of disconnected stories, confusing and pointless, like the tale of Fenata, the beautiful princess who died when her dog ate a mamba snake and licked her hand. Fenata's mother buried her in an anthill and the ants carried her through the earth, back in time, to an underground lake where fish had wings and elephants had hair. These were ancient BaKii stories and tales the Bushmen told the BaKii when they first met in the deep Kalahari so long ago. The tales contained secrets of roots and prayers to certain stars on certain nights that touched the world beyond. Dimly but deeply Ma-Mojamaje felt the march of time, and this too she passed on to Naledi, tales of men returning from the mines and keeping their wages to themselves, plowing their own fields with hired labor and no wife. She poured her own regrets into Naledi's child head, the essence of Bushmen, BaKii, and BaNare womanhood, the wisdom of age, the joys of her life and the memory of a young boy who made the mistake of trusting her love. This was Naledi's education, the life of an old woman becoming her own, the experience of a lifetime and the secrets of the past.

Maka and Mojamaje worried about Naledi, why she neither spoke nor walked. Ma-Mojamaje reassured them. "She will walk when she sees something important to do. She will speak when she has something important to say." And so they left Naledi to her grandmother.

Their joy at having twins, seeing the compound fill with the neighborhood's children, the squawk of young voices, overpowered their worries and filled Mojamaje and Maka with a contentment and pride. Mojamaje taught Ma-Boko to speak, read, and write English and Boer, and she learned fast. She divided her time between Mojamaje's lessons and Ma-Mojamaje's homilies. Ma-Boko struggled to decipher her old grandmother's meanings, grappling with the allusions and metaphors, but try as she might, none of it made any sense to her. Still Naledi sat listening, and Ma-Boko took her placid countenance as the glow of comprehension. In this way Ma-Boko became the first of the BaNare to look to Naledi as a privileged sharer in secrets of the earth and heavens.

Naledi paid such close attention to Ma-Mojamaje that she learned a secret that Ma-Mojamaje tried her best to conceal. For months Ma-Mojamaje had blinked and rubbed one eye and then the other. She tried medicines and chants, but nothing did any good. As throughout her life, Ma-Mojamaje postponed regret and sprang into action while her condition steadily worsened. She walked over to Mojamaje and reached up to take his head between her hands, inspecting every line of his face, squinting to memorize every mark, the sweep of his high Bushman cheekbones, one of her many gifts to her son. Her scarf fell so low over her eyes that she had to tilt her head back far to see his face, her wrinkled eyes cloudy, glistening. Then she moved on to Maka, struggling to focus one by one on the freckles that lay like fine powder along her cheeks, wrinkling with age. Ma-Mojamaje swallowed this hard truth, that even her son's young wife grew old. Then on to Ma-Dinti, who so long ago had ushered her into the Tladi compound the first time she came from Loang to Naring—an age past, a lifetime. Then Leana, Koko and Keke, finally Ma-Boko and Naledi her pupil, into whom she had poured herself, then out the compound gate through the winding paths of Naring, fixing in her memory for one final time the home she had won for herself and her son, the dream of her life fulfilled. Every day she walked, bent at the waist, stubbing her bare dry feet on stones. Each day the scene grew dimmer, each pointed thatch roof seemed rounder than the last. Children tumbled across her path and she could only guess their ages, boy or girl. She had long since forgotten names, wandering for hours until she barely made out the turn that took her back to the Tladi compound before darkness descended completely.

Then one day a gust of wind blew off Ma-Mojamaje's head scarf. She fell on her knees and felt for it along the compound floor, as the wind blew the scarf first to one corner and then the other. Naledi decided she had seen enough. She placed her palms on the dirt floor of the compound, straightened her legs to thrust her bare bottom in the air, and stood up for the first time in her life. Then she walked, shakily at first but then quickly steadying, to retrieve the scarf and help Ma-Mojamaje to her feet.

Ma-Boko came upon this scene and ran to Maka smearing mud over a crack on the outside of the compound wall. Ma-Boko cried, "My grandmother is blind and my sister walks!"

The Tladi family compound erupted in commotion. Neighbors ran to see for themselves, word spread and everyone found out. Naledi assumed full responsibility for her blind grandmother, helping her with her chores, sleeping beside her in her house, brewing her endless cups of tea. Naledi's face wore a calm seriousness beyond her five years, beyond even Ma-Boko's precocity. She cut a morula branch from the hills, carved smooth both ends and took Ma-Mojamaje on daily walks through Naring, holding one end of the stick while the blind woman held the other. Ma-Mojamaje called out directions she had memorized on her last days of sight.

Still Naledi spoke not a word.

The children skipped along behind Naledi and Ma-Mojamaje, inventing rhymes, matching them with tunes. They fetched sticks of their own to hold out between their hands, forming a long chain behind Naledi and her grandmother, winding along the village paths like a snake through rocks. This is the song they composed:

> Naledi!
> Why is your grandmother blind?
> Naledi!
> What did she put in your mind?
> A giant Bushman played a trick
> Lit a grand fire with a stick
> Tladi begged to taste her charms
> Instead she slept with empty arms
> And raised a son in lonely bliss
> Who is she who did all this?
> Mojamaje's mother

Inside the cool darkness of her sightless eyes, Ma-Mojamaje smiled sadly at the children's song, remembering Tladi's son, her love.

5

Company

Perhaps because of what came later, the BaNare remember the years of the twins' childhood as their golden age. The rains were good and they planted vegetables behind their compounds with seeds from De Swart's and Big Boots's shops. Red, orange and green harvests from their gardens joined the yellow melons and pumpkins and early corn at the first-fruits celebration. Their hero Mojamaje was safe and happy. The women piled their thanksgivings at the gate of their chief's compound, and Pule's family took in everything but the corn, which the BaNare girls set to stamping and grinding, malting and brewing into beer for all Naring to drink.

At one of these first-fruits celebrations, Naledi produced an onion of prodigious dimensions. She had tended only this one plant and balanced it on her head, basketless, as she walked to the ceremony, an innocent smile on her thin lips. The onion was as large as her face. Instead of depositing the thing with the other first fruits, Naledi slipped through the gate and into the house where Chief Pule still lay surrounded by his sorcerers. Naledi hummed to herself as she reached up with both hands and removed the onion from her head. Peeling away the papery purple skin, she dug her fingernails into the soft flesh and the aroma of onion rapidly grew to overpower the room. She worked her fingers into the heart, and with one snap of her lithe wrists the fragrant bulb broke open. Naledi leaned forward to place one of the halves over Chief Pule's face. The sorcerers watched in fascination, then nervously eyed each other, wondering why they themselves knew nothing of this trick. Pule's puffy, immobile face disappeared under the purple onion, and in a moment he coughed, then sputtered. Naledi withdrew the half onion and the inactive chief opened his eyes for the first time in months.

After this demonstration, Naledi made mysterious appearances at various gatherings of Naring's magicians, or so the old professionals reported. Out in the wilderness at night, when they crowded around a fire of antelope dung and the leader asked for the next ingredient, the hand that reached into the firelight to deliver the tiny, bloody pigeon liver would be thin, freckled, and pale. When they turned quickly to look into Naledi's face, she was gone. Rumors spread, the BaNare demanded more proof. Still Naledi spoke not a word.

Mojamaje and Maka continually tried speaking with Naledi, asking questions, one of which always was "Please child, why will you not speak?" They noticed a deliberate air to the girl, a calm calculation, a faint grin tugging at her thin lips. "She plans something," Maka suggested to Mojamaje. "What do you think it will be?" And Ma-Boko began to look up to her sister, judging Naledi's education superior to her own, noticing how Naledi's eye already glinted with authority, a career chosen.

Ma-Mojamaje spent less and less time on chores, eventually retiring to sit on the compound floor while Naledi did all her work, cooking, cleaning, sweeping, brewing beer and tea. Naledi was the only girl in Naring to abandon the makgabe before marriage, wearing instead a dull green cotton shift several years too large. She wore a head scarf, too, the mark of a woman. Old BaNare wandered in to sit beside Ma-Mojamaje and drink Naledi's brews. More and more children filled the compound, and Ma-Boko led them in games and songs. Their mothers gathered to gossip with Maka:

"Why did I marry him? He eats chickens in bed."

"At least you know where he is."

"I have not seen mine for weeks."

"He is at the mines for sure."

"He will come home and sleep with your sister."

"He will ask your sister for money."

"I know her sister—she will give it to him."

"The money or the other thing?"

"Both."

"He need only whisper those township words."

"The men spend too much time in those holes."

"The mines are terrible."

"I am not speaking of the mines."

Old men coaxed from Mojamaje stories of South Africa, of the English war against the Boers. Six months after Mojamaje's return, Dr. Stimp had exulted from his pulpit that the war had ended in English victory. No redcoats came to arrest Mojamaje or his wagonful of Boers, but far away in Taung, at Kalahariland Territory headquarters, an office clerk filed away the report on Mojamaje's desertion from the Scorch Squad, to yellow and gather dust behind the report of his desertion from Sweete's column as it butchered the Kgama army.

Among the old men who sat with Ma-Mojamaje was Chief Pule, who recovered steadily after Naledi's ministration, enough to walk and talk but not to think. Pia the Scornful remained Acting Chief. Bloated from years of prostration and sorcerers' potions, Pule waddled through the village to perch beside Ma-Mojamaje. Naledi smiled down serenely and pressed a small, peeled onion into his puffy hands. He sniffed it once and took a healthy bite. A welter of scars covered his nose, but Pule's eyes still danced with mischief, though he sometimes forgot his own name.

"Who am I?" he whispered to Naledi, who smiled benignly, turning her head back from the potful of porridge she stirred. She brought one finger up to her lips and Pule winked back.

Old Man De Swart wandered in too, stinking of brandy. Bald as Pule now, he still wore his rough leather jacket, as Pule still wore his leopard suit and copper earrings. "Any snicker?" Old Man whispered, pouring an invisible bottle of brandy into his beer. Naledi shrugged her shoulders, pointing her chin to the swarm of women chatting around Maka. Old Man nodded his comprehension, content to slop his finger into the beer to stir in his imaginary snicker.

Chief Pule, Old Man, and a changing dozen other old BaNare kept Ma-Mojamaje company every day. They asked her questions and listened to her stories. When her scarf fell completely over her eyes, Naledi pushed it back up. They all came for company as much as to give it, especially Old Man, who never forgave his son, Paulus the erstwhile Lover, for taking over his shop, stocking it with the same goods that English Big Boots sold, turning a neat profit. Big Boots had sold out to another Englishman, whose footwear concealed only his ankles, earning him the name Little Boots. He sold out to an Englishman who wore shoes instead of boots, whom the BaNare called No Boots. This constant turnover at the English shop gave Paulus the chance to reconquer some of the Naring trade, since Old Man had been too pokey and besotted to seize the advantage. No one blamed Paulus for usurping his father's place, for now he had a wife and children to support and he supplied his father with all the brandy he desired.

Every week a larger crowd filled the Tladi compound, the consequences of which perhaps only Naledi foresaw. She waited. The BaNare watched her and waited too.

6

A Grave Moment

It was the missionary Stimp who finally forced Naledi to act. He joined forces with Pia ya Pipa, Scornful Acting Chief, who had learned enough English from Big Boots to speak frankly and intimately with the zealous Stimp. They saw eye to eye from the first.

After delivering the twins and claiming credit for Maka's survival, Stimp had enjoyed the first trickle of acceptance by the BaNare. A few women took their children to his clinic, appreciating Stimp's medicines as a supplement to the sorcerers' potions of beetle blood, goat urine, herbs and ash. Some adults began attending Sunday services, then some sent their children for Saturday lessons. Stimp's confidence grew to smugness when Pia the Scornful asked him to marry his sons to Koko and Keke in Naring's first Christian wedding. This was the BaNare's first whiff of intrigue between the missionary and their Acting Chief.

Koko and Keke had grown up only in form, with breasts and hips blossomed to full plumpness, revealed to all the world by their skimpy childhood makgabe. The two girls still scampered side by side, their hands over their mouths, their eyes darting furtively to each other. Pia's sons, on the other hand, rarely made public appearances. Or rather, there was so little to note about them that the BaNare glimpsed them often without recalling who they were. Peke, the younger, resembled Pono, the elder, only in utter featurelessness, an uncanny blandness that failed to fix either one in the BaNare's memories. The BaNare had long dreaded this union, and now the Christian ceremony added a measure of insult. What was wrong with a BaNare wedding?

Nevertheless, curiosity and jealousy brought the BaNare to Stimp's mud-brick church to witness the event. Koko and Keke wore high-collared white dresses, ruffled and laced at every possible place, hiding their ankles and wrists. Their hands covered their mouths, their eyes darted in constant conspiracy. Pono and Peke wore proper black suits like their father's, shiny black shoes and black bowler hats. Tabo Cross-Eyes was there in a black suit too, but his huge body overwhelmed the stiff clothing, poking massive forearms out the arms, thick calves out the trouser legs, a trunk of a neck out the collar. His bald head gleamed and he refused to wear shoes. BaNare crowded inside and outside the church, unable to understand the English ceremony. They noticed Naledi in the back row with her family, holding the other end of Ma-Mojamaje's stick. Would Naledi act now, use whatever mysterious powers she possessed, to stop this union of Naring's two largest inheritances, this wedding of heirs? But no, Naledi stood wordless, preoccupied, uninterested in the proceedings. The BaNare closest to her did report later that she smelled distinctly of onion.

Encouraged, emboldened, Stimp judged his position strong enough to pronounce his first edict. One Sunday a month after the wedding, he declared from his pulpit that he would admit no little girls wearing makgabe to his clinic. Henceforth, girls must wear dresses. At first Stimp's announcement shocked the BaNare to outrage. What kind of debased viper would pay such attention to little girls? Grown men never looked twice at little girls.

The BaNare regarded Stimp anew, noticing now the seedy curl of his collar, the lumpy cut of his black suit, the frayed cuffs of his white shirt. His scrawny neck and scruffy brown beard, his long nose, beady goat eyes, balding head and sunken cheeks, his hunched walk, huffy voice, every choppy gesticulation, every pimple, every sniffle, every word, now confirmed his foul lechery. Why did he not have a wife?

But Stimp had written to his home church in England, which sent him dresses for the girls of Naring. He announced that he would distribute them at the clinic, giving one to each little girl in return for her makgabe. The BaNare were skeptical, wondering what the vile lecher wanted with all those makgabe. But the lure of free clothing won them over, so the girls of Naring skipped up to the clinic to exchange their makgabe for dresses.

The girls ran back from the mission in shame, feeling thoroughly naked without their makgabe despite the dresses they wore. Each one dashed into her house, pulled off the dress and tied on another makgabe. Her mother washed and folded the dress neatly and put it away for the girls to wear on special occasions, but always with makgabe underneath. The only exception was their visits to the clinic, when the girls, trembling with mortification, wore their dresses without makgabe underneath so Stimp would not realize the deception. Their mothers stayed close by while he examined them. Stimp seldom walked through the village, so he thought that his war against the makgabe was won. He flushed with triumph, eager for the next campaign.

Stimp and Pia turned now to serious conspiracy. Together they directed correspondence to Kalahariland Territory headquarters, requesting an English officer posted to Naring. Headquarters replied that its budget allowed only essential staff and Naring was too peaceful to merit a posting. Stimp and Pia replied that an insurrection brewed among one of Naring's leading families. Every week more and more BaNare met in the compound of Mojamaje Tladi, conspiring to drive out the Christian missionary and unseat the present chief, himself a loyal Christian, and instate Mojamaje in his stead. Stimp and Pia composed a brief biography of Mojamaje to buttress their case for alarm:

1. His grandfather, Tladi, murdered the grandfather of Acting Chief Pia ya Pipa.

2. As a boy, Mojamaje slaughtered ten Boers by crushing them with boulders he rolled down from a cliff.

3. In Taung, he stole a Zulu stabbing spear and used it to pierce its owner's heart, from the back.

4. He cut off the shaft to the spear to make a dagger. He used it to cut up one hundred Taung Boers.

5. He became a Christian, selling a thousand illegal rifles every year to the Kgama army, for war against the English.

6. The English rewarded his Boer-killing by giving him command of a thousand English soldiers. He led them into a trap by the Kgama army. Then he deserted.

7. He came back from South Africa with ten thousand cattle. This spread the rinderpest and killed millions of innocent cattle.

8. In the great South African war, he used his dagger to kill a thousand Boers. Then he switched sides and killed a thousand English.

At Taung headquarters, the Kalahariland officials checked their files to find Mojamaje's records of two desertions. They dispatched an officer at once to take up the post of Naring District Commissioner.

To this day the BaNare wonder why Stimp and Pia demanded an English official. Were they not better off alone? They had no part in deciding which officer the English would post to Naring. They must have known that they might receive not a spit-and-polish major but Willoughby the Young, Willoughby the Beardless, Willoughby the Throb of Hearts of Young Girls Just Past Puberty.

The BaNare remember Willoughby well: a pale wisp of a boy with a wild crop of red hair. Or was it black? Some claim his hair was brown. Others say he was short and swarthy. This confusion derives from the fact that few BaNare ever said a word to any of their District Commissioners, who lived in a square brick house behind a square brick office in a clearing in the center of Naring, behind a ring of fast-growing shade trees. The BaNare knew him only as Willoughby. They called his successor the same name and every replacement after that. They thought "Willoughby" meant "District Commissioner."

The first Willoughby was indeed a fair, lanky red-haired young man with a pleasant, smooth face and a smiling mouthful of small, beautiful teeth. His ears were enormous, shaped like melons, and every girl of marriageable age aspired to peer inside them, touch them, lay her cheek against them. His gray uniform surprised the BaNare, who expected the red coat that Sweete's column wore. Willoughby never learned a word of the language, but once every fortnight he walked through the village, smiling and waving, calling out greetings in English, breathing deeply the air of late afternoon when the dust of the day mingled with the scented haze of cookfires, fine lines of blue smoke weaving through the still air, flattening to hang in a dreamy cloud above the village. Cowbells, goats bleating, children's tired voices straining to stretch their mirth until sundown, the red glare of dusk splashed against the Naring hills—Willoughby took in the scene with his hands shoved in his trouser pockets, whistling a tune, wistful, lonely for England.

Willoughby's nonchalant indifference so impressed the BaNare that they blamed him not at all when Stimp declared from his pulpit:

"The law of Kalahariland henceforth forbids the unsanitary custom of interring the deceased in Naring proper. This church will provide a cemetery outside the village limits."

The BaNare were aghast. They had always buried their dead in the center of their compounds, smoothing over the graves with mud, to keep them safe from jackals, which dared not come near an occupied compound.

"Jackals!" they cried aloud.

Out at Stimp's graveyard, far from the village, the jackals would come at night, dig up the graves. . . . It was too horrible to imagine. And to have a spot on the earth marked out only for corpses, waiting—every time the BaNare passed it, they would think of death.

Did Pia conspire in this with Stimp? What about Tabo Cross-Eyes? Tabo had just fulfilled his public plan to marry his daughters to Pia's faceless sons, Pono and Peke. Certainly this dynastic union threw Tabo in with Pia once and for all, but no one offered a shred of evidence that Tabo shared any responsibility for Stimp's heinous decree.

Whereupon, as with Pia's cattle schemes exploded by rinderpest, Tabo provided the evidence the BaNare needed. The bad eye overpowered the good, offering Stimp's cemetery its first victim: Tabo's mother, Ma-Dinti. Lately her stoop had come to rival Ma-Mojamaje's, her scarf also fell over her eyes, and she sat with the other old BaNare in the Tladi compound to keep Ma-Mojamaje company. When she died in her sleep, her son gave her up to the jackals. When Tabo announced the funeral plans, every mother in Naring eyed her son with suspicion, wondering whether she would meet the same fate.

The cemetery was south of the village, past the canyon, along the Naring ridge, nestled among the rocks. An eight-strand wire fence enclosed the bare rectangle with Ma-Dinti's bleak grave lying alone in one corner. Few but the Tladis attended the funeral. Stimp hurried through a few prayers and ran back to his mission. Ma-Boko noticed Naledi alight with curiosity, carefully taking in the surroundings, measuring the graveyard with her eyes.

Aggrieved, the BaNare cursed Tabo for abandoning his mother to the vermin of the dark. Then a week after the funeral, in the middle of the night, the fiercest hailstorm in history struck the Tladi neighborhood. It bypassed the mission and Willoughby's brick house to descend with terrifying force on the Tladi family compound. One moment the night was still, the next moment hailstones roared down. After clobbering the Tladi compound, the hail swept around the neighborhood, killing goats, chickens, one dog and two sick milk cows. Tabo had just become the first of the BaNare to follow Stimp and Willoughby in building a square house and roofing it not with thatch but with two sheets of corrugated metal, which cost a fortune at No Boots's shop and then rang and rang with a deafening din when the hailstones hit them. Everyone in Naring heard the sound. Tabo ran out in terror, stumbling naked into the night. The hail knocked him down, but no one heard him scream over the clatter of the hail. When the storm ended as suddenly as it had begun, the BaNare stepped into the quiet night to see Tabo, dimly through the dark, sitting upright on the ground, crying, "Forgive me, Mama!" again and again.

The hailstorm confirmed what everyone suspected: Stimp's graveyard was an insult to the dead. The missionary expected others to follow Tabo's example and bury their dead in the new cemetery, but no one did so. Months passed. Stimp assumed that illegal burials must be taking place in compounds at night, for surely BaNare still died. He watched the decline in his old patients at the clinic, but their relatives stopped taking them for treatment when they approached death, so that Stimp would not know when they passed away.

Irony of ironies, affliction of fate, Mojamaje's family broke the deadlock. Tabo's hailstorm had come at the beginning of summer, and at the season's end, just before dawn, another violent storm crashed into Naring. A bolt of lightning struck Ma-Mojamaje's grass roof, which erupted in fire and collapsed to the ground. Tabo and Mojamaje dashed to pull Naledi out just as the pouring rain extinguished the fire.

As the first light of day gave shape to the rubble, Tabo and Mojamaje carefully pushed away the roof beams and charred, soggy, sweet-smelling grass. There, beneath a singed gray blanket, lay Ma-Mojamaje, suffocated by smoke. They pulled out the thin, old woman's body, shrunken with age to the size of a child's, light in their strong hands, and gently placed her on the ground outside the ruined house. The dim light smoothed her wrinkles and she looked young, her high Bushman cheekbones round and unbroken, proud. Mojamaje knelt over her, his long body bent to shade her from the rain, his eyes staring down at her face. The BaNare gathered around, numb with loss.

Everyone in Naring heard the crack and saw the flash, including Stimp, who rushed out of his house to peer out through the rain and locate the flames. The downpour faded and then stopped as the missionary raced down through the village just as Mojamaje stood up, Maka's arms consoling him.

The BaNare noticed Stimp and exclaimed, "Now he sees!"

"The missionary knows she is dead!"

Stimp pulled Pia out of the crowd. The two men spoke in English, then rushed to wake Willoughby. They directed the young man to issue a warrant for Mojamaje's arrest.

"He hasn't buried her yet," Willoughby protested.

"He will bury her in the compound," Pia insisted. "This is his chance to rebel."

Back at the Tladi compound, Maka settled the issue of Ma-Mojamaje's burial, which Mojamaje was too sad even to discuss. "We must bury her somewhere," she said. "I think it will be right here."

They announced that the funeral would take place the next morning in the Tladi compound. The first of the luckless BaKii to conquer Naring and become BaNare, so long ago, Mojamaje's mother spent her first night of death on a wooden plank, waiting for the dawn to see her to safety in the compound floor. A crowd of mourners formed long before sunrise as young men from the neighborhood dug Ma-Mojamaje's grave. The young girls in the crowd wore dresses, for this was a special occasion. Underneath, all wore their makgabe. The BaNare crowded around Ma-Mojamaje's famous woodpile, encircling the Tladi and Potso compounds, standing on wagons and mud walls to see Ma-Mojamaje's open grave, on the very spot where Tladi had faced the BaNare, dagger in hand, alone on the day of Battle of the Rocks. Even the youngest child knew the story of Tladi and Ma-Mojamaje, and also the measure of her success, Mojamaje, the first BaNare to work in South Africa, to learn English, returning at the head of thousands of English soldiers and juicy cattle. The passion and tragedy of her early years yielded to calm as Maka filled the Tladi compound with children. Ma-Mojamaje was already old when the light in her eyes went out, and her death when it came was a quick one. The children began to sing her song, adding new verses for the occasion:

> A giant Bushman played a trick
> Lit a grand fire with a stick
> Tladi loved her and his son
> There never was another one
> She saved a child from demon's death
> She gave it sight and words and breath
> And died on fire, in lonely bliss
> Who is she who did all this?
> Mojamaje's mother

The sun rose over the ridge, the door to Ma-Mojamaje's house creaked open and four young men carried out her body, wrapped in gray blankets. Mojamaje and Maka followed, huddled together, struck with sorrow. Mojamaje wore his long gray army coat and hat; Maka wore her old yellow dress and a black scarf over her head. They stared ahead, lost in memory. The twins emerged last from the house, Naledi in her green dress and Ma-Boko in a white lace dress from the mission. Breasts and hips poked against the lace, showing a shadow of black through the tight white webbing. Naledi remained as thin as the stick she had used to lead her grandmother through the village. She carried this stick now, splotched with black char from the fire as huge black freckles dappled Naledi's yellow skin. In only a few years she and Ma-Boko would reach the age of marriage, but still Naledi had never spoken a word. Her dress hung loosely from her shoulders, its fall interrupted by no hint of a bosom, or maybe her breasts sagged against her chest like an old woman's. She wore her scarf low on her forehead, pushed low over her eyes, bent forward at the waist, hands clasped behind her back, holding the stick, which now seemed to join Ma-Mojamaje and Naledi in the same person.

The crowd sang, the young men lowered Ma-Mojamaje into the grave, but before the first clod of soil hit her blankets, Stimp arrived with Willoughby, Pia ya Pipa, and Tabo Cross-Eyes. The melody died on the

BaNare's lips. They stared with hatred at the intruders' faces. Stimp's beamed triumphant; Willoughby's glazed with embarrassment; Pia's puffed with smug scorn; Tabo's wrinkled with perplexity. Tabo had worn his black suit, but he still refused to wear shoes. The BaNare cursed him for standing with Stimp and Pia, for casting his bulk on the side of the cemetery jackals. His poor wife Leana, having long ago abandoned his defense, now stood inside the Tladi compound to number herself among Mojamaje's supporters. Pia's spent father, Chief Pule, also stood among the loyal mourners, beside Old Man De Swart and the other old BaNare who had spent their afternoons keeping Ma-Mojamaje company. The battle lines were clearly drawn, though the Potso and Tladi families each had members on opposite sides.

Stimp's unwelcome party had stopped before the gate to the Tladi compound, at the edge of Ma-Mojamaje's famous woodpile. Willoughby shifted uncomfortably from foot to foot. Everyone observed that his uniform resembled Mojamaje's. Stimp said something to Willoughby, who stepped forward to say, "See here, I'm sorry, all this is terribly illegal." He spoke in English, so only Mojamaje, Stimp, Ma-Boko, and Pia understood.

"Go on," Stimp goaded. "Arrest him."

"Quite a crowd," Willoughby replied. "Might get ugly."

As Stimp and Willoughby argued, Naledi stepped forward, brandishing her stick, pointing it toward the unwanted visitors outside the compound. Whereupon, for the first time in her life she began to speak.

Patiently, hopefully, the BaNare had waited years for this moment, a promise fulfilled, for certainly this was the proper occasion for the mysterious twin to make her debut as whatever Ma-Mojamaje had made of her. Witch? Sage? Avenger? Oracle? Jester? One by one the BaNare turned their eyes to Naledi, whose freckled face glowed with the passion of consummation. All voices stilled and mouths dropped open, dogs in the distance ceased their barking, birds overhead shut their beaks, the wind died and infants stopped bawling and smiled knowingly at their elder about to reveal the secrets of childhood, mysteries learned before speech, only to evaporate in the first heady flush of language.

In a voice high and soft, resonant, eager and weary, filled with the wisdom of ages and the innocence of youth, Naledi spoke these words:

"BaNare, people of Naring, listen!
What does my grandmother say?

When we came here the earth was wet
We wore flowers for clothes and prayed to
    the air
All fish had wings and elephants had hair
Around the fire we shook with sweat
No Zulu burned us, no Bushman ate us
No one on earth had the power to hate us
Now strangers come
See by their skins how they make the earth dry
They make clouds vanish and crack the sky
Where are they from?
They walk on our sweet earth uninvited
While my grandmother already grows thirsty
    inside it
Prepare for the Great Thirst!
BaNare, take care!
Bare all for the Great Thirst!
BaNare, beware!"

At Naledi's exhortation to "Bare all for the Great Thirst," Ma-Boko stood up and pulled off her white Christian dress, revealing the developing curves of her adolescent body and the childhood makgabe around her waist. Other girls followed her example, and the BaKii in the crowd broke into an ancient BaKii song, their accents so heavy that the other BaNare could not understand, singing praises to the dead woman who brought them their first dignity, pushing forward to surround the grave. Now the whole crowd surged and sang, scooping up dirt to heap onto Ma-Mojamaje's grave. The handfuls of dirt fell one against the other and the last to back away from the spot, smoothing the earth over and over, were the old BaNare who had kept her company, remembering their youths, tears moistening the grave soil beneath them. The very last to turn away was Old Man De Swart, now in rags, toothless, kneeling, a wispy white beard drooping to the dust, remembering the story of the mother who pulled from the rocks the boy-hero of the battle he himself had fought from the other side.

Stimp thundered at Willoughby, but the young officer waited until the BaNare had finished their work and then replied, "Sorry, Reverend, they buried the evidence."

When the excitement died down and the crowd thinned out, the talk of the day turned to Naledi's performance, her perfect timing and lovely pitch, such precise pronunciation for a child who had never spoken before. Some mentioned Ma-Boko's contribution, how the stick Naledi used to lead her grandmother through the village made for a nice touch, but few discussed the meaning of Naledi's words. Some praised the rhymes, some said they wished she had sung them. Only years later did the BaNare struggle to understand the complicated message of Naledi's first speech. Some suggested that Ma-Mojamaje spoke through the child, some hinted that Mojamaje wrote the words, but only long afterward when they finally deciphered exactly what Naledi said over her grandmother's grave did the BaNare agree that this was the moment when the Great Drought began.

7

Tabo Closed-Eyes

Mojamaje coughed once, coughed again, then found he could not stop. He sat on a chair atop his mother's grave, before a cookfire where Naledi brewed tea. He fell over, coughing again and again. Throughout Naring, old men coughed, then old women, then children, then everyone else. Noses filled with drizzle. The BaNare sneezed. They ran to Stimp, who gave them pills. After the second week the oldest and youngest began to die. It was like the rinderpest the English had sent to sweep away cattle, to force men to the mines. The BaNare had slowly rebuilt their herds, bought plows and wagons, but now the English made everyone cough, snort and die, to take their cattle and come take their land.

"What is happening?" they demanded of Stimp.

"Flu," the missionary said.

"Where is it from?"

"England," Stimp replied.

"I knew it," the women wailed.

"The English are killing us."

The first cough followed Ma-Mojamaje's funeral by a week. After a month there were dozens of BaNare to bury, too many funerals each day for everyone to attend. They were unable to dig the graves fast enough, so Pia ya Pipa ordered all the young men out to the missionary's cemetery to dig rows of graves all at once. Bitter with grief, no alternative in sight, the BaNare drove their wagons out to fill Stimp's graveyard with their dead: Old Man De Swart, the other old men and women who once spent their afternoons in the Tladi compound, infants, children already sick when the flu struck. Tabo Cross-Eyes, the oldest living member of the Tladi family, fell into a stupor but recovered after only a day. After that, no one worked harder driving the wagons between Naring and the cemetery. Yet the BaNare still held him partly to blame for the catastrophe: he took the side of Stimp against his own people. His rapid recovery from the flu only doubled BaNare suspicions. What medicine had Stimp given Tabo to make him immune?

Tabo hitched his ten best oxen to his wagon, the same one that had carried Maka and her twins back from Stimp's mission. Among the oxen was Dupa Red, born during the rinderpest and grown in the last twelve years to the largest ox the BaNare had ever seen. His hide was completely dull red, without a trace of the white or black splotches most cattle had. Dupa Red's horns were immense, as wide as a man's arms, solid, thick, constantly carving up the sky above its massive head. Red resembled Tabo in power and contradiction, for behind Red's bland, obedient face lay a sparkle of murder, a beast of burden's knowledge that its strength exceeded its master's. Tabo worked Dupa Red to his limit during the flu. After three months, Red pulled the wagon all by himself as the other nine exhausted oxen tramped along, listless in their yokes.

The last funeral was Chief Pule's. Despite his years of illness, he had survived the flu until the very end. The BaNare mourned both Pule's loss and the accession of Pia. They sang their old chief's name as they moved down to the cemetery, chanting, their feet kicking up clouds of dust, remembering details of Pule's life, bogwera, his earrings, traders, his people commended to jackals.

Tabo drove his wagon to the graveyard for this last burial. He stopped it just inside the fence, blocking the gate. Five men unloaded Pule's coffin and then Dupa Red snarled, maddened to mutiny from overwork. He twitched, bucked and threw off his yoke with one furious flick of his huge neck. The crowd panicked, but there was nowhere to run. The ox stood free, its red eyes luminous with violence, merciless, glaring into the crowd. The BaNare stood silent, and still, listening to the snorts of the ox. They knew that when he stopped snorting, the enraged ox would charge.

Tabo stepped forward, reaching out his arms to grab the ox, and Dupa's horns swept through the air to pierce Tabo's chest. The children screamed. Tabo splashed against Red's hooves, then lay face up, eyes closed, bloody and completely still. The smell of blood frightened the other oxen, who started to pull at their yokes, rattling the wagon. Trapped against the fence, the BaNare looked down at Tabo and then up at the ox, wondering which direction it would charge, whom it would puncture next.

Then a blur, someone rushed out from the crowd and the ox's right foreleg snapped. The ox crumpled to the ground and his horns were twisted until a dull crack signaled that Dupa's neck was broken. Truly it was a miracle.

It was Jacob, known thereafter as the Ox-Killer, who darted out to fell Dupa Red. He was a poor BaKii boy, known to be strong, but no one imagined that Jacob was stronger than Tabo or Tabo's prize ox. And he was still a boy, too young for marriage, nonetheless a vanquishing champion, his colossal shoulders hiding the startled eyes of Dupa Red, its horns turned upside down.

The BaNare rushed to Tabo. He was dead. The children screamed again and the women wailed as a dozen men helped Jacob drag the ox outside the fence, where other men began to collect wood for a fire. Men picked up spades and began digging another grave for Tabo. The BaNare cut Dupa Red apart and roasted him over the fire. As they chewed they reviewed Tabo Cross-Eyes' life and admitted that perhaps they had made a mistake. Perhaps they had given him the wrong name. Measured against his charities, Tabo's transgressions withered to insignificance. His attempt at Seantlo had failed, overshadowed by Paulus the Lover's secret tryst with Bosio Night Girl. His delivery of cattle to Big Boots served Pia's wicked ends, but the rinderpest swept them away before anyone profited. Tabo delivered Stimp's graveyard its first victim, his innocent mother, then stood with Stimp at Ma-Mojamaje's funeral, but the flu overwhelmed any verdict in that case. Despite the gleam of trickery in one eye, Tabo did little harm, while his childhood protection of Dinti the Ostrich and Mojamaje, his deference to Leana, his rescue of Maka on the stormy night of the twins' birth, his tireless toil during the flu and his fatal attempt to save the BaNare from his rampaging ox, all made the BaNare think twice as they digested roasted Red, then think a third time as they sang one last time over Tabo's grave. They decided finally to exonerate him, judging his life a balanced one, forgetting his offenses.

This, as it turned out, was a mistake.

8
What Mojamaje Felt in His Bones

While Dupa killed Tabo and Jacob slew Dupa, Mojamaje lay in his blankets, shivering with flu. Maka fell ill beside him. The BaNare interpreted her ailment as spiritual rather than bodily. She insisted on sharing Mojamaje's fate, lying huddled in his blankets, cold and wet with the same fever that raced through his shivering form. Maka's skin paled, even the freckles, to a ghostly translucence that frightened Mojamaje when he opened his bleary eyes to peer through the dark at her wraith's face, wet with tears at the thought of his passing.

Every morning Naledi served her parents tea. She was the only BaNare to escape the illness completely, a fact that everyone noted well. Ma-Boko's fever was mild and brief. She and Naledi rebuilt Ma-Mojamaje's charred roof and occupied the house, visiting Mojamaje and Maka together every sunrise.

"If you die," Ma-Boko scolded, "I will never forgive you." She stood with her hands on her blooming hips, thrust coyly to one side, her eyes rolling with mock scorn. "If you live, I will give you a treat. Both of you. The treat of your lives. Everyone will envy you both. If you die, the BaNare will remember you as fools, but not for long, because who remembers fools? Not me." On and on she chugged, her voice no longer a little girl's, humming with a husky rumble appropriate to her growing curves. Word followed word at breathtaking speed, until Mojamaje and Maka struggled to open their eyes and ask weakly, "Please . . . stop . . . tell us, what is the treat?"

Ma-Boko pursed her full lips to whisper, "If you live, I will teach you this dance." And she launched into a swirling, whirling, rhythmless wriggle, hopping on one foot, whistling, spinning, clapping her elbows together, bending over to tuck her head between her legs.

The dance grew wilder each morning. At first Mojamaje and Maka barely looked up from their beds, bewildered, then they smiled, laughed, until their sore lungs ached and they begged helplessly for Ma-Boko to stop.

She froze in midwhirl. "Promise not to die?" she asked, tossing her hips, folding her arms across her rising bosom. Then she stood on her hands to kick her feet in the air.

"Yes," Mojamaje and Maka gasped, clutching their ribs, light-headed from sickness.

"All right," Ma-Boko replied, righting herself and smoothing her lace dress, like a fancy lady. "But if you break your promise, I swear by my sacred makgabe, by the blood of my great-grandfather Tladi, by the hair of the lion that ate him, by the stars and moon and the wild, secret thoughts in my sister's head, by the scar on the neck of Seele Seantlo Child—I swear to you, parents, if you die I will do it again."

Most BaNare agree that Ma-Boko's performances saved Mojamaje's life. She kept blood flowing through his head and lungs. Others argue that Naledi's tea contained a magical elixir. Finally he grew strong enough to walk outside the compound, and neighbors called out greetings, reminded of the many who had not survived the flu. Suddenly Mojamaje was the oldest living BaNare, the only living survivor of the Battle of the Rocks. He sat in the Tladi compound hunched in his low wooden chair, his skin sallow, hanging in folds from his high Bushman cheekbones, his gray English army coat draping his bony shoulders. Maka recovered quickly, completely. She bit her lips in silence, fearing even to hear Mojamaje speak, cringing at the croak of his sick man's voice.

"Maka," Mojamaje called one moonlit evening as he sat alone on his chair before their house. The twins were off with the other children singing in circles, Ma-Boko leading, Naledi watching. Maka pretended not to hear her husband as she clanged the tin dishes she gathered from the branch rack where they had dried all day. "Maka," he called again, then coughed into the deep collar of his coat. Maka dropped her hands to her sides and wiped them on her dress, the same yellow dress, patched and mended, that she had worn when he first saw her in her mother's Taung fields. She stepped through the moonlit dusk to stand by Mojamaje's chair.

"I will not die now," he said quietly, reaching out his hand to take hers. "You fear it. Do not be misled." Maka sat down beside him, her legs outstretched on the compound floor. "I sit here each day to save my strength," Mojamaje continued. "I cannot leave you now. I will grow stronger. I once watched old men, wondering how it would feel in my bones, in my heart, my fingers, mouth. Naledi knows. She was born an old woman, grown up."

Maka pulled up her knees, wrapped her arms around them, and softly began to hum. "I have not changed," Mojamaje said. "Do not fear my old man's voice. Remember its sound on your mother's farm? Remember the ride to the diamond town, my whistle and snap of the whip? You are still the girl who rescued me on her horse, stern and serious, carrying me away. You are still that girl, dear Maka, and I, in my old man's body, will always be that boy."

9
Ma-Boko's Fire

The twins approached the age of marriage. Ma-Boko's white lace dress had already grown too small to hide the woman's body beneath it. Deep black peeked through every stitch and loop. Now when she stood with her hands on her hips, a rush of words bursting from her lips, she looked like a sultry vamp, daring any man to approach.

Just as all the boys waited for Ma-Boko to grow up, all the girls waited for Jacob the Ox-Killer. After his dazzling display at Pule's funeral, no month passed without some comely vixen accosting the young Ox-Killer in the shadows. But Jacob ran like a mouse from a cat. Not only was he still too young for serious seduction, he was a poor BaKii boy with no kin able to contribute cattle for a wife.

One day at the end of the flu winter, as Jacob strolled whistling along the Naring paths, shoeless, shirtless, in torn short trousers, a buzz-hawk streaked down toward a nearby compound. Lone buzz-hawks often circled lazily above the village, high in the air, watching for anything small that moved. Mothers feared for their children. Mostly the hawks stole chickens. Some observers swore that the bird had already taken an infant in its talons, while others reported that it had only begun its descent when the Ox-Killer scooped up a rock from the path, hurled it overhead and crushed the hawk's head in midair.

Six months later Jacob performed his next heroic feat. Summer was ending and his band of herdboys prepared to drive their cattle back to Loang from the drying rainpools in the Kalahari wilderness. Jacob always carried a heavier stick than the other herders, one appropriate to his great size. The youngest herdboys were unable even to lift it. As the Ox-Killer and four companions beat the brush for stray calves, a fury of barks suddenly crashed toward them.

"Mateane! Wild dogs!"

The ferocious pack flew through the bushes, snapping their jaws at anything that moved. Just as a wild dog leapt, its round, flat ears drawn back like wings, for the throat of the youngest herdboy, Jacob's thick stick whizzed through the air to crack the dog's neck. The animal fell dead, fangs bared, its mud-brown fur quivering from the blow.

A year later Jacob threw himself between a child and a poisonous cobra, which drilled its venom deep into Jacob's leg. The snake died.

Finally, two years after the flu, Jacob had passed enough tests to prove himself worthy of Ma-Boko. She, meanwhile, had ripened even more, and the BaNare judged that both were ready for the match. Jacob took a job with Paulus De Swart, lifting merchandise off De Swart's wagon into the shop, lifting furs and hides off the shop floor into the wagon. This gave the BaNare girls frequent opportunity to observe Jacob's flexed muscles, for still he never wore a shirt. Jacob was truly a man now, having abandoned his short pants for baggy black trousers that managed to cover only half his calves. His leg muscles strained against the thin cotton, tearing it from the bottom hem. Week upon week the girls followed the rip's progress up Jacob's leg.

Paulus spent part of each day exchanging boasts on the veranda of his shop with Ro Roodie, Maka's half brother whom Mojamaje had rescued from the South African war. Ro made a miserable living from his black-smith trade in the middle of the neighborhood of Boer compounds. Sometimes the two Boers fell into argument, which always ended the same way.

"Your children are black," Paulus sneered. "What kind of Boer are you?"

Ro pulled his sleeves back from his freckled red forearms, swelled with sinew from the blacksmith's hammer, and replied, "I have a horse. What kind of Boer are you?"

Indeed, Ro Roodie's compound swarmed with dark-skinned children. Ro's original wife, Paulus's sister, had died giving birth to a son, whom

Ro named Bowman but whom everyone called Bo. The BaNare found a wet nurse, Ata, a husbandless BaKii girl whose infant had died the same week as Ro's wife. Ata moved into Ro Roodie's compound, clasped little Bo to her breast, and within a year she had borne Ro a lovely brown daughter. A year later she bore him a second daughter, moved Bo off her breast, shifted the first daughter over and clamped the new infant to her other breast. Every year a new child appeared, to move from breast to breast, then off Ata's chest to make room for the next.

But it was also true that Ro owned a horse and Paulus did not. Though the De Swart shop now carned Paulus a good income, a horse was risky business. It fell sick in the hot summer, and died before new-born calves in a drought. But Ro Roodie had saved all his money to buy a horse from No Boots, the English trader. As Old Man De Swart used to say, "Boers ride horses. Boers carry rifles. Boers keep pigs." Even if his children were a bit dark, Ro Roodie's horse proved conclusively that he was truly a Boer.

Ro entrusted his horse to his son Bo. Bo grew to hate the horse as much as the De Swart children had hated Old Man's pigs. Every day through every winter, Bo had to lead the horse into the Naring country-side to hunt for rare spots of delicate grass. The coarse, dry pasture that cattle survived on was indigestible to horses. When Bo Roodie found a distant spot of sweet pasture, he could not leave the horse there for several days, for it needed water every day. He spent every winter leading the horse back and forth from pasture to stream through the Naring canyon, carrying stones in his pockets to hurl at the horse when they passed out of sight of his father.

A month after Paulus De Swart hired Jacob the Ox-Killer, Ro and Paulus stood on the shop veranda, trading insults and discussing No Boots, whom they both hated. Bo Roodie trudged past leading his fa-ther's horse to pasture.

"What is this?" Paulus exclaimed, his handsome face twinkling with glee. "A Bushman mouthful. A walking graveyard. That is no horse, and you, Roman Roodie, are no Boer."

BaNare idling past the shop stopped to listen and look. The horse was indeed a miserable creature, once an elegant steed but now ribs showed through its black hide. Bo Roodie halted too. He was tired of wasting his time keeping the horse alive. The horse stopped too, happy to rest its creaky bones.

"No meat," Paulus laughed. "A man could throw it over his shoulders like a goat."

Ro fumed and flushed, hissing a reply through his teeth. "No man can lift that horse."

"Wager five pounds?" Paulus snapped.

"Done," Ro replied.

"Jacob!" Paulus yelled, folding his arms, leaning back against one of the beams that supported the veranda.

Ro realized his mistake. "Scum," he spat, narrowing his eyes at his gloating tormentor.

Jacob the Ox-Killer stepped into the sun, his muscles shimmering with sweat. As Paulus explained the task, Jacob grinned, his white teeth sparkling in the sunlight. One by one passersby had gathered to listen to the Boers and now more BaNare came running when Jacob appeared. The Ox-Killer stood before the horse, took four deep breaths, his chest rippling as it rose and fell. The girls in the crowd giggled. Bo Roodie held the horse still. The BaNare stood hushed. Jacob slid his arms under the horse's belly.

Then a voice called out, "If he does this thing, does he keep the horse?"

The crowd laughed.

"Yes!" another voice cried.

"It is only fair."

"He should keep it."

"Right," young Bo Roodie added, wishing never to see the horse again.

The first voice had been Ma-Boko's. When she called out her question, Jacob looked over and found her eye. She stood with her arms folded over her ample chest, one leg forward to give tilt to her hips. Her eyes danced with invitation. Jacob's winked with acceptance. He lifted the horse.

Paulus clapped his hands, Ro Roodie cursed, Bo Roodie sighed with relief, the crowd cheered. Sputtering with anger, Ro accepted the crowd's verdict and awarded the horse to Jacob. The five-pound bet enraged him for this was three pounds more cash than he possessed.

Jacob the Ox-Killer led the horse away, following Ma-Boko to her family's compound. He offered the horse to Mojamaje for Ma-Boko's hand in marriage.

Maka led Mojamaje to the privacy of the rear of the Tladi compound.

"I have seen her with this boy," she began. "He seems a good one. But what do we want with a horse?"

Mojamaje leaned gingerly on a stick cane, coughed into his hand and replied, "We do not know much about him. A horse is too much trouble."

"Ma-Boko knows everyone," Maka said. "The boys are hers for the taking. Everyone knows this. She chose Jacob."

Men, women and children in the neighboring compounds stopped what they were doing to listen, moving nonchalantly to where they could better overhear. Some ended up no more than ten yards away, only low mud walls separating them from the concerned parents in the Tladi compound.

"The future worries me," Maka continued. "He is poor. Does he have relatives to help him?"

"I think not," Mojamaje replied. "Ma-Boko has us."

"Will we live forever?" Maka asked.

At this point one of the neighbors called over, "There is an uncle at Loang. Many goats, no cattle."

"His land is worthless," another neighbor added. "Sandy, far from water."

Mojamaje said, "But he is strong. He can plow our fields."

"Yes," Maka agreed. "Does he drink beer?"

"No," a neighbor answered.

"Has he been to the mines?" Mojamaje asked.

"Not yet," another neighbor replied. "But I wonder whether he has other girls."

"No," a young woman said from the next compound. "You can believe me, I tried."

"I think," Maka concluded, "Ma-Boko knows what she is doing. She selected this one."

A neighbor added, "He will protect her from crazed oxen."

"Snakes," another said.

"Wild dogs."

And so Ma-Boko, Mother of Brains, married Jacob, Killer of Ox. He was sweet, loyal, the girls all lusted for him, but still BaNare adults wondered why Ma-Boko chose him. He was far from rich. No one had ever accused him of intelligence. Ma-Boko spoke three languages with fantastic speed. Despite the final consensus that her pale sister was the more remarkable twin, everyone agreed that Ma-Boko deserved her name. What made her choose Jacob?

When the BaNare tell the story of the Great Thirst on cold winter nights, crowded close to the fire, they extract their brittle hands from under their blankets to reach toward the yellow flames licking the hard, twisted logs, crackling, hissing, rumbling, a background of low voices now prominent, loud against the sound of the story. The listeners watch the shadows play on their outstretched hands and look to the flames themselves, the violent red undersides of the wood glowing against the white ash below. Tiny twigs catch, flare, disappear. The listeners shrink, small, drawn into the fire, imagining themselves within it, safe from the cold but perishing in one sudden flash.

"Look," the teller of the story says, "how quickly this wood burns away. If we place all our wood on this fire, our whole night's supply, the flames will leap to the height of a tree. Hot air will carry flat bark ashes high in the sky, out of sight in the dark. Everyone will jump back, eyes wide with fear and admiration. Such wonderful, flickering light. The night around suddenly turns to day. But after two hours, when the wood burns down, the cold will return to our marrow. For the rest of the night we can only pray for the fire to last until morning. Our wood will be spent."

As the listeners nod their heads, leaning closer to the fire at the thought of it burning out, the teller asks, "Is this Ma-Boko or Naledi? As a child of five, Ma-Boko stood with her hands on her hips, tossing back her head, a husky laugh in her throat, a wink in her eye, a storm of clever words on her tongue, a vision of Drift. At the age of five she was fifteen. At the age of ten she was sixteen. At seventeen, she acted seventeen. Her wood was spent. A woman, she cast her eye for the same prizes others pursued. They all wanted Jacob, a sweet strong boy never gone to the mines to lose his manners and fall in love with gold. Jacob's heart was pure. His face was clean and simple. Ma-Boko took what everyone wanted. She married for love, hoping that Jacob's strength might carry her through the night."

The flames of the fire both draw and repel the listeners as they remember their own lives, the youthful bursts of flame falling back to bare embers, sinking, threatening to expire.

"But do we tend this fire like that?" the teller now asks. "We lit the fire log before the sky blackened, before it was dark enough to see the flame. Slowly the night crept over us. Slowly the flame grew visible. Log by log we add more wood. We keep the fire at an even pitch, never too much, to make sure that our supply will last through the night. Is this not Naledi, the conservative twin, saving her flame for when it would be needed most?"

Three languages, yes, but what use were they, except in South Africa, and Ma-Boko knew from her father's stories that this was the last place she ever wanted to go. As childhood's end approached, she saw her choices narrow to nothing, while Naledi's odd behavior made more and more sense. Under Ma-Mojamaje's tutelage and then on her own, Naledi prepared herself for the career she now practiced, occasional oracle, keeper of secrets, as sorcerers and midwives came more often to seek her advice.

Ma-Boko turned to Jacob's bulk, and in his powerful arms she felt safe. He lifted her with one hand under her back, with the other hand he caressed her breasts and belly, fingers spread, breath calm. Sometimes as he slept she whispered encouragement, exhorting him to wake the next morning and thrill Naring with more heroic deeds. She pressed her breasts against his face, and he reached out without waking, on instinct, to cradle her in his arms.

After their wedding, a joyous event that all Naring attended, Ma-Boko and Jacob took up one of the empty houses in the Tladi compound. Their first child was a boy. The BaNare called him Boko, meaning "Brains," for what other name was appropriate for the first child of a woman with her name? Their second child was a girl, named Nea. Neighbors brought their children to play and again the Tladi compound bubbled with tiny voices and tripping steps.

Mojamaje sat among them, warming himself in their glow.

10
Drought Sky

And so Maka's twins left childhood as different from each other as when they had entered it. No one in Naring failed to notice. The BaNare did not yet realize, though, that Naledi's speech over her grandmother's grave marked the onset of the Great Drought. It was not always easy to tell the difference between ordinary bad years and drought. The first summer after the flu, when they wanted to plow, no rain fell for months and months. At the very end of summer, enough rain fell to wet the fields but it was too late to plow. There was no harvest despite plenty of rain. During the second summer, rain fell only twice, in two showers. The first rain fell at the start of summer. Everyone plowed. The second shower fell just as the fields almost dried to powder. The harvest was good and the children grew fat. Yet the grass in the pasture was dry most of the year. There were no rainpools for the cattle to drink. The crops were good, but cattle thinned.

In neither year did the BaNare speak of drought. Everyone prayed for rain and tried not to notice when the rains failed to come, when the Kalahari threatened to crawl over the sand slope and smother them. The BaNare hoped for the best. What else could they do?

And then every summer thereafter, the same pattern repeated: Enough rain fell to plow and then halfway through the season, when the crops were almost dry and dead, a small shower revived them. The harvest fed the BaNare. But out in the pastures the first signs of drought appeared. The plow-season rain brought some new green grass and the midsummer shower brought more. But after that came nine rainless months. The odor of wet earth quickly yielded to the smell of dry dust, which the wind whisked high in the air even before harvest, to eddy and cloud and block the sun. Where wind penetrated, dust followed, into eyes, throats, nostrils, ears, pores, between teeth. As the grass turned brown the wind blew it away to leave bare soil and sand that rippled whenever the wind changed direction.

By harvest the nights were already cold as the heat of the day escaped quickly through the cloudless sky. The Tladi family stood in the sunshine by day, to stay warm, following the sun around Ma-Mojamaje's house, keeping out of the shadows and the wind. Every morning the sun rose low in an icy blue sky, the west wind rushed over the sand ridge, through the eaves between the mud wall and grass roof of every house in every compound. Maka, Leana and the twins finished the harvest quickly, tucking their numb fingers into their mouths to warm them. They skipped the last gleaning to hurry back to Naring. There was nowhere to hide from the cold. Even in the sun, out of the wind, the cold dried Maka's face, shrinking it so her black freckles met to obscure the yellow skin beneath.

The cloudless nights left no heat in the earth to last the winter. After the last measure of warmth floated up through the sky, a bank of gray clouds rolled over the sand ridge to cover Naring, keeping out the winter sun, freezing the water in every pot in the village. Children reached up to touch the ceiling of dark cloud, so low did it seem to hang. The wind doubled in force. Maka, Leana and the twins fetched water wrapped in gray blankets, with openings only for their eyes, tearing with grit. Gray spectres of all sizes moved soundlessly through the village, while the wind whistled through slats in the oval wood corrals dotting the neighborhoods. It was an eerie, empty sound, as when Bushmen bit off the end of bones to blow through their hollow shafts.

Year by year, drought crept up on the unsuspecting BaNare, until at last came evidence impossible to ignore. The Loang wells dried up. At the time, the BaNare pointed to this event as the beginning of a drought, finally speaking the word, but no one yet looked back to trace the dimmer beginning at Ma-Mojamaje's graveside. The drought was not yet a great one. The Loang wells had dried up before. No one doubted they would soon fill with rain again.

Loang's thirsty herders drove the cattle back to Naring, following the Kalahari wind over the sand slope. The river through the Naring canyon now dried too. Men dug holes in the riverbed to uncover pools of water underneath. Herdboys dipped buckets into the pools and sloshed water into troughs of dugout tree trunks, from which the cattle could drink. Because the trees were all skinny and twisted, the troughs were small and misshapen, slowing the work and creating a queue of thousands of cattle waiting to drink. The animals grazed where they stood, waiting, until all the grass at the canyon mouth disappeared. The cattle grew hungry now, so the herdboys drove them away to find grass, then back to the river pools to drink. In this way a widening circle of grass disappeared as all the BaNare cattle congregated to drink and graze at this one spot. Each animal ate and drank only once a week. Their heads lolled as they waited on the plain at the canyon mouth. Now the site of the Battle of the Rocks filled with drowsy black flies feasting on the multitude of cattle droppings that dried quickly to the same dull brown as the dust around them. Dung beetles flew like hummingbirds onto the plain, their black teardrop bodies glistening like fresh manure.

The cattle roared with anxiety. Every day at least one went berserk, delirious with thirst, smelling the stagnant, fetid water above the stench of dung, and here Jacob the Ox-Killer's talents proved invaluable. He spent each day heading off the frenzied beasts that aimed their faltering, meatless frames in one desperate charge at the pools. Their eyes glowed with terror, foam spewed from their parched lips, and once, as Jacob threw his arms around a cow's neck, its eyes popped out and rolled in the dust.

New calves tugged at the empty udders of their mothers. Bull mounted bull. Old plow oxen sat quietly on the sand, chewing air, their flinty eyes calm, waiting for the drought to end. Wandering through the village, blinded by the wind, lowing, trembling, the thirsty cattle gnashed their jaws in frustration, then one by one they collapsed, senseless with cold.

When summer came, the wind abated and the cloud bank rose high in the warming air, finally dropping the moisture that had made it dark. The BaNare picked out cattle strong enough to pull plows, sowed their fields and took to the shade as the skies cleared and turned white-hot. Some new grass sprouted but the sun burned it back. Three months later a cold, misty shower refreshed the young crops, but again the pasture died back. Long before harvest the cattle fell back again to queue on the plain between the hillock and the canyon. Each winter they died sooner, and after six years there were hundreds dead by the time the grain was gathered in. The BaNare cut up the casualties, stringing the fatless strips of beef from their eaves. The slow blackflies from the riverbank found their way to the drying meat. The village buzzed in a still, somber drone, but only for a week, until the cold winter wind shriveled the meat to such desiccation that even its smell disappeared. The flies wandered off.

The goats fared better than the cattle. They cast their dirty, shifty, bulging eyes on anything remotely green or wet. The herdboys never let goats drink from the river, reserving its water for the precious cattle, but still the goats survived on the minute drops of moisture in the tiny leaves of bushes and shrubs in the hills and surrounding plains. Poking their pointy muzzles deep into thorn brush, they evaded the long white thorn spikes to nip the leaves. Their fiendish bleats rivaled the flies' buzz in feeding the BaNare's unspoken dread. Only flies and goats thrived in their country. This was not a good sign.

The next summer's return brought the BaNare out of their houses into the shade. Ma-Boko's children, Boko and Nea, played among the others whom Maka welcomed into the Tladi compound. Mojamaje sat in the shadow of Ma-Mojamaje's old house, conversing with the old BaNare who came to drink Naledi's tea. In fits and starts, involuntary glimmers of sense, the frazzled BaNare began to acknowledge the drought, turning to Naledi for deliverance. Rumors of witchcraft, her magical powers, wound their way through the village paths like the children who still played the game of Naledi and Ma-Mojamaje, forming a snake with sticks, composing a new song with words taken from Naledi's speech at her grandmother's grave. Neighbors asked her opinion on the weather, but Naledi only smiled and hummed the children's song.

Mojamaje watched the skies with growing unease. So far in the turmoil of South Africa the BaNare's luck had held out. Tladi, raids, refugees, Boers, English, Stimp, perfidious Pia, all these disruptions produced lasting strains and cracks that a drought might multiply, shattering the BaNare after all, to share the same fate in the end that South Africa suffered.

11
Lost in the Mines

One summer the rains failed completely. Winter's cloud bank lifted without a single drop reaching the ground. Empty skies replaced it. High overhead the sun roasted Naring. The air became solid, hot to the touch. Not one plow dipped through the soil. Not one ox was strong enough to pull a plow. No cow bore a calf. Through the previous bad years BaNare men had left one by one for the Joburg mines, and now the remainder departed all at once, Jacob the Ox-Killer among them.

Jacob's departure rattled Ma-Boko to the core of her confidence. She had accepted the life of an ordinary BaNare woman, a disappointing end to a promising childhood, while Naledi's reputation only grew. Jacob was her reassurance. At night she clung to his neck, her arms locked in a wild embrace that would have strangled a weaker man. When he left, she turned to Naledi, who began to speak more, and the two sisters spent more time conversing, trading couplets and puns. Their chatter grew raucous, compensation for Naledi's years of silence, sisters swept up in reacquaintance.

In the Joburg mines, Jacob earned the wages of two and fame as the greatest fighter the mining barracks had ever seen. The cement-brick shacks, roofed with tin, crammed with cement bunks, encouraged foul crimes and sinister retribution. At night miners reduced to the souls of wild animals crawled on all fours, daggers in their teeth, to stalk the cement floor in search of their prey. A muffled gasp told the other miners that one of their numbers no longer breathed. The knife always penetrated cleanly between the ribs, for the best killers went years uncaught, gaining valuable practice. Jacob the Ox-Killer protected the BaNare in his barracks—one hundred bunks, one hundred blankets, still his nose and ears covered them all. He would not let a single BaNare suffer the fate of Dinti the Ostrich, undefended, alone in the mines. The BaNare slept together, crowded to one end of the cement block, but still Jacob knew when an animal touched ground at the opposite end. Soundlessly, his enormous form moving like a bat through the dark, Jacob slipped to the floor and broke the intruder's neck. After Dupa Red, the buzz-hawk, the wild dog and the cobra, miners were easy game.

Jacob earned double wages for working deeper than other miners, while most BaNare stayed on the surface, sweeping floors, afraid of the dark, earning miserable wages. Blasters set off charges at the end of the tunnel and the explosion rocked the shaft, filling it with dust and debris, and then the Ox-Killer and a Bhaca strongman, Texi Za, tore away the rubble and crawled through the new gash to see whether gold lay beyond. In the last month of Jacob's first contract, as he and Texi approached a fresh gash, the earth around them rumbled a second time. A wave of dust whooshed through the shaft, dimming the gaslights on the wall behind them. Jacob instinctively reached up to the ceiling, to ease its falling weight onto his shoulders, but not even he could hold up a mile of rock. The tunnel collapsed. When the dust cleared, Jacob found himself sitting upright against the wall, his left leg tucked back under his body, his right leg stretched out before him, buried below the knee in broken black rubble. Texi sat beside him with both legs under rock. His big Bhaca eyes were closed, his head slumped to one side. The gas lantern above them still shone as before the cave-in, as if nothing had happened.

"Texi," the Ox-Killer called, breaking the silence. He tossed a stone at Texi's shoulder. The huge man fell over, one leg pulled clean away from the mound of broken rock. It was cut off at the knee. Jacob looked down in horror at his own leg, imagining it severed too. He felt nothing below the knee. Terror flushed through his nerves.

For hours Jacob sat still, numb with fear, certain his leg was gone, trying not to move, afraid that his leg would roll away from the rubble to reveal its bloody stump. The gas lantern died out. The cavern fell dark. The Ox-Killer stayed awake, looking out into the darkness with wide eyes, afraid to fall asleep for fear he might roll over. The earth at that depth was warm to the touch, filling the air with a sweltering heat, forcing streams of sweat to Jacob's creased face. It took the other miners a day to dig through to where Jacob sat. They cleared away the rock to free his leg. It was not even broken. They pulled him to his feet, but he fell over, transfixed with disbelief, afraid to test the leg he had given up as lost.

The company sent him back on the train. At Lorole Station, returning BaNare miners lashed together a litter from thorn tree branches to carry the Ox-Killer back to Naring. He kissed Ma-Boko and Nea, rubbed Boko's and Patrick's heads, and dropped in a heap on the compound floor.

"My leg!" he cried, eyes wild with memory. He could see that his foot still clung to the far end of his leg, but he now feared that part of the middle might have disappeared in the mound of rubble. So Jacob began to walk with a limp, convinced that his leg had lost length in the mine. He folded a rag and stuffed it in his right boot.

"There," he sighed in relief. Then he thought, "Poor Texi. If only he had tried this."

After a week, Jacob's limp returned, but no more cloth would fit in his boot. So he tied a wad of rags under the boot with string. Every week he added more cloth. The rags wore out quickly, so the BaNare saved scraps for him. The Ox-Killer sat with the old BaNare in the Tladi compound while Mojamaje helped restuff his boot. Naledi served Jacob tea. The huge, sad man grinned with joy, happy to be alive, when she thrust the cup into his vision.

12
The Black Slaughter

Willoughby left Naring at the end of the flu. His replacement lasted a year; the next, six months; the next, two years. The BaNare called them all Willoughby. No one took much note of the District Commissioner except for Pia, who befriended each one upon arrival. Stimp disappeared soon after Willoughby, replaced by a succession of younger men, none of whom shared Stimp's zeal. Pia befriended the missionaries too. Now chief in full, Pia tried to renew the deal he once had struck with Big Boots, the English trader. But Big Boots's latest successor, a boozer named Ugly Boots, refused Pia's offer. The drought already gave the English trader more cattle than he could manage as desperate BaNare sold their herds before they died on the hoof. Pia approached Stimp's and Willoughby's successors with other shady proposals, but none expressed interest. Frustrated, scornful, friendless since the death of Tabo Cross-Eyes, Pia could only wait for a change of guard to deliver him a cooperative English trader, missionary, or Willoughby.

Meanwhile, Pia groomed his faceless sons and took a second wife. The flu had carried off his first wife and his youngest daughter. Pia's new wife quickly bore him a son, named Patrick, so her own name became Ma-Patrick. Although the epidemic had passed months before, Patrick was born with the flu. He spent most of his first seven years on his back. When he finally grew well enough to walk, Ma-Patrick led him to the Tladi compound to join the mothers and children congregating there.

In truth, Koko and Keke drove them out. The flu never left Patrick's lungs, so he coughed and sneezed his way through childhood. When he came too close to them, Koko and Keke slapped him away, snapping, "Stop sniveling, you snotty child." The children softened their insult into a nickname, and dubbed him "Patrick the Sniffler." The Tladi compound welcomed Ma-Patrick and her sniffling son, and in no time they became part of the family. Though returning each night to the other side of Ma-Mojamaje's woodpile to sleep in the Potso compound, Patrick and his mother spent every waking moment with Mojamaje's family.

In the beginning, Patrick the Sniffler spent most of his time sitting with Mojamaje and the other old BaNare who gathered to drink Naledi's brew. His mother never stopped eating as she helped Maka, Leana, Ma-Boko and Naledi with the work of the compound, snapping kernels of boiled corn from a cob she held in one hand, the thumb flicking the grains into her mouth. Then Patrick grew a bit stronger and began helping take care of Ma-Boko's children. The BaNare approved of this arrangement, for an ailing child seldom kept busy, and often became frustrated and sad at being excluded from surrounding activity.

Even after his injury, Jacob the Ox-Killer gave Patrick and his son

Boko rides through the village on his colossal shoulders. Sometimes he carried them down to the hillock where he worked at watering the starving cattle. Boko grew into a strong, healthy boy. These trips on Jacob's shoulders were the only times poor Patrick ever left the Tladi compound.

Patrick loved Boko, but he saved the full measure of his affection for Nea, Ma-Boko and Jacob's second child. Patrick was already fourteen years old, still scrawny and haggard, looking half his age, when he took into his arms the only girl he could ever hope to hold. The BaNare wept to think of the loving attention he lavished on Nea, and predicted the old story, unrequited love. For Nea was a beauty from her first breath of life, with full-moon eyes, round cheeks, blushing lips, and the smooth black skin of her mother. When she grew up, such a lovely girl would not look twice at Patrick the Sniffler. The BaNare settled back to see exactly how it would turn out.

Meanwhile, Patrick composed a song to sing as he fluttered through the Tladi compound, his delicate feet barely sounding against the dry mud floor:

> Remember me for what I am
> A child with children of my own
> I crossed the woodpile long ago
> To make this place my home
> A wizened youth, an early grave
> These things I all expect
> Pots clatter, tots chatter
> Tea leaves brewing, toothless chewing
> Tiny army around my neck
> Never will I plow a field, crack a whip
> Hunt the wild wood
> O, thani ay! Ay, thani o!
> Life is good

At the time, the BaNare did not appreciate the significance of Patrick the Sniffler's presence in the Tladi compound. Mojamaje kept an extra eye on the boy, though, for he was the third son of Chief Pia, and thus stood third in line for the chiefship. Although Pia's scheming had suffered recently from lack of collaborators, Mojamaje continued to expect some new plot. Despite Patrick's fragility, Mojamaje might some day need him.

Then a new District Commissioner arrived who played right into Pia's greedy hands. His name was Stone, but the BaNare called him Willoughby. Few noticed Stone's advent until Pia spread word that the new Willoughby had asked the English government to send South Africans to dig for water in Naring District. The BaNare flinched, expecting a column of Boers to march into their midst with spades on their shoulders, like rifles. Instead, two Englishmen drove up with a wagonful of tangled metal wires, tubes, bars, shafts, and four massive wooden barrels, all pulled by twelve uncannily healthy oxen.

A crowd quickly formed around the wagon. Stone pushed his way through to climb aboard.

"BaNare," he announced in a lovely deep peal, "this is a drilling machine." But he spoke in English, so no one understood. He looked around for Pia to translate, but the chief was nowhere to be seen.

"Ma-Boko!" the crowd volunteered, pushing her toward the wagon. Barefoot, a green scarf tied on her head, her white lace dress tight against her flesh, showing substantial patches of black skin through the stitch loops, its hem hanging barely to her thighs, Ma-Boko looked to Stone like the other women of Naring, only more so.

"Go on," Ma-Boko said loudly, in clear English. "I will tell them what you say."

Stone was taken aback, but he did as she said. "This machine heats water," he said. The BaNare liked his voice of authority. "The water turns to steam. The steam pushes a piston, the piston drives a pipe into the ground." The BaNare looked carefully at Stone's receding black hair, his intelligent eyeglasses, his strong chest. The English had sent a real man at last.

"If there is water," Stone boomed, "it comes up the pipe. These gentlemen will put a pump on the pipe that will bring water to the surface." He motioned toward the two Englishmen, who leaned against the wagon, smoking, eyeing the young women in the crowd. "Someone must stand there to work the handle. The wooden barrels on the wagon hold the water that turns to steam. The wagon drops the machine someplace and goes back and forth to fetch water from the nearest well or river. This keeps the drill working. This is a very expensive machine. We must thank His Majesty for helping us find water."

Stone's voice died and he looked to Ma-Boko to translate. She smiled back at Stone, turned to the crowd, threw out her arms and shouted, "This thing finds water!"

The BaNare cheered.

Stone was disappointed that Ma-Boko had omitted the details of the machine's operation. Yet he enjoyed the crowd's enthusiasm.

"Willoughby! Willoughby!" the BaNare chanted.

Stone leaned forward to ask Ma-Boko, "Who is Willoughby?"

"You," she replied.

The two Englishmen set up the drill by the bank of the stream through the canyon. The pools in the stream were almost dry, their green, shiny sludge barely sustaining the BaNare and their cattle. The drill struck water before nightfall. The Englishmen fixed a hand pump to the pipe, and the BaNare crowded around the new well. The Englishmen pumped the handle a dozen times, sending a stream of water rushing out.

"Water from a stick!" the BaNare exclaimed. Quickly they brought their buckets. Young boys took turns pumping the handle. The BaNare drank freely for the first time in years.

The Englishmen then moved the drill to the District Commissioner's house, striking fresh water in two days. Stone allowed only people near this well. Livestock were to use the one on the stream bank. The BaNare danced for days on end, splashing each other with bucketfuls of water, dousing their remaining cattle, permitting even goats to drink. Stone hired Ro Roodie to accompany the English drillers into the countryside to find more water. Ro was a blacksmith, he knew the language and the territory, and he had nothing else to do. The drought had stilled every wagon and plow in Naring. There was nothing for Ro to repair.

The BaNare swooned with excitement as they tried to guess how many hundreds of wells the drill would discover. They watched the wagon return periodically to refill its casks at the two Naring wells. The wagon broke down and Ro repaired it. The stream bank pump broke and Ro repaired it. Months passed, then a year, but still no new well appeared.

The BaNare's cattle drank greedily on the battlefield of the Battle of the Rocks, but no rain fell to revive the pasture. Winter returned, the wind blew away the last brown tufts of grass, so again the cattle could not eat. Only shrubs and trees dotted the bare soil. Cattle milled through the village, barely alive, their ribs barely covered with flesh, their hides hanging loose, fluttering in the biting wind. The ceiling of dark clouds returned, hanging so low that children again reached up to touch it. Trees died, the BaNare pulled them apart for firewood. Summer returned, the air warmed, the cloud bank rose high, higher, forming tall white, billowing columns but loosing no rain. The sky cleared to a daz-zling, painful blue. One by one, regardless of age, the BaNare cattle died.

Despite the general depression, the Tladi family compound found reason for cheer. Ma-Boko was happy to have Jacob back, even in his somewhat addled state. She carried water constantly from the new pump for her compound garden, and prepared special dishes for him with onions, potatoes and peppers. By night he was the same old Jacob, with his masterful animal sense and touch. By day she set him a schedule of tasks. Sometimes she sent him out into the countryside to collect fire-wood, where he uprooted dead trees and splintered them with bare fists.

Maka shared her daughter's contentment, but she was also the only BaNare to welcome the drought. While Leana, Ma-Patrick and even Ma-Boko thickened each year, Maka stayed lean and trim, her breasts and hips still invisible in the contours of her yellow dress. She was happy because the long drought cleared Mojamaje's lungs. The flu slowly drained away, evaporating in the dry air. Some BaNare concocted a rumor that Naledi had conjured the drought to cure her father.

Two years after the drilling machine first came to Naring, Pia the Scornful called a special meeting at Stone's office, insisting that every BaNare adult attend. Stone strung a brown canvas canopy, shading two rows of chairs, to the corrugated iron roof of the office veranda. Stone's house stood behind the office, in the shade of white gum trees planted by successive Willoughbys.

At noon on the appointed day, the chairs filled with the current En-glish missionary and the current English trader, Paulus De Swart, Ro Roodie, the two English drillers, Pia the Scornful, Koko, Keke, and two balding fat men whom the BaNare identified after considerable debate as Pono and Peke. The BaNare assembled slowly, to sit in the dust on the treeless expanse before Stone's office. It was summer, and the mid-day sun beat down on the crowd as they sat, waiting for the meeting to begin, smelling of dust and sweat. Men slumped forward, elbows on their upraised knees, while women sat upright, legs stretched straight before them, their hands shading their eyes. The crowd buzzed with anticipation and flies. Finally Stone arrived to take a chair. With him came his wife, whom most of the BaNare had never before had a chance to see.

Pia stood up to speak. For the first time the BaNare noticed that their haughty chief looked old and worried. His elegant black suit hung loosely from his shoulders. His white shirt collar was torn and ragged. His hands trembled, slicing the air, as he droned on and on about his grandfather Potso, his father Pule, himself, and his sons Pono and Peke. He conveniently left out any mention of Patrick. The BaNare's eyes moved across the small group in the comfortable shade of the canopy. The English missionary reminded the older BaNare of Stimp. He was a new man, only two months in Naring. Most BaNare confused him with the new English trader, a surly brute named Black Boots, who sat to his left. Both men had oily skins and fat cheeks. The two English drillers picked their teeth with partridge quills and ran their eyes along the crowd in search of young women's breasts carelessly exposed above their loose, frayed dresses. Koko and Keke looked thin and hard as flint but older now. They sat side by side, hiding their mouths with their hands, exchanging conspiratorial glances. Behind them sat Pono and Peke—or was that Peke and Pono?—characterless mounds of flesh.

The BaNare saved their final and most intense scrutiny for Stone and his wife. Her skin was as white as her long, straight teeth. Her neck was thin like a crowned crane's. The heels of her shoes came to a point, leaving an empty space between her foot and the ground. She wore a skirt that bound her legs like a bandage. Her hair was long and black, falling off the back of her high head. What a handsome couple they made, Stone strong and fit in that elegant gray uniform, lucky to share a bed with a queen. She ran an idle finger across her delicate lips and the crowd uttered a silent gasp.

Pia droned on and on, recounting now the history of his foes, the Tladi family. The BaNare yawned, settling in for a long, pointless meeting. They turned now to examine the Tladi contingent, sitting toward the back of the crowd in full strength. Mojamaje was there, august in his faded gray uniform barely recognizable as a mate of Stone's. Mojamaje's skin spread in myriad creases from his high Bushman cheekbones. Beside him Maka looked regal, sitting straight and tall. Then there was Ma-Boko, with the feisty bounce to her eyes and growing plump in the rear, her bosom expanding its territory. And then Naledi, the mysterious child never married, her splotchy freckles creased with almost as many wrinkles as her mother's. Her face was calmer than usual, stony.

Behind Naledi sat Jacob the Ox-Killer, retying the rags under his boot. Patrick the Sniffler assisted, his bony body no larger than a child's. All the other young men Patrick's age had long since gone to the mines. He held Nea in his arms as he leaned toward Jacob—such a lovely little girl, a bright flower blooming in desert dryness. Beside Patrick sat Boko, a brooding, intelligent boy, almost old enough to go to the mines, listening intently to Pia's every word.

It was Mojamaje who first grasped the import of Pia's speech. He said calmly to the BaNare around him, "Pia is stealing the well."

Mojamaje's words rippled through the crowd, silencing the idle chatter, turning all ears to the canopy. They finally realized that Pia was recounting the Potso and Tladi family histories in order to claim for himself the water that the English drillers had at long last found in the Kalahari, in the middle of the Loang pan.

"As we all know, BaNare," Pia expounded, "Loang was conquered by Tladi, Man of Lightning, after he blew apart the face of beloved Potso, chief of his people, grandfather of me. No matter, Loang belonged to Tladi. Tladi passed Loang to Tumo, Boy of Thunder, his elder son. His younger son was tricked into marriage by a sinister BaKii wench. No matter, Tumo inherited Loang. Tumo passed Loang on to Dinti the Ostrich, who died without an heir. The son of that treacherous BaKii woman wheedled Dinti into a futile marriage with a girl who lived at night, like a hyena. No matter, Dinti passed on Loang to his younger brother, Tabo. The descendants of that BaKii female schemer tried to ruin Tabo's good name, calling him Cross-Eyes. No matter, Tabo passed on Loang to his daughters, Koko and Keke. As we all know, BaNare, these girls grew up to marry my sons, Pono and Peke. I am old, BaNare. I have served my people, taking the whip from my father's feeble yet loving hands. No rewards matched my burdens. Is it not fitting, here at the end of a difficult time, for my sons to reap the harvest I sowed? Loang belongs to Koko and Keke. We rejoice, BaNare, for my sons' good fortune in marriage, receiving for their bridal cattle not only fine wives but the new well at Loang. Their cattle will graze there freely. All others will pay five shillings for every animal, every year."

As the BaNare unraveled the thread of Pia's address, a powerless rage replaced their confusion. Pia was stealing more than water: for dozens of miles the grass around the two Naring wells was completely gone, eaten by the BaNare's dying herds of cattle and goats, blown by the wind. But out at Loang the grass, though dry, remained ungrazed. For a year, maybe two, a herd could thrive there, so when the drought finally broke, if Pia succeeded in enforcing his claim, only Koko, Keke, Pono and Peke would have any cattle left.

Then word rumbled through the horrified crowd and the BaNare watched Naledi rise to her feet, Ma-Mojamaje's stick in her hand, still

black from the fire that took the old woman's life. Naledi raised the stick
above her head, then pointed it at the canopy. The BaNare turned their
faces to hers for deliverance. Afterward they swore that they stuck out
their tongues that moment and tasted rain. Naledi's high, strong voice
rang out:

> "BaNare, listen!
> What does my grandmother say?
> When we came here the earth was wet
> Now a cloud of dust has finally burst
> My father clutches his throat from thirst
> BaNare, did you forget?
> Strangers make the earth dry
> This beautiful child, my sister's child
> Must wander the dangerous empty wild
> Can she drink an empty sky?
> If this chief steals our well, we will die of thirst
> BaNare, I warn you to steal it first
> I have seven black goats, I will not stay
> Myself, this Great Thirst drives me away
> Where will I go?
> BaNare, Loang
> Loang! Loang!
> *Loang!*"

As Naledi cried, "Loang!" again and again, her eyes glowed white and
wide like an animal's, her freckled face turned up to the sun. Ma-Boko
jumped to her feet and repeated Naledi's call, and now the BaNare did
the same. Pia the Scornful fell back into his chair, struck dumb with fear.
Then Ma-Boko ran toward home, calling over her shoulder, "BaNare,
follow!" As the crowd surged behind, she reached the open space between the Tladi and Potso compounds, where a small herd of goats
poked their snouts among the thorn brush.

"Our animals!" Ma-Boko declared. "We must spare the black and kill
the rest!" Enraged, consumed with despair, the BaNare fell on the startled goats and fanned out through the village, hooting, chanting, slicing
the gullets of any goats, cattle, or sheep that were not black. No BaNare
cattle were completely black, every one had at least some patch of red or
white, so they all died. Only black goats survived. Soon the BaNare were
covered with blood, wild-eyed and furious, shrieking and weeping. Em-

bracing defeat, they licked the blood from their knives. Dogs howled, dying animals screamed. Naring smelt of blood. Streaks of red ran along the ground. Black Boots hurried to stand guard with his rifle over the three horses he kept in a shed behind his shop. Every compound stoked their cookfire, roasting the meat they butchered, eating the meat before it was done.

Naledi strode through the village, holding her stick like a staff, surveying the Black Slaughter. Ma-Boko pranced from neighborhood to neighborhood, shouting encouragement, screeching with glee. At first Mojamaje set out to subdue his daughters, appalled that they would urge the BaNare finally to succumb to the drought, to abandon all reason, to destroy their last wealth. Maka grabbed his arm and held him back. "Let them do it," she said calmly. "The cattle are dying anyway."

But the chaos did not end with the slaughter. That night the BaNare began streaming across the sand slope toward Loang, driving their black animals before them.

13

Pia's Fate

The exodus to Loang split the Tladi compound as it split the BaNare. Boko and Nea accompanied their mother and aunt on the long, dangerous walk. Jacob the Ox-Killer went along too, carrying one of the water barrels from the English drilling wagon. Ma-Patrick and Leana started out with the march but Leana died on the third day out, old, forlorn, still wondering whether her husband Tabo's eyes were crossed. Many BaNare died along the way, especially the young and old.

Maka remained behind with Mojamaje and Patrick, who were too weak to make the journey. She served tea and beer to the old BaNare who also stayed in Naring. Patrick helped Maka with the chores. It was a sad time in the village and no face reflected more remorse than Patrick's. His precious Nea was gone, certainly forever.

Those who stayed behind wondered about the settlers' fate.

"They will come back."

"They are too many."

"They have no food."

"The English will shoot them."

"Bushmen will eat them."

Once Pia realized he was not among the creatures the angry crowd wanted to destroy, he thundered at Stone, "They are stealing my well!" But his voice rang hollow like a rainless storm. "Arrest them!" he shouted after the slaughter, as the column departed.

Stone wrote to Kalahariland Territory headquarters, requesting instructions, while the empty compounds stared back into Pia's tired eyes. Round and round he wandered, surveying his desolate domain, running out to the sand ridge to cry, "Come back! Come back!" Then he sat in the dust and fell asleep. He awoke, returned home, cut holes in his clothes and meandered through the village, sleeping in empty houses. Faceless Pono announced he was taking over as Acting Chief, relieving his father of his official duties.

Pia stumbled one night into Ma-Mojamaje's woodpile, fell, and slept against the dry wood. He awoke early in the morning, stood up and staggered into the Tladi compound. Mojamaje sat in his low-slung wooden chair while Maka bent over her cookfire. Mojamaje glanced up at Pia, then with one long arm he pulled another chair next to his own. Pia slumped down onto it. Maka pressed a cup of tea into Pia's empty hands.

CHIBI

Tladis

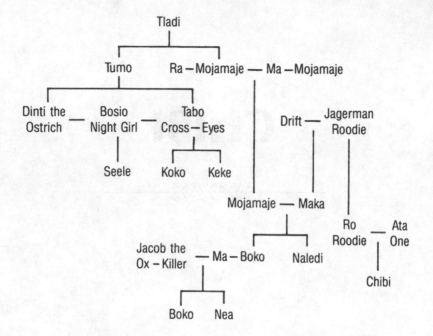

Potsos

De Swarts

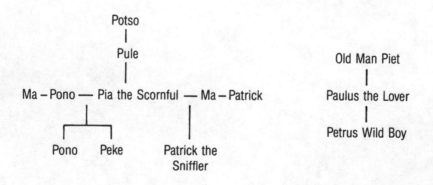

1
Wild Boy

The march to Loang came just as the drought squeezed for the first time against the BaNare's bellies. Hunger invaded Naring. The men at the mines found that the drought affected all South Africa, though not as severely as Kalahariland, but enough to send so many men begging for work that the mines lowered their wages. BaNare men brought back less money precisely when their families needed more. Children cried all night for food, their elders went hungry to feed them.

After these grim details of the ghastly drought, the tellers of the story of the Great Thirst are relieved to inform their listeners that the story of Chibi comes next. Without Chibi, the story of the Great Thirst would have come out very differently. She won her first fame when the children sang this song about her:

> Hot as a chili
> Milk the cow
> Snake snakes a wiggle before it can stop
> Chibi's so happy
> On her fat bottom
> Petrus the Wild Boy is happy on top

This is not the song of a hero. Chibi first made her mark in Naring for exploits that no one considered noble: Chibi the trollop, the butt of ribald jokes, every gossip's favorite prey. Only later, assisted by hindsight, did the BaNare note her indirect membership in Mojamaje's family, her faint resemblance to Ma-Boko and Naledi, the courage bristling from

her brow. Short on mystery but full of surprises, Chibi's life yielded
richer victories than even her ample bosom heralded.

At the time, none of the BaNare realized that Chibi had composed
the sweetest of the many songs to win popularity during the Great
Thirst:

> Come with me to paradise
> A rainbow in the clouds
> Swim in milk
> Trees full of fruit
> A wreath of berries for your head
> My dear, this life is hard for you
> A heart so bold and proud
> Dust fills your empty soul
> So dry you think it dead
> My love will rain for you!
> Do not give up hope, my dear
> My love will rain for you!

Of the many songs composed during the Great Thirst, only this one
survived to become part of the story. Most of the songs Chibi sang as a
child were original rhymes, which other children quickly spread through
Naring. Chibi received no credit for her drought song because it was a
woman's lament directed at a man. Who could Chibi have swooned for?

This song explains much about Chibi, for she was a dreamy, sweet
child, ignorant rather than scornful of social propriety. In her naive way,
and despite her early reputation, Chibi was the most serious character in
the story of the Great Thirst.

No one remembers Chibi's childhood. She was a Roodie, and she was
the reason that Mojamaje's rescue of Ro Roodie from war-torn Taung
was so important for the story of the Great Thirst. After Ro's wife died
and Ata the wet nurse replaced her, the BaNare lost count of the offspring passing across Ata's chest. Although Paulus De Swart needled Ro
by calling these children black, in truth their hues varied considerably.
The youngest and lightest was Chibi. Her amber skin, marked with faint
freckles, identified her as a Roodie. Years later, some BaNare said that
when Chibi's frame filled out it resembled Ma-Boko's, while her skin
resembled Naledi's. Through Ro and Maka, the two children of
Jagerman Roodie, the villainous Taung Boer, Chibi was a member of
Mojamaje's family.

The first of Ro's countless children with Ata was a girl, named Atanyana, meaning, "Little Ata." The BaNare called her Ata Two. At a very young age Ata Two began bearing children, each by a different man. Her first child was a girl, whom the BaNare named Ata Three. Every year each Ata produced another child. Though some of their offspring died in infancy, the Atas' prodigious fecundity developed into a legend that stuck to each of their daughters, even those with other names, like Chibi.

The BaNare first noticed Chibi among the Roodie children when she appeared on the back of Wild Boy's horse. "Where did Wild Boy find a horse?" the BaNare asked, until someone identified it as the very same steed that Jacob the Ox-Killer had lifted and presented to Mojamaje for Ma-Boko's hand in marriage. How did the horse stay alive in the drought, and how had it found its way into Wild Boy's untrustworthy hands?

First the BaNare remembered that Mojamaje had made this offer: "Feed and water my horse, it is yours to ride." Everyone knew how much trouble a horse was to keep, so Mojamaje had entrusted it to the only taker, Wild Boy Petrus, son of Paulus De Swart. Mojamaje expected the lad to give up quickly or else to neglect his duties and let the horse die.

Petrus had inherited none of his father's gorgeous features, or so the BaNare assumed. Wild Boy's hair grew every which way around his head in a jungle of greasy, straggly blond locks, obscuring his face. When his voice deepened and his leg hair darkened beneath his short pants, a scraggly beard further hid his face. His toes were hairy too, long and sinewy, capable, children claimed, of gripping the mane of his horse.

Miraculously, despite the worsening drought, under Petrus's care the horse's health had improved until its coat shone black and clean, its red eyes healed to liveliness, its bare ribs retreated behind layers of firm new muscle. Snorting proudly, leaving sprawled in the dust all memory of its former decline, the horse bore Petrus through Naring.

"Yi-yi-yi-yi-yi!" Wild Boy yelled, whacking the horse's flank with his hat, snorting along with the horse in violent glee. Every so often one of the older BaNare girls raced past with her arms tight around Petrus atop the horse, giddy with fear and excitement, to disappear into the countryside, out of sight. Children reported that Petrus clung to the mane with his toes while he pulled off the girl's dress and ravished her in midgallop.

The only girl seen more than once on Petrus's horse was Chibi, youngest child of Ata One, the only passenger to cry "Yi-yi-yi-yi-yi!" along with Wild Boy. While girls her age still wore makgabe, Chibi's breasts rose high off her chest. Her thighs and buttocks rounded early as well. Often her blue dress fell off one shoulder as she rode through Naring, exposing one voluminous breast to the keen-eyed BaNare public. Adults called Chibi and Petrus "The Slovenly Riders," while children called them "Wild Boy and the Slut."

Ro Roodie would have yanked Chibi off the horse and thrashed her, but this was still before the discovery of the Loang well and he was off with the English well-drillers in search of water. As the drought dragged BaNare spirits lower and lower, the last entertainment left in Naring was the spectacle of Chibi and Wild Boy on the horse.

As for how the horse thrived in the drought, the answer to this question involved Black Boots, the English trader. He fed his own three steeds with hay grown, cut and baled in Taung, railed to Lorole Station and carried by wagon to Naring, then stored in a shed behind his shop. A twenty-strand wire fence enclosed his compound, including the hay shed, horse corral, shop and house. To protect his property, Black Boots at first had hired a night watchman, but he never managed to stay awake past midnight, so instead Black Boots bought a dog in South Africa. Naring dogs were all dun-brown, short-haired wretches with weaselly snouts, bony tails, fetid breath, smashed ribs, torn ears and bleeding sores from the sticks and stones children used to torment them. They ate rats, lizards and whatever else they could steal. Black Boots's new South African dog was a monster, twice the height of the Naring dogs, black as its master's boots, with short, glossy hair and the teeth of a lion. Its chest resembled Jacob the Ox-Killer's, a knot of sinew on two powerful, graceful forelegs. Its abdomen thinned to a tight waist and its tail shot straight up like a warning. Tying the beast inside the hay shed by day, Black Boots loosed it to prowl the compound by night. BaNare walking past the fence after dark nearly left this earth when the fearsome dog erupted in bloodthirsty barks.

Wild Boy found a way to befriend it. Every night he crawled through the underbrush to the trader's compound fence, behind the hay shed, to talk softly to the beast. At first the dog woke the whole village with its fiendish howls, pulling Black Boots out of bed to investigate, sending Wild Boy scurrying away. Eventually the dog calmed down, answering Wild Boy's voice with querulous growls, then curious whines, until Petrus vaulted the fence, patted the animal on the head, and stole bales of hay from Black Boots's shed. In this way he fed the old black horse in style. Black Boots invested such confidence in his monstrous watchdog that he grew careless about inventory. He never discovered the theft. This was how for several years Petrus had fed the horse he borrowed from Mojamaje.

Some BaNare argue that Wild Boy was an animal himself and thus spoke to the ferocious dog in its own tongue. Others say that a dog is a dog and all crave affection. Or perhaps Petrus fed the dog meat. Sometimes on moonlit nights, when the cocks crowed and dogs joined in, Black Boots's fearsome beast could be heard above the rest, baying in plaintive peals at the distant moon, and some BaNare insisted they heard alongside this deep dog sound, above the commotion, the howl of a human voice.

2

Dazzling Vina

When Chibi's father returned from finding water with the English drillers, she wisely ended her daily rides with Petrus. The BaNare made sure old Ro heard none of the rumors about his daughter, but Paulus De Swart had his own thoughts on the matter.

"You miserable excuse for a Boer!" he screamed at Ro. "Keep your half-breed daughter away from my son!"

"You have two sons, man," Ro blandly replied, washing his face in a barrel of water all the Ata children filled from the two pump wells he had helped install in Naring. "Janie is married, Andries works in Joburg. You have two daughters. Marthe married my own son, Bowman. Ruthie married your sister's son. Soon she will bear a brood of idiots with hair on the nose. Do you have another child I know nothing about?"

"Petrus," Paulus growled. "You know I mean Petrus."

"Petrus?" Ro replied. "I thought you meant one of your human sons."

Paulus leapt for Ro's throat, and the two old Boers tossed in the dirt until enough neighbors came to pull them apart.

That night, Ro Roodie called his family into the two-room shack he shared with Ata. Dozens of children and adults jammed against the mud walls, their eyes glinting in the light of the oil lamp on the table before Ro. Ata sat on the floor at his feet, cradling two infants against her enormous chest.

"Are these all mine?" he asked her, amazed. Ata called out for the grandchildren and great-grandchildren to scat, leaving Ro's ten daughters, only Chibi still a child, standing in the lamplight.

Ro said, "Which one keeps company with Petrus De Swart?"

Chibi stepped forward to say, "I do, Papa."

Ro peered at the girl, noting the tremendous breasts and hips, the patches of freckles. "What is your name, child?"

"Chibi," she answered, holding both hands to her chin.

"What has he done to you?"

"Nothing, Papa."

"That boy is no Boer," Ro continued. "He is an animal, a devil. I warn you, Chipi, do not let him touch you."

"Chibi, Papa."

"His father thinks his filthy son has a hope with you, the child of a Boer. He would like that, the scum. You would make a respectable wife. These wily De Swarts all want the Roodies. I am a real Boer, Shibi, and no De Swart will ever use me."

"Chibi, Papa."

"Or you. Do not let this boy use you. Remember, your father is a Boer."

Petrus, of course, had already used Chibi many times. He did not grab the horse mane with his toes and disrobe her in midgallop, as reported, but took her along on his hay heists. She would remain outside Black Boots's fence as Wild Boy lifted a bale out of the compound. He had urged her to climb in to pet the dog, but she refused. They carried the hay to the back room of the De Swart shop. Paulus had immediately discovered this cache, which pleased him for two reasons. First, Paulus hated the English trader. Second, it suggested that his wild son might be able to make a living someday as a thief. At least the boy showed aptitude for something.

After Wild Boy and Chibi set the hay bale down in a dark corner of the back room, Chibi lay back on the pile of furs the BaNare sold to Paulus. She pulled up her dress. Wild Boy pulled down his pants and lay atop her. Even after a year of riding through Naring, Chibi had not overcome her fear of falling, so when she lay in the shadows of the De Swart back room, her eyes lost direction and she felt as if she were falling backward off the horse. She threw her arms around Wild Boy to hold on, a gesture he took as affection.

"So you like it?" he grunted, losing himself in the folds of her skin, as Chibi imagined herself not under his hips but on the horse, the room too dark to decipher up from down, wrapped in empty space, a bewildering vertigo that sent her arms flying around Wild Boy's back. Sometimes the moon cast enough light through the small window above her to make shapes visible in the gloom. Objects hung from the ceiling beams and Chibi tried to guess what they were: bridle, spade, basin, dress, shoes, bullwhip, bucket, ax handle, jute bags, yoke chains.

"So you like it," Wild Boy mumbled again, falling asleep on her breast.

Did Chibi love Petrus Wild Boy? Perhaps she loved him the way Black Boots's dog did. Petrus was the only human being who gave Chibi or the dog any attention.

Then old Ro returned from the Kalahari with the English drillers, after successfully installing a pump well at Loang. So as not to offend her father, Chibi abstained from her wild rides with Petrus. Then Pia's meeting at Stone's office sparked the Black Slaughter, and Petrus rode out of Naring until the danger passed, thus sparing the life of his horse. But that was the last straw for Black Boots: he sold two horses to Stone, rode his third horse out of Naring, and never came back.

As soon as Black Boots disappeared, Petrus rode into the trader's compound and tore open the hay shed door. The monstrous South African dog bounded into his arms, yipping with joy and relief. From that day on the contented beast ran alongside Petrus's horse through the village. The BaNare called it Wild Boy's Dog. But Petrus also faced a new problem: Where was he to find another supply of hay?

A month after Black Boots's departure, a new trader arrived in Naring to take over the English store. Who would buy a business in the middle of a crippling drought? Since the Black Slaughter there had been no cattle for sale and no oxen to pull a wagonful of merchandise from Lorole Station. Yet coins still tinkled in the pockets of men returning from Joburg and the BaNare still snared wild furs in the Kalahari. In fact, hunting had never been easier, as the drought drove game east from the deep sands, desperate for water. Hunters walked out only a day from Naring to find herds of antelope, packs of gold-nosed foxes, standing, staring, begging for death.

Who was Naring's new trader? Who bought Black Boots's shop?

"A dirty Englishman," the BaNare guessed, watching a donkey cart pull into Naring. The new trader sat proudly on the seat, his family huddled in the cart behind. His hair was straight, black with streaks of white, and puffs of gray hair sprang from his ears. His face was round, darker than dust, with a pointed nose and invisible cheekbones. He wore a long black English suit, as did his son, a lovely boy with thin features and long, white nails grasping the side of the lurching cart. Two women sat wrapped in gossamer veils, purple and red, masking their forms and faces, except for their dark eyes. They darted inside Black Boots's shop the minute the cart rolled up to it, only their ankles and bare feet exposed in a jeweled flash to the BaNare crowd forming at the compound fence.

A former miner pushed to the front of the crowd to explain, "Those are the Indians we told you about. Thousands in Joburg. Cheaters and bandits." This man had no direct experience, of course, for rarely did miners see the sprawling Joburg townships, where Indians ran shops. The mining companies kept mine workers confined to barracks, feeding them from iron cauldrons, doling out their pay at the end of contracts, tossing them onto trains back home.

"What are those animals?" the BaNare asked, pointing to the donkeys hitched to the cart. Another miner stepped forward to say, "Those are the donkeys we told you about. Thousands in Joburg. Stupid and stubborn."

The crowd stared at the four beasts, lashed four abreast, motionless in front of the empty cart, eyes closed, ears erect. Furry, gray, the size of a two-year-old cow, the donkeys kept the BaNare amused until night darkened the sky.

Chibi had no way of knowing at the time, but the donkey cart delivered her rival to Naring. Ahamed the Indian trader installed his wife, his son, and Dazzling Vina, his daughter, in Black Boots's square brick house. Vina was the only one of the Indians with kinks in her hair, the only one who would have passed the potato test. Ahamed's wife was very pale, almost as white as the English, leading the BaNare to suspect Vina was not of her flesh. Ahamed's son supplied more evidence for this conclusion when he began fooling around and within a month begat his first illegitimate child. The BaNare surmised that Vina was the result of Ahamed himself fooling around in the Joburg township. Ahamed took in his son's unfortunate girl, to work in the store and bear her child in the

privacy of the Indian house. Ahamed's son scampered out to fool around
some more.

No fool, Ahamed sat Vina at the cashbox. She sat quiet, coy, her long
lashes dimming the smoky haze of her eyes, in the shadows of Ahamed's
shop, poorly lit so as to obscure the poor quality of his wares. As a result,
Ahamed won at once all the business in Naring. Paulus De Swart considered burning down the Indian's house, but Stone would surely know who
had done it. Stone arranged for Ahamed's donkey cart to pick up hay at
Lorole Station to feed the two horses he had bought from Black Boots.
Petrus Wild Boy and Chibi crept into Stone's storage shed to steal the
hay.

One glimpse of Dazzling Vina made Petrus forget Chibi. In the darkness of Ahamed's shop, Vina's color faded to show only the slim outline
of her face and body, which resembled closely that of Stone's seldom-
seen wife. Vina looked like an Englishwoman in the dark. She even
walked like one, slowly, her head held high, a queen unaccustomed to
sweat. Dangling gold chains bound her bare ankles.

More tempting yet, Vina soon abandoned the flowing robes she arrived in to don instead a sleeveless cotton dress that hung so loosely from
her slender shoulders that it seemed about to fall off. The miners took
one look at Vina's delicate bronze arms, naked to the shoulder, disappearing into the cotton dress to connect at some breathtaking point with
the elegant body beneath, and they bought the same sleeveless dress for
all their female relatives. Ahamed charged as much for this sleeveless
dress as De Swart charged for a long-sleeved dress, but because the
sleeveless style required less material, Ahamed made a whopping profit
on every dress he sold.

Certainly Chibi was no match for this Indian Temptress. Yet who
expected Wild Boy to pursue Vina in earnest? He appeared one day in
Ahamed's shop, invisible as a dog, wandering between the bolts of cloth,
along the counter, ignored by Ahamed and his customers. Only Vina,
her pointed nose tuned to sniff out lewd advances in advance, noticed
Wild Boy lurking in the shadows. He meandered toward her cashbox, to
lean against the counter as customers handed over their coins. He looked
at the spoons, enamel plates and cups in the cabinet under his arm,
raising his head only when Vina reached out her arm to return a custom-
er's change. Perfectly positioned, his head adjusted to just the right
angle, Wild Boy could see, under her outstretched arm, the full curve of

Vina's pointed breast through the shadowy armhole of her sleeveless dress.

Day after day, Wild Boy edged closer to Vina, unnoticed by Ahamed or the customers, encouraged by the steamy glances Vina flashed at him the moment her breast appeared in his vision, striking him dumb. Her eyes seemed to whisper, "This is my breast, Wild Boy, my gorgeous copper breast. See how perfect its shape in the shadow of my dress? Someday, Wild Boy, if you are lucky, I will let you touch its beautiful skin." As Wild Boy inched closer each day, Vina's glances lengthened and she took to biting her lower lip or placing her tongue between her teeth as she leaned forward.

At last Wild Boy made his move. One moment Vina's breast appeared in the armhole of her dress, the next moment Wild Boy's hand reached toward the opening. From across the store, Ahamed caught a glimpse of a hand moving toward his cashbox.

"Thief!" Ahamed cried, at the precise moment that Vina's right hand slapped Wild Boy's away and her left hand smacked him across his dirty face. Ahamed darted toward Wild Boy, shouting, "Thief! Rapist! Animal!" He grabbed the stunned Wild Boy's hair to tug him toward the door, but Petrus recoiled like the mongrel he was, pushing away the Indian's bony arm and bending his knees, poising for action, growling a garbled protest. The only customers in the shop were three miners, their helmets glinting in the dim light, and now they leapt at Wild Boy, overpowered him, pummeled him bloody and deposited him in a heap in the dust outside Ahamed's shop.

The miners thrashed Petrus Wild Boy because all miners hated Boers. The English mine owners made a rule that the Boer foremen were not allowed to strike their miners unless the miners hit them first, so the Boers used every vile curse they knew to tempt the miners to violence. Sometimes a miner lost his temper and attacked his foreman. The Boer took pleasure both in the brawl and in reporting the incident, knowing that the English owners banished violent miners from the mines. And the Boers took special care to single out the most experienced miners, who knew enough to qualify soon as foremen. In this way the Boers protected their jobs. The three miners in Ahamed's shop thus took out their anger on Petrus, a Wild Boy, no foreman but still a Boer.

After Petrus suffered this beating, he never let his ferocious black dog out of his sight. At first, after Black Boots had quit Naring, the dog had only run alongside the horse as Petrus and Chibi rode. When Petrus dismounted, the dog wandered away. After the whipping, Wild Boy resolved to take the dog everywhere, hoping to run into the same three miners. After the incident in Ahamed's shop, Wild Boy's Dog never left Wild Boy's side.

3
Talons

Petrus ignored Chibi during his quest for the Indian breast. She moped through the village, singing her song, and wandered into Mojamaje's compound, where Maka served her a cup of tea. Mojamaje recognized her as his wife's half brother's youngest daughter.

"My niece," he greeted her.

Abandoned by Wild Boy, just another face in the Ata compound, saddled with a bad reputation, Chibi began life anew in Maka's shadow. She gazed up and saw an alternative, the famous wife of Mojamaje, who rode into Naring at the head of an enormous herd of cattle. Did not Chibi also ride a horse? Was she not Maka's relative?

Chibi finished her tea, chatted with the women in a circle around the cookfire, then rose to help two little girls, great-granddaughters of Mojamaje's comrades, stamp corn at the back of the compound. Ahamed and De Swart sold flour and grain corn, but the latter was cheaper so BaNare women bought it to turn to flour at home. These two girls stood face-to-face over a wooden mortar, as tall as the smaller girl's waist, each thumping a long wooden pole into the hollowed bowl in the top of the mortar. The poles were carved thin at the center, to allow little girls to grasp them with two hands and older girls and women to grab them with one. The fringe of the girls' makgabe twitched and flew as they raised their poles high and brought them down against the grain in the bowl of the mortar. *Poomf—poomf—poomf* . . . First one pole, then the other, drummed against the corn, the girls maintaining a steady rhythm, one pulling her pole out just as the other's came down. Chibi stood watching for a moment, then seized the pole from the younger girl's hand without interrupting the pattern. The older girl smiled and picked up the tempo. Chibi dropped one hand and grabbed the older girl's pole, again without breaking the rhythm. The two girls stepped back to clap and whistle as Chibi continued stamping, one pole in each hand, the beat slowing, poles rising lower each time but still falling with enough force to crack the corn. Huffing now, straining against the weight of the wood in her hands, Chibi finished the job.

Maka then came over to help Chibi scoop the pounded corn out of the mortar and spread it on a mat to dry in the sun. Chibi quickly regained her breath and, some BaNare claim, began that moment to come to her senses. Later they winnowed the grain, kneeling on the edge of Mojamaje's circle of conversation. Maka chatted to the girl, hands gripping the flat, wide winnowing baskets, laced bark strips tossing powder into the air, wind drooping over the compound wall to brush the chaff to a dark pile on the floor beyond the basket's edge, leaving only white flour scratching the basket weave.

Chibi came every day to the Tladi compound, helping Maka work, crouching by Mojamaje as he conversed with his friends, sometimes accompanying Mojamaje and Patrick to public meetings. Lost in the cadence of work, she seemed to forget Wild Boy. One day, she skipped through the compound gate to the kakwa tree against the compound wall, where chickens still roosted despite the leafless branches. Chibi carried an egg back to the compound, balancing it on her head, to add it to a fresh potful of hot porridge. She cracked it against the rim of the cast-iron cooking pot, pulled apart the two halves of the shell, and a black lump tumbled into the gruel. All the chickens in the Tladi neighborhood were white. Chibi thrust her hand into the pot to rescue the mysterious dark thing.

Others came to see, crowding around the tiny, quivering black mass. It was a falcon, its gray beak and talons already sharpened to hooks. Its mother, perhaps dazed by drought, must have dropped the egg into the nest at night. Chibi knelt beside the tangle of wet feathers, lifted the bird with one hand and pressed it down the front of her dress, to the warmth between her breasts. Its talons scratched her skin. For days she carried the trembling creature this way, between the Ata and Tladi compounds, dribbling thin porridge into its twitching beak, wrapping it in rags and setting it to sleep in a corner of the compound as she helped Maka with chores. When it disappeared, the other regulars in the Tladi compound were certain that a dog had eaten it, but they reassured Chibi, "Yes, we saw it fly away."

Some BaNare claim that Chibi sought out the company of Maka to

learn from her lessons that would come in handy when the Great Thirst
tested her powers. But how could Chibi know the future? No, she was
still a silly, lonely girl with the body of a woman, talonless, drawn like the
old to the Tladi fire.

Then Ro Roodie left town again, hired by Stone to string telegraph
wire from Naring to Lorole Station, where a wire already ran alongside
the tracks to Taung headquarters. Until the Black Slaughter, the District
Commissioner had communicated with Taung by letters carried by the
English trader's wagon. Black Boots's departure had forced Stone to seek
an alternative. So Ro took along his son Bo, five miners and a donkey
cart supplied by the Lorole police post. Because of this job, carrying
poles from Lorole, digging holes to set them in, tying the wire to the
poles, Ro Roodie missed the spectacle of Chibi's belly swelling with
Wild Boy's child.

"Child, you grow fat," Maka noted as Chibi knelt to blow air into the
smoldering logs of the Tladi cookfire. Her huge blue bottom menaced
the old BaNare sitting behind her, and they averted their eyes from the
awesome sight.

"I will speak to Wild Boy's father," Maka continued.

Chibi gave no reply but stood up, smoothed her blue dress, walked out
of the compound, through the village and into the ridge of hills, to sit
with her head in her arms.

"I am ruined!" she cried aloud. Poor Chibi! To everyone else she had
been ruined long before, when her bare breast flew past, Wild Boy's hair
flying back into her mouth, when she gained her reputation as Wild
Boy's slut. Filled with the same feeling every Ata girl felt when her belly
rose with her first child, ending her chance of marriage, Chibi sang with
a quavering voice to the tiny yellow desert birds sleeping in the spindly
trees above her head:

> Dust fills your empty soul
> So dry you think it dead . . .

Luckily, she had heard enough of Mojamaje's wondrous stories, of
Maka's encouraging entreaties, for resolve to overcome her remorse. "I
will show that animal," she said at last, wiping away her tears to look
upon the world with new eyes. She picked her way through the thorny
brush to stand on the rim of the ridge, looking down on Naring, her
tormentor about to become her prey.

"I am a falcon!" she shouted, frightening the birds around her, whose thirsty throats gasped at the hot air, squawking, as their tiny yellow wings, dry and brittle, pulled them up into the cloudless sky.

4
A Devil in Fur

The drought drove the baboons to desperation. They lived in the Naring hills, which stretched for fifteen miles in a line from north to south, broken by clefts and canyons, hiding a thousand crooks and caverns. The Battle of the Rocks took place at the mouth of the largest of these canyons, which served as Naring's door to the east, to the rolling plain that led to South Africa. Before the drought, herders drove their cattle through this canyon to graze on the plain, so baboons avoided it, keeping instead to smaller, remoter crevices. Children gathering wild plums in the hills often startled a troop of baboons, which sometimes bared their teeth, barked, and ran screaming, screeching away.

When the drought blistered the plum bushes to dormancy, the children no longer scrambled through the hills. Sour green jojane berries withered on the vine. Tiny, bitter white mokgolegetwa bulbs blew away in the wind, caterpillars and grubs shriveled to dust, the plum bushes died. Baboon stomachs growled with hunger. They found water in the deepest crannies of their caves, but the endless chain of rainless weeks wound around their bellies and pulled tight. They attacked starving rock rabbits, they attacked each other, and then they attacked Naring.

Because the sprawling Boer compounds were closest to the hills, the baboons attacked there first. Late one moonless winter night the BaNare woke to the hideous squeals and barks of the baboons descending the hills, enraged with hunger. The night was completely black, a canopy of thick, cold clouds obscuring the stars. The thump of baboon feet bounding toward the Boer compounds brought men and women running with spades, axes and sticks to drive the animals back. A few old men brought guns, but it was too dark to aim. Snarling, grunting, ripping the air with their fangs, the baboons rampaged through the grounds of the Boer compounds, picking up each loose object, sniffing it, tossing it into their elongated jaws if it smelled like food. The baboons made the greatest racket at the Roodie homestead, which was littered with hundreds of scraps of metal and wood from the wagons and plows Ro and Bo had repaired. *"Uhr-unnh! Uhr-unnh!"* the animals shouted, barking with frustration as they threw down each inedible morsel, mouths frothing with madness.

The cowardly, starving dogs of Naring ran to the scene, hurling impotent high-pitched barks from a distance on the perimeter of the Boer neighborhood. Shouting and cursing, the BaNare swung their weapons into the dark, hitting each other instead of the baboons, tripping over the junk in the Boer yards.

Suddenly the baboons broke through a window, pulling back the wooden shutter to rampage through one of the houses. The children inside shrieked with terror and flew out the door as the frenzied animals tore the room apart, poking their pointed snouts into every corner, slurping down day-old porridge, swallowing eggs whole, drinking from the water bucket, chomping uncooked corn. Bursting back out through the window into the night, they moved toward the center of Naring.

The BaNare were helpless, unable even to count the invisible monsters. A hundred? Five hundred? Had all the baboons in the Naring hills massed to storm the village? The air was cold and the Kalahari wind blew dust into the BaNare's blank eyes, muffling their shouts, adding to the terror of the night. The baboons swept out of the Boer neighborhood, the Naring dogs turned and ran, the BaNare evacuated their children from their compounds. The baboons had free rein. Naring was theirs.

But suddenly a blood-chilling howl tore through the commotion. A baboon screeched in agony. The rip of flesh filled the air as one baboon after another screamed and cried a dying howl. A frantic scrambling, a confused skirmish, a succession of murderous, roaring admonitions turned the tide of battle and the baboons retreated through the Boer compounds up into the hills, their leaders casting a final salute of anguished barks as their defeated troops receded to silence.

The first gray of dawn streaked over the ridge as the BaNare waited anxiously for night to end and morning light to reveal their deliverer. Had Jacob the Ox-Killer returned from Loang? As the ceiling of cloud illuminated slowly, filling the air with a pale, icy glitter, the BaNare counted the shapes of the dead baboons, mystified by the spectacle. They counted nine dead: three huge males with powerful chests, teeth like knives, bodies the size of Bushmen; four females, thinner and smaller, one with a darker coat than the others; two tiny babies, almost human in the softness of their shadowed faces. Even in the gloom the BaNare could see the dun-brown fur blotched with fresh blood. When the sky brightened enough to see colors, the BaNare adjusted the count to eight, for the dark female baboon turned out to be Wild Boy's Dog. This fearsome beast was their savior.

The BaNare crowded around the bloodied dog. A horrible gash extended the full length of its spine. Dust-caked blood obscured almost its entire coat of glossy black. Its fur quivered.

"It lives!" the BaNare cried. But their amazement faded to realism.

"Not for long."

"It will die."

A few Bushmen in the crowd, driven by the drought to settle in Naring, pulled the baboon carcasses into the canyon, collected firewood, skinned and ate the fallen invaders. No BaNare dared touch baboon meat. Such animals were too human, a consideration that meant nothing to Bushmen.

The crowd dispersed, relieved to escape a full baboon assault. The Boers set to cleaning up the mess in their homesteads. Thankful but helpless, they left Wild Boy's Dog to die. Wild Boy himself paid the dog no mind, showing not the slightest sorrow, mounting his horse to gallop into the countryside. Chibi did not ride with him.

"What a dog," the BaNare lamented.

"Never another the same."

"A devil in fur."

"Wild Boy never deserved such a thing."

The dog survived. It opened its eyes to see Petrus riding past. Struggling to plant its forefect on the ground, dragging its bruised hind legs, Wild Boy's Dog pulled itself into the De Swart compound, under an abandoned wagon frame. Black flies covered its wound, swarming with delight, crawling deep into the raw flesh. The youngest Ata children found the animal's hiding place and brought it water and porridge. The dog's wound took months to heal, leaving a wide, purple, hairless scar down its back, an ugly stripe to mark its victory over the baboons. It never recovered enough to run again beside Petrus's horse, but when Wild Boy walked on his own two feet, the dog limped close behind.

5

A Boer Wish

Chibi asked Maka not to speak to Paulus De Swart about marriage.
"I will speak to Wild Boy myself," Chibi said. "Did not Ma-Mojam
aje win her husband by her own wits?"

Maka was pleased, for this was the closest thing to wisdom Chibi had
shown. Yet she feared that Chibi made too much of the tale of Ma-
Mojamaje, a forlorn outcast who won respectability through the sheer
force of her own will. If Chibi hoped to win Wild Boy through sexual
trickery, she was in for nothing but rude disappointment. Dowdy Chibi
was now far behind Wild Boy, who had already abandoned his dreams of
Dazzling Vina to move on to stalk even more brilliant game.

One early summer night two months after the baboon attack, Chibi
crept to the De Swart compound and tossed stones against their water
barrel, rousing the family. Old Paulus bellowed for Petrus to investigate.
Wild Boy came out, ax in hand, ready to smite baboons.

"Wild Boy," Chibi hissed from the shadows. Petrus moved forward,
ax raised. "I am here to help you steal hay."

Wild Boy dropped the ax, rubbed sleep from his eyes, and whispered,
"Chibi?" In truth, he had forgotten about her. Now he remembered her
huge breasts and hips. "Follow," he ordered, his bare feet slapping the
dust as he ran toward Stone's house. Chibi ran after him, as Wild Boy's
Dog dragged itself from under its shelter and hobbled along far behind.

Wild Boy opened the door to the shed that housed Stone's two horses.
Purring to the animals, he led Chibi to the rear where a stack of hay
bales climbed the wall. They pulled one of the bales off the pile and
Chibi hefted it onto Wild Boy's bare back. They skulked out of the
shed, Chibi closing the door behind. A light flashed on in a window of
Stones' square brick house, not ten feet away. One red-curtained window
now glowed with light. They heard voices as two silhouetted profiles
moved across the curtain. But the voices spoke on, unaware of the
thieves outside.

Relieved, Petrus and Chibi breathed deeply and whispered reassurances. Wild Boy added a vow, "I will burn that one," moving past the window.

Chibi's heart plummeted to her feet. "No!" she cried, loud enough for the Stones to hear. Wild Boy broke into a run and Chibi followed. The door opened and Stone stepped out into the dark. He discovered nothing and disappeared again into the house.

"No!" Chibi cried again when they found themselves far enough from the Stone house. "She is English. You are a Wild Boy. The Indian slapped you. Willoughby will arrest you. You are mine!"

Wild Boy ignored Chibi's plea. He licked his lips and hefted the bale higher on his shoulders. Entering the De Swart shop, he dropped the bale on the floor. Chibi pulled up her dress, Petrus pulled down his trousers, Chibi lay back on the soft pile of furs and Petrus lay atop her. As the black room circled above her head, Chibi felt as if she were falling backward off the horse. She threw her arms around Wild Boy, holding on for dear life.

"So you like it?" he mumbled, wiggling in delight.

As they slipped out the shop door, Petrus said, "You are fat."

"It is your child," Chibi replied.

"Keep it," Wild Boy said. "A gift. I do not want it."

Next morning, Ro Roodie returned from laying Stone's telegraph wire. He took one look at Chibi and stormed to the De Swart store. He fell upon Paulus De Swart without uttering a word and the two old Boers fought until customers pulled them apart.

No one knew what poor Ro Roodie said to his errant daughter, the chattel of Wild Boy Petrus De Swart, half man, half beast, but the punishment he devised for Chibi provoked much debate. Piecing the story together, the BaNare decided that poverty, not pride, inspired Chibi's sentence. The drought and then the Black Slaughter had destroyed every ox team in Naring. Every plow and every wagon lay still as death in the dust and thus never required repair. Ro Roodie's blacksmith hammer lay idle, reducing him to impoverishment. While BaNare men flocked to South Africa, some forever, Ro hesitated to send his son Bo. Ro himself was old and worn, unable to whack the anvil with force, so Bo stayed in Naring to take the rare smithing jobs that did come up, to keep the Naring business in Roodie hands. A second son should have gone to South Africa, but Ro had no second son, only ten daughters by Bounteous Ata One. Perhaps, speaking Boer, Chibi the Young, Chibi the Pale, might find work in South Africa as a Boer and send Boer wages back home. Or so Ro Roodie hoped. In any event, this was to be Chibi's punishment.

"When I bear this child," she said to Maka, "my father will send me to work in Taung."

Maka dropped a freshly brewed pot of tea. She seized Chibi's shoulders and sat her down between Mojamaje and Patrick the Sniffler. "This child is going to South Africa," Maka announced. "Tell her what she needs to know." Patrick leaned back to listen too, for he had never left Naring. He coughed into his hands, wiped them on his torn trousers, and stretched one arm around Chibi's shoulder. The old men began telling stories and the old women cranked corrections when the embellishments exceeded belief. Chibi looked into Patrick's young face, still a boy's despite the aged infirmity of his body. Patrick listened carefully. Chibi's mind wandered.

For four months, until she bore her baby, Chibi sat listening to tales of South Africa. When her child finally came, a healthy, pale daughter, she delivered it to Maka, who found a wet nurse in the village. The Tladi family gained a new member, whom the BaNare named Wild Infant. But it lost one too, as Chibi left for South Africa.

"I leave now," she said to Maka, a blanket rolled up atop her head, her blue dress cleaned and hanging freely, no longer taut from the child underneath. "I will send money to you. You are my grandmother. You love me here. Patrick will be chief. I will send money to make him rich. Everyone will listen then. I will make my child proud of me. Everything will be all right. I speak Boer."

Maka dropped her teapot again, pulled the rolled blanket off Chibi's head, and tugged the girl over to the circle of old BaNare. "What did you tell this child?" she demanded. "Did you explain about life in South Africa—how hard, how cruel, her skin, the English, the Boers? Or did you spin silly fables, confusing her mind?"

"Maka," Mojamaje replied, removing his old gray English army hat. "Clouds can do no more than rain. We have rained for months. But sometimes a thirsty man holds his hat out like this." He held out his hat before him, right side up, the bowl facing down. Chibi was completely baffled, but Maka understood. The old group had tried their best, but Chibi held her hat the wrong way.

Maka turned to Chibi, pointing a wrinkled finger at her eyes. "Child, listen to me. You do not look like a Boer. You will work like a dog for terrible pay. Be careful of men who promise you things. . . ." Maka rushed to cram Chibi's head with useful advice, but the girl only smiled and waved Maka's words away.

"Let me explain," Chibi replied. "My father is sending me to Taung. The Roodies have a farm there. My father's father's brother's son owns it. He is a Roodie, like me. I will work as a maid in his house. One of the family."

Maka shook her head in dismay. Surely Chibi knew the true story of Jagerman Roodie, his murder by Drift, his conniving Griqua widow taking in his brother, the details of Maka's own past. But Chibi seemed immune to facts.

"Maka," Mojamaje interrupted, looking up from his low-slung chair. "The child will learn. She is going. She will learn or they will eat her. You yourself, and I, your husband, learned things in Taung. Do not try to spare this child. You cannot. Tell her only one thing: Tell her to return. She must stand and fight, as you did, but in the end she must remember this is her home."

Maka turned to Chibi and said, "Go, child, your life is yours. Try, and when they beat you, try again. When they beat you, try a third time. But if they beat you again, come home."

6
The Black Goats

And what of Loang?

Most of the black goats had survived the trek, to bear a flock of new offspring soon after arrival. The tough, dry grass surrounding Loang revived them and the abundant water from the new pump well, with no cattle to monopolize it, gave the black goats their first taste of luxury. Not all the infant goats came out black, so the Loang people castrated the male deviants and allowed only the pure black to reproduce. They ate the female deviants as tender, young meat. They slaughtered the old black goats before they died of old age. Young men among the settlers stitched the black goatskins into sacks. Eyes radiating violence, they threw the black sacks over their shoulders and set out from Loang, through Naring to Joburg. Soon on the gold fields other miners knew and feared the black goatskin sacks of the Loang men, who slept in the same barracks, sported knives in their belts and saved all their wages. They returned to Lorole Station, walked back to Naring, loaded their sacks with flour from De Swart's shop and set out for Loang. Everyone called them the Black Goats.

The Loang settlers also ate wild animals from the desiccated wilderness around them, dazed docile antelope, duikerbok, hartebeest, wildebeest, gazelle and even eland, their wildness sucked out by the searing summer sun. Their secret waterholes dried to dust. No moist grass grew in all the Kalahari. They wandered onto the flat, wide Loang pan, heels clicking lightly on the baked clay floor, the smell of water from the well pump drawing them from hundreds of miles around. The BaNare slaughtered them at will. Bushman bands ringed the pan to join in the harvest and beg for water from the well. Eventually the smell of blood grew so strong on the pan that it drove the animals away again.

Ma-Boko knew that the Loang people could not survive long on only their goats and occasional sacks of flour. The goats had already begun to strip the area of its every blade of grass, every last leaf, to leave it as bleak as Naring. Already the children, thirsty for cow's milk, fell ill with reeling heads. They stopped growing, their height stunted forever. The next generation of BaNare would resemble the Bushmen—a nation lost to the wilderness, shrunken and listless, doomed to misery.

Ma-Boko tried to discuss these problems with Naledi, but her mysterious, freckled sister took a grand turn to face her and replied:

> "I raise my stick and here we are
> You wonder how we came so far
> Now you ask me what to do
> I leave that to you
> But doubt not the wisdom of these things
> Do you ask how the sky or why birds have wings?"

Ma-Boko fumed in response, but mostly she was tired. True, the excitement of the Black Slaughter, the arduous journey to Loang, had stimulated her sparkling wits, but she fell into lethargy once the hubbub died down. Loang settled into routine. Every movement was a struggle for Ma-Boko. Jacob the addled Ox-Killer came to her each morning for instructions on the day's tasks. She sighed as she remembered his magnificent youth, and then her own. Now she set Jacob to building houses, using his bulk to spare the rest of the settlers the effort of strenuous work. This saved food.

Boko, son of Ma-Boko, left for the mines with the Black Goats. Nea, her daughter, grew into the sweetest child in BaNare history. Nea cried when her brother left Loang. She cried each time her father Jacob grinned at her mother and asked, "Next?" She wept for her mother, her father, for all the BaNare.

"Why must we fight?" Nea asked Ma-Boko.

Her mother laughed "Ha!" as Pia the Scornful once had done before he ended up humble and spent, around the Tladi compound cookfire. Nea felt her mother turn bitter, a cold wind following summer. The girl grew no taller, stunted by the drought, and her round cheeks retained an infant flush. As she approached marriageable age, she seemed to grow only younger, a helpless child lost in a world of suffering.

"Why must we fight?" Nea asked Naledi, but her mysterious aunt only smiled.

7

An English Prayer

Stone ran a hand through his thin black hair. Removing his eyeglasses, he folded his hands on the desk before him. Acting Chief Pono leaned back from the desk, in a metal chair that creaked under his chiefly weight. Stone cocked one eye at Pono, a large, aging man. He preferred Pono to his father, Pia the Scornful, a haughty, arrogant rascal. Pono was serious. His bland face never flashed with deceit. He seemed to view chiefship as service to his people.

After the Black Slaughter, when Stone had requested instructions from Taung, his superiors sent him a copy of the old profile of Mojamaje that the missionary Stimp and Pia himself had drawn up to convince the English to send the first Willoughby to Naring. Pono came to the office to examine the document with Stone, validating each item.

"Interesting," Stone concluded, his deep, clear voice filling the tiny brick office. "Why does this matter now?"

"Master Willoughby," Pono began, spreading his fat hands in front of his face, "Mojamaje is my enemy."

At first Stone had tried to purge the title "Master Willoughby," but finally had to accept it. Even Pia and Pono believed it meant "District Commissioner."

"So?" Stone asked, raising one eyebrow.

"Long ago," Pono explained, "when his grandfather Tladi murdered my father's grandfather Potso, gunpowder, boom, no face, the Tladi hate the Potsos. The woman with the stick. That was Naledi, Mojamaje's daughter. Naledi and her sister led the people to the Kalahari. They killed our cattle."

"Where is this Mojamaje?" Stone asked.

"Loang. With his knife." This was untrue, of course, but Pono did not want Stone to look for Mojamaje in Naring. Mojamaje spoke English much better than Pono did and he would explain the truth of the whole situation. "You must send soldiers to Loang," he implored Stone. "The Tladis are keeping that well for themselves. Please, Master Willoughby, my people kiss your feet."

"I shall write to headquarters for instructions," Stone replied. "I promise, Chief, justice will be done."

Pono stood up, bowed, and backed out the office, closing the door behind. He breathed a sigh of relief, smiled up into the sun and walked back home to the Potso compound. Each step lowered his spirits until he reached the site of Ma-Mojamaje's famous woodpile. There he paused. Listening carefully for the voices of Koko and Keke, he heard their shrill giggle from the back of the compound.

"They are home," he whispered to himself. "My day is ruined." He kicked a twig. "My life is ruined. Koko and Keke, Keke and Koko, Koko and Keke. Which is which? Not even I can tell." As he stood immobile, his brother Peke rushed out of the compound to his side.

"Brother!" Peke called. "Never leave me so long." Together they walked out of the neighborhood to find some beer.

"I think soon Willoughby will bring soldiers," Pono explained. The two men still looked alike: round faces, graying hair, sagging paunches, pale eyes.

"Will the soldiers bring guns?" Peke asked.

"I hope so," Pono replied.

"Will they give us Loang?"

"I hope so," Pono answered.

"Will they shoot our wives?"

"I hope so. We must ask them nicely, in English. Let us practice, brother. Here is what we say." In English now, Pono said slowly, "Please, dear English, shoot Koko and Keke."

Peke knew very little English, so he missed several words when he tried to repeat the phrase. After a dozen tries, with Pono patiently correcting him, Peke said it perfectly, then the brothers said it in unison, falling in step, tramping through the village, singing with glee:

> Please, dear English
> Shoot Koko and Keke
> Please, dear English
> Shoot Koko and Keke
> Please, dear English . . .

And so on to the beerhouse, where they taught the chant to the assembled old drunkards, who delighted learning the English words, endorsed their meaning, and joined Pono and Peke in singing the song until they all fell drunk in a heap, asleep.

8
First Try

While Pono and Peke slept in the beerhouse, Chibi set out for South Africa. Buffeted, tainted, reviled, Chibi left Naring without bidding Wild Boy farewell. The tales of South Africa that Mojamaje and his old cronies told her rolled out of her mind as smoothly as her father's warning about Petrus. Despite his pursuit of Dazzling Vina, his dreams of burning the Englishwoman, his indifference to the Wild Infant he implanted in Chibi, she still remembered Wild Boy fondly, especially the hay thefts, dropping the bale onto the De Swart shop floor, pulling up her dress, lying back on the furs, smelling of wildness . . .

Chibi tripped, waking from her reverie, losing her balance and catching herself before she fell. She looked at her feet, at the iron rail she had stubbed. Another track ran alongside it, to Lorole Station, to Taung beyond. She stepped between the rails and walked on. Carrying corn flour but no money, she stopped in Lorole village to offer some flour in return for the use of a fire and a pot to cook it. Lorole was close enough to the South African border to have escaped the worst of the Great Drought. Their rains had been paltry, but every year yielded at least some harvest of grain. South Africa itself had suffered even less. The Wall-Makers had seen a constant stream of BaNare climb on the train at Lorole Station, driven to the mines by drought. The Wall-Makers called it justice, atonement for the Battle of the Woodpile.

"BaNare?" the Wall-Makers snarled at Chibi. They had never forgiven the BaNare for turning them away. Ten thousand skeletons, naked and cold . . .

"No," Chibi corrected. "Boer."

The Wall-Makers laughed. They hated Boers, too, but Chibi was too dark to pass for a Boer, so they took her claim as a joke. "Eat, child," they offered, refusing payment.

Chibi thanked her hosts and set off down the tracks toward Taung. Her bare feet stumbled on the wooden ties until she fell into a steady stride: two feet between, then one between, then one foot, then two feet. She sang her song, especially the refrain, letting go both hands to balance her rolled-up blanket on her head, her arms sweeping the air:

> My love will rain for you!
> Do not give up hope, my dear
> My love will rain for you!

She encountered two women from the distant north, Kgama country, on their way to Joburg. They traveled together until Chibi turned off the tracks at Taung. The town had grown to a remarkable size since Mojamaje and Maka had left it so many years before. The great South African war had demolished it, but now it had grown as large as Kimberley in the days when Mojamaje sold grain there, with sprawling wide streets and townships.

It was a mild, early summer morning, with a skyful of white billowing clouds whose bottoms darkened to drop a light shower of rain. Chibi turned her face to the sky, dropped her bundle and rubbed her hands across her face, washing away the dust. After a chain of inquiries, she turned up a long lane that led to the Roodie farm. Rows of tall, white-trunked trees cut the horizon at every angle, and two of these rows lined the dirt path she now traversed. The farmhouse came into view, a stately white-plastered building. Chibi gasped in delight, proud to be part of such a fine family. Glass windows neatly divided the front. Behind, Chibi could see a huge farm shed, wagons, plows, and bare fields rising gently over the land.

This fabulous house looked nothing like Ro Roodie's scrap-strewn Naring compound or the plain mud house Maka and Mojamaje had described Drift building and Jagerman Roodie seizing for his pale Griqua wife. After Jagerman Roodie's murder and his Griqua widow's marriage to his brother, Brakman, the eldest son of this new union had inherited the farm. His name was Karman, and he turned his inheritance into a tremendous success, expanding acreage, breeding prize bulls and wool ewes. He refused to take in his disinherited siblings, who fled to the slums of Joburg to look for work, cursing Karman's soul. This was why Ro Roodie had stayed in Naring after Mojamaje rescued him. It was with the likes of Karman Roodie that the English made peace after the great South African war.

Chibi knew all these details, or at least her father had explained them to her. Ro did not expect his half brother Karman to welcome Chibi with open arms, investing her with the inheritance that Ro once claimed, but certainly she would find work in the house as a kitchen girl or maid, decent wages, a clean bed. That was all he told Chibi to expect. She embellished these hopes, installing herself as a full Taung Roodie, hurrying to the grand white door of the elegant white house. Chibi stopped, looked in a window, and called out "Hello!" in Boer.

The door opened. A woman in white, several shades lighter than Chibi, emerged to spit, "In the back, pig."

Bewildered, Chibi walked around to the rear of the house, where the wall facing the fields was composed of crumbling unpainted brick. A canopy of tree branches shaded the ground. Chickens skittered across the dust. An old man the color of Chibi stood thumping a hammer against a cow's hindquarter. For four smacks the animal held its place. On the fifth it roared, bucked, and loped off into the fields. The old man turned to Chibi, a five-toothed gappy smile on his wrinkled face.

"Leg falls asleep," he explained. He spat a stream of tobacco juice into his hands and rubbed them through his nappy, dust-colored hair.

"I called out front," Chibi said shyly.

"Blackies in the rear," the old man scolded.

"I am a Roodie," Chibi protested. "From Naring. My father is Roman Roodie, son of Jagerman Roodie."

The old man whistled and laughed. "Mama?"

"Ata One."

"Boer?" the old man asked.

"Not exactly."

"Black?"

"Not exactly," Chibi mumbled. "Darker than me."

"Very black or just black?"

"Just black," Chibi admitted.

"Child," the old man said, "you are a lucky little girl. Rain started, time to plant, I will hire you for the season. Never let Old Karman see you. The worker compound is over the rise. Go down and tell them Pyk sent you. The Roodies will never know you came."

"I want them to know," Chibi insisted. She bit her lip, scratched her back, still with the blanket roll on her head. "I am a Roodie."

"Child," Pyk counseled, "Boss Karman hates Ro Roodie. Hates blackies. He would really hate you."

"I am a Boer," Chibi replied.

"Boer?" Pyk sputtered. He raised his hammer. "Leg asleep? Get down to that compound!"

Chibi hurried away in the direction Pyk pointed with the hammer, her tired head swirling. As she trudged through the fields, her toes sinking in the soft, moist soil, she pondered her predicament, and remembered Maka's advice.

"My first defeat," Chibi said to herself. "Two more and I can go home."

9

Bushy

Chibi's life on the Roodie farm was very different from the one Mojamaje and Maka had led there. Chibi was just another field hand. Karman Roodie owned twenty plows, each pulled by a team of twelve mighty oxen. Women walked behind them dropping corn seeds carefully into the fresh furrows. Up and down the fields they walked, bent at the waist, as Pyk and four other overseers watched out for careless workers. Up before dawn, to sleep after dusk, Chibi felt her adolescent fat turn to taut muscle in the Roodie fields. When weeding time came, the women took hoes and bent double again, thwacking away the vines and punk-grass from the tender grain shoots. At harvest time they moved through the fields tearing the cobs from the towering stalks, shucking, threshing, bagging the grain in jute sacks, heaving the sacks onto Karman Roodie's wagons for transport to Taung station. Pyk paid out wages. Chibi counted her shillings, folded them in a rag, tied the rag around her waist.

At first Chibi heeded Pyk's warning not to divulge her identity as a Roodie. But as she made friends in the workers' compound, a miniature township of mud houses and tin shacks, Chibi gradually revealed clues to her parentage. Sometimes she stole glimpses of her relatives, creeping up to the house at night to crouch in the shrubbery, peeking in the win-dows. The residents all looked so white. "Real Boers," Chibi sighed. Karman himself was a despotic, dour, irascible brute. He sat all night in a huge armchair, scowling at his children and grandchildren. Sometimes he threw a liquor bottle across the room. Chibi watched each nighttime's drama and longed to share it. Furniture crammed the house, oil lamps lit it brightly, the smell of fried meat filled it. When Pyk hired Chibi for another season, he croaked, "Everyone knows you are a Roodie. Karman will find you and whip you. You ask for trouble."

The next work year was easier, as Chibi learned all the tricks: sneaking into the shade for naps, hiding the yoke chains to delay plowing, weed-ing the same row over and over, hiding among the tall stalks at harvest, holding the oxen still while others loaded sacks onto the wagon. In the compound at night, men on their way to and from the Joburg mines stopped to look for fun, drinking beer and forcing themselves on women. Chibi fought them off. Her resolve weakened, though, at the end of her second year in Taung, when Bushy arrived. An expert foreman from a farm near Joburg that put Karman Roodie's to shame, Bushy took over management of the Roodie fields at a princely wage. Pyk retired as head overseer but remained in the compound, content to crab away at the younger generations. All the women fell in love with Bushy. Tall and lean, with deep black skin, hands the size of pumpkins, and soft, femi-nine lips, Bushy was an instant success in Taung.

Bushy was a religious man. Every Sunday he donned a white robe festooned with purple sashes, shoes, and a narrow-brimmed stiff black hat to pray beside the Taung River. As he walked from the farm to the riverbank, lost in reflection, men and women gathered behind him. At first they were only curious, but gradually he developed a following of believers. Bushy led his congregation in hymns, baptizing new adherents in the Taung River. A rumor rapidly developed that each female convert underwent a second baptism in Bushy's arms. Bushy also demanded half his followers' wages. In return they received beautiful white gowns like Bushy's, which they wore to weekly services by the river, singing songs Bushy composed:

> Your kingdom is a place
> I know in my heart
> Plenty of meat
> Nice beer
> Money
> Aah

The Bushyites overheard Chibi singing her song as she worked:

> A rainbow in the clouds . . .

and they begged her to join the church and write songs for them. She refused. "I am afraid to talk to God," she explained. "Use my song, please. You do not need me. I do not want Bushy to push me in the water."

Fear of baptism kept many from joining Bushy's flock, especially in midsummer when the river ran deep and fast. For Chibi, though, the real reason was fear of Bushy's arms. Although her loins ached with desire, Chibi kept her mind on her Wild Infant and stuck to the business of saving money. "I am a nice girl," she said to herself.

The Bushyite ceremonies grew more difficult to resist. Bushy's reputation spread, and every Sunday he strode toward the river, his white robes ruffling in the breeze, black skin sparkling against the white, followers thronging behind, singing songs as Bushy called out, "My people, come!" in a smooth, leathery voice. He appointed ten young women his "Holy Zion Angels" to flank him as he sermonized. Each Angel wore a colored sash pulled tight around her white robe to accentuate her nubile bust. The youngest wore a green sash, the oldest yellow, while reds and blues draped the ripest Angels. Bushy gave each one a tin cowbell to clank as they sang praises to the sky:

> He got something
> Everybody wants

He gave it to me
O Lord

Halfway through his sermon, Bushy fell to his knees, threw up his arms, shook his shoulders violently, grunted like a pig, then rolled his eyes toward his congregation, whose song died on their lips. He jumped to his feet and cried out, *"Mor blalan elf peekina!"* No one understood the phrase. *"Shing ook po vavik toom!"* No one understood. On and on Bushy rambled, his eyes rolling in their sockets, spittle dripping from his chin. His bones rattled, his knees twitched, until he fell in a convulsing heap on the riverbank. Finally he lay still.

His followers waited in silence. Suddenly Bushy stood up. All signs of his frenzy had disappeared. "Did you understand my words?" he asked solemnly. His followers shook their heads no. "This happens when God enters my soul. He speaks English through me. That was English. I do not know it myself. That was God, speaking through me."

None of the congregation knew any English, so they accepted Bushy's pronouncement. Word spread. More and more farm workers came to join the church to hear God speak English through Bushy. He doubled the number of Holy Zion Angels and declared his intention to cure the infirm. His first patient was a woman no one had ever seen before, claiming to be crippled below the hips. She crawled up to Bushy in the middle of one of his seizures and kissed his feet. Bushy cried out as if in agony, "Aaarrgh!" Then he raised his hands, fingers extended like lion claws, to fall upon the woman, pry open her mouth, reach in one hand and pull out a live lizard. The youngest of his followers fainted. The woman cripple jumped to her feet and began a dance of thanksgiving, swirling in circles, her arms spread like bird wings, an ecstatic grin on her face. The Bushyites watched with awe-filled eyes as her hips began to sway. She turned her face to the congregation, sweat streamed down her cheeks, her eyes clouded, she pumped her hips, tossing her pelvis toward the crowd, moaning with delight. Then the Holy Zion Angels began to rock slowly back and forth where they stood, until one after another they too broke into lewd gyrations. The rest of the Bushyites followed until Bushy led them into the calm river to cool off.

The first beneficiary of Bushy's healing touch, the stranger who crawled on her hands, joined the church as leader of the Angels. Some followers voiced doubts, pointing out that she looked enough like Bushy to be his sister. Yet week by week, Bushy's fame spread. Once a month he performed a new miracle, always on a stranger who joined the church after the cure, ending the meeting with a dance. Chibi's gentle lyrics were forgotten as Bushy's services grew rowdier. Once he sacrificed a live hornbill, cutting off the wild bird's huge beak, spraying his followers with its blood. When the river flooded with summer rain, Bushy tossed a bleating sheep into its froth and the congregation listened as the screams of the dying animal receded in the surging current that sped it downstream. Once the new leader of the Angels tore off her robe to run naked through the Bushyites, pulling out her own hair and babbling incomprehensible phrases. "English!" Bushy exclaimed. After that she and Bushy ran the service together and he called her "Queen of the World."

Despite Bushy's increasingly spectacular success, Chibi refused to join him. The Bushyites whispered that even the Queen submitted to baptism in Bushy's bed, and everyone now agreed that she was indeed his sister. The ceremonies sounded exciting, but Chibi held firm her resolve.

"I am a nice girl," she said aloud, an assertion that those working near her who heard it, so far from Naring, had no reason at all to dispute.

10
Asleep on the Step

Back in Naring, Petrus Wild Boy missed Chibi only for the two hands she had lent him on his nocturnal hay thefts. One night soon after her departure, he struggled out of the Stones' shed with a bale on his shoulders, kicked the door shut with one foot, refastened the latch with his teeth, straining to balance the heavy bale. The latch bolt snapped into place with a resounding crack. The two horses whinnied and a light flashed on in the Stone house. The back door burst open. Stone's wife rushed out with a pistol in her hand. Her shadow blocked the light of the window from illuminating Wild Boy's face.

"I thought so," she declared in English. "You miserable worm. Think I can't count?"

Silhouetted by the lighted window, her face was a black blank, invisible to Wild Boy. He froze where he stood, silent. Petrus knew no English and she knew no Boer.

Stone's wife moved toward Wild Boy. "I counted the bales. You waited for my husband to go to South Africa. I am not stupid." Drawing close to Petrus, she stepped aside to let the pale window light fall on his face. The bale still hung on his bent back, his arms folded behind to support it. He groaned softly from the strain. Stone's wife said, "So it is you. I see you ride." Petrus understood nothing but the softening of her voice.

Reaching out a hand, she brushed the mat of blond hair from his face. Petrus looked up. Stone's wife gasped. His face was beautiful. He had shaved and washed it every time he stole hay, in the hope of meeting her. No one else, not even Chibi, had ever peered under the tangle of blond hair hiding his features. He had inherited the looks of his father, Paulus the Lover.

"My husband bought me a horse to ride with him," Stone's wife whispered, running one finger along Wild Boy's perfect chin. "I refused. I will ride with you." Shadow still hid her face. She turned on her heels and disappeared into the house. Wild Boy blinked, smiled slyly, and shook his head until his matted hair tumbled back over his face. He hefted the hay bale higher on his back and hurried to stash it in his father's shop.

Petrus understood none of Stone's wife's words, but he guessed from her tone he had made some progress. Next morning he cut off all his hair, shaved again, washed all over, pulled on short trousers, left off his shirt and shoes, mounted his horse and rode back and forth in front of the Stone house. Neighboring BaNare came out to stare at his magnificent chest and calves, his tanned back, the marvelous angles of the bones of his face, the beautiful burnished arms, the glamorous glint of seduction in his eye.

The BaNare asked each other, "Who rides Wild Boy's horse?"

"It looks like Paulus the Lover as a boy."

Slowly the BaNare realized the truth.

Petrus rode back and forth, ignoring the crowd, his romantic eyes fixed on the Stones' door. Suddenly Stone's wife emerged from the house, dressed in a long, tight gray dress that covered her collarbones, wrists, and ankles. Her silky hair coiled in a bun on her head. Black flat-heeled boots disappeared under her skirt. She hurried to the shed. In one hand she clutched a short, shiny stick with a leather band around her wrist. She opened the shed door, saddled her horse, led it out into the hot morning sun, mounted smoothly and rode to Wild Boy's side. The two horses pranced off through the village.

Word flashed through Naring like a bolt of lightning.

"Wild Boy is beautiful!"

"The Englishwoman loves him!"

Everyone ran outside to see, but the riders disappeared into the countryside, through the canyon in the ridge. The BaNare waited patiently. Late in the afternoon the riders returned. Stone's wife rode her horse to the shed and Wild Boy rode home.

Wild Boy rambled through the village on foot, his maimed dog trailing behind, wagging its crooked tail, slobbering through its mangled jaw. The vicious scar along its back reflected the setting sun. Wild Boy whistled, kicking stones along the path. Night fell. The compounds near the Stone house filled with observers. The sky was moonless, too dark to illuminate the Stones' door. Toward dawn a slivered moon rose to reveal Wild Boy's Dog sleeping on the wooden step of the Stones' back door.

11
The BaNare Way

Stone was a complicated man. He loved humanity, including his wife. Considerably older than preceding Willoughbys, he had requested a posting to Kalahariland Territory out of concern about the drought.

"My experience is needed," he said to Bagley, Senior Commissioner at Taung. "Send me to the worst place."

Bagley hesitated, worried about sending a married man to remote Naring. But Stone insisted, and who could turn away an experienced officer willing to take a beginner's pay?

Establishing an efficient routine in his Naring office, Stone wrote lengthy monthly reports, in duplicate, which put Bagley to sleep. Stone proposed dams, wells, irrigation canals, ranches, the importation of olive, lemon and gum trees. Every monthly report included a project proposal with an itemized budget and timetable. Bagley stopped trying to read them and wrote back to remind Stone that any projects must keep within the budget supplied by the ten-shilling-per-compound district tax.

Stone persevered. When Bagley announced that the Kalahari govern-ment would hire a drilling machine, Stone traveled to Taung to argue for the drill to come first to Naring. So when the BaNare split over the successful well at Loang, he was baffled but undaunted. He stayed cool through Pia the Scornful's collapse and Pono's accession to acting chief-ship. Yet he took the BaNare rift personally, and it wounded his heart. Searching for explanations, he snapped up the new chief's version of the story.

"Of course," Stone said to himself. "A troublemaker."

As Stone's sensitive spirit left him only two options, to blame himself or to blame someone else, Mojamaje was the obvious choice. Despite his military bearing, Stone craved the love of everyone in the world, espe-cially those he served. Slowly, without the two men meeting, Mojamaje became Stone's rival for the BaNare's affection.

He craved his wife's affection too. He loved her in the same way he loved his work: blindly, passionately, dutifully, on principle. Her name was Edna. She rattled through her Naring brick house like gravel in a gourd. She sat before a mirror in an unlit room, brushing her hair, peering through the gloom for wrinkles, marking time, growing old. During summer she waited for the onset of winter, and during winter she awoke early each morning to see whether the cloud bank had lifted, counting the days it hung over Naring—thirty-eight, her age. There were no children. She stood for hours on the wooden steps of her porch, watching the spare compounds around her, separated by a hundred yards of open space, a ring of white gum trees, miles of distress. She refused to ride the horse that Stone bought her, afraid to venture into the village, afraid to wander over the sand slope into the Kalahari and never come back.

When Edna noticed Wild Boy and Chibi riding past, she longed to mount her horse and join them. When she counted her hay bales and noticed some missing, it took no time at all to arrive at a culprit. Each time Stone left for Taung or Lorole Station, she hoped for Wild Boy to make his move, sleeping with one ear to the window, pistol in hand. When Wild Boy stumbled into her trap, caught in the light, a bale on his back, she was disappointed at his youth. But when she brushed aside his hair, the face that stared back was far too beautiful to resist. Next morning, when Wild Boy strutted before her house, Edna took a cold bath, washed her hair, read a magazine, kissed her husband's photo-graph, pulled on her riding boots, grabbed her whip, and rode out to meet her new lover. Unable to speak each other's language, Edna and Petrus cantered in silence, weaving through the village, bounding into the countryside halfway to Stinkface, the pasture where Jeedo Parido once tried to hide from Old Man De Swart, Wild Boy's grandfather, where the railway curved north from Lorole Station.

Stone returned, left again, now Petrus arrived at night to reap his reward. Wild Boy's Dog curled up on the steps of the Stone house to sleep. Petrus tried the door. It opened with a dull creak. He stepped inside, clad more soberly in full-length trousers and a shirt. His bare feet slid along a thin carpet. Wild Boy's eyes swept the dark, his knees bent slightly, like a stalking animal's. Truly, Edna knew full well that Petrus was a beast of the wild. No illusions marred her plans. She waited in her bed, listening for Petrus's entrance, her heart racing with anticipation. Disturbed by the emptiness of the parlor, Petrus sank to all fours, expecting ambush. He crawled to the bedroom, teeth bared, ready to pounce, and crept inside. Hearing Edna's breath, he leapt atop her, pulled down the sheets, tore off his clothes, wrapped himself around her, grabbed for her breasts, sitting on her stomach. Edna pulled the pistol from under her pillow and clonked him on the head.

Petrus awoke some time later, splayed on the floor. A lamp lit the room. Edna sat in a white nightdress, brushing her hair. She turned around.

"You hit me," Petrus said in Boer, rubbing his bruised forehead.

"No animals allowed in this house," she replied. Neither understood a word the other said.

"I am doing you a favor," Petrus said. "I have other calls to make."

"We will try again. Be a gentleman."

"Do you want it or no?" Petrus asked, rising to his feet. Edna rose too and held out her arms. Petrus charged like a bull. She brandished her brush.

"Gently, ox," she said. Petrus paused, confused, and Edna stepped forward to lay her palms against his naked chest. He recoiled. Taller than Petrus but slender and pale, Edna set out to tame this Wild Boy. "No fear," she whispered, moving forward to press against his chest, forcing him down onto the bed, kissing his face, closing her eyes and breathing hard. Petrus grabbed her, rolled atop her and reached for her breasts. Still clutching the hairbrush, she whacked him on the head until he stumbled to one corner of the room, blushing and dazed.

Again and again she took the offensive, teaching him to treat her like the queen the BaNare thought her to be. It took until morning, but as the sun rose to light the window above her bed, Edna won her battle. Petrus conformed without comprehending, disappointed at the slow pace. Eating was more exciting. But he left feeling thrilled, if not in the hips then in whose hips they were.

Thereafter, whenever Stone left for Naring, Wild Boy's Dog appeared at Edna's door, sleeping like death.

"He will find out," the BaNare declared.

"He will kill her."

"Wild Boy too."

"And himself."

"Why?"

"Despair."

In the Tladi compound, Mojamaje's old companions proposed informing Stone of his wife's infidelity. This would force them to leave Naring in disgrace and the next Willoughby might press Pono to abandon his claim to the Loang well, thereby ending the schism.

"No," Mojamaje said firmly. "Willoughby has nothing to do with our troubles. Pono is not our main problem. Our problem is the drought."

Protests followed. "But Pono and Peke stole the well."

Mojamaje replied, elbows on his knees, tapping his fingertips together, narrowing his eyes. "The well is useless now," he replied, "during the drought. The grass will soon be gone from there too. My daughters acted rashly. Once the drought ends we can see about the well. We can make Patrick chief. He will do what is right. But today, in the absence of rain or even its smell, we must pay close attention to causes. We must think clearly."

Unconvinced, still following their original line of argument, Mojamaje's companions replied, "But why not talk to Willoughby? You know English. Tell him the truth."

Mojamaje paused to collect his thoughts and then stuck out one bony finger. "One, there is nothing Willoughby can do about the drought. He can maybe depose Pono, but that is a BaNare affair. Do you want the English to decide who is chief?" He held out a second finger. "Two, if I talk to Willoughby, the BaNare will all expect miracles. I know them. When nothing results, they will blame Willoughby. Attention will fall in the wrong place."

Unsatisfied by Mojamaje's subtle theories, his companions returned again and again to Willoughby. "Talk to his wife," Maka now suggested.

"Bring her here. That will impress the BaNare. They cannot think Willoughby an enemy then. And through her maybe Willoughby will understand things."

Mojamaje shook his head, but the others clapped in joy. "Of course!" they exclaimed.

Maka's eyes from the corners of her lids assured Mojamaje of her intent, that of course nothing would come of it, but it would pacify his cronies, giving them the illusion of action. She said, "Cheer up, Mojamaje. Write the poor woman a letter."

Word reached Petrus Wild Boy that Mojamaje wanted to see him. Petrus walked to the Tladi compound, his miserable dog, once a proud warrior, dragging behind. The full complement of Mojamaje's aged associates sat waiting in a circle, including Patrick and casual comers like Bat-Ears, Kebatlagotsenyadiatla, Obu, Desire, and the Snake. Maka served tea and beer.

"Petrus," Mojamaje called when Wild Boy appeared at the gate. Wild Boy's Dog collapsed against the compound wall and fell asleep.

Petrus shuffled in to greet the assembly curtly.

"How is my horse?" Mojamaje began. Wild Boy stood at the edge of the circle, his blue animal eyes flashing with distrust.

"Old," Petrus replied. "Soon I will kill it and eat it."

"The meat is mine," Mojamaje reminded. "You ride it, but the thing belongs to me."

"I will ride it until the meat is gone from its bones."

Mojamaje smiled. "Such a wild one! They say you changed. Shaving, washing, cutting your hair. I see inside you are still a leopard. Is that right, Petrus De Swart?"

Wild Boy tried to hide his pleasure at Mojamaje's remarks. Proud of his wild image, Petrus feared his success with the elegant English lady might have ruined his reputation. A grin forced its way across his face. He shook his head yes. The assembly exploded in creaky laughter. A jumble of pride and humility tumbled through Petrus's mind. He sat down on his haunches by Mojamaje's chair, a newly tamed animal awaiting its master's first command.

"The horse is yours," Mojamaje continued, "if you do these BaNare a favor. They are very old. Do not do it for me, the owner of your horse, do not do this thing because I ask you. Do it for your elders. But if you do it, I give up all claim to my horse. Sell it, eat it, ride it until it drops dead. This horse was a gift from my daughter's husband, Jacob, after he lifted it up. It means much to me. Do not take my words lightly."

Petrus asked warily, "What do I do?"

Mojamaje reached into his worn gray English army coat and pulled out a slip of paper. "Take this message to the English lady."

Petrus leapt to his feet and howled like a wounded lion, betrayed, embarrassed, stamping his feet, beating his chest with his fists. Edna was the one sore spot in his leathery armor. He stomped around the circle of BaNare, ending up again at Mojamaje's chair. He fell silent, crouched down, and caught his breath.

"I will do it," he said.

Mojamaje held the message out to Petrus. "What does it say?" Wild Boy asked. Mojamaje unfolded the paper, taken from the pad he had used in the great South African war to issue writs of safe passage, one of which had saved the lives of Ro Roodie and the wagonful of Boers Mojamaje brought to Naring.

Mojamaje read the message aloud, translating it for his listeners: "Madame Willoughby, this is Mojamaje Tladi writing to you from the village of Naring. I offer you fond greetings from my people. As you may know, my people clutch their stomachs. Why do they do this? The reasons are many. Many things complicate the issue. Myself, I am very old. In fact, no one in Naring is older. I learned English long ago in Taung. I write this message to ask you to come speak about things with us. The old BaNare wait here by my side. I will change English for them to let them understand you. Do not think we want you only to listen. That is not the BaNare way. You speak also. We want to hear. I do not write to your husband because Chief Pono has his ear between his teeth. Chief Pono hates me. If I speak to your husband, he will look up records and find reports that I deserted the English army. These things are untrue. The records are lies. Would your husband believe me? It is his job to believe the reports. But you are a woman. You will hear me out. You will believe your heart. This fine young man, Petrus De Swart, is like my grandson. He rides my horse through Naring. I am glad you enjoy your rides with him. Please write an answer to this message. Give it to Petrus. He will bring it to me. I am hoping for a favorable reply. I hope you are enjoying our village. Welcome. Respectfully yours, Mojamaje Tladi, Eater of Rocks."

12

Savages

Mojamaje gave Petrus precise instructions. He folded the paper and placed it in Wild Boy's rough palm, closed his thick fingers around it, and said, "Willoughby is not in Naring. It is safe. Keep your fist tight. Walk to the English lady's house. Go inside. Stand before her. Open your fist. Give her the message. She will write an answer. Put the answer in your fist. Walk here. Open your fist." Mojamaje repeated these commands over and over, for Petrus was truly a Wild Boy, with the memory of a moth. Petrus repeated his instructions aloud. "Go quickly," Mojamaje concluded.

Petrus ran through the village, his bare feet kicking up clouds of fine sand. Wild Boy's Dog roused and lumbered far behind. Petrus burst into the Stone house, stood before Edna, opened his fist and the message floated to the floor.

Edna picked it up, read it, smiled, sat down at a table to write a reply. Petrus had crumpled the note so badly that she used a sheet of her own paper. *Dear Mr. Mojamaje*, she wrote. *Yes, I would be delighted to speak with your friends. Would this afternoon be convenient? If your reply is yes, Mr. De Swart can show me the way.* Edna rolled up the message, handed it to Petrus, and pushed him out the door. Turning back, she lit a match and burned Mojamaje's crumpled note.

Alas, Petrus truly was a Wild Boy and as Mojamaje had feared, his list of instructions was too long. Back outside, in front of Stone's house, Petrus looked up into the blazing sun and tried to remember what to do next. He opened his fist, unrolled the paper, and looked at the neatly formed letters, arranged in mysterious English words. He closed his eyes, ran over Mojamaje's instructions in his head, but failed to follow the chain even as far as where he now stood. He forgot how he had ended up on Edna's steps with a slip of paper in his hand. His miserable dog finally reached the house. Its purple scar glimmered in the sun. It snuggled up to Petrus's bare leg and the Wild Boy kicked it away.

Edna lay down for a nap, so she missed the spectacle of Petrus standing forlorn out front. He sat down to think. The dog crawled back to climb into his lap and lick Wild Boy's cheek. Its breath reeked of stale porridge. Petrus was lost in painful thought. Then his eyes sparked up and across his vision sailed Dazzling Vina, the Indian Temptress. Gone was her sleeveless shift. Her sinuous form was wrapped instead in filmy folds, a swirling mist of a dozen colors, offering nakedness underneath, a loosely bound package easily unwrapped. Elegant red slippers hid slim feet, gold dangled from her ears, her ankles, her slender wrists. Her hair had grown to a massive brown halo enshrouding her head. Hidden in this glorious vision was the angular, smooth dark face, in shadow the same as Edna's. Now in the bright sun its dark skin glowed like a beacon, announcing the mysteries hidden in the Indian cloth around her.

Petrus stared, struck with awe. Vina winked and rolled her hips toward her father's store. Petrus stood up and followed her slowly. His dog padded behind. Step by step he closed the gap, transfixed by her figure. Amid the blue, violet, scarlet, orange, and silver of the twisting cloth, exploding against Naring's Kalahari brown, Petrus caught glimpse after glimpse of Vina's magnificent copper breasts, sometimes both at once, a full chest bare beneath the billowing silk. The BaNare in the vicinity stopped to watch, following Petrus's dazed progress, his arms moving up, forward, as a puff of wind blew backward a fluttering fold of Vina's garb. The Wild Boy raised a hand to grasp it, to touch its tip, a gesture of longing the BaNare all appreciated, and in this fleeting moment of exquisite romance no one noticed the slip of paper floating out of Petrus's open hand, wafted aloft by that same gust of wind.

Four steps more and Vina disappeared into her father's shop. Petrus stopped short at the door. His senses paid a return visit, warning that perhaps the same three miners waited inside, while the message floated high in a twisting column of warm, rising air. A second breeze blew from the east, easing the message over the sand slope into the Kalahari.

Mojamaje and his associates waited hours for Edna's reply. Finally they sent a messenger to Wild Boy, who returned with Wild Boy's report: "She tore up the paper."

Edna waited for Wild Boy to come lead her to Mojamaje. When the sun set without his return, she fell back to bed, depressed and hurt. Afraid to probe the village on her own, she had leapt at this invitation. Wild Boy would have escorted her past the staring eyes. The old man would have spoken to her in English, introduced her to others, made her feel at home in Naring. Irritable, uncomfortable, Edna tossed and turned until midnight, when her husband came home and crawled into bed beside her. She pulled away, rolling to the edge. Stone sighed a familiar sigh. "Good night, Edna," he said.

Edna stared into the dark, listening to the barking dogs of the empty Naring night. "Savages," she whispered to herself, crying silently into her hands.

13

Paradise

Sound carried well across the Taung plain. In Chibi's fourth year in South Africa, a tremor rumbled across the northern tip of Taung, east of Mmi, and quickly spread to the ears of every field hand on every farm in the district. By planting time, the onset of summer, the quaking reached the Roodie farm. Chibi and her comrades clapped their hands to their ears as the clanking, smoking, shuddering thing approached them. Some ran screaming to hide beneath blankets. Some stared with dread. Others, including Chibi, rushed toward the thing for a better look.

"What is it?" they cried, but everyone knew the answer. Everyone knew it was coming. The only question was who would ride it into their midst. Everyone guessed Bushy and everyone was right. He sat atop the red tractor like a king, his hands clutching the steering wheel with the grip of a strangler. His legs pumped away under the wheel. Sweat streamed from his brow. Two huge black wheels spun slowly, relentlessly, carving deep tracks into the soil of the Roodie farm. He steered the tractor into the barn close to the Roodie house.

Word spread that all the plow teams were fired. The men who yoked and drove the oxen and held the plow, the women who planted the seed behind, were all given a day to vacate their houses in the worker compound. The tractor was here to do their work. It needed no grass, no water, no protection from wolves. It needed only Bushy, expert foreman.

They had all heard the rumble for months, watched hundreds of refugees straggle past the Roodie farm, driven out by tractors. They had known their day would come soon. All had hoped for one more season, for the tractor to delay another year before reaching them, giving them time to think of somewhere else to go. It was the same story throughout Taung—wishful thinking, the hope of time. Nothing could slow the tractor.

"Bushy is killing us all," some fired workers muttered.

"Traitor."

"But Karman Roodie owns the tractor."

"He owns Bushy too."

"He owns us."

"I will kill him with a long knife."

"Like that Zulu killed the other Roodie."

"The knife was Zulu. The killer was BaNare."

Chibi overheard this conversation and interrupted to say, "I know him."

"Who?"

"Mojamaje," Chibi replied. "The BaNare who killed the Boer with a Zulu knife."

"That was long ago. You are only a girl."

"He is old now," Chibi explained. "He lives in Naring, my home."

The other workers fell silent, eyeing Chibi with new respect. They knew she was a Roodie, a distinction that slipped to disgrace in her present occupation—fallen kin, poor relative, scratching in the dirt, now unemployed. Chibi's new revelation changed things.

"You know this man?"

"I know him," Chibi repeated. "He is the husband of my father's half sister."

"Do as he did."

"Kill this Boer, Karman the Tractor Owner."

"And Bushy."

"You are a Roodie."

"This is your farm."

"They cannot force you out."

Searching for words, Chibi gazed at the crowd formed to interrogate her. She pushed her way out of the circle, rushed out of the compound and into the empty fields, moist with rain, ready for the tractor.

That same afternoon, Bushy held another Bushyite service. Every field hand in the area joined in. Their bitterness that he drove the tractor gave way to awe that he was the only one immune to its curse. Confirmed skeptics fell on their knees to beg Bushy to baptize them. "Save me! Save me!" they cried. A steady wail rose from the growing horde crowded onto the riverbank. Heavy storms on the Foelberg Plateau had flooded the Taung River to a mighty, roaring torrent of white. Bushy's glistening robe was soaked from the baptisms as convert after convert braved the surging current to fall into Bushy's arms, slip backward into the water and emerge a Bushyite.

Chibi wandered to the edge of the crowd. The songs pressed against her ears, forced their way into her throbbing head and finally came out her tongue. She sang with all the feeling her wrenched heart could muster. Slowly she floated toward the line of converts waiting for baptismal dunking. The Holy Zion Angels closed their eyes as they sang, waving their hips and clasping their breasts in their hands. Chibi closed her eyes too, thinking of Petrus Wild Boy, the wind on her face as she rode through Naring, her arms clutched tight around his strong chest. Step by step she approached her baptism into the Bushyite church. A dreamy smile tugged at her lips as she remembered opening the hay shed door, creeping to the De Swart shop, the eerie shadows of the merchandise hung from the ceiling. Suddenly she was at the water's edge, with no one before her save Bushy himself. She opened her eyes. Bushy took her hand, pulling her into the river. Chibi closed her eyes again, thinking of Petrus pulling down his pants, her own hands lifting her dress above her waist. Bushy placed one hand against Chibi's spine. With the other hand he firmly shoved her backward into the rushing water. Chibi remembered now lying against the soft furs on the De Swart shop floor, as Petrus lay atop her, how this always made her feel as if she were falling off the back of Wild Boy's headstrong horse. Instinctively she cried out and threw her arms around Petrus, but this time the chest was Bushy's. Years of grueling work had made Chibi's arms lean and muscular, so her panicked grip held Bushy like a trap around his chest, pinning his arms to his side. The Bushyites screamed. Some rushed into the water to help, but too late. Bushy fell over into the current, locked in Chibi's deadly embrace. They disappeared downstream.

As Bushy opened his mouth to shout at Chibi to let go, water rushed in to choke him. He sputtered and gurgled but no word escaped his lips. The Bushyites ran along the bank, following the bobbing pair as they sank below the surface, to reappear far downstream. They ran for miles until Chibi and Bushy spun too far ahead to be seen. The Bushyites walked. Toward dusk they came upon a wide bend in the river and there sat Chibi, knees up, head in hands, before Bushy's bloated body, ready for burial in its long white gown. She thought of Maka and the old

woman's parting advice to try three times. "My second defeat," Chibi
muttered, regarding Bushy's body at her feet.

The Bushyites whispered, "She killed him."

"She murdered our leader."

"Who will drive the tractor?"

"We are saved!"

"Roodie will find another driver."

"First he will kill us for murdering Bushy."

"Who is she?"

"Her father killed the first Roodie with a Zulu knife."

"Karman will kill her."

"How did she kill Bushy? He was strong."

"She is a Roodie."

"Her father is famous."

"She came here to save us."

"She will be one of the Holy Angels."

"She will be Queen of the World."

"What is her name?"

"Chibi."

"Queen Chibi."

"Give her Bushy's robe and sash."

The Bushyites rushed forward, stripped Bushy's corpse of his gown
and purple band, pulled Chibi to her feet and draped the vestments over
her torn dress. Dazed, cold, trembling with fear and excitement, Chibi
regarded her new followers, who stepped back to hear her first prayer.
Bushyites became Chibiites. Their pain and desperation concentrated on
the freckled, pale-skinned young BaNare before them.

Chibi's mind raced. There was no turning back to the Roodie farm.
She had murdered the tractor driver. No Boer would believe it was
accidental. Her new followers were homeless. They had nowhere to turn
so they turned to her. She wore Bushy's clothes. Looking out on the
haggard faces before her, tinged orange by the setting sun, Chibi rummaged through the underbrush along the bank, found a dead tree
branch, tore off the twigs and raised the stick to point over the heads of
the crowd, as she had watched Naledi do when announcing the exodus
to Loang. Affecting Naledi's distant bearing, Chibi waved the stick and
cried out, "The mission!" Her followers echoed the call and surged east-
ward across the open fields.

The journey took three days. Some Chibiites ran to fetch their children and belongings. Others marched along with only the clothes on their backs and the hope that Chibi inspired in their hearts. Chibi expected the police to arrest her, to intercept the crowd before it reached the Taung Mission. But although Karman Roodie mourned the loss of his expert tractor man, the willing departure of his entire work force more than compensated for the damage. On other farms field hands had refused to leave, sometimes smashing tractors and burning barns. In the yellow Tsa Valley three Boer farmers died at the hands of their furious dismissed workers.

As with Mojamaje and Maka's ride so long before, word of their impending arrival reached the mission ahead of the Chibiites. There were five English missionaries now, two drilled wells, a solid fence, a large school, a hospital, and hundreds of refugees from the tractor. They all begged for conversion and once a week the missionaries baptized two, married them, and wrote their names on a waiting list for mission accommodation. Every week more refugees arrived, filling the grounds with a desperate mob.

Chibi and her followers entered the mission at night and dispersed throughout the crowd. The other refugees noted their white robes.

"Bushyites?"

"Chibiites," came the reply.

"Who is Chibi?"

"A Roodie."

"A Boer."

"She owns a farm."

"God speaks English through her mouth."

"He told her to lead us to paradise."

"She killed a tractor driver."

"She tore apart a tractor with her bare hands."

"She ate the pieces."

"She leads us to paradise."

One by one the other refugees announced their conversion to Chibiism. Since there were not enough white robes for all, the original Chibiites ripped their robes into strips to give everyone a white sash. By morning every refugee on the mission grounds wore the white mark of Chibiism.

"Heathens," the English missionaries spat. "Remove those pagan garlands." The Chibiites refused. "Out!" the missionaries ordered. "Out or we call the police."

The Chibiites discussed their predicament.

"We can kill the missionaries and live here in the mission."

"This will be paradise."

"The English police will surround the fence."

"They will shoot us like cattle."

"Bullets cannot hurt us when we wear this white cloth."

"Who told you that?"

"No one, exactly, but I heard—"

"You are stupid to believe it."

"We must leave."

"Where can we go?"

For the first time since their conversion, the new Chibiites realized they did not know who Chibi was.

"Which one is Chibi?"

Luckily some of her original followers had thought to preserve Chibi's robe from division into sashes. She alone wore a full white gown. Bushy's purple sash hugged her chest, wrapped over one shoulder and around her waist. Chibi's eyes bulged from worry, hunger, lack of sleep. She had hoped to stay at the mission for years, as Mojamaje and Maka had, learning the lessons they learned. But this demanding multitude spoiled her plans. The missionaries would drive her out. "My third defeat," she said to herself.

The crowd buzzed with trepidation and debate as Chibi climbed the steps of the brick mission school.

"My people!" she announced in a small voice unused to attention. One by one, her followers hushed.

"We must go," she continued. "We cannot stay here. Is this paradise?"

"No!" the Chibiites cried.

"I will take you to paradise," Chibi said in a stronger voice. "The journey is hard. Do you think paradise is easy to get to?"

Some cried "Yes," some cried "No."

"Paradise is hard," she said. "I will take you there if you want to go."

"We go!" the crowd shouted. They had no choice.

Chibi descended the steps, her followers parted to let her pass, she led them out the mission gates, through Taung town, where English police stood ready with rifles. Chibi turned at the train station. Her flock hurried behind, followed by the blue-coated police. Chibi stepped between the rails. The Chibiites followed in a single line. The police watched the refugees disappear down the tracks, west toward Kalahariland Territory. Chibi trudged on and her spirits rose as Maka's parting advice rang in her ears. It was time to go home. With a thousand Chibiites in tow, she was on her way back to Naring.

14
Conceit, Deceit

Stone looked into the empty summer sky, then out at the bare Naring countryside. The drought was wearing him down. He felt powerless, useless, his years of experience wasted, baked to dust by the relentless heat. Removing his eyeglasses, wiping them on the sleeve of his gray tunic, he set off for a walk across his domain. The first person he passed was a handsome young Boer, clean-shaven and dustless, lounging against a compound wall. A dying black dog slept at his feet. There was a long purple scar along the dog's back. Stone avoided the Boer boy's eyes but his vision caught a twinkle of mockery in the boy's face.

Every week, Stone took a stroll through the village. Since the schism, the retreat to Loang, he had met only silence and stony glances. During his first years in Naring there had always been at least one person, child or adult, who called out, "Willoughby!" as he passed. At first he had replied, "My name is Stone," but eventually he gave in and called back, "Well, hello there." He loved the BaNare as he loved his wife, and lately both had grown cold and distant.

When the slip of paper bearing Edna's message soared out of Petrus Wild Boy's hand, up with hot air, to rise over the sand slope and disappear into the Kalahari, it fell to earth amid the tangled thorn brush a mile outside Naring. Those BaNare who saw it float by made no move to retrieve it, another harmless scrap captured by the empty dry wind. How could they have known the role it had still to play in the story of the Great Thirst? There it lay in silence, undamaged by rain.

Out collecting firewood one day, Kina Cross-Eyes, a granddaughter of Koko and Pono, lifted a newly fallen branch and there lay a slip of paper. Or was she the granddaughter of Keke and Peke? All their grandchildren looked alike. The BaNare gave Kina the name Cross-Eyes in honor of her grandmother's father, Tabo Cross-Eyes, the ambiguous giant felled by the beast that gave Jacob the Ox-Killer his name. Kina rushed home to show the paper to her grandmother, Koko. Keke? In any event, the paper ended up in Chief Pono's hands. He passed it on to Stone.

That night, Stone confronted his wife with the evidence. "Conspiring with the enemy?" he boomed in his lovely deep voice. He read aloud Edna's message: "Dear Mr. Mojamaje, Yes, I would be delighted to speak with your friends. Would this afternoon be convenient? If your reply is yes, Mr. De Swart can show me the way."

Edna's eyes filled at the memory of her humiliation, rejection, her hope for contact with the BaNare.

"Which De Swart?" Stone demanded.

"The old shopkeeper," Edna replied and then held back a sneer.

"Mojamaje is a criminal," Stone continued. "He lives in Loang. He led the rebels to seize the well. What was he doing in Naring?"

"Read the note," Edna said.

"I read it," Stone replied. And then, cringing with anticipation, he asked, "Did you meet him?"

"Of course," Edna replied, her tears freezing in her eyes, a light of vindictive deceit suddenly replacing them. "His English is beautiful."

"What did he say?" Stone asked. "What is he like?" Scorn mixed with curious awe in his voice.

Edna replied, "He told me he wanted to kill you. He told me to change your mind about that well if I wanted you to live."

"You never told me," Stone said.

"I did not want you to live," Edna answered.

They stood in the bright light of two oil lamps in their spare, square bedroom. The white sheets of the bed glowed yellow in the glare. They faced each other at the end of the bed, Edna in her long gray dress, her black hair curled and pinned tight on her head, above her long nose and drawn cheeks. Her tears dried in her eyes and the whites sparkled with venom. Stone's uniform seemed to shrink on his shoulders.

"What did he look like?" Stone demanded, his face worn with fear.

"Strong," Edna replied. "Your age. Tall. Kind face. Gentle voice. Serious, but kind. He looks like a powerful man. I am sure he means what he says."

"Who else was there?"

"A few others," Edna replied. "No, more like a crowd. They called out his name. They love him."

Each new lie from Edna's lips cut away more of Stone's confidence. By the end of the night there was nothing left. He stormed out of the house, across the dusty courtyard into his one-roomed office, lit a candle, and sat down to work. The picture Edna painted of Mojamaje was exactly the man Stone himself wanted to be, wanted Edna and the BaNare to acknowledge him for being: powerful, serious, kind, loved by all.

Stone pulled out his file on Mojamaje and read through the list of his criminal accomplishments: murder, treason, and so on. He looked to the telegraph key, thinking of the wire strung across the plains to Lorole Station, beside the rail to Taung, to Kalahariland Territory headquarters. Edna had reported that Mojamaje had threatened to kill him. This was a serious matter. Stone's hand moved toward the key on his desk. He would report the threat to headquarters. Mojamaje, the fierce rebel firebrand, was already back in Naring, perhaps preparing for the final assault on Stone's person. Stone's hand trembled. He withdrew it from the key and placed his head in his arms.

The candle burned low. Slowly Stone struggled to regain his composure. He cleaned his eyeglasses with a handkerchief, ran a hand through his thin black hair, and took out the file on his next monthly report, which would ride tomorrow on Ahamed's donkey wagon to Lorole Station. Stone opened his report to the last page and added these lines:

The rebel leader, Mojamaje, has threatened the life of the District Commissioner and is massing his followers for an armed attack on Naring. There is no immediate danger, but further instructions would be greatly appreciated.

Ahamed's donkeys carried the report to Lorole, a train carried it to Taung. Senior Commissioner Bagley opened the envelope and withdrew Stone's report, flipped to the last sheet, and read the number. "Forty pages," he muttered. "Too bloody long again." Bagley thumbed through quickly and tossed it on the growing pile of Stone's reports.

Stone awaited instructions from Bagley, but none came. Neither did Mojamaje lead a swarm of rebels over the sand slope to slit Stone's throat. Nevertheless, the damage was done. Stone carried an image of Mojamaje forged by the calumnious list and Edna's fantastic description. At night as he fell asleep, Stone dreamed of the horde pouring over the ridge, spewing from the Kalahari, led by a figure who resembled himself, eyeglasses, thin receding hair, except for the blackness of Mojamaje's skin.

Stone's obsession with Mojamaje made him miss the clue about Wild Boy in Edna's note. The possibility of his wife's infidelity never occurred to Stone. She hated him for this conceit. She longed to shout that De Swart was her lover, the young, wild, beautiful boy with the pitiful black dog. But this would be too kind. He would have to learn the hard way. She would not help him.

15
The Truth

Maka poured a last cup of tea and sat on the ground beside Mojamaje's low chair. It was the end of the day, and his cronies had just departed.

"Alone at last," she whispered.

Mojamaje pulled his wide-brimmed hat lower on his forehead. "You do not like my friends?" he asked. "Tsema who takes off his wooden leg to lean his chin on it? Shadi who blows his nose in his hands? Mmaana who spits tobacco juice into her tea to spice it?"

"Or that bore Mojamaje," Maka added. "Little does he know that these old coots listen to him only because they want my beer." She smiled up at her husband, counting again the deep lines in his face. Every year the wrinkles pushed his Bushman cheekbones higher, narrowing his eyes until they seemed to disappear.

Mojamaje chuckled, turning to look into Maka's cloudy brown eyes. Often when he did this, he remembered her as a young woman, her slim waist in his arms as he rode behind her.

It was a calm summer evening, the air cooling quickly beneath a cloudless, darkening sky. The sun disappeared over the sand slope. Maka took a last sip of tea and stood up to toss the dregs over the compound wall when she noticed unusual activity across the neighborhood. She peered through the dim dusk light to see figures running in circles before a cluster of compounds. The figures moved toward her. Then she recognized them as women and heard their voices. They screamed, kicking up dust, falling to the ground to writhe in torment. A gentle breeze carried their anguished cries to the Tladi compound. Maka slipped out the gate, walking carefully on her aged bones. "I will see," she called over her shoulder to Mojamaje, who by now had stood up to watch other women rush to join the wailers. Round and round these women ran through the village, tearing their hair, grunting like animals. Older women raced to calm them, cornering them like cattle against compound walls, embracing them with strong arms, speaking softly, urging them to explain, to reveal their affliction.

At midnight a half-moon rose over the Naring hills and Maka returned home.

"The women are finished," she said through the dark. "It has been a year. They hid the fact from their husbands. From each other. The strain of secrecy grew too great to bear. The shame, the fright. It was too much." Her voice shook and she paused to regain its meter. "Finally one broke. She ran out crying the truth. Other women heard. They ran out to concur. All the women in Naring came out to tell the same story. The truth is here."

Maka fell silent, her breath blowing lightly on Mojamaje's face in the dark. "What is the truth?" he asked.

"For a year," Maka explained, "longer for some, the women of Naring have failed to bleed in their monthly way. The drought has dried their wombs. There will be no more children. The BaNare are dying out."

16
Three Rabble

In no time at all the dry-womb panic spread to Loang. Women there came forward to confirm the aridity of their wombs. Although the panic was briefer than at Naring, it fueled the desolation already infecting the Loang settlers.

The night after the revelation, Ma-Boko whispered aloud, "Enough." She woke her husband Jacob and led him out of their house. "Ssh," she whispered, holding one finger to her lips. The Ox-Killer stood in the dark, ready for her next command. She pulled him by his tattered shirt, making her way down to the flat floor of the Loang pan. The cloth wedges from Jacob's boot brushed along the dust, past the three brush fences that hid the gaping holes that had once watered Tladi's cattle, into the center of the pan, toward the well pump that had split the BaNare in two.

"Jacob," Ma-Boko said aloud, "break the well."

The night was warm, with the half-moon low on the horizon. Jacob's hulking form towered over the pump, a pipe set in concrete with a curved metal handle and spout. The joints were firmly bolted. Jacob nodded in the dark, wrapped his hands around the handle and with one grinding yank ripped it off the pipe.

"Good, Jacob," Ma-Boko commended, patting his forearm. She led him back to their house, neglecting to tell him to let go the handle he still clenched tightly in one fist.

Next morning, Loang erupted in consternation. Then Jacob emerged from his house, pump handle in hand, like a club ready for action, and the commotion died. No one complained. The pump head was twisted and torn. No one knew how to repair it. There were no tools. Everyone was glad for a reason to quit Loang. Naledi pointed her stick, the settlers rounded up their black goats and headed back to Naring.

Naring, Loang, the word was out. News of the crisis, the death of the BaNare future, no more children, made its way across South Africa and down into the mines. And here it was Boko, Ma-Boko's son, who decided what the BaNare miners should do about it. Unlike the other Black Goats, Boko had renewed his contracts immediately, avoiding sojourns home. He sent his wages back in the pocket of a cousin. Rumors thrived in the stifling Joburg barracks, and soon it became widely known that Boko was the son of the dreaded Ox-Killer and grandson of Mojamaje, famous Boer-stabber, runner of guns, owner of the largest cattle herd in Taung history, honorary Englishman. Boko took advantage of this notoriety and rose quickly from digger to one of the foremen's helpers, whom other miners hated for abusing their privileges. None did so more ruthlessly than Boko. Back in the barracks he fought with knives and united the Black Goats into a private army. Others sang this song:

> Some day, some day
> I will kill that little bastard
> Some day

Upon learning of the BaNare dry-womb crisis, Boko marshaled his Black Goats into regiment formation and marched to the mine manager's office. The mine police rushed to the scene, eager to gun down the rebellious strikers. But all Boko wanted was to cancel the BaNare contracts and go home. Without hesitation, the mine manager shoved them onto the next train, which arrived in Lorole just as the Chibiites swept past the station.

Some BaNare dispute the chronology of these events. They claim that the Loang settlers and their black goats, the white-sashed Chibiites, and Boko's Black Goat troops with their black sacks on their shoulders, all arrived in Naring on different days. Some say that hours separated the arrivals. Most agree, though, that all three hordes burst into Naring at precisely the same moment. Children collecting firewood in the countryside saw them coming and ran to tell their parents, who notified Chief Pono, who told Stone, who ran to his office to tap out this telegraph message: SEND HELP. MOJAMAJE'S REBELS ATTACKING.

From the Tladi compound Mojamaje and Maka looked out at the sand slope, where hundreds of Loang settlers drove thousands of black goats out of the Kalahari into Naring. Then they looked to the canyon, to the site of the Battle of the Rocks, where hundreds of Chibiites emerged with white sashes flying. Beside them marched Boko's disciplined black-sacked miners, half wearing metal helmets, BaNare manhood come home. All three hordes surged into Naring in a swirl of dust.

Naring descended to chaos and panic. The hordes met on the clearing between the Tladi and Potso families, filling the paths of the entire neighborhood. From the cascading crowds a stick pointed up, Naledi stepped forward, and the crowd cleared a space for her to be seen. The commotion calmed, hysteria subsided, Naledi spoke:

"BaNare, listen!
What does my grandmother say?"

Quiet descended, a sudden snap of silence, as Naledi continued, pale eyes shining, her slender form rigid and fierce:

"BaNare, hear these voices—
This earth we love is bleak and dry because of strangers
There arrive now those who know the answer to such dangers
BaNare, you have three choices—"

Now Naledi's voice rose and the crowd twitched, incited, as Naledi finished her speech:

"Bare all for the Great Thirst!
BaNare, take care!
Share all for the Great Thirst!
BaNare, prepare!
Dare all for the Great Thirst!
BaNare, beware!"

The crowd erupted in cries of passion, the Black Goats chanted, the earth thundered from pounding feet as the BaNare jumped in the air again and again, swarming over the clearing and absorbing Naledi into its fray. The Chibiites shouted, "Beware the tractors!" and the BaNare looked to the canyon to see whether this new scourge, whatever it was, would descend on Naring as well, surely come to end their days. The BaNare fell on the ground and tore their hair, terrified, spent.

Mojamaje and Maka watched from their doorway, shaking their heads at the spectacle, Naring gone wild, desperate with hunger and thirst.

"Nonsense," Mojamaje muttered.

Stone sat in his office, waiting for the attack, his finger on the telegraph key. Naring was full again, overflowing with frenzy. Certainly, Mojamaje was back. Somewhere in Naring's maze of compounds lurked Stone's assassin, the man he wanted to be, the famous Mojamaje with his monstrous knife, as long as a Zulu spear, aimed at Stone's heart.

In Kalahariland Territory headquarters, Senior Commissioner Bagley read Stone's telegram with dismay. "Mojamaje's rebels attacking indeed," Bagley scoffed. Sighing with frustration, he took up the stack of Stone's old reports to look for clues to the meaning of this cryptic message. After an hour he found the addendum that Stone had written to report Edna's bilious lie about Mojamaje's threat: *The rebel leader, Mojamaje, has threatened the life of the District Commissioner and is massing his followers for an armed attack on Naring. There is no immediate danger, but further instructions would be greatly appreciated.*

Rummaging through other Naring files, Bagley found Pia and Stimp's list of allegations against Mojamaje. "Murder, desertion, treason, smuggling, rebellion," Bagley mused. "Quite a character." Pondering what action to take, Bagley telegraphed to Stone, SEND DETAILS.

The hordes headed for the Tladi and Potso compounds, not Stone's office. The chaos died down. As night fell around his tiny office Stone telegraphed Bagley, UNDER CONTROL. WILL INFORM. He sat at his desk, looking out the window at the darkening village. The swirling commotion, the marauders advancing from all directions, cut like a personal insult into Stone's bristling pride, another indication of his squandered love. As he sat for hours by the telegraph, Edna and Wild Boy staged their most daring rendezvous. Petrus slipped in the Stones' back door facing the hay shed. Wild Boy's Dog curled up on the step. Edna opened her arms in passionate abandon, sucking wildness from Petrus's animal flesh, losing herself in swooning desire. As night fell Petrus slipped back out the door. His dog roused, struggled to its feet, and ambled after him. Edna bathed. Stone stood up from his desk, ran his hands through his hair, stepped into the dry summer air, locked his office, and crossed the dark courtyard for home.

17
Chibi's Boon

And what of Chibi? Swept forward by her followers, Taung field hands orphaned by the tractor, Chibi bore no resemblance to her former self, Wild Boy's tramp. Related to Maka and Naledi by her Roodie freckles, Chibi now took her place among such notable women, contributing one third of the force that engulfed Naring from east and west.

Yet Chibi's real importance sprang from another cause. Clearly, Mojamaje rescued Ro Roodie from the smoking cauldron of the South African war so that his blood would mingle with Ata's to produce Chibi. But Chibi ended up adding more to the Tladi cause than white-sashed minions and a darling Wild Infant. It was a tribute to her new maturity that she handled her role flawlessly. She did exactly the right thing. Despite Mojamaje's protests, the BaNare blamed their fractious fate, and even the drought itself, on the battle over the Loang well. Then Chibi's arrival changed everything. But before explaining how and why, the tellers of the story of the Great Thirst remind their listeners of the convoluted inheritance of the Tladi family fortune.

Tladi conquered Loang by leading his Imitation Zulu against the luckless BaKii. Tladi's legacy passed through his elder son, Tumo, to Tumo's elder son, indecisive Dinti the Ostrich. Poor Dinti married Bosio Night Girl, whom the BaNare had expected to fall for Paulus the Lover.

When fire scarred shy Bosio's face, she rebuffed her husband Dinti, who escaped, disheartened, to die in the mines beneath a mile of earth. Dinti's younger brother, Tabo Cross-Eyes, announced Seantlo rights over Bosio. He entered her house to beget a child in the name of his departed brother, Dinti. By law, the child would be Dinti's. When Tabo stepped into Bosio's house, she clobbered him with an iron pot. A child appeared, though, for Bosio Night Girl walked at night and rolled in the shadows with Paulus the Lover. The child was born with pale skin and a purple scar, identical to her mother's, across her neck and cheek. Bosio loved her infant daughter, whom the BaNare named Seele. One night mother vanished with child through the canyon, lost in South Africa. The BaNare sang this song in Seele's memory:

> Face of beauty, child of woe
> Dinti the Ostrich dead below
> Face like nighttime, empty dreams
> Tabo Cross-Eyes what he seems
> Face of lonely, blind allure
> Paulus, bashful Lover, Boer
> Face of blackness, jealous sun
> Bosio Night Girl trusts no one
> Face of beauty, marked for life
> Seele child of Seantlo wife

Legally, Seele was the heir of Dinti, Bosio's legal husband. Her departure to South Africa on Bosio's back removed her from her rightful position as Tladi's heir. So the inheritance passed from Tladi to Tumo to Dinti to Dinti's younger brother, Tabo Cross-Eyes. Tabo's wife, Leana the Loyal, lost five sons before bearing Koko and Keke, evil pranksters, one year apart in age but identical in everything else. Tabo's inheritance passed to Koko and Keke, who married Pono and Peke. Though Tladi had conquered Loang for all the BaNare, Koko, Keke, Pono and Peke invoked this chain of descent to claim the place for themselves.

The first night after the three hordes swarmed into Naring, Chibi slipped out into the village with a familiar stranger in tow. They wound up to the Tladi compound. Chibi knocked on Mojamaje and Maka's door.

"Who is there?" Maka called.

"Chibi Roodie," came the reply, a whisper clipped and sure. After a long pause the door opened and Chibi hastened the stranger inside.

Maka lit a candle. The dim yellow light showed deep hollows in Chibi's newly mature face.

"You have changed," Maka said, tying a scarf around her head. She sat beside Mojamaje on their blankets on the floor, Maka in her old yellow dress, Mojamaje enshrouded by his old gray army coat. The wrinkles of their old faces stood out as bold stripes in the candlelight. "We have waited for you to call," Maka continued. "Wild Infant asks for you. Welcome home, Chibi. You have done well for yourself." Pointing her chin toward the stranger, noticing the white emblem, Maka added, "I see this is one of your followers."

Chibi spoke in a harried, hurried voice: "My father and mother cannot help me. My elders, I turn to you. Look close in the face of this woman."

Mojamaje and Maka peered across the room. The woman sitting on the floor beside Chibi wore an old green dress. A gray scarf covered her hair and the white Chibiite scarf hid her neck and cheeks. Above the white swath her eyes were dark and clear, her skin was a shimmering, pale brown, the color of Maka's beneath her freckles before wrinkles merged the lines.

"She is beautiful," Maka said.

"Look closely," Chibi urged.

The woman looked back at Mojamaje and Maka, wrinkling her brow in dismay, almost in fright.

"Please lower your scarf," Mojamaje asked. But he and Maka had already guessed. The mysterious stranger untied her white cloth and let it fall to the floor. Her face was somewhat older than Ma-Boko's or Naledi's. Her features seemed more lovely in full view. Mojamaje's and Maka's eyes fell together to her neck and cheek. There, in exactly the shape they expected, was the violet scar. This was Seele, child of Seantlo.

"Welcome home, my child," Mojamaje said. "I am Mojamaje, cousin of Dinti, your mother's husband. And where is your mother?"

"She died," Seele mumbled, retying the scarf.

"Do you know the story of your birth?" Maka asked.

"I know it."

"By law you are Dinti's child."

"I know it," Seele replied.

"Do you know you are Tladi's heir?"

"I know it," Seele replied.

"What will you do?" Maka asked.

"Tell me."

Mojamaje nodded and said to Chibi, "You must protect her. She is a secret. The BaNare are too ruffled now. We must plan this thing carefully."

"Seele," Maka continued, "no one will hurt you. My grandson rules the miners who came home with you. My daughter's husband is here with a pump handle in his hand. They call him the Ox-Killer. He is a giant."

"I know," Seele replied.

"Show no one your neck," Mojamaje said. Seele nodded, rising to go. Chibi rose too and followed Seele to the door.

Chibi stopped and turned around to ask, "Can I take my child?"

Maka replied, "Of course. She is in the house behind this one." Chibi nodded and disappeared through the door. "We are proud of you, Chibi," Maka called after her, blowing out the candle.

Back through Naring the two figures wove, silent in the hot summer dark, one with a sleeping child in her arms, to disappear into the crowded Ata compound.

That was how Chibi the trollop, the sullied slattern, every gossip's favorite prey, won a place of importance in the story of the Great Thirst.

MOJAMAJE

❦❧❦❧❦❧❦

Tladis

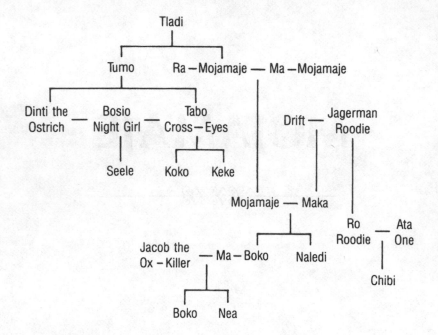

Potsos

De Swarts

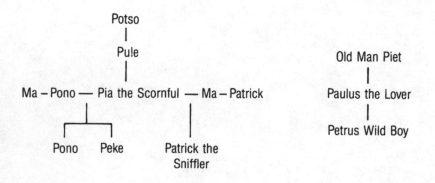

1

Witchcraft

Onc night as the compound slept, the old woman slipped out into the night to run toward the hills, moving much faster than an old woman, as fast as an ostrich, or a hawk through the air. Witches are known for speed. Distances cannot deter them. She entered a cave in the rocks, twice darkened by depth and the black night. She crawled between the smooth rock walls until the air was hot and thick. With a crisp whistle she called to the bats, whose fluttering hummed and echoed dully through the cave. She saw them through the dark. Witches can see in the dark. One bat flew to her and raised one paw, strung with the filmy web of a wing. The bat reached up to its noseless face, plucked out its own eyes and handed them to the old woman. With the two slimy pellets in her hand, the old woman crawled back out into the night, sped back to her compound and skulked into her house to feign sleep. The compound awoke to a normal morning, unsuspecting, unaware. Through the day, the old woman hid the bat eyes in her mouth, where no one could see them, working silently through the day. She went to sleep early, before the last light of day disappeared. When the rest of the compound retired, the old woman crept through the dark, her witch's eyes glowing in the gloom, to the infant sleeping against her mother's breast. She spread the child's tiny eyelids with her withered fingers, pressed her face over the child's small head, placed her cracked lips over each eye in turn and sucked out the infant's eyeballs. Quickly, before the flesh closed around the empty sockets, the old woman wiped off the bat eyes and pressed them into the child's skull. Next day, the old woman worked silently again, the eyes of her granddaughter invisible in the sagging folds of her cheeks. That night she slipped out again to the hill of the bats, crawled again on her belly, squirming like a lizard, to the end of the cave. With a shrill whistle she called to the bat, who took from her the tiny child's eyes. The bat's wet, winged paw touched the old woman's leathery hand.

Next day, as the children played in the compound, one of them held a mirror close to the infant girl's face. The older children turned the tiny head so her eyes turned to the mirror. The sun's reflection flashed brilliantly in the infant's face. The little girl's eyes remained wide open. The children screamed. "Blind!" they cried, and their parents ran to see.

Somewhere a bat flew by day, the eyes of an infant freeing it from the night.

This is one of the oldest stories the BaNare are able to recall. The name of the old woman, the infant, the location of the bat cave, are details long forgotten. Some think the events took place in Taung, before the BaNare came to Naring. Others point out that the story must be more recent because mirrors did not exist until Hrikwa the Griqua brought them in his wagon. Still others maintain that the bat story is ancient and the mirror appeared only in later versions.

The bat-eye switch features in the story of the Great Thirst because it won new popularity after the arrival of the three hordes. The drought had finally pushed the BaNare to their limit, and they fell at each other's throats, exchanging blame, abandoning reason. All order fell away. The Black Goats spent all their wages buying grain from Ahamed to make beer. A few old men tore off their clothes and sang forgotten songs of beastly lust. Public meetings degenerated into brawls. In searching for an explanation for the drought, the BaNare turned to witchcraft. They suddenly noticed how much the old crone in the bat-eye tale resembled Ma-Mojamaje, and how much Naledi resembled the granddaughter who lost her daytime eyes.

Mojamaje called together all his old companions, the oldest of the BaNare. He had two things to tell the BaNare, but not in a public meeting, where anything could happen. If he told his cronies in the morning, by afternoon all Naring would know. The Tladi family assembled to listen, including Chibi plus one of her followers, a shy woman who hid her face in her white Chibiite scarf. Maka, Ma-Boko, and Nea sat with their legs outstretched on the compound floor, while Jacob stood over Mojamaje, pump handle in hand. Boko crouched on his heels by his grandfather, brooding, a miner's helmet on his head. Patrick the Sniffler and his mother stood at the compound gate. Ma-Patrick was the only Loang settler who had gained weight during the five years there. She still ate constantly, growing larger every week, chatting away with a porridge spoon bobbing in and out of her mouth.

Mojamaje waited for the last of his companions to arrive. Then he stood up from his low chair and spread his arms wide. "BaNare," he said. "I will not waste your time. I have two things to say. First, Patrick has asked to marry Nea, child of my daughter. She seems small, yes, but my wife was the same age when she married her husband. The Tladi family approves. And BaNare, would Boko the Big Miner let anyone else come near the poor girl?"

Boko's tense frown melted to a wide grin. The old BaNare smiled. A clever joke, but they knew what Mojamaje was up to. Someday soon he would propose Patrick as chief. The boy's marriage to Nea would yield a rival union of the Tladi and Potso families, in direct competition with the notorious cabal of Koko, Keke, Pono, and Peke.

Now Mojamaje reached into his coat and pulled out a pair of spectacles. "I asked my grandson Boko to bring these from South Africa. I am teaching Patrick English. When he learns enough I will give him these eyeglasses. No one in Naring will seem more intelligent." The others nodded their heads. This was Mojamaje's first public hint that he might someday propose Patrick as chief. Mojamaje returned the spectacles to his coat.

Mojamaje continued, "There is a second thing. Chibi, would you please introduce your follower."

By this time a crowd had begun to form at the Tladi gate, as Naring noticed the unusual size of the gathering in the compound. A few onlookers had overheard the announcement of Patrick and Nea's betrothal and spread the news quickly to the rest of the crowd. Now they witnessed Chibi gently leading one of her followers to the center of Mojamaje's circle and helping her to remove her scarf.

The crowd gasped. Mojamaje's cohort smiled again and some even whistled, as Seele hastily retied her scarf and retreated to the shade of one of the Tladi houses. Then the crowd erupted in confusion, in debate, in furious hope, and a few BaNare began to sing Seele's song:

Face of beauty, child of woe . . . .

Then someone in the back of the crowd cried, "Naledi!" and everyone turned to see the mysterious woman approach the Tladi compound with her stick in her hand and a bundle of wood on her head.

"Notice her eyes," someone muttered, and indeed Naledi kept them hidden now, as her scarf fell low over her forehead.

The crowd parted to let Naledi pass. She made her way to the center of the site of Ma-Mojamaje's enormous woodpile, now marked by only a few remnants of bark and twig. Naledi twirled her stick and tossed it into the center of the bare circle. Then she dumped her headload of wood on top of the stick. Then she returned to the Kalahari for more wood, again and again until a woodpile began to take shape.

"What does it mean?" the BaNare asked.

"What is Naledi up to now?"

The news of Patrick and Nea's engagement, of Seele's reappearance, and of Naledi's revival of Ma-Mojamaje's famous and certainly magical woodpile drove Acting Chief Pono to panic. He did not know what to do, how to respond to this triple challenge from the Tladi family, to his village falling apart.

Koko and Keke's grating laughter echoed through the Potso compound, flushing Pono out, past Naledi's growing woodpile, to search out his brother. He found old Peke in a murky beerhouse, slumped against the grimy wall with a gourd of swill in one hand.

"Pono, my brother!" Peke greeted.

"Drunkard," Pono scolded. "There is no time for drink. We must plan."

"Plan what?" Peke asked, narrowing his eyes to focus on Pono, who sat down beside him, taking a gourd from the hand of the toothless woman serving the beer from a barrel. Other customers murmured lazily, slouched like Peke against the round wall.

"Plan our defense," Pono said. "Everyone loves Patrick. He will marry Nea Sweet Child, a Tladi, and declare himself chief. Seele Seantlo claims Loang. That witch builds her grandmother's woodpile. Mojamaje is turning the BaNare against me. To blame me for the drought."

"Drought," Peke slurred.

"What?"

"The drought is the cause of our troubles."

"Worse than our wives?"

"Much worse."

"Make rain," Peke suggested.

"Drunk," Pono replied.

"Chief," Peke answered, "I do nothing but drink, you are a chief. A drunkard drinks, a chief makes rain. Ask anyone."

The two brothers fell quiet. Then Peke said, "Potso made rain. And Potso's father, what's his name."

"Puka."

"Puka made rain. And Puka's father. Chiefs make rain."

Pono emptied his gourd, struggled to his feet, and stepped back outside. The summer sun immediately drew sweat to his skin. He looked up into the blazing white sky. "Rain," he said aloud. "Chiefs make rain."

Next day the BaNare learned that Pono their chief, concerned for the security of his authority, would prove his worth by making rain in the tradition of Potso the Great Chief Murdered by Tladi, Man of Lightning, who was grandfather of Mojamaje and great-grandfather of Seele Upstart, Seantlo Child, thinking she can wander back to Naring any time she wanted to claim Tladi's fortune.

"I will show them," Pono vowed, succumbing at last to the comfort of witchcraft.

2
Making Rain

To this day, no one denies that Pono pondered carefully the risks of making rain. He consulted his sorcerers, watched the skies, judged with remarkable sensitivity the mood of the BaNare. No champion schemer could have plotted a better course. Yet were there not at least some hints that events would overrun his cool calculations? Was he truly the victim of consequences beyond his prediction? In the end, the BaNare acquitted Pono of the charge of stupidity, but not of blame. These were difficult times, when anyone could make a mistake, but in the end the mistake was still Pono's.

Pono had the choice of five wizards who had inherited from their fathers knowledge of the rainmaking rite. No living BaNare had ever seen such a ceremony, not even Mojamaje, the eldest. The last one had taken place early in Chief Potso's reign, before Mojamaje's birth. Pono chose the wizard who charged the highest fee, surmising that he would render the best service. The exact sum was never disclosed.

Pono's choice was Squirrel Man, famous for squeaking and scratching at the ground as his enormous tail of woven ostrich and chicken plumes waved in the air. His most popular cure involved finding eggshells in the entrails of a goat, placing the eggshell between his withered lips, swallowing, and vomiting back up a pouchful of ashes and spider webs. He smeared this mixture over a child's sore eyes and led away four goats as payment. Fees had risen so high only during the drought, as each BaNare family took action against its own misfortune, refusing to acknowledge impotence in the face of disaster, hiring sorcerers to find more concrete causes and devise appropriate cures.

Squirrel Man consulted a circle of wizards, all of whom received payment from Pono, to decide the best day to hold the ceremony. Squirrel Man announced the final choice. "When the moon approaches Kopadi-lalelo, the evening star, we will wait until I find an eggshell in the entrails of a donkey."

Pono groaned when he heard this verdict. Donkeys were expensive and Ahamed the Indian trader would surely raise the price as soon as he heard the news. Ahamed imported donkeys from South Africa for resale in Naring: they required less water than cattle, ate anything, like goats, and never died from disease. Squirrel Man's elaborate method of deciding when to hold the ceremony was his own invention: the rainmaking ceremony never changed, so wizards displayed their creative talents in conceiving their own preliminary rites. So Pono bought a donkey a week for six weeks until Squirrel Man found an eggshell.

"Aiyee!" the sorcerer yelled, raising the tiny white fragment in the air, flashing it before the BaNare crowded around the bloody donkey corpse.

The news of Squirrel Man's discovery brought new hope to Naring. It was as if rain had already fallen, as if white clouds had already filled the sky, as if moisture had already soaked the soil red, thrusting supple green shoots into the humid air. It was as if grass had already sprung back lush and thick on the barren wastes of pasture, as if the men of Naring had already led fertile cows back from South Africa to repopulate Naring with cattle, as if tottering calves already tugged greedily at their mothers' swollen udders, as if tots drank milk every morning and roasted green corn until their bellies ached, as if every storehouse bulged with squashes and pumpkins and shiny red beans, and baskets taller than a child old enough to slaughter a chicken brimmed with ripe grain. It was as if every

BaNare bore a bundle of long green sweet-reed stalks, one stalk held in one hand, broken at its juicy joints, the fibrous outer hull stripped away with eager teeth to reveal the sugary white pulp beneath. Tear, bite, chew, swallow, spit out the pulp, tear, bite, chew, swallow, spit out . . . The BaNare dreamed of the harvest, the glorious rain, the magnificent bounty delivered them by their Great Chief Pono, son of Pia, son of Pule, son of Potso, son of Puka, son of Palolo, son of . . .

"If I fail, they will kill me," Pono told Squirrel Man. "You raise their hope too high."

"That is my job," the shriveled sorcerer replied with a wag of his fluffy tail.

Squirrel Man buried the eggshell in the sand at the base of Pono's compound wall. The summer sun rose lower in the sky as winter approached. The wind gained force and changed direction, gusting from the Kalahari over the sand slope into Naring. Sand piled up against houses and walls in softly rolling dunes. When Squirrel Man dug up the shell a week later, it was clenched in the jaws of a rotting donkey head. That was how deep the dunes had grown around Naring: a donkey head could lie completely unseen, covered by sand. Mothers feared for their children disappearing into the swirling dunes. Squirrel Man tossed the eggshell into the air. The wind caught it, lifted it high in a twisting gust, then dropped it swiftly to the ground a few dozen yards from the Potso compound. Squirrel Man hurried to the spot.

"Here," he announced. "This is the place to make rain."

The sorcerer ordered a fire built over the eggshell. The BaNare gathered to watch—first a few sticks, then logs, until the blaze leapt to the height of a tree. Squirrel Man folded his tail under his legs and sat watching the flames. Night fell. The crowd wandered away. The fire burned day and night as the winter cloud bank rolled over the sand ridge to cover Naring, an icy gray ceiling obscuring the sun, moon, and stars. Never before had the bank appeared so early, at the very end of summer. The BaNare shuddered: "This winter will freeze our blood. Our skins will crack like Squirrel Man's eggshell."

Still the wizard sat by the fire, which his assistants kept ablaze. One by one the BaNare donned their blankets whenever they ventured outside their houses, until only formless shades moved silently through the village. Still Squirrel Man sat, with only his loincloth and feathered tail to keep him warm. His ancient, wrinkled skin rippled with cold as he sat watching the fire, too far away to feel its heat.

"He will die," the BaNare concluded.

After a week, Squirrel Man jumped up to declare that the ceremony now would commence. The wily, wiry sorcerer brought Chief Pono to the scene, sat him on the ground, sent blanketed girls to fetch water, which he sprinkled on the ground around the fire.

"Magic," he explained to the BaNare assembling again to watch. "Sing," he ordered, and his assistants launched into a popular rain song. The growing crowd joined in. Squirrel Man brought out the donkey head and heaved it onto the fire.

Pono sat beside the pyre, wrapped in a huge yellow blanket, staring dejectedly into the flames. "This will never work," he muttered.

The singing rose louder. More BaNare rushed to the site. Stone stepped out of his office to see what the commotion was about. He wore a gray English army coat, like Mojamaje's, buttoned to the neck. His eyeglasses whistled in the wind. His thin black hair tossed in curled wisps. He drifted toward the fire, marked more by smoke than by flame in the light of day. As Stone disappeared into the maze of paths that led toward the Potso compound, Petrus Wild Boy slipped into Stone's house and Wild Boy's Dog dropped to sleep on its step.

Stone pushed his way through the crowd to Pono's side. "Good day, Chief," Stone said politely. "What have we here?"

Pono replied from deep in the folds of his blankets, "I am making rain."

Stone surveyed the scene: Squirrel Man's ridiculous outfit, the fire, the earnest faces of the BaNare singing to the skies. Stone looked above the fire, where the smoke merged with the low ceiling of continuous clouds. Now, Stone was a man of science and generally kept an open mind about the practical functions of ancient rituals. "Hmmn," he murmured. "Potential."

"Chief," he said to Pono, "if you make the fire much bigger, it will heat the air above, lift the cloud bank, the water in the cloud will turn to rain and fall to the ground. But you need a much bigger fire. More wood. A tremendous fire." Excited now, as when he had explained the drilling machine's operation, Stone looked about for more wood. Not twenty yards away, between the Potso and Tladi compounds, Ma-Mojamaje's famous woodpile, rebuilt by Naledi, climbed higher than a compound roof. Stone snapped his fingers. "The perfect thing!"

"Chief," Stone said to Pono, "that woodpile there is just the right size. More wood, more heat. We can raise the cloud bank and really make rain."

Sure enough, Stone looked up again to see a tiny spot of deep black forming where the column of smoke touched the low cloud ceiling. It looked like a miniature thundercloud. "See, Chief," Stone said, pointing to the spot. Noticing Stone's pointing finger, the BaNare looked up too. They scanned the sky from zenith to horizon, craning their necks as they sang.

"There!" someone cried, pointing toward the Naring hills.

"Yes!" someone else confirmed.

"Look!"

Sure enough, above the ridge of hills, beyond, far away, a dark patch of cloud hung below the unbroken gray ceiling. It grew larger, racing toward the ceremony site. The BaNare stared in tense anticipation. The singing stopped. Only the wind and the sputter of the fire broke the wintery silence. Dark, swirling, like a rain cloud dancing across the sky, the dark mass skimmed under the cloud bank, passed over the Naring hills, and headed for the fire. Stone stared in silence too.

A voice suddenly cried, "The wind blows the other way! It cannot be a cloud!"

The sense of this comment struck every BaNare to the heart, turning hopes of rain to fear of unknown disaster. Clouds do not fly against the wind. Too frightened to scream, the BaNare waited for the mysterious darkness to reach them.

"Locusts!"

Humming, buzzing filled the air, the flutter of countless frenzied wings, as the BaNare fell to the ground, pulling their blankets over their heads. The insects' stiff bodies beat against them, against the walls of their houses, crackling like wood on a fire. Children bawled under their blankets. But the locusts found no grain drying on the compound floors: there had been no BaNare harvest. Confused, the locusts perched everywhere, chomping firewood, thatch, mud walls, blankets, and now the hungry BaNare regained their wits and fell on the attackers, cracking their long, stiff insect bodies in two, and stuffed the locusts into their mouths.

3
Cold Skin

The wedding of Patrick the Sniffler and Nea Sweet Child took place during the weeks that Squirrel Man consulted the donkeys. Despite its humble trappings—there were no cattle to change hands in payment for the bride, goat meat was the only food, the beer was brewed from old corn bought in De Swart's and Ahamed's shops—the BaNare took solace in the event. The sight of the two young lovers hand in hand gave every adult a fleeting sense of possibility. Nea still seemed a delicate desert flower, in a red dress falling decorously to her knees. Her eyes sparkled with love. Patrick was twice her age, but he too looked like a child. A rumor arose that Nea's monthly bleeding had not stopped, that only she among the BaNare was able to bear a child. Though a mild breeze might blow them both away, Nea and Patrick stood alone like brawny bororo trees as the BaNare's last hope for the future.

"Our finest examples."

"Our new generation."

Boko led his Black Goats to and from the wedding in disciplined ranks, reminding the BaNare of the stories of Tladi's regiment. Boko marched them through the village once a week thereafter. Their helmets gleamed with menace. Stone noticed this martial display and asked himself this question: "Is that Mojamaje?"

The rainmaking failure, the marriage of Patrick and Nea, Boko's wild antics—to Chief Pono, the news was all bad. What now? "Simple, Chief," Squirrel Man counseled. "Time for a diversion. Keep them all busy and eventually rain will fall again."

And so Pono surprised the BaNare by ordering all young men to report for bogwera initiation. No one obeyed until Pono fired Squirrel Man as his official sorcerer and announced that the initiation would be harmless, no beatings, no naked nights by the fire, no circumcision. The men of Naring heaved sighs of relief.

"I will go," each one said.

"I have nothing else to do."

"Except go to the mines again."

"I can do that after."

One by one the men of Naring agreed to join Pono's initiation.

Another surprise, but not the last one, came when Boko agreed to take his Black Goats to the ceremony. He also urged Chibi to send her male Chibiites. Boko's endorsement of the initiation immediately kindled Pono's suspicions. But events were already out of control, the ceremony would take place, not even Pono could stop it.

Patrick the Sniffler decided to go too.

"You are too weak," Nea pleaded.

"No," Mojamaje declared.

"Do not go," Maka ordered.

"Be careful," Ma-Patrick advised, shoving a spoonful of porridge into her mouth.

"I must go," Patrick insisted. "The honor of my family is at stake. I crossed the woodpile long ago to become a Tladi, but really, I am a Potso. The deeds of my family scald my heart. I must cool the wound. Too long. I have waited too long. I am a man. I must be a man."

Boko understood. "He will keep warm. I will carry blankets for him. He will be safe."

Patrick ignored all warnings and walked alongside Boko out to the wilderness for the ceremony. This was the first time Patrick had ever left Naring. Pono chose a site only two hours away. That very afternoon, he sat the novices down and invited the old men to sing songs and give instructions. It was a tame event. Neither Mojamaje nor Jacob the Ox-Killer attended. Perhaps if they had been there, things would have turned out differently. Many BaNare blamed Boko for what happened, but the truth was not so simple.

The first night of the initiation ceremony, when the novices snuggled into their blankets, nestling around the fire, Boko leapt to his feet, threw off his overalls and mining helmet to cry, "Bare all for the Great Thirst! Share all for the Great Thirst! Dare all for the Great Thirst!"

On cue, all the Black Goats jumped up, threw off their clothes and helmets, and lay down naked by the fire.

"We are the only true BaNare," Boko declared. "Our chief is a woman, an infant. Will he lie beside us as the ancient law says?"

Pono roused from his mountain of blankets to listen to Boko's tirade. He made no move to take off his clothes.

Someone threw more wood on the fire. No one spoke. Boko and the

Black Goats lay motionless and naked. A cough rang out, then a sneeze, followed by a wheeze, a sniffle, a throat cleared. Patrick rose to his feet and cast off his blanket. The BaNare men watched in silent horror. Patrick threw off his clothes to reveal the scrawniest skeleton ever to appear before their eyes. He lay down among the Black Goats, shivering with cold.

"What do I do?" Pono gasped. "He will die."

"Cover him with a blanket," Peke advised.

"A chief cannot force an initiate to break rules."

"Then he will die," Peke admitted.

Then Boko's muscular frame gleamed in the firelight as he picked his way over the trembling bodies of his men to fall to the ground and grab Patrick's arm and pull him closer to the fire than anyone else could bear. Boko had inherited from Mojamaje, his mother's father, a mysterious resistance to fire. Remember the infant Mojamaje crawling through the towering blaze at the Battle of the Woodpile? Sleeping close to the fire at his own bogwera?

Boko turned his back to the fire and curled his body around Patrick's. The heat grilled Boko's back shiny but reached Patrick only through the warm air surrounding him. Protected from the flames but bathed in heat, Patrick's shivering body warmed to a soothing glow.

The BaNare men watched in fascination. Pono and Peke passed their bottle of brandy. "They will be heroes," Peke whispered. "Patrick is brave. They will make him chief. You are finished."

"Yes," Pono muttered, closing his bleary eyes to sleep.

To this day, the BaNare debate Boko's motives. Some say he hoped to make Patrick chief by aiding the sickly young man in this feat of endurance. But like Nea, Boko was a child of the times. Serious, intelligent, he grew up to face a world not of his making, too wide for his arms but not for his mind. He grew up beside Nea on Patrick's lap, loving them as no one else on earth. As the BaNare envied Nea and Patrick their gentle spirits, their innocence, Boko knew the dangers lurking in the wind, in the dunes building steadily, silently, against Naring's walls, in the steamy Joburg mines, everywhere.

The mines were to blame. Boko was lost in their tunnels, blind to open light. By example at least, he urged Patrick along the path to bravery, to honor, beyond the limits of Patrick's weak body. Without the violence of the mines dimming his senses, Boko might have covered Patrick with a pile of ten, twenty blankets. But he belonged to a generation who sweated their lives away for someone else's gold, to return home youthless, strangers in their own compounds. So instead, Boko wrapped his beloved's naked skin in only his own mortal flesh. The night was bitterly cold. The other men fell asleep, leaving Patrick in Boko's hands. Patrick dozed, his toes and fingers tingling with the first draft of cold from the night beyond as a stiff wind blew around and around the blaze. The wind changed direction and pushed the warm air away from the entwined friends, whistling out into the blackness. Patrick quivered. Boko fell asleep.

Cold crept along Patrick's skin and by morning he was dead.

4
A Perfect Trick

Pono awoke to a skyful of low, gray clouds, the relentless ceiling. He rubbed his eyes and looked out at the BaNare men standing in a silent circle around the fire. He had fallen asleep expecting the men to declare Patrick chief in the morning, but he woke instead to find Patrick's corpse. Boko knelt over his dead friend, crying with rage, pounding his fists on the ground, a blanket over his shoulders, his head bursting with frustration. He stood up. Some Black Goats helped him lift Patrick into the air and they set off back to Naring. Pono and Peke took their time rolling up their blankets. No young men stayed behind to carry their belongings.

"You are still chief," Peke reassured his brother.

"Will they kill me?" Pono said. "The BaNare loved Patrick. I called bogwera. I am responsible."

Peke replied, "They will blame that madman Boko. No worry. His whole family is crazy. His aunt builds that woodpile again, like her crazy grandmother did."

"Why?" Pono asked.

"No one knows."

When the BaNare men reached Naring with Patrick's body, the village exploded in recrimination.

"It is all your fault," neighbor accused neighbor.

"Coward."

"You would not stand up against Pono and Peke."

"Patrick's blood is on your hands."

"He died of cold—no blood."

"See what you have done?"

"The rainmaking should have convinced you."

"Waiting killed Patrick."

"He should have been chief."

"Why did you wait?"

"Fool."

"Coward."

"Witch."

Squirrel Man's business boomed as BaNare paid him to determine which of their neighbors were casting spells in their direction.

"Idiots," Koko and Keke snarled at their husbands. Almost old women now, they stood with their hands over their mouths, their eyes darting furtively, their childhood makgabe securely tied around their waists beneath their prim long dresses.

"It was not our fault," Pono protested.

"You are chief," Koko snapped. "Everything is the chief's fault. One more mistake and you will step down. Puo my son will take your place."

"Never." Pono howled, storming out of the Potso compound, past Naledi tossing another bundle of wood onto the enormous pile. Peke hurried after his brother.

"Which one is Puo?" Peke asked.

"I have no idea," Pono replied. "Probably the eldest."

Pono and Peke maundered through the village, overhearing the heated discussions of Patrick's tragic end. Some BaNare expected them to cut holes in their clothes and end up in the Tladi compound, drinking tea, like their father, Pia the Scornful, taking refuge in the last calm eye of Naring's storm.

Patrick's death stunned Nea Sweet Child to numbness. Poor confounded girl, she had not known that death was so final, so possible. Her chubby child's cheeks ran with salty tears that evaporated into the biting dry air, the chill wind, before reaching her cracking lips. Boko sat against the Tladi compound wall with his helmet on his head, arms wrapped around his sister, staring into space. Mojamaje, Maka, the old BaNare, all sat silently sad. Jacob sat blinking, pump handle in hand. Naledi added wood to Ma-Mojamaje's pile.

No one rebuked Boko. It was too late. Patrick was dead without once wearing the eyeglasses Mojamaje had asked Boko to bring from Joburg. They remained in the folds of Mojamaje's gray coat.

Patrick was buried in the Tladi family compound. This was illegal, as Stimp had dictated so long ago. The same flu that soon after had filled the missionary graveyard filled Patrick's lungs throughout his short life. No one informed Stone or the missionary of Patrick's illegal burial. The BaNare concentrated not on questions of law but on the fact that Patrick's grave was dug in the Tladi compound, not in the Potso compound. As they lowered Patrick out of sight, the BaNare sang his childhood song:

> Remember me for what I am
> A child with children of my own . . .

When the song ended, the BaNare fell silent, remembering Patrick the Sniffler. Then suddenly a noise broke the quiet. The crowd looked to Naledi's woodpile. Clacking, huffing—it was Pono, climbing his way to the top. He looked ancient, odious, a victim of the drought. He struggled to the peak of the mountain of wood, to sit atop the highest log, facing the BaNare. Wild eyes stared out from his puffy face. More clacking and huffing, and Peke sat down beside him. No one could tell them apart.

The crowd muttered, "Thieves."

"Fools."

"Murderers."

When Pono spoke, one arm looped around his brother's, the BaNare judged that what he said could not have been their own idea. So diabolical, so neat, such a perfect trick, it bore the unmistakable mark of Koko and Keke, perfect scoundrels. The evil sisters had waited patiently, resolutely, to spring their ultimate trap.

"BaNare!" Pono declared. "Pono and Peke make a decision. There lies our poor brother Patrick, son of our dear father's second wife, Ma-Patrick the Eater. A lovely boy. His death is a terrible waste. And BaNare, we know your desires. Mojamaje sent this Seele, child of Seantlo wife, to walk arm in arm with that Chibi tramp, exciting your greed. Seele says she will throw our well at you. It will belong to everyone. Mojamaje told her to say that." Pono paused. "Very well. The well is Seele's. It is hers. It is yours. Koko and Keke do not need it. They do not need you. They do not need us."

The BaNare could not believe their ears. Pono and Peke were giving up the well.

"In return," Chief Pono concluded, "we claim only our legal due. Patrick was our brother, as Dinti the Ostrich was brother to Tabo Cross-Eyes. Seele is the fruit of Tabo's Seantlo with Dinti's widow. We claim Patrick's widow as our own Seantlo wife."

5

War

Sweet, helpless, childish Nea, claimed by abominable Pono and Peke, each four times her age, three times her weight, Patrick's poor meatless body still warm in its grave!

The BaNare erupted in confusion, but one by one they realized the connection between Seele and Nea. If Seele's claim on the Loang well held good, it was through Seantlo, justifying Pono and Peke's claim on Nea. Refusing the Seantlo claim meant giving up the Loang well.

Suddenly Boko vaulted over the compound wall toward Patrick's graveside and called out a command to his Black Goats, who rushed into the compound to encircle Nea in a shield of miner's helmets and overalls. Boko stood at their head and shouted, "Try it! I will kill you all!"

Someone rushed from the crowd with a burning stick, to set fire to Naledi's woodpile and roast Pono and Peke in its flames, but someone else knocked him down. Others joined the battle. The scene descended to riot.

At this point, some tellers of the story of the Great Thirst move quickly to the next events. Only the most disciplined tellers bite their lips and admit to their listeners that not everyone sided with Nea. When night fell, knife fights flared, gunshots rang out, the BaNare were at war with themselves. All along, Pono, Peke, Koko, and Keke had many supporters, as had Tabo Cross-Eyes and Pia ya Pipa before them. Friends, relatives, acquaintances, lackeys, conspirators, impartial observers, all found reason to side with Mojamaje's enemies. That night after Pono's announcement, many BaNare argued that the law was the law, Seantlo was a brother's right, Nea deserved sympathy but the law vindicated

Pono and Peke. In a public meeting, how would the BaNare decide? Honest tellers related that the debate would have been a close one, with perhaps the weight in Pono and Peke's favor. After all, the drought had been a disastrous struggle, drying the wombs of BaNare women, smothering all Naring's cattle, baking their fields to dust, driving their men to the mines. Nea was only one. There were worse fates. A small price to pay for relief from the drought.

Cooler heads, though few in number, realized that the ownership of the Loang well meant nothing as long as the drought gripped their throats. Their pleas of peace fell on deaf ears. Nea disappeared, as Boko moved her under cover of night from compound to compound so no one might follow her trail. Meanwhile, the Black Goats prepared for war, carving long poles with tapered tips, which they held under their arms like Zulu stabbing spears. Some carried rifles over their shoulders. Some tucked knives in their belts. They marched up and down the paths of Naring, shouting, filling the air with violence.

Mojamaje sent for Boko, but his grandson was out of control. Remorse and guilt over Patrick's demise sent Boko careening in violent spasms to leap at the head of his Black Goats and shout their bloodcurdling yells at the top of his miner's lungs. Ma-Boko considered ordering Jacob the Ox-Killer to subdue their son, but Mojamaje stopped her.

"The drought," he explained. "This is all the fault of the drought. I hoped we could settle it among ourselves. We cannot. Ma-Boko, tell your son not to kill tonight. Tell him I will speak to Willoughby in the morning."

Ma-Boko ran to tell her son, who reluctantly passed the word to his Goats, who spread the news throughout Naring.

6

A Gun and a Knife

Through the night, the story of the old grandmother who traded bat eyes for infant eyes transformed itself into a very different tale. First, Pono became the old woman, Nea the child. By morning, Stone was the crone and the BaNare were the infant. The details of this process never came clear, though supporting evidence helped it along. Someone counted back through the years to declare that Stone and the drought had dwelt among the BaNare for exactly the same time. Others disputed this notion, calling it a vile fabrication, but by morning it ruled Naring.

"Why else would Mojamaje go to Willoughby?"

"Willoughby is the cause."

"Mojamaje will kill him."

"Willoughby brought the drought!"

And now the BaNare recalled that in all Naledi's speeches she blamed strangers for the drought. They asked themselves who these strangers could be. Naledi pointed her stick at Pia the Scornful, Tabo Cross-Eyes, Stimp and Willoughby and declared,

"When we came here the earth was wet. . . .
Now strangers come,
See by their skins how they make the earth dry,
They make clouds vanish and crack the sky"

The BaNare now asked, "Who are these strangers?" Pia and Tabo were not strangers. Stimp was gone. That left Willoughby. The last Willoughby was the stranger Naledi blamed for the drought.

Slowly the BaNare's anger swung from Pono and Peke to Stone, the current Willoughby. During the day a crowd formed around the Tladi compound, waiting for Mojamaje to emerge. Instead, the circle of old men and women assembled once more to discuss what Mojamaje would say to Stone. Maka came out to join them, then Mojamaje. The crowd outside the compound grew large and restless as the west wind whipped Kalahari sand in their faces. Blankets covered their heads and bodies. Beneath their blankets the men carried guns and knives.

The day wore on, growing colder as the thick gray ceiling of clouds pressed lower on the earth. The goats of Loang picked through the spare underbrush for dried leaves. Their black coats rippled with wind, their anxious bleats lost in the whistling gale. One by one the old cohort agreed on the message Ma-Boko would speak in English to Stone: "Please, sir, Mojamaje must speak to you about important matters. The BaNare will kill each other if you do not come. Blood will soak the sand. Please follow me. I will lead you to Mojamaje and his advisors."

Jacob stayed behind, guarding the Tladi compound with his pump handle.

Naledi added firewood to the towering woodpile.

Nea blinked in the dark of her hideout, a strange storehouse in a strange compound somewhere in the maze of Naring. She cried softly in misery and confusion, the image of Patrick the Sniffler floating before her in the gloom.

Boko drilled his Black Goats in Zulu formation.

Ma-Boko ran to Stone's house and knocked on the door. Stone opened the door. "Please," she said in English, out of breath, "Mojamaje must speak to you. Blood will flow. Please follow me."

Stone stood still on the threshold, eyes narrowed at Ma-Boko. Wind whistled into the house. She stood barefoot, her white lace dress torn and dirty. He marveled at her command of English, then remembered her translation when the drilling machine arrived.

"Tell him to come to my office," Stone replied, turning back to the house and slamming the door.

"Mojamaje," Edna called, drawing a brush through her hair. "I heard that name. At last you will meet him. Be careful. He is a better man than you. Perhaps he will kill you. As he promised me."

Stone reached into a drawer and pulled out a revolver and smooth leather holster. "We shall see," he answered, stalking through the house like a caged animal, tying the pistol onto his hip, disappearing out the back door without closing it behind, leaving it flapping in the wind.

Back at the Tladi compound, Ma-Boko repeated Stone's message.

"I will go," Mojamaje said.

"He will go," his old friends said to each other.

"He will go," repeated one of the BaNare in the crowd outside.

"He will go!"

"To Willoughby!"

"To kill him!"

Maka pulled Mojamaje into their house, alone. The room was dim. Mojamaje stood in his heavy gray English army coat, tying the waistbelt tight around his body, closing the skirt from the cold air.

"Be careful," Maka said.

"No danger," Mojamaje replied.

More BaNare joined the crowd outside. Boko led his Black Goats in chants.

Maka's face was barely visible in the room.

"Will you tell him about Nea?"

"Nea, Seantlo, the well. Willoughby must abolish Seantlo and make the well open to all."

"Do you remember," Maka said, "driving me to the diamond town in the wagon for guns?"

"Of course, Maka."

"You are old, Mojamaje."

"I know it."

"We had guns then. Willoughby will not listen. You are old."

The crowd outside called Mojamaje's name, shouting, chanting, singing.

Maka pushed him gently toward the door, a dark object in one of her hands, which she reached to his waistbelt as he stepped out into the late afternoon light. He looked down at his waist and there, tucked in his belt, was Vlei's huge dagger, the one Drift used to kill Jagerman Roodie.

The BaNare shrieked.

"The knife!"

"Mojamaje's knife!"

The crowd parted as Mojamaje stepped out the Tladi compound gate. The BaNare swelled behind as he marched slowly toward Stone's office. The commotion, the wind, the swirling sand, clouded Mojamaje's eyes and ears with memory. His English army hat hung low over his brow, his old man's legs moved painfully forward. The BaNare remembered the song of the Battle of the Rocks and sang it to the sky:

All through the night
Through the terrible fight
Mojamaje kept watch by the door
First he ate a rock
Then he ate a bullet
Then Mojamaje ate a Boer

Boko heard the news and dashed with his Black Goats to the scene. The Chibiites wrapped their white scarves around their necks and flooded behind Chibi in her white robe, falling in step behind Mojamaje. Ma-Boko sent Jacob the Ox-Killer to walk alongside Mojamaje, to protect him with the pump handle just in case.

Chaos reigned as Mojamaje shuffled toward Stone's office. Verse followed verse, until the BaNare arrived at a new rendition:

All through his life
With his terrible knife
Mojamaje kept his people free

First he ate a Zulu
Then he ate a Boer
Now he will eat Willoughby

7

Mojamaje's Life

Mojamaje struggled against the biting wind, laden with grit and sand.
His high Bushman cheekbones rumpled against his narrow eyes, almost
closed to the outside world. Inside his eyes, it was nearly dark. Shadows
danced before him as the crowd parted and surged behind. The singing
receded in his ears. The wind howled, whistling between the brim of his
hat and his ears. "The knife," Mojamaje said to himself, mouthing the
words but speaking no sound. The Ox-Killer walked alongside, confused
by the furor, the pump handle light in his massive paw. Dusty cloth
streamed from his boot. Jacob kept one eye on Mojamaje, ready to catch
him if his old man's legs failed.

Mojamaje's head swam with exhaustion, cold, and memory in the
dimness of his slitted eyes. "Maka," he whispered to the wind—the
knife against her spine as they rode toward the dawn from the Roodie
farm, Maka tense in his arms on their horse. She knelt over him, shaking, her father's stink, his bulk, pushing the knife down against Mojamaje's clenched throat—Maka, so wild, lost to her past, recovering her
breath, her sense, her love for Mojamaje, determination to endure. Now
the knife was in his belt. Maka and the knife. Mojamaje's life.

Stone heard the noise, stepped out of his office onto its tiny, roofed
veranda, and gazed in horror at the crowd storming, approaching him.
Truly, as Edna had spat, this Mojamaje had the love of his people. All
Naring followed behind two distant figures moving slowly toward Stone.
One was Mojamaje. Edna was right. A better man than he. The man he
wanted to be. The love of Naring. Stone unhitched his holster guard,
stepped down off the veranda into the dust, his eyeglasses whistling as
the wind flew by. "I will show her," he said to himself. "I will show
them." He considered running back into the office to telegraph head-

quarters for reinforcements. "I will stand and fight," he said instead, and this is what he did.

Petrus Wild Boy ambled past, waved to Stone, disappeared around the corner of the office, and ran to the back door of Stone's house. He slipped inside. Wild Boy's Dog curled up on the step, his mangy coat bristling with fever, his flesh quivering in the cold.

Step by step, Mojamaje fought the wind. He was pleased with himself that he coughed not once. The drought had dried his lungs. For years, since the devastating flu, he had saved his strength, sitting in the winter sun and summer shade of the Tladi compound, discussing, planning, observing, happy to survive another day. The huge Zulu knife pressed against one leg, then the other, as he stepped along the sand, winding his way up to Willoughby's office. A long arc past the last cluster of compounds, their grass roofs dried to tinder, rustling in the wind, and the shadows in his narrow Bushman eyes fell away to only two: the square shape of Stone's office, and before it, the figure of Stone.

The crowd whooped as Stone came into their view. The last hundred yards were a straight line across a bare clearing of dust-covered rock, swirling with sand blown over the ridge from the Kalahari. Stone flinched as Mojamaje and Jacob turned the corner to make straight for him. Behind them a column of helmeted men, black goatskins thrown over their shoulders, pointed poles clutched under their arms, behind the column a white-scarfed, chanting throng, behind them the entire BaNare people.

Stone moistened his cracked lips and peered closely at Mojamaje and Jacob. On the left, a gray English army coat, exactly like his own, and a wide-brimmed army hat. A weapon—a pistol?—hung from the coat belt. Mojamaje was still too far away for Stone to see his face. Beside him strode a giant with something resembling a pump handle gripped in one hand. "Which one is Mojamaje?" Stone asked himself. He wanted to run inside, lock the door, telegraph headquarters, but this was his last chance to redeem himself in Edna's eyes, in the eyes of the BaNare.

At that very moment, Edna's eyes were closed. Wild Boy's lips pressed against her mouth, his rough hands clasped her breasts.

"Hurry up," Stone hissed through clenched teeth, one hand rubbing the leather of his holster, his image of heroism as ancient as Boko's.

Mojamaje began to huff as he walked. His head began to spin. The cold began to penetrate his skin. Turning to Jacob, he said, "Wait here."

The Ox-Killer stopped. The crowd stopped. Mojamaje continued on alone, the new song rising behind him to the gray ceiling of clouds:

All through his life
With his terrible knife
Mojamaje kept his people free
First he ate a Zulu
Then he ate a Boer
Now he will eat Willoughby

The crowd spread out along the open clearing, working its way along the perimeter until Stone's office was completely encircled, ringed at twenty yards by a bloodthirsty mob. He swallowed hard to moisten the dry inside of his mouth. Worried by the racket, Jacob crept a few yards behind Mojamaje, just in case.

Mojamaje stopped, then raised his head. His broad hat brim rose up and at last exposed his face to Stone.

"My God," Stone gasped, eyes wide with fear and disbelief. "He's old!"

It was the oldest face in Naring, wrinkled almost beyond recognition, its fine youthful features withered by ten years less than a century of life. Stone watched as Mojamaje stood motionless a yard away. The crowd was hysterical, yelling encouragement, urging Mojamaje to slay Stone.

But Mojamaje was thinking of something else. Lost in reverie, the cold seeping up through the skirt of his coat, Mojamaje forgot for a moment why he had come. He looked quizzically at Stone through his narrowed eyes. Then he thought of the knife, the knife that had made him famous. He had only touched it once, for a brief instant, when he bought it from Vlei with his beautiful fur cloak. He remembered sewing the skins, the smell of the animals who had died to make it. When he stepped back, naked, into Drift's lightless house, she snatched the knife from his hand. Maka had kept it thereafter, strapped to her back, concealed in her blankets, hidden from sight. Stopped before Stone, dust swirling in his eyes, Mojamaje wondered what the knife felt like. He reached to his belt, drew the huge dagger and raised it high in the air.

The crowd went wild. Stone fell back, turned, ran into his office and bolted the door behind. The BaNare surged forward, certain that Mojamaje had drawn the knife to plunge it deep in Stone's heart. "Kill him!" they shouted.

Mojamaje snapped out of his dream, staggered toward the office veranda, and called out to the Ox-Killer behind him, "Stop them, Jacob."

Jacob's face screwed to concentrated fury as he darted forward, swept Mojamaje onto the veranda, and spun to face the crowd, brandishing the pump handle. The first to reach them was Boko, Miner Out of Control. Jacob cracked his pump handle down on Boko's metal helmet. The resounding gong froze the BaNare in their tracks. They pulled back. Boko fell unconscious in the dust. Jacob raised the pump handle again, ready to smite the next comer.

Inside the office, Stone pounded on the telegraph key, UNDER ATTACK . . . Before he had time to tap out another word, the Black Goats climbed the roof and jerked the cable from its mooring. The line went dead. They beat the corrugated metal roof with the butts of their pointed sticks.

Mojamaje and Jacob stood alone on the veranda facing the confused crowd. The sight of Boko sprawled on the ground brought even the Black Goats to silence. Mojamaje returned the knife to his belt. The Black Goats climbed down to the ground. Mojamaje raised his arms, coughed his first cough since the drought had cured his flu, and began to speak.

"Kill Willoughby," he declared, "and the English will come through the canyon, like Zulu, like Boers, but with guns and cannons to destroy Naring. I have seen them. They will do it."

The BaNare looked at each other. Mojamaje continued, "I will talk to him." He turned to knock on the office door.

"Who's there?" Stone called, cringing against his desk, pistol drawn.

"Mojamaje."

"Go away."

"You asked me to come to your office," Mojamaje said.

"Go away. I telegraphed the army. They are on their way. Leave me alone."

Mojamaje turned back to the crowd and said, "We need time to think."

The BaNare were ready for action, any action at all. Years of drought had driven them to despair, like Boko, thirsting for remedies, refusing to admit that none existed. Then what? Killing Stone was something to do, action, taking charge, battling the drought. Mojamaje led them to the slaughter, raised his terrible knife for the kill—then he let his prey escape. He told Jacob to clonk his own grandson, and now paused to think.

"Why?" the BaNare cried.

"Why?"

"Why?"

Mojamaje gave no answer. The crowd parted slightly as Maka and Ma-Boko pushed through, bearing three of the low wooden chairs that Mojamaje and his aged confidants slouched on in the Tladi compound. They placed them on the tiny veranda of Stone's office. They returned, with helpers, to fetch more chairs and the cooking pot for brewing tea. They made a fire close against the veranda. Maka brewed tea. Mojamaje sat down. His cohorts pushed through the crowd, took their places around Mojamaje, sipped Maka's tea and discussed the matter at hand. Ma-Boko removed Boko's helmet, pressed his skull with her fingers, rolled back his eyes. "No damage," she decided.

"Poor Boko," the crowd muttered. "He loved Patrick so."

Men brought their chairs, women brought cups, blankets, cookpots and firewood. The BaNare sat down. Their throats were dry and their faces were cold. They wrapped their hands around their hot cups and thought long and hard about what to do. Even the Chibiites cooled their fervor and sat down. Only the Black Goats refused to relax, prowling the clearing like wildcats, waiting for Boko to wake up, pressing their faces against the small window of Stone's office.

"Where is Nea?" Ma-Boko asked the Goats.

"Only Boko knows," they replied.

Ma-Boko shook her son, worried now. "Where is Nea?" she repeated, but Boko heard nothing.

8

A Vigil

Night fell, the BaNare brought porridge flour to cook in the clearing before Stone's office. They brewed more tea and roasted black goats. The children fell asleep in their blankets. The Black Goats drummed on the office roof but Stone refused to come out.

Nea crouched in her hiding place, warm under the dozen blankets her brother had thrown over her. Hunger and thirst tugged at her stomach and throat, for Boko was long overdue for a visit. She had heard the uproar, the chanting, the shouts, the new song about Mojamaje. The crowd sounded very close. Then the noise died down. Night fell. The smell of cookfires and charred meat crawled under her blankets to lick at her nose.

"Where is Boko?" she wondered. "Where am I?" The air was warm from her breath and sweat, the coarse wool of the blanket, the smell of woodsmoke, meat, the heavy aroma of cow dung, the— Cow dung? Naring was cattleless. Nea furrowed her brow in concentration. Her little nose flared. Not cattle manure, more like goat. No, a horse. Nea had never sniffed a horse up close, but perhaps this was what it smelled like. The blankets muffled all but the loudest sound from Nea's ears, so perhaps she was near horses but could not hear them. Or donkeys. Was she in Ahamed's storage shed, not in a compound at all? She pushed back blanket after blanket, layer after layer, until fresh cold air hit her face like water. She was surrounded by hay. She climbed up the bales, pulling a blanket around her shoulders. At the top, she looked down through the darkness on two enormous, motionless animals. "Horses," she concluded.

Nea worked her way to the ground, blinking in the dark, feeling her way along the stalls to the door, found the latch, and stepped out of Stone's famous hay shed. She groped her way through the dark and started in fright at a black shape in the dim shadows at the Stone house back door. The shape made no move. Nea leaned toward it, bringing her face closer, closer, refocusing her eyes, trying to identify the thing. Finally she recognized a pale stripe wiggling the shape's length, just as she smelled dog. "Wild Boy's Dog," she decided. She backed away and stepped through the dark toward the conversations, fires, smoke and goat meat around the corner, past the next building, Stone's office, to the clearing where the BaNare sat.

Shyly, Nea walked to the edge of the crowd, past the first cookfire, her blanket hiding her face. At the third fire someone recognized her. "Nea!" the cry went up.

"Nea is here!"

The BaNare were now all on Nea's side, united behind Mojamaje. Someone swept her off her feet and carried her up to the veranda, to Ma-Boko's eager arms.

Nea ate some goat meat, drank tea, sat on the front step of the veranda with Boko's head in her lap, his body covered with blankets.

Mojamaje coughed and Boko woke up. The first thing he saw, through eyes struggling to focus, was the ancient face of his grandfather. He saw him clearly, pain pounded between his temples, Jacob's blow at last had knocked some sense into Boko's hard head. As he gazed through half-opened eyes at Mojamaje, he understood a true lesson of heroism. The seriousness of his actions now struck him to shame, to culpability. Had the Black Goats killed Willoughby? The BaNare were starving, children's bellies swelled with air, and Boko had offered them only more trouble. If they killed Willoughby, who knew what terrible vengeance the English would wreak? It would be the last blow to the BaNare, the end. Mojamaje had known all along.

Nea noticed movement beneath Boko's eyelids. "Brother," she said, "are you awake?"

Boko reached one hand backward, up to her face, feeling its contours. "Nea?" he asked weakly. She was safe. Somehow his grandfather had seen to that too. The crisis was very different from what he had conceived. "Is Willoughby dead?"

"No," Nea replied.

Boko dropped his hand. "I cannot think. A sound in my ears."

"Father hit you with his pump handle," Nea explained. "It rang like a cowbell. I heard it from far away."

"Yes," Boko said. "That is the sound."

"It will go away. Sleep."

The Black Goats tired of terrorizing their trapped prey and gathered around their inert captain, but Nea chased them away. So they sat down to listen to the BaNare's discussions and took up cups of tea. Mojamaje spread the news that Stone had called the English army before the Black Goats tore out the wire.

"We are doomed!" the BaNare cried.

"No," Mojamaje insisted. "Willoughby's boss will come. We will talk to him."

"Will he listen?"

"I hope it," Mojamaje replied.

"Will they shoot us?"

"No," Mojamaje assured.

"Do you know it?"

"I hope it. I will speak to them. This Willoughby made a mess. He refuses to talk to me. We must send the people home."

"They will not go."

"If they go," Mojamaje explained, "maybe Willoughby will talk to me."

"They want to see."

"To protect you."

"Willoughby will shoot you."

"Some would go, but not the Black Goats."

"The others stay to see what the Black Goats will do."

The night wore on. Mojamaje coughed, Maka dozed in her blankets. Boko woke up again, fell back to sleep. Nea told her friends who came by that Wild Boy's Dog slept on the Stone house step.

"Willoughby is a fool," the BaNare agreed.

"So brave against us."

"Wild Boy burns his wife right now."

Maka woke, threw another blanket on Mojamaje's shoulders, and looked out on the scene before her. Dozens of cookfires burned low in the dark, their red glows empty of flame, casting faint shadows on the blanketed forms around them. The wind blew stronger, blurring the last conversations of the sleepy BaNare. She urged Mojamaje to come home, to sleep in their house. Worried, Maka counted Mojamaje's coughs, but she knew how volatile the BaNare remained. If he or Jacob left the veranda, some firebrand would whip up the crowd again to murder Stone. As Stone himself saw it, that troublemaker was Mojamaje, holding vigil on his veranda, waiting for the moment to strike.

9

Wilderness

At Kalahariland headquarters in Taung, Senior Commissioner Bagley read Stone's telegram with irate impatience. "Under attack," he spoke aloud.

"Then the line went dead," his lieutenant explained.

Bagley stood in his nightshirt, holding his eyeglasses to his face with one hand, grasping the telegram with the other. His instinct was to dismiss the message as another false alarm. The dead telegraph line argued otherwise. Bagley said, "Very well, meet me at the office." The lieutenant saluted and disappeared out the door, closing it softly behind. Bagley shuffled back to the bedroom.

"Arnold," his wife called from bed. "What is it?"

"Nothing, dear."

"The ship leaves in four days," she warned, sitting up in her night-dress. Electric light from the next room fell across her face.

"I know," Bagley sighed.

"If we miss it, I shall leave you. I am serious, Arnold."

Bagley sighed again and looked at the drooping, intelligent face of his wife. Her hair was gray, thinning, white shoulders gleamed in the pale light. Their biennial home leave began in four days: submarines in the Atlantic had already sunk two South African merchant ships. Bagley knew, and his wife guessed, that the ship they had booked for home would be the last to travel safely. If they missed it, they would spend their home leave in South Africa. His wife would never forgive him. Bagley shared her anxiety, for different reasons. If he arrived in England and war closed the ocean behind him, he would be on the spot, ready for a military commission and promotion. If they missed the boat, he would spend the war in South Africa, left behind, out of touch.

As he climbed into his uniform trousers, Bagley considered his options. If he ignored Stone's telegram, there were two possibilities: in case of a false alarm, Bagley was safe, aboard ship, headed home; or, in case there really was an attack, ignoring the telegram would leave an indelible stain on Bagley's record, especially if Stone were killed. If he waited for more information, he might find out in three days that the message was genuine and he would miss the boat fixing the mess.

No, there was only one thing to do. He would rush to Naring, set things right, rush back and make the boat. He pulled on his tunic, dropped a hat on his head and hurried out the door, closing it gently so as not to disturb his wife. Bagley strode into his office, brightly lit against the dark Taung night. "Asquith, I need ten men."

"Impossible, sir," the lieutenant replied.

"Impossible?" Bagley boomed. "I have fifty men at my disposal. Immediate, personal disposal."

"Fifty, yes," Asquith replied. "Ten, no. I am your only officer. Buell, MacRea and Burns will be back on the day your own leave begins. Sir."

"So?"

"One officer must remain at post. This officer in charge cannot command troops. A second officer must be present."

"So?"

"If you go, you must take all fifty. None can stay here with only one officer at post. Me."

Bagley raised a fist to punch his lieutenant, then restrained himself. Turning to the map of Kalahariland on the wall, Bagley huffed, "How far is Naring from the rail?"

"Fifty miles from Lorole Station, but the tracks wind to only twenty miles farther north. There is no station. No stops except by military order."

Bagley asked, "Can I stop the train?"

"Of course, sir."

"Do I need your permission, Asquith?"

"I do not understand, sir."

Bagley changed the subject. "I won't walk twenty miles out there. Load my car on the train."

"But sir, there is no road. The terrain—"

"Asquith, shut up."

And so Senior Commissioner Bagley left on the midnight train with fifty English soldiers and a motorcar. He loved that car, especially after his struggle to procure it. The first motorcar he ordered had been seized off the docks by the High Commissioner. The present one took another year to arrive. Bagley drove himself to work every day along the half mile between his house and the office. There were four paved streets in Taung, and Bagley loved them all.

The train steamed through the night across the border to Kalahariland, north along the edge of the Kalahari, to Steenbok, Aurora, then Lorole Station. Bagley stretched his legs and entered the station house to read one last time the old report on Mojamaje, the rebel leader. "Murder, smuggling, cattle theft, treason," Bagley read. "Quite a fellow."

The train dropped Bagley, his troops and the car along the tracks. The first light of dawn cracked over the South African border to the east.

"What is this place?" he asked his scout, the grandson of a Wall-Maker refugee whose father had served in the great South African war.

"Stinkface," the guide replied. "Naring is twenty miles there, behind those hills."

Bagley's troops set out along the flat plain, marching in double file, their rifles over their shoulders. Bagley putted ahead at the wheel of his long, wide army-green car, rolling and bouncing over the dusty ground. Bare thorn bushes bent under the car's body, to spring back in place after the car passed. The dark ceiling of clouds brightened as the sun rose higher behind it. A thorn punctured Bagley's right front tire. He leaned against the hood while his men made the repair. They continued on. Flies rushed in through the open windows to cling to Bagley's face. He rolled up the window. The heat of the engine warmed the air inside to a stifle. Bagley rolled down the window, gasping for air. Flies jumped on his face.

They reached a dry creek bed, two feet deep. The car's rear wheels stuck in the sand. Bagley drummed his fingers on the steering wheel as his men pushed the car out. Another creek bed, another puncture, overheated radiator, flies on Bagley's face. Each bump, each delay, drained more of Bagley's self-esteem. He deserved London, a clean office, high ceilings, not this empty nowhere of dust and scrub. In Taung he had been able to make himself forget that the territory he administered was nothing but this. Now the truth of his station overwhelmed him, Bagley cursed and sweated as his car bumped over the stubbly ground, his domain.

They reached the canyon through the Naring hills in late afternoon. The soldiers' disciplined ranks had melted away to random straggling toward the hills. They had all drained their water jugs. The wind whipped through their gray uniforms to chill their skin and bones. Their lips cracked. Bagley's engine churned louder and louder with overwork.

The sentry on the ridge reported the English advance. The BaNare's worst fears had finally come true. First the Zulu, then the Boers, Wall-Makers, now the English, complete with motorcar to crush them under its wheels. The Black Goats rose from their blankets and grabbed their spiked poles. Some drew their knives. "English!" the BaNare cried, still crowding the clearing in front of Stone's office. But the mood of violence had passed, the taste of blood receded from their tongues. The weary BaNare had spent the day hoping that Stone's telegram had fallen on deaf ears, that the English were not on their way to shoot them down.

Bagley's car clanked along the canyon rocks, finally emerging on the other side, on the site of the Battle of the Rocks, turning onto one of the paths worn through the thorn brush leading to the center of Naring. His soldiers regrouped, marching in quick step behind the car.

The approaching engine frightened the children and sent the Black Goats running to Boko, able now to sit up on the step of Stone's office, a blanket around his shoulders. The wind carried the engine's roar toward the BaNare, then away, then toward them again. Boko held his head in his hands. The assault on Willoughby had taken the last of the BaNare's strength. Even the Black Goats sank into despondency. They would be helpless against the English. "Do nothing," Boko told the Black Goats. "My grandfather says do nothing. He will speak to them. Return to your fires. Eat."

"Yes, we will eat," the BaNare said.

"They will not shoot us if we eat."

"Eating is harmless."

Every fire received more wood. The last chunks of goat meat returned to the fire. The BaNare pulled them out and sat munching the bones as the English came upon them.

Bagley stopped the car on the edge of the crowd and turned off the engine. He carefully surveyed the scene. Thousands of BaNare huddled around dozens of cookfires, eating. No one looked up. The English soldiers stood in rank, salivating, eyeing the goat meat and tea. Bagley stepped out of the car into the wind, to weave his way, alone, toward Stone's office.

There on the veranda sat Mojamaje, slumped in his chair, his English army coat pulled tight around his waist, his hat pulled low on his eyes. Maka stood behind him as Bagley approached. Her hands clutched a gray blanket over her shoulders and a black scarf hid her hair. Ma-Boko stood beside her, also in a blanket, and Chibi too, a blanket covering her bright white Chibiite robe. Jacob the Ox-Killer stood against the office door, the pump handle against his shoulder like a rifle. Boko and Nea Sweet Child sat below on the step of the veranda, her arms around her brother's shoulders, holding a blanket tight around him. This was what Bagley saw, the Tladi family together on the office veranda. Except for Naledi, who was busy adding wood to Ma-Mojamaje's famous pile.

Bagley stopped at the steps, a foot before Boko and Nea. "Not much of a revolt," he said to himself but loudly enough for Mojamaje to hear.

"No," Mojamaje replied. "Only talk. Now we eat."

Bagley was shocked. "You speak English," he said.

"And my daughter," Mojamaje replied, pointing at Ma-Boko. She stared back impassively at the English officer.

Bagley was nearly invisible in the depths of his thick overcoat, collar turned against the wind, hat pulled low. "Where is Mojamaje?" he asked.

"I am Mojamaje."

Bagley almost laughed. "The District Commissioner said you were attacking him. There seems to be some mistake."

"I am too old," Mojamaje explained.

"You are too old," Bagley agreed.

"And you?" Mojamaje asked.

"Arnold Bagley, Senior Commissioner, Kalahariland Territory administration."

"Pleased to meet you. Welcome to Naring."

"Where is Stone?" Bagley asked.

"Is that his name?" Mojamaje replied. "We call him Willoughby. We call them all Willoughby."

"Where is he?" Bagley asked.

"In the office."

"Safe?"

"Safe," Mojamaje replied. "Frightened."

"Can I speak with you in private?" Bagley said.

"I am old," Mojamaje answered. He coughed as if to demonstrate this fact. His body shook with pain. Recovering, he continued, "No BaNare is older. I sat in this chair last night. It will take me an hour to rise. I am comfortable now. This chair and I are one. We can talk here."

"In front of the others?"

"Only my daughter speaks English," Mojamaje assured him. "She will listen to us and tell the BaNare everything we say."

"I see," Bagley said. "No secrets in Naring."

"Some," Mojamaje corrected. "None for you to know."

Bagley stepped carefully past Boko and Nea, to take one of the empty chairs beside Mojamaje. The Ox-Killer took a step forward, raising his pump handle in alarm. Bagley flinched and Mojamaje waved Jacob back.

"Charming," Bagley murmured, thrusting his hands in his coat pockets, leaning forward to talk. He peered past Mojamaje's hat brim into the reddened eyes of a sick old man.

Mojamaje told Bagley the details of Seantlo, Seele and Nea, Loang, the demon drought, children crying for food, Patrick's tragic death, Mojamaje's walk to Stone's office. "He misunderstood," Mojamaje explained. "This knife I carry is old, like me. Older than me. A gift from my wife." Mojamaje turned to point at Maka, who stood fuming with mistrust behind him. She feared that Bagley would arrest her husband. "I raised the knife," Mojamaje continued, "because I was thinking of it.

My wife has kept it for all these years. I only touched it once. I wanted to touch it again."

Bagley looked at the crude iron blade in Mojamaje's belt. It looked like an old Zulu stabbing spear with the shaft cut off. Bagley had never seen one before. "May I see it?" he asked, reaching out his hand.

"The BaNare watch us," Mojamaje replied. "They would not understand if I gave you my knife." Bagley turned his head to see thousands of eyes turned up from beneath their blankets.

"I see," Bagley said. He leaned back in his chair to think. Ordinarily, he supported chiefs and District Commissioners, fined troublemakers, banished them or sent them to jail. If he did this in Naring, there would only be more trouble, perhaps serious. Next time they might kill Stone.

"You see," Mojamaje offered, leaning forward to place his elbows on his knees, "my grandson Boko worked in the mines. He wanted to come back home and do something valuable with his youth before the mines took it all. He found there was nothing to do against the drought. The Kalahari has swallowed us. We can only wait for rain. I do not know Willoughby, he refuses to talk to me, but the drought must be hard for him too. It is hard for us all. Do not blame him. Perhaps he is like Boko. He wants to end the drought but he found no practical way to do it. Maybe in frustration, something we all know, he blamed me for the drought. Things like that happen all the time in Naring."

Bagley listened carefully to the old man before him, and each word, every phrase, told Bagley that this land was not empty after all. Bagley smiled to himself, satisfied beyond expectations with the Mojamaje he had finally encountered.

Mojamaje watched Bagley's face and took this opportunity to say, "You are thinking what to do." Bagley nodded. Mojamaje continued, "Declare Seantlo illegal. That will mean Seele does not own the well, Pono and Peke cannot take Nea. This child, Nea, is too young for this. She is too sweet and simple. This is Nea here." Mojamaje pointed to his granddaughter, who turned her face up to Bagley.

"I see," Bagley replied, convinced by Nea's cherubic cheeks.

"And this is Chibi, a brave girl who brought Seele back. My wife's brother's daughter." Mojamaje pointed to Chibi, saying to her, "Show him your robe." Chibi pulled open her blanket to reveal her white Chibi-ite robe.

"I see," Bagley said.

"After you ban Seantlo," Mojamaje continued, "take back the well as government property. Then give it to all the BaNare. I do not know why Willoughby did not do this from the beginning."

"Is that all?" Bagley asked.

"One more thing," Mojamaje replied. "Take Willoughby away."

Bagley leaned back again in his chair. Before he could say, "Impossible," Mojamaje continued.

"Do not report this thing as trouble. That would look bad for you. Report that Willoughby does a good job. Give him a holiday. Then send him to another place." Bagley smiled in appreciation of Mojamaje's delicate suggestion.

"When you tell Willoughby the news," Mojamaje concluded, "tell him a young Boer steals into his house when he is not there. But Mrs. Willoughby is there. This thing has gone on for years. It embarrasses the BaNare. We feel sorry for him. We feel sorry for his wife. The Boer is the father of my wife's brother's daughter's child." Mojamaje pointed to Chibi again and leaned back with finality into his chair.

Bagley pondered Mojamaje's proposal. He feared delay above all, missing that ship. Seconds ticked away in his head. Mojamaje offered him a quick getaway.

"I accept," Bagley said, standing up. "Can I see him now?" Mojamaje told Jacob to stand aside. Bagley called to Stone through the door. It opened and Bagley disappeared inside.

"Ma-Boko," Mojamaje said. "Tell the people."

Ma-Boko stood on the veranda step and called to the crowd:

"BaNare, listen! Mojamaje has saved us. The English will follow his orders. They agree. They will not shoot us. They will do these things Mojamaje wants. One . . ." Ma-Boko held up one thumb. ". . . Seantlo is forbidden. Nea is free." Before the BaNare had time to consider this ruling, Ma-Boko held out her forefinger alongside the thumb. "Two," she bellowed, "Loang well belongs to all the people." The BaNare began to cheer as Ma-Boko added her middle finger to the other two and cried, "Three, the English will take Willoughby away!"

The BaNare threw off their blankets and danced in the howling wind.

10
Doom Igniting

Bagley's troops sat down to eat their tinned rations. The BaNare served them tea while Bagley spoke with Mojamaje and then stormed into the office. Stone shut the door behind and saluted.

"Willoughby," Bagley said, "you leave with me. You can send for your belongings."

"My name is Stone, sir."

Bagley turned to leave, adding, "And your wife sleeps with a Boer." He disappeared back outside, walked to his car, waving hello to the cheering BaNare, and sat behind the steering wheel to wait for Stone. The sky had darkened as he talked with Mojamaje. The dying cookfires glowed red. A woman brought him a cup of tea.

Stone sat back down at his desk. "No," he whispered. "Impossible." The rejection of the BaNare was bad enough, now Bagley too, in name of the entire Kalahariland administration. Worst of all, most impossible, was Bagley's report about his wife. "Impossible," Stone repeated. He stood up again, opened the door and stepped onto the veranda. It was empty. BaNare carried their chairs, cups, and pots back to their compounds, the excitement over. "No," Stone whispered. "Impossible." He cursed the blame and punishment pressing down on his shoulders. "But surely the fault was the drought's, not his." He hurried toward his house, picking his way through the few dawdlers still huddled around their fires. They laughed as he rushed past. The drought was not over. The dry wind still blew. Stone looked up at the ceiling of gray clouds turned black, oppressive. No stars appeared to fill the void. The drought was still here. Bursting into his house, Stone slashed his fists through the shadows, threw open the door to the bedroom. Edna lay in bed, feigning sleep. He sniffed the sheets, pulled open the closets, stormed through the house in pursuit of the Boer. Stone dashed back out the front door to circle the house, but once again Petrus Wild Boy had made his escape in time.

Stone sighed with relief. "Lies," he reassured himself, grasping at the last threads of self-esteem. Exhausted, he sat down on the darkened back step—and jumped up again in alarm. He touched fur. Bending down, Stone peered through the gathering gloom at the dark shape on the step. It was Wild Boy's Dog, dead. Petrus never noticed it, for years the BaNare had expected it to fall asleep and never awake. From its hideous scar, Stone recognized the dog as the one beside the handsome young Boer he often passed on the way to his office. Of course. It was true. Here was the evidence. Edna and the Boer.

Stone sat down beside the dog, its mangy coat still warm to the touch. He patted its head in sympathy. The ceiling of clouds had turned black, though the air below still held its last rays of daylight. Stone looked up. "The drought," he said.

Stone was right. The BaNare's relief was a false one. As Mojamaje had argued from the first, the drought was the cause of their misery. Not Pono, not Willoughby. The crisis was over only for now. Salvation would come only with rain. Stone said, "Can Mojamaje make rain?"

For the love of Edna, the love of Naring, even the love of Bagley, Stone set out to make rain. He ran to the last cookfires in the clearing before his office. Grabbing a glowing branch, he set off through Naring. The last BaNare around their fires wondered what he was up to. The BaNare he passed on the paths ignored him. His mind raced with dreams of atonement, the magic of science, warm air, condensation. He remembered Pono's feeble attempt to make rain, when the cloud of locusts swept over Naring. He had urged Pono to build the fire higher, to heat the air below the ceiling of cloud. The rising air would raise the bank. Its vapor would turn to rain. The rain would fall to earth and save the BaNare. Stone rushed along the paths, struggling to remember the location of the enormous woodpile, taller than any tree, that he had seen not twenty yards from Pono's measly pyre. Stone's torch flared against the wind, doubled in force by the approach of night. Objects turned to shadow, but still enough light reached Stone's wild eyes for his search to continue.

He found it. Between the Tladi and Potso compounds, Ma-Mojamaje's famous woodpile, rebuilt by Naledi to its former splendor, towered above the other shadows. Stone dashed to its base and held his torch against the nearest twig. The compounds around him were silent, wrapped in darkness, all sound lost to the swirling wind. The cold air bit Stone's tired face, tore across his torch, almost killing the flame. Then a few twigs erupted. The fire spread to others, whipped by the wind, first one way then the other, the wood dry as dust from rainless years. In no time at all the woodpile blazed. The flames leapt, whirled, devouring the wood, thirsty for fuel, crackling, roaring.

The BaNare ran screaming to the scene. The grass roofs of their houses were dry too: if the flames only touched them, the village would vanish, the fire leaping from compound to compound, roof to roof, borne by the ferocious wind. Doom ignited Naring. They beat their blankets against the inferno's edge, but the heat drove them back. Smoke clogged their nostrils. Why had Naledi rebuilt this pile? Who had set it afire? The flames lit their terrified faces, driving away the winter cold, replacing it with icy fear. First the drought, now destruction. The ceiling of clouds glowed in the flickering light. A deafening rush of wind bent the flames across to lick a compound roof, bursting into a searing dance of death, ready to leap from roof to roof throughout Naring. The BaNare had survived the Zulu, the Boers, their men lost to the mines, through the birth of a new world they remained intact, through chaos and tragedy, still they fulfilled Mojamaje's hopes, until now. Now they would not survive this fiendish drought. The brittle brown grass of every roof in Naring stood ready for flame to devour it, to destroy in one final conflagration their last possession, their last pride, the Naring of Tladi and all the BaNare who came before. One by one the BaNare ceased their futile battle against the blaze and screamed their despair to the sky.

Then it began to rain.

11
A Final Song

The BaNare remember that year as the wettest in their history. The rain fell in heavy night storms at first, yielding to clear days. Grass sprang back quickly, leaves of trees and bushes followed, tall, white clouds billowed from horizon to horizon. Rain washed the dust from the sky so that blue and white, the red and purple of thunderstorms, the green of new pasture, replaced the chilling gray and dusty brown that had blanketed Naring through the Great Thirst. The world returned to color. Men hurried to South Africa to buy cattle, but not enough yet to plow.

The early rainstorms calmed to a gentle, constant shower that bathed every object in wet, silvery light. Such moistness brought out the hoes, and BaNare women scratched the eager soil and dropped in seeds from Ahamed's and De Swart's shops. With only hoes, the BaNare reaped their greatest harvest. The few cows from South Africa all bore female calves, so within a few years the BaNare herds were large again, the pastures filled with cattle, the days of black goats ended. Melons, squashes, pumpkins, beans, corn, sweet reed stalks, all popped from the earth into the BaNare's blissful mouths. Few bothered to chew. Children drank milk again. There was corn enough for beer and old men drank it.

The sound of rain filled the sky with salvation. The BaNare danced every night, even in the rain. Cattle ranged out to drink from the myriad raltipoole and graze day and night until every last one was fat and strong. Girls sang softly as they carried water from Naring's two wells. Their feet scraped not coarse sand and dust, but a carpet of new grass growing faster than cattle could chomp. Their pails swung loosely from their hands, the water sloshed down onto their shoulders as they raised the full buckets onto their heads. The water felt cool and clean on their dry skin, tingling cold as a light breeze swept past. Walking home with the pails on their heads, they rubbed the drops deep into their flesh. When the water splashed down the fronts of their dresses, the wet cloth clung to their breasts and young men's hearts turned to love.

By this time the listeners and teller of the story of the Great Thirst are cold and weary, as dawn pushes its way to the eastern horizon above the Naring hills. Dogs bark, cocks crow. One by one blanketed women and girls emerge from their compounds, buckets clanging dully in the hazy, half-lit morning air. The listeners and tellers still huddle in their blankets in a circle. Their eyes beg for sleep, but now they press close to the dying fire. Almost in a whisper, as if to keep the waking village from overhearing, the teller tells the end of the story.

While Bagley gave Stone his bad news, while Ma-Boko related the news to the jubilant BaNare, Maka pulled Mojamaje out of his chair, tugged one of his arms over her shoulders and helped him back toward the Tladi compound. Maka led him into their darkened house, a circle of mud with a grass roof, home. She closed the door behind. Light filtered in through the open window but Maka closed this too, snapping its wooden cover in place. Mojamaje lay on his blankets, coughing. Maka sat down beside him, removed his hat and eased his head into her lap. Dark hid their faces.

Mojamaje's lips moved as if to speak. He was too weak for sound. Now in the dark, eyes closed, he was back against the rocks. Boer bullets exploded around him. The rock turned cold and the sunlight vanished. He was alone. The fear of death crept through him like the cold of the night. After that day it never left him. He waited for the impact, the torn flesh, the end of his thoughts. After that day he searched the world for someone else and found her in a Taung field with an ox whip high in her hands. He could not have asked for more than that, year after year in her arms, facing the dark together. So much had happened but really it was very simple. After that he was always with her. There was doubt before Drift's death and trouble at the mission, but then they met in the swirling herd on the road to Naring and he knew it was all behind them. He loved the children and told his stories but truly he lived for only her. His herdboy dreams were nothing but this. In this he attained the goal of his life. It was over now and he had not lived it alone.

He coughed again and tried to speak. Already he felt far away and turned to shout back all he had waited to tell her now, as he lay in her arms, where he hoped he would be when it ended. She was younger and beautiful still. Now he was frightened, terrified as he had been on the rocks, for he was leaving her alone. He could not bear it himself and now she would have to. Oh, Maka, I am so sorry.

He tasted them now—the rocks, hard and dry, cold against his lips. He coughed again, deeply, from the bottom of his ancient lungs. The oldest BaNare, famous. His feet slapped the warm sand, his herdboy's stick whistled against the cattle's hides. Cold skin. Against the rock.

Maka clasped his hairy head to her breast. He was quiet now and Maka was ready. She knew it would come. This was all she could hope for, they were old and together still. It was too much to think how to go on without him. She had lived this moment again and again, wondering what it would be like. It was as bad as she had expected. But she had a plan. She had it worked out. She would think of him young, how handsome he looked in her mother's fields, so tall and eager and wild. He rode behind and she longed to turn and embrace him at last. She loved his arms around her waist but hated the thought of more, the risk of her heart. But he stayed and won and was always there with his eyes on her own and she knew he needed her too. Against all her might, the full weight of South Africa, the world she was born to, against all odds, Mojamaje had saved her and saved himself. In this only she would ever know the true measure of how good and kind was Mojamaje, Eater of Rocks, cold and lifeless in her arms.

The roof above Maka erupted in flame, charging the room with bursts of light, the only roof to burn before rain poured down to drench Naring, ending the Great Drought. Boko rushed in through the smoke to pull Maka out—brave Boko, misguided miner, who had inherited Mojamaje's magical resistance to fire. The roof collapsed behind, covering Mojamaje with flaming grass. The cascading rain now quenched the fire and the BaNare ran, some crying out in fear, to bear witness to their terrible loss. They pulled away the smoking rubble. There he lay, beneath his blankets, untouched by the fire. Ma-Boko reached into Mojamaje's coat and drew out the eyeglasses he had asked Boko to bring from Joburg for Patrick the Sniffler. Tears clouding her eyes, mixing with the pounding rain, Ma-Boko held the spectacles against Mojamaje's lips. She pressed his chest.

No smoke! She announced the verdict to the BaNare wailing around her.

"No smoke! He did not die from the fire."

The crowd buzzed with speculation. What was the cause?

"Sickness," the BaNare guessed.

"Old age."

"A cobra bite?"

"Impossible."

Finally the crowd achieved consensus. Mojamaje had given up his life to bring rain. He sacrificed himself to end the Great Drought, dying so his people might live. This was the miracle of Mojamaje's death.

The BaNare stood in silence as the rain poured down, flashing silver and black in the night, the smoke of Ma-Mojamaje's famous woodpile thinning to wisps. They gazed forlornly at their dead hero. Then above the drenched cries and moans of the mourning crowd, a song rose:

> All through the night
> While the fire burned bright
> Mojamaje said his last good-bye
> First to his wife
> Then to his knife
> Then he lay down to die

12
The End of the Story

So ends the story of the Great Thirst. Many unanswered questions remain: For example, what happened to the heart Mojamaje mistook for Hrikwa's pouchful of beads floating in the Loang well? Such questions have answers but the BaNare do not know them. Remembering the important points of a long story is a complicated task, so over the years minor details have dropped by the way. Neither do the BaNare explain the fates of the other characters in the story, for these are familiar details that even children know. In the future, though, they might be forgotten, so it is wise to record them here.

Stone and his wife disappeared, perhaps in Bagley's motorcar. No one remembers. Another, meeker Willoughby took his place. Pono died the next year and Koko's son Puo became chief. Shy Seele the Seantlo girl lived in the Ata compound, loving children. Chibi and Petrus Wild Boy built a compound of their own near the canyon. Wild Infant grew up. Boko never went to the mines again. A year after the Great Drought ended, the English hired Boko and his Black Goats to ride by train to the coast, sail on a boat to Egypt, and dig trenches for English soldiers fighting German tanks in the sand. Naledi and Ma-Boko ruled the Tladi compound while Jacob the Ox-Killer performed the heavy work. He gave up his pump handle to the new Willoughby, who sent Bo Roodie out to fix the Loang well. All the BaNare were free to use it, and they did so.

Six months after the end of the drought, Nea Sweet Child bore Patrick's child. She married again and settled with her husband in an empty house in the Tladi compound. Still she seemed never to grow a day older.

Old men and women returned to their places in the Tladi compound, sipping tea and beer, discussing the day's doings. The Black Goats returned with bicycles. Boko married Keke's youngest daughter and took up a house in the Tladi compound. Chief Puo squandered district funds on a motorcar for himself, and the BaNare called a meeting and deposed him. They chose Boko, now an undisputed Man of Reason, as their new chief.

South Africa grew only worse, but that is another story. Peace returned to Naring.

But the world was different without Mojamaje. Two months after his death, Maka died in her sleep. There was nothing left for her but death. For the BaNare, though, there are memories and stories, of a time when Bushmen and Zulu warriors roamed the earth, of a time before gunpowder, horses, mirrors, and wheels, when Tladi, Man of Lightning, conquered the Kalahari. Mojamaje, Eater of Rocks, son of Ra-Mojamaje and Ma-Mojamaje, grandson of Tladi, father of Ma-Boko and Naledi, grandfather of Boko the Miner and Nea Sweet Child, husband of Maka who was the daughter of Drift, who descended from those who remained in Taung when the BaNare first came to Naring—Mojamaje is their hero, their champion, their legend, a memory of another age. To this day they discuss the meaning of his life, whether times today are better, disagreeing, arguing, and in typical BaNare fashion, concluding only after endless hours of debate that the reason to remember Mojamaje's world is that it is lost forever.

AA34